Praise for these
bestselling authors

Jayne Ann Krentz

"A master of the genre...nobody does it better!"
—*Romantic Times*

"Who writes the best romance fiction today?
No doubt it's Jayne Ann Krentz."
—*Affaire de Coeur*

Jasmine Cresswell

Jasmine Cresswell "delivers glamour
and sizzling passion."
—*Romantic Times*

"Romantic suspense at its finest."
—*Affaire de Coeur* on *Secret Sins*

Marie Ferrarella

"Marie Ferrarella's cute
Hayley Mills-like tale will charm."
—Debbie Richardson, *Romantic Times*
on *My Phony Valentine*

"Once again Ms. Ferrarella demonstrates
a mastery of the storytelling art
as she creates charming characters,
witty dialogue and an emotional storyline
that will tug at your heartstrings."
—*Romantic Times*
on *In the Family Way*

Jayne Ann Krentz is one of today's top contemporary romance writers, with an astounding twelve million copies of her books in print. Her novels regularly appear on the *New York Times,* Waldenbooks and B. Dalton bestseller lists. First published in 1979, Jayne quickly established herself as a prolific and innovative writer. She has delved into psychic elements, intrigue, fantasy, historicals and even futuristic romances. Jayne lives in Seattle with her husband, Frank, an engineer.

Jasmine Cresswell is the multitalented author of over forty novels. Her efforts have gained her numerous awards, including the RWA's Golden Rose Award and the Colorado Author's League award for best original paperback novel. Born in Wales and educated in England, Jasmine met her husband while working at the British Embassy in Rio de Janeiro. She has lived in Australia, Canada and six cities in the United States. The parents of four grown children, she and her husband now make their home in Sarasota, Florida.

Marie Ferrarella earned a master's degree in Shakespearean comedy and, perhaps as a result, her writing is distinguished by humor and natural dialogue. This RITA® Award-winning author's goal is to entertain and to make people laugh and feel good. She has written over 100 books for Silhouette, some under the name Marie Nicole. Her romances are beloved by fans worldwide and have been translated into Spanish, Italian, German, Russian, Polish, Japanese and Korean.

JAYNE ANN KRENTZ

JASMINE CRESSWELL
MARIE FERRARELLA

Everybody's Talking

HARLEQUIN®

TORONTO • NEW YORK • LONDON
AMSTERDAM • PARIS • SYDNEY • HAMBURG
STOCKHOLM • ATHENS • TOKYO • MILAN • MADRID
PRAGUE • WARSAW • BUDAPEST • AUCKLAND

HARLEQUIN BOOKS
225 Duncan Mill Road, Don Mills,
Ontario, Canada M3B 3K9

ISBN 0-373-83586-8

EVERYBODY'S TALKING

Copyright © 2003 by Harlequin Books S.A.

The publisher acknowledges the copyright holders
of the individual works as follows:

THE MAIN ATTRACTION
Copyright © 1987 by Jayne Ann Krentz.

EDGE OF ETERNITY
Copyright © 1994 by Jasmine Cresswell.

MY PHONY VALENTINE
Copyright © 1997 by Marie Ferrarella.

This edition published by arrangement with Harlequin Books S.A.

® and TM are trademarks of the publisher. Trademarks indicated with ® are registered in the United States Patent and Trademark Office, the Canadian Trade Marks Office and in other countries.

Visit us at www.eHarlequin.com

Printed in U.S.A.

CONTENTS

THE MAIN ATTRACTION

Jayne Ann Krentz

Prologue

TRENT RAVINDER STOOD in the deep shadows of the old lodge building and listened to the whisper of wind in the trees while he watched a redheaded elfin queen take a secret midnight swim.

She was a very charming elf: small, slender, mischievous, intriguing and maddening. He had been trying to get a good grasp on her for days, but she'd always managed to slide through his fingers whenever he'd gotten close.

Elf magic.

She thought she was alone tonight, and she would have been if Trent had not decided to try working off some of his restlessness by taking a midnight walk. But luck or fate or simple coincidence had brought him around the corner of the lodge just in time to see her glide beneath the surface of the pool. Trent had frozen the instant he'd sensed her presence, afraid to disturb the magic.

He stood watching her frolic by herself until she emerged at last from the water. Pale, silvered light gleamed on her soft breasts and the sensual curve of her flanks.

When she reached for a towel, Trent debated whether to make his presence known. It was, after all, her fault he'd felt the need for this late-night walk in the first place. It was Filomena Cromwell who had added this new, unsettling restlessness to his life. The elf should be made to take responsibility for her actions.

But not tonight. Tonight he would allow her to disappear back to the safety of her bedroom or her mushroom castle or wherever it was she vanished to at night. There was no need to rush, Trent told himself as he faded into the shadows. Time was running out for his elfin lady. Soon she would discover that no matter how swiftly she danced or how adroitly she sidestepped, she couldn't escape him.

One of these days Filomena Cromwell would be his.

Trent smiled at the rash promise he had made to himself. All he had to do, he thought, was get her attention. It wasn't as simple as it sounded.

Chapter One

FILOMENA CROMWELL WAS HAVING a very good time. The music was enthusiastically played, even if it was being provided by a small-town band. The Gallant Lake Country Club restaurant was filled to capacity with locals out for an evening of dining and dancing. True, the food and the atmosphere were a far cry from New York, San Francisco or Seattle, but Filomena found it deliciously amusing to know that every eye in the room was upon her and the man with whom she was dancing.

She tipped back her head, aware that her long red hair was falling intimately over Trent Ravinder's arm as he held her close. As usual when she danced with a man as big as Ravinder, she was having to exert an unrelenting amount of physical resistance in order to keep from being pulled even closer in his grasp. Large men always tended to overwhelm a woman as short and slender as she was.

But she was accustomed to the maneuvering required to survive on a dance floor, and her eyes were alight with mischief as she looked up at him through her lashes.

"I'm glad to see you function well under pressure, Trent," Filomena murmured.

Trent looked down into her face, his striking green gaze hooded and watchful, although his expression was coolly polite. "This is like dancing in a goldfish bowl. If I'd known we were going to attract this much attention, I would have worn my neon tie and spats."

Filomena laughed in delight. "That certainly would have livened up everyone's evening."

"Oh, I don't know," he said thoughtfully, running a critical eye over her gown. "I have a hunch it would have taken more than a neon tie to compete with that dress you've got on." His hand moved on her back, his fingers warm and deliberate on the shoulder-to-waist triangle of feminine skin exposed by the outfit.

Filomena frowned in mocking concern. "You don't like the dress? I'm crushed. It was designed by my partner. Glenna always knows what looks good on me. I've learned to trust her implicitly when it comes to my clothing."

"Is that right?" Trent's deep, quiet voice sounded unruffled, but there was a distinct note of challenge in it.

"Oh, yes. Glenna always knows what she's doing when it comes to dressing me. She's the one with the talent for design in our firm. My instincts are for fabric and color. We make a good team."

Filomena smiled to herself as Ravinder gave the dark green dress another assessing glance. She knew the gown was one of Glenna Sterling's brilliant combinations of the demure and the disconcerting. The clinging jersey was beautifully fitted to her slender frame, hugging every soft curve. Long sleeves and a high neckline provided an illusion of discreet reserve in front, which was instantly shattered by the daring plunge to the waist in back. The flowing fabric fell into a long sarong skirt that moved beautifully around her legs. The expanse of skin exposed along the length of Filomena's spine left the viewer with the strong conviction she was not wearing a bra. The conviction was correct.

"My congratulations to your partner. She knows how to dress you in a way that makes a man want to undress you. That's a hell of a talent, I suppose, in the fashion business."

Filomena grinned. "Why, Trent. You sound disapproving. More than disapproving. One might almost say prudish. Priggish even? Or puritanical? Downright Victorian, perhaps? I'm left wondering why you asked me to dance?"

"You know damn well why I asked you to dance."

Filomena's grin became a throaty laugh. "Of course I do. I shouldn't tease you about it. I know you're trying to do my family a favor, and it's very generous of you. Not every man would volunteer to try to keep me occupied and out of trouble this evening."

"You think that's why I asked you to dance? I'm doing your family a favor?"

"Certainly." Filomena nodded with absolute conviction. "It's been obvious since I arrived two weeks ago that they're all scared to death I'm going to embarrass them beyond recovery and thus ruin my sister's wedding, not to mention the family's social standing here in Gallant Lake. But there you were staying conveniently at the lodge for most of the summer. My mother took one look at you and decided you were going to be the family's salvation. They're hoping you'll keep me out of mischief at least until after the wedding. Actually I think half the town is waiting to see if you can do it. The other half hopes you'll fail, naturally. The gossip of a really big scandal would be wonderful. Gallant Lake is such a quiet little town most of the time."

Trent studied her vivid gaze for a long moment before he spoke. "You're certainly doing your best to put on a show for the hometown crowd, aren't you? It's been one staged event after another since you arrived, starting with that high-school-prom replay you put on last week."

"That was the prom I never went to," Filomena explained. "I wound up baby-sitting on prom night because I didn't have a date. Hardly a surprise, given the fact that I didn't have a date all during high school. Actually I'm glad I waited ten years for the big event. I'm sure I had a much better time last week than I would have had ten years ago."

"You caused quite a stir when you wrote 'no ex-cheerleaders or football players allowed' on the invitations. Your mother nearly fainted when she got hold of one and read it. She was sure you managed to alienate some very important people in town."

"I wanted this prom to be for those of us who were always on the outside looking in during our high-school years. We had a great time the other night. Spent the evening admiring one another for having proven there is life after high school. Most of us have been quite successful."

"Most of Gallant Lake talked about the party all last week, your mother tells me. Your father says you spent a fortune on champagne and caviar and all the trimmings."

"What's the point of replaying your high-school prom if you don't do it up right? Besides," Filomena added carelessly, "I can afford it."

"You don't mind being the subject of all that speculation and gossip?"

"Not this time," Filomena assured him.

"What do you mean by that?"

"I mean that the last time I gave the town something to talk about, everyone felt sorry for me. I was an object of pity and the subject of a great many I-told-you-so's."

"I find that hard to believe. When was that?"

"Oh, a long time ago," Filomena said smoothly. "Nine years ago to be exact."

"That would have been when you were nineteen?"

"Umm. Some women are quite sophisticated and mature at nineteen. I, unfortunately, was a late bloomer. I was also rather plump, dowdy and not terribly good at making scintillating conversation with a man."

Trent smiled faintly. "I can't imagine you at a loss for words. What happened to bring about the flowering of Filomena Cromwell?"

"Getting away from Gallant Lake helped immeasurably. I shed some pounds that first year in college and began to learn some social graces. It wasn't a big change, not at first, but it was enough to attract the interest of someone back here in Gallant Lake. We started seeing each other when I came home on weekends and vacations. He was a few years older, sophisticated, suave, handsome and all the rest. I was terribly flattered. By spring of that first year in college, I was actually engaged. I couldn't believe it. Some man actually wanted me. *Me*, Filomena Cromwell.'' Filomena shook her head, smiling indulgently at the memory of the naive young woman she had once been.

"I get the feeling there's a punch line coming.''

Filomena shrugged. "No punch line. The remainder of the growing-up process was completed for me in a hurry one day when I found my fiancé in bed with another woman. Someone who had been in my graduating class. One of the in crowd.'' She smiled. "I'm sure you can imagine my surprise. Everyone in town heard about it within twenty-four hours. My fiancé broke the engagement and told everyone he planned to marry the other woman, that it was her he had loved all along. I, apparently, had just been a way of passing time and I had totally misunderstood his intentions. I wondered at the time if I would survive the humiliation. You know how it is when you're only nineteen.''

But Trent Ravinder wasn't smiling. He was still watching her intently. "It must have been quite a shock for a gentle, insecure young woman. Mind telling me who the fiancé was?''

"Don't you know?'' Filomena was honestly surprised. "How unfair of my family to assign you the duty of keeping me out of trouble without telling you the exact nature of the problem. It's no secret, believe me. His name is Brady Paxton. He's here with his wife tonight. They're sitting right over there.''

She turned her head and looked directly at a big tawny-haired man sitting at a table across the room. The man had been watching her as she danced, and his gaze collided awkwardly with hers when she glanced in his direction. Paxton turned away quickly, but not before Filomena caught the hint of embarrassment in his expression. She smiled to herself.

Ravinder sucked in his breath, his hand tightening with unexpected fierceness around Filomena's waist. "You little witch,'' he muttered. "He's fascinated with you, isn't he? And you're getting a kick out of putting on a show for the town.''

Filomena shook her head, and her smile faded. "No, I'm not particularly enjoying it, but everyone else is certainly excited.

It's been like this since I arrived. I gather Brady and his wife are having domestic problems and everyone knows it. It's impossible to keep secrets in a small town. I've been away a long time, and I'm a little out of touch with local events. During the past few years, I've just been home for short visits at Christmas and the occasional weekend. Not long enough to even run into Brady, let alone seduce him. But now I'm here on the first long vacation I've had in nine years. And I look somewhat different than I did when I left under a cloud of humiliation at the age of nineteen.''

"It isn't just your looks that have changed, is it?" Trent asked shrewdly. "In fact, that's probably the least of it. You've also got style and a considerable amount of financial success. Your folks tell me you're doing very well in the fashion business. You've lived in San Francisco and New York learning the trade and now you've got your own sportswear design firm in Seattle. Your dad said that for the past couple of years you've traveled all over the world looking for exotic fabric and design ideas and setting up business contacts. He said your little company, what's it called? Cromwell & Sterling? had a small fortune in orders last year. He said you'd probably double that this year.''

Filomena laughed. "I'm afraid that doesn't make me or Glenna self-made millionaires. At least not yet. If you know anything about the apparel business, you know that most of the profits have to be channeled right back into the operation.''

"That's true of most young firms," Trent said seriously. "But I get the feeling there's still a fair chunk of change left over for you to play with, isn't there? The entertaining you've been doing here in Gallant Lake has been first-class all the way. That flashy green Porsche you arrived in didn't come cheap, and those earrings you're wearing tonight aren't made of plastic.''

"What good is success if you can't enjoy it a little?" Filomena responded.

"So now you've got everything you didn't have nine years ago," Trent observed, sizing up the situation. "Style, polish and money. You've come back to the old hometown to show it all off. And the old flame, now married and apparently feeling restless, is gnawing on his own insides wondering what he's missed. No wonder your family is worried. That's a recipe for disaster.''

Filomena considered that. ''I'm not so sure,'' she finally said. ''I know that's what everyone thinks, but I learned a lot about Brady nine years ago and I'm here to tell you that he's a businessman first, last and always. It's amusing, I'll admit, to imagine him drooling over what he threw away all those years ago, but I have a hunch there's something more involved.''

''Such as?'' Trent asked bluntly.

''Such as you,'' she returned sweetly. ''I'm not the only one giving the gossips a field day here in Gallant Lake, Trent. You're doing an equally good job. You must know as well as I do that no one believes for a moment that you're spending six weeks in the Oregon woods just to do some fishing.''

Trent smiled slowly, but there was a hard edge to the curve of his mouth. ''It's the truth. I'm here on vacation.''

''But everyone is convinced that's just camouflage. They think you're here to scout the territory for your development firm. It's called Asgard Development, isn't it? Take a look at all the people sneaking little glances at us. They just know you're going to end up buying a big piece of land near the lake and put in a multimillion-dollar resort. They're all trying to figure out how they can get rich off the deal, Brady Paxton included.''

''If you think it's me he's eyeing tonight, you're out of your redheaded brain. He's salivating over you. As for the other angle, I give you my word, I'm here on vacation.''

''Whatever you say,'' Filomena assured him, her eyes gleaming with amusement. ''You're entitled to a little business privacy. Believe me, I'd be the last one to deny you that. We keep all kinds of secrets in the fashion-design business.''

''You don't believe me?'' Trent asked roughly. There was no answering amusement in his green eyes.

''Why should I?''

''Because,'' he stated with a cool arrogance that was amazingly intimidating, ''when I tell you something, you can believe it. I don't lie, Filomena, and I don't tolerate anyone lying to me. I might not talk about a certain matter for a variety of reasons, but I sure as hell wouldn't lie about it. That's something you had better understand up front.''

Filomena's eyes widened in astonishment. It seemed to her he was overreacting to a very casual, teasing comment. ''Good grief, I didn't mean to insult you. I'm sure you're as honest as the average businessman.''

''I'm honest, period. And I expect the people I deal with to return that honesty with interest.''

''Or what?'' Filomena couldn't resist the soft, goading taunt.

''Do you really want to know?''

She blinked, assimilating the blunt warning. It was obvious she had strayed into dangerous territory. ''No, I don't suppose I do. I take it you believe in revenge as much as you believe in being trustworthy? Your word is your bond and everyone else had better prove just as reliable or you'll hound him or her to the ends of the earth? Have I got that straight?''

Trent inclined his head with an arrogant motion. ''You seem to have grasped the essentials.''

''Why?'' Filomena asked softly.

It was Trent's turn to blink. ''Why what?''

''Why should I take you totally on trust? Why should I or anyone else believe you?''

Trent looked down into her face. ''Because I say so.''

''That's supposed to be enough to satisfy me? I should trust you completely just because you say so?''

''You take me on trust, Filomena, or you don't take me at all.''

His words sent a chill down her spine. ''Well, at least you've allowed me some choice in the matter,'' she retorted dryly. ''I'm relieved to know I have the option of not taking you at all. If you'll excuse me, the dance seems to be over.''

She stepped back in a firm bid to break his grip. For an instant nothing happened. Trent didn't release her, and Filomena realized she couldn't escape until he voluntarily let her go. She could feel the easy, unconscious strength in his arm as he held her close, and it disturbed her.

"Scared?" Trent asked softly.

"Not in the least. Just annoyed. Large men always seem to take advantage of their size when they deal with someone smaller than themselves."

"I didn't mean to frighten you," Trent said earnestly as he ignored her subtle efforts to free herself. "I just wanted to get things clear between us."

"The only thing that's clear is that we're the last two people on the dance floor. Whoever might not have been staring at us earlier is certainly doing so now."

That got his attention. He glanced around at the sea of interested faces and scowled. Without further comment he took Filomena's arm and led her off the floor. Filomena's sense of humor quickly reasserted itself.

"I'm sure my family will thank you for taking the tactful approach. Lecturing me on the subject of truth, honesty and integrity while standing in the middle of a dance floor was probably not on the list of duties they expect you to fulfill."

"You can be a sassy little thing at times, can't you? Typical of the species, I suppose."

"What species?"

"The one that includes elves, pixies, imps and assorted mischief makers." The harshness was fading from his expression as he guided her back to the large table occupied by her family. "No wonder your relatives and most of the town are on pins and needles waiting to see what you'll do."

"I think they're equally interested in seeing what you'll do. You seem to have been assigned responsibility for handling me," Filomena shot back. "But I'll give you full marks for being able to dance in a goldfish bowl. Not everyone could have handled that. Did it bother you?"

Trent gave her a sidelong glance. "I'll admit I like my privacy. Especially when it comes to dealing with you. But I can handle a little heat when it's necessary."

Filomena laughed. "I'll just bet you can. Thank you for the dance, Trent. I enjoyed it. At least until the lecture started."

"My pleasure, Filomena. I feel the experience gives us a sort of common bond, don't you? We've faced the assembled society of Gallant Lake together."

"That's one way of looking at it." Her tone was sardonic.

Filomena studied him out of the corner of her eye as they moved back toward the table. She wasn't the only one studying Trent Ravinder, she knew. She was well aware of the interested gaze of her parents and her Aunt Agnes and Uncle George as well as her sister Shari's curious glances. Shari's fiancé, Jim Devore, appeared amused by the whole event. But there was a certain respect in his dark eyes as he watched Ravinder lead Filomena back to the family fold.

Trent bore the scrutiny well, but that came as no surprise. Filomena had seen the calm inner fortitude in him the moment they had been introduced almost two weeks ago. He was staying at her parents' lakefront inn, the Gallant Lake Lodge, and right from the start he had apparently become more than just a paying guest. He was rapidly assuming the status of an old friend of the family. It was a clever trick. The Cromwells were gracious hosts, but they rarely adopted their clientele.

Trent Ravinder's inner strength had an outward manifestation. He was a big, lean, broad-shouldered man who moved with a confident, contained vitality. He was over six feet in height, and that made him too tall as far as Filomena was concerned. She was only five feet three inches, and she had an instinctive dislike of being towered over by other people, especially men. The only exception to the rule was her father.

The shards of green jewels that formed Trent's eyes were the most riveting element in a face that was composed of hard ridges and stark planes. Those eyes betrayed a cool intelligence and a fierce will that made it easy to believe he would be successful at whatever he chose to do. But even the brilliance of his gaze couldn't make him a handsome man; there was too much power and too much rough-edged determination in that face to allow room for good looks.

Ravinder's hair was thick and dark with a sprinkling of silver at the temples that made it clear he was well into his thirties. Filomena had automatically assessed his clothing with a knowing eye the day she'd met him. It was immediately obvious that Trent wore his clothes; they didn't wear him.

There was nothing flashy or trendy about his taste. In fact, he appeared to have a decided preference for conservative styles. They suited him. He looked good and was comfortable in everything from the faded jeans he wore during the day to the expensive slacks and jacket he had on tonight. He'd paid good money to get that jacket to fit his hard, massive frame that well, Filomena knew.

All in all, there was no doubt that Trent looked successful and motivated. He didn't look like the kind of man who would take six weeks off in the middle of summer to go fishing in the Oregon woods. It was far more likely he was in town for the business reason everyone assumed.

But he'd claimed he was here only for a vacation and, Filomena reflected with a smile, Trent certainly didn't take to having his word questioned. The arrogance of the man was amusing now that she was no longer dealing with it in the middle of a dance floor.

For a woman who was rather enjoying the stir she was causing in her hometown, she had discovered an alarming dislike of being involved in a public scene with Trent Ravinder. Perhaps that was because she suspected that if push ever came to shove, she probably wouldn't win in any confrontation with the man. Filomena didn't like the feeling. These days she was accustomed to winning.

During the past few years she had learned the pleasures of her own personal strength, determination and abilities. She was not the weak, naive little fool who had once made such an idiot of herself over a man from Gallant Lake, Oregon. Business success, extensive travel and the necessity of working with a variety of top-level creative, often temperamental people had taught her just how much internal power she had. She had an abundance of confidence and poise now. She didn't appreciate the notion that Trent Ravinder, a man she barely knew, could ruffle those hard-won qualities, even for a moment. She had been right to keep him at bay for the past two weeks.

As they approached the table, Trent reluctantly released his hold on Filomena. He smiled at her parents. Filomena had to admit he had certainly charmed them.

"I've brought her back safe and sound."

Amery Cromwell smiled pleasantly. Filomena's father had bequeathed her his red hair and hazel-gold eyes. "Of course you did. What could happen on a dance floor? Sit down, both of you. Agnes and George have ordered some champagne to toast the engaged couple."

"Just the thing for celebrating engagements, I always say," Aunt Agnes declared cheerfully. She was older than her brother, somewhere in her sixties. The deep red hair of former years had long since turned gray, but Agnes refused to accept the inevitable. Agnes also refused to pay the fees charged by professional hairstylists. She bought her own hair-coloring supplies at the local drugstore, and she never quite followed the instructions apparently. Either that or she preferred to exercise a measure of creativity. The result was a halo of short curls dyed a vivid shade of orange.

George Buckner, Agnes's husband, was a self-made man and proud of it. He had put his money into real estate for the past forty years. He loved land and had a deep, abiding faith in it as an investment. He was also a big man, and Filomena and her sister had learned from the cradle that his spirit of generosity was as large as the rest of him.

George and Agnes had never had children of their own, and they had delighted in giving their nieces presents on all major occasions. They would have given Filomena and Shari more down through the years if Amery and Meg Cromwell hadn't taken a firm stand against too many gifts. The parents had been afraid the girls would be spoiled. But George and Agnes had found ways to smuggle small, delightful presents to their nieces at odd moments when everyone thought Amery and Meg weren't looking. Filomena knew Uncle George and Aunt Agnes loved the pleasure of surprising her and her sister.

Trent's gaze swept the family group as he seated Filomena. He noticed that Agnes was sipping at another martini. It was her third. After knowing her for a couple of weeks, he was not surprised.

He smiled at the older woman as he took his own seat beside Filomena. "You surprise me, Agnes. I would have expected you to order a bottle of gin for Shari and Jim, not champagne."

"Never let it be said I don't respect the traditions," Agnes said firmly. "Besides, gin is expressly designed for retired schoolteachers. Young ones such as Shari should still try to get a variety in their diet." She toasted her soon-to-be married niece with her martini glass.

"Too bad not everyone around here has some respect for the traditions," George inserted with a glowering look at Filomena that only barely masked his amusement.

Filomena's expression was innocent. It was something she did well, Trent had decided. It worked because there really was a genuine, fundamental innocence about her that seemed to go hand in hand with the underlying spirit of mischief. She smiled serenely at her uncle. "Are you implying I lack suitable respect for wedding customs and conventions, Uncle George?"

"We've been hearing about that so-called 'ladies' night out' party you gave for Shari night before last."

Shari spoke up. "That was my 'farewell to singlehood' party. Every woman is entitled to one. Men have bachelor parties, don't they?"

"That's not the point," Uncle George declared. He turned to Shari's fiancé. "Have you heard about that party?"

"I've heard," Jim said dryly. "Frankly, the less I hear, the better. I have a feeling this may be one of those cases where ignorance is bliss."

Agnes lowered her voice and glared at Filomena. "Well, out of sight is definitely not out of mind. Not in a town this size. You know what everyone's saying, don't you? Gossip has it that you imported a male stripper along with the wine and canapés. But no one knows for certain because none of the women who attended is talking. I have been told," she concluded ominously, "that a condition for attending the party was a vow of silence. Nothing was more likely to get everyone talking about it, and you know it."

"I would like to take this opportunity to state categorically that I definitely did not import a male stripper for Shari's party," Filomena said piously.

Shari nearly choked on her wine. Jim Devore gave his bride-to-be a severe look.

Trent, who, along with everyone else at the lodge, had heard the laughter that had emanated from behind the sealed doors of the lodge's old ballroom the night of the party, raised quizzical eyebrows at Filomena. Mischief he would tolerate but the elf needed to learn that he wouldn't allow any outright lies. "Is that a fact?"

Filomena lifted her chin, her eyes filled with laughter. "Yes, it's a fact. Damian Fontaine is no sleazy stripper."

"What is he then?" Trent asked politely, remembering the glimpse he had caught of the lean, muscular young man he had seen being smuggled in amid a crowd of caterers who had arrived from a larger, neighboring town.

"Mr. Fontaine bills himself as an exotic dancer," Filomena explained in haughty accents. "He's had classical ballet training, you know."

A groan echoed around the table. Shari had to work to suppress her giggles.

"I should have known the rumors were true," Jim remarked, looking resigned. "Be warned, Trent. The women in this family need a firm hand on the reins."

"Oh, dear," Filomena's mother said in pained tones. "Then

it's true, there *was* a stripper at the lodge the other night. How will I ever explain it?''

"He was not a stripper!" Filomena declared staunchly. No one paid any attention to her denial.

Trent gave Meg Cromwell a reassuring look. "My suggestion is that you rise above it and pretend it never happened. Hope and pray that the ladies who attended will keep their vows of secrecy and that the gossip will fade.''

"I seem to have done a lot of pretending and hoping and praying in that regard since Filomena showed up a couple of weeks ago.''

Trent slanted the older woman a quick, sympathetic grin. He liked Meg. She made an excellent hostess for the Gallant Lake Lodge. There was an air of tranquil relaxation about the place, but under the surface everything was run with efficiency. He had a hunch that underlying efficiency was largely due to Meg Cromwell. Her husband's talents lay in other directions. Amery was a first-rate accountant and fly fisherman. The lodge relied on his skills in both areas.

Aunt Agnes intervened. "I warned you we were going to have to keep an eye on that redheaded gal of yours while she's here. She's in a mood to cause trouble. Just look at that itty-bitty scrap of a dress that shows half her backside. A few years ago Amery would have sent her back upstairs to change if she'd showed up ready to go out to dinner in a dress like that.''

Filomena gave her aunt a fond look. "Just be grateful it doesn't show half of my front side, too, Aunt Agnes. I've got another one that does.''

Agnes plunked her glass down on the table and gave a shout of laughter. She pointed a bright red fingernail at Trent. "You see what I mean? Nothing but trouble, that gal. Sassy, independent and reckless. You need a husband to look after you, Filomena Cromwell. Someone to keep you in line.''

"You know how I feel about marriage, Aunt Agnes.''

"You'd change your mind if the right man ever came along.'' Agnes gave a woeful sigh. "Who'd have thought someone that small could cause so much mischief? Think you can handle her, Trent?''

Trent was aware of Filomena's quelling glance but he chose to ignore it as he answered her aunt. He knew that even though it had been Agnes who had asked the question, that same anxious query was in the minds of the rest of the family. Amusement lit his eyes. Filomena really had them going, he thought. ''Trust me, Agnes. I'll keep her out of trouble.''

Everyone except Filomena laughed as if he'd made a clever joke, but Ravinder heard the underlying note of relief buried beneath the humor. Filomena said nothing. She sipped her glass of white wine and looked at him over the rim as if he were an alien entity she had accidentally stumbled upon. She was deciding what to do with him, Trent knew. The cool, calculating expression in her hazel-gold eyes told him she hadn't yet figured out just what approach to use. Once she made up her mind, she would be a formidable opponent.

Unless he disarmed her first, Trent thought. *Unless he turned her into a sweet, loving lady who would save all that fire and ice for the bedroom. His bedroom.* He felt himself tighten with an annoying but increasingly familiar rush of desire. He had begun suffering these unexpected bouts of sensual arousal soon after he'd been introduced to Filomena Cromwell, and he was a long way from getting accustomed to them. For years he had been coolly in control of himself in virtually all areas of his life, including his own sexual needs. It was both irritating and exciting to discover that this redheaded slip of a woman had the power to threaten his masculine control.

He glanced at Filomena as the conversation changed to a discussion of the new house Jim and Shari planned to buy. Filomena appeared to be interested in what was being said, but Trent sensed she was still very aware of him. Good. It was some consolation to know that she couldn't dismiss him completely from her mind when something else caught her attention. But her absorption in the topic of house buying gave him a chance to examine her thoughtfully.

As usual she looked like an elfin queen among a flock of handsome giants. That had been Ravinder's first impression of her, and it returned every time he saw her surrounded by her family.

The fact was, Filomena was quite short by Cromwell standards. Even the women in the family were tall. Her mother and her sister and her aunt were all six or seven inches taller than she was and built along Junoesque lines. The men were even larger. Filomena's father and her Uncle George were well over six feet, and there was a sense of solid density about both of them. The newest member of the family, Jim Devore, was built like a football player and probably stood six-one or two.

Filomena was petite, slender and delicate. Trent knew he could cup one of her round, pert breasts easily in the palm of his hand. He could wrap both hands around the enticing swell of her derriere. The knowledge didn't do much to drain the sensual tension from his body.

The slinky gown Filomena was wearing emphasized her narrow waist and the lush, sweet flare of her hips and thighs. She might be diminutive in height, but she was a good object lesson on the wonders of proportion, Trent told himself. For the past two weeks he had known beyond a shadow of a doubt that she would be absolutely perfect for his bed. The thought of her lying beneath him, responding to him was enough to make him work to stifle a groan.

Filomena turned her head at that moment, her gaze locking briefly with his, and Trent knew she had read his thoughts. He saw the faint, betraying flush in her cheeks, and he smiled. He wanted her aware of him. She had been staying out of reach for too long. Her response to his knowing smile was a quick flash of feminine anger in her wide eyes, and then she looked away again, refusing to meet his gaze any longer.

Trent took a sip of his beer and considered Filomena's profile. The red hair flowed in luxurious waves down her back, practically begging a man to twist his hands in its depths and feel the fire. Her large hazel-gold eyes were framed by soft, casually brushed bangs that had obviously been professionally styled to compliment the shape of her face. She was no riveting beauty, but it took quite a while to realize it because her features were so expressive. When a man did realize it, he no longer cared one way or the other about classical beauty. Filomena offered so much more. Laughter, anger, passion—all those expressions came easily to her elfin face.

Trent remembered what she had said about once being plump. It amused him to think of her that way. He was willing to bet he would find Filomena just as sexy with twenty pounds more on her bones as he found her now, and that was very, very sexy, indeed.

Trent considered the role the Cromwell family had more or less assigned him. He knew Filomena's people were worried. Even he had heard the gossip about the Paxtons' domestic problems. He'd seen Gloria Paxton earlier this evening sitting with her husband. It was obvious she had once been a very attractive young woman, but her natural beauty was hidden tonight beneath an expression of resentment and pouting depression. Gloria Paxton was a sad, bitter, discontented woman, and it showed.

Trent had heard Meg Cromwell remark privately that Gloria had put on weight since the birth of her second child. But it need not have affected her attractiveness, Trent decided, if she had dressed to suit her changed figure. Unfortunately it was obvious Gloria Paxton was still trying to pretend she was a size eight. The result was that she looked as if she'd been poured into the silver lamé dress she was wearing, her large breasts threatening to spill out of the front while the seams around the hipline appeared ready to burst. The skirt was much too short. Nothing seemed in proper proportion.

Gloria's hair was an unnatural shade of platinum blond, stiff with lacquer and done in a wild, flamboyant style that seemed all wrong for her face. It was a style that might have looked cute on a coed a decade ago. On top of everything else, Gloria's makeup was far too heavy.

All in all, Trent decided, he felt sorry for Gloria Paxton. It was hard to imagine her as the woman who had stolen away Filomena's fiancé nine years before.

Trent's sympathy for the Paxtons ended there. Every time he caught a glimpse of Brady Paxton he felt nothing but a cold need to assert himself and make it clear that Paxton no longer had any rights at all to Filomena Cromwell.

Because in spite of what Filomena had said on the dance floor, Trent was certain of what he had seen in Paxton's gaze when the other man had looked at Filomena. There was no doubt that Paxton wanted another shot at the woman he had once rejected. The man had hardly been able to take his eyes off Filomena all evening. The humble daisy of yesterday had bloomed into a brilliant, exotic flower, and Paxton wanted to pluck it.

Which, of course, was precisely why Trent Ravinder had been drafted into the role of escort for Filomena. The last thing the Cromwells wanted was a scandal on the eve of Shari Cromwell's wedding. Filomena could go back to Seattle after it was all over and laugh to her heart's content; the rest of the Cromwells would have to stay in town and endure the aftermath.

Filomena Cromwell was, in the eyes of her family and most of the neighbors, a wild card, unpredictable and potentially dangerous.

Trent found himself smiling in anticipation.

Chapter Two

FILOMENA STAYED on her best behavior for the remainder of the evening. She was well aware that Trent Ravinder was poised like a hunting cat, waiting for her to put a foot wrong. It amused her to wonder what he thought he could actually do if she did decide to cause trouble.

She was warmly polite to all the people who came by the table to congratulate Shari and Jim and say hello to her. She chatted briefly with several old acquaintances with whom she had once gone to school. Many of them couldn't help sneaking amazed glances at her. Obviously Brady Paxton wasn't the only one who seemed to be wondering what had happened to the previous version of Filomena Cromwell.

But the evening didn't get really exciting until Gloria and Brady Paxton left their table and started toward the Cromwells. Even from this distance it was easy to see the idea of saying hello was not Gloria's. It would be the first time Filomena had confronted Brady and Gloria in person since her return. She heard her sister's quick intake of breath as the Paxtons made their way across the crowded room. Then she saw Jim reach over to pat his fiancée's hand reassuringly. Meg Cromwell shot Filomena a quelling glance. Amery eyed his daughter warily. Aunt Agnes and Uncle George had the same expressions they always got just before the fireworks started at the town's annual Fourth of July celebration.

Trent didn't move, but he picked up his glass of beer and smiled deliberately and dangerously at Filomena.

Filomena had to struggle to keep from laughing. She thought of telling everyone not to worry, that the last thing she wanted was Brady Paxton back, but then she asked herself why she should spoil the fun. The rest of the family and half the diners in the room were obviously suffering that delightful sense of terror and anxiety one experienced at the top of a roller coaster.

Instead of offering reassurance to her nervous relatives, Filomena took the opportunity to examine Brady Paxton in detail. No doubt about it, she must have been a fool nine years ago. She really couldn't imagine what she had ever seen in him. As she looked at him, she realized she felt absolutely nothing except regret at having wasted her freshman year in college pining for him.

Brady had played football in high school, but now he had a distinct businessman's bulge at the waistline. Too much time spent behind a desk and not enough at the gym, Filomena decided. The additional weight was minor, however. It wasn't sufficient to detract much from his open, outdoorsy good looks.

He still had those blue bedroom eyes and that wealth of tawny-brown hair. Dressed in a properly fitting jacket he would always be a handsome man by most standards, but Filomena thought he looked oddly soft and uninteresting to her now. She hadn't noticed it when she'd been on the verge of turning twenty, but now she realized what was missing in Brady. There was no sense of depth to him, nothing that demanded respect or promised emotional strength when it was needed.

It was then Filomena acknowledged to herself that those were precisely the qualities she had sensed in Trent Ravinder. There was a steel core in Trent that was totally lacking in Paxton. She knew instinctively, and with a certainty she couldn't explain, that while Ravinder might be arrogant, demanding, stubborn and difficult at times, he would also be a rock when he was needed.

Fortunately, she thought, she didn't need any rocks in her life.

"Good evening, Amery, Meg..." Brady Paxton greeted everyone politely until he'd made the rounds of the table. Amery introduced him to Ravinder, explaining that Trent was staying at the lodge for the summer. The two men exchanged short, stiff nods. Brady's eyes kept returning to Filomena, who smiled her most dazzling smile in response. "Good to see you again, Fil. It's been a long time."

Aware of the hostility in Gloria's eyes, Filomena sorted through several rejoinders and finally came up with the blandest one she could find. "Yes, hasn't it? Time flies when you're having fun. How's the insurance business?" Brady had joined Gloria's father's insurance agency shortly after marrying Gloria. The agency's name had promptly been changed from Halsey Insurance to Halsey-Paxton Insurance. At the time, that had seemed more important than anything else in the world to Brady.

Brady nodded complacently. "Can't complain. We hear you're doing very well, Fil. Quite the little entrepreneur, huh?"

Gloria spoke up. "Yes, Fil, we hear you're involved in the fashion business. Lots of travel and shows and wheeling and dealing. Who would have guessed you had any talent in that direction?"

Filomena turned up the voltage of her smile. "I certainly didn't show much flair for it in high school, did I? But that was because I hadn't had any training in the principles of design. I've always loved color and fabric and style. I just didn't understand them or how they applied to someone my size when I was a girl."

Gloria's expression soured at the good-natured response. "That's right, you concentrate on styles for short women, don't you? Nothing I'd be interested in."

"That's correct. My firm designs exclusively for petite women," Filomena murmured, remembering how she had once envied Gloria's five feet seven inches of model-perfect figure. "Officially the term refers to women five foot four and under. There are millions of women who aren't tall enough to look really good in the standard sizes."

"I know," Gloria said with an acid pity. "Poor things. They tend to look swamped in their clothes, regardless of how much they pay for them. Sleeves are too long, waistlines don't fit right, hem lengths are dowdy-looking. Must be very depressing."

Out of the corner of her eye, Filomena saw Shari bite her lip. Filomena had once looked that way in her own clothing, and everyone knew it. Her plumpness at the time hadn't helped. She knew her sister was about to jump to her defense, even if it did mean creating the scene the family had hoped to avoid. Filomena kicked her sister under the table in an old warning left over from childhood. Shari frowned but swallowed whatever it was she had been about to say.

"It's all a matter of proportion, Gloria, as I'm sure you realize," Filomena said easily, determined to defuse the situation. She had no quarrel with Gloria Paxton. If anything she felt sorry for her. "The right fit in clothes makes all the difference."

"Well, your clothes have certainly made a difference in you," Gloria observed coldly. The implication was clear. Gloria was attributing all of Filomena's obvious success and style to her clothes alone.

Filomena's eyes danced as she thought of the years of hard work, tension and penny-pinching anxiety behind her. The clothes she now wore were the least important change that had occurred in her life. Her laughter bubbled forth, warm and genuine. She picked up her wineglass.

"Thank you for noticing, Gloria. I realize I've changed during the past few years. Lucky for me, hmm? I don't even want to think about what a disaster it would have been for me to have married and settled down when I was nineteen. It's so easy to make foolish mistakes at that age, isn't it?" She grinned. "Just think of what I would have been like if I'd stayed here in Gallant Lake. No style, no Porsche, no travel, no fun at all. A woman sometimes needs time to come into her own."

There was a moment's silence around the table as everyone absorbed the underlying fact that Gloria Paxton probably thought she had been the one who had made the mistake when she was nineteen. Gloria's face turned a dull red.

Shari and her mother made a few frantic but false conversational starts in an effort to smooth over the awkward situation, but it was Amery who coughed and looked determinedly at Brady.

"Say, I think my fire insurance policy is about due for renewal, isn't it, Brady? Let me know if I need to update the coverage. Can't afford to be without decent insurance in my business, you know."

"I'll review the policy for you, Amery," Brady said absently. He seemed unaware of his wife's hostility. He switched his attention to Trent. "How are you enjoying your summer on the lake, Ravinder?"

Trent smiled meaningfully at Filomena. "I don't think it's going to be boring."

Filomena sensed the cool claim Trent was making and knew it had not gone unnoticed by Brady or anyone else. She didn't like it, but there wasn't much she could do about it at that moment. Brady frowned. "I hear you work for Asgard Development."

"That's right."

"They've been doing a lot of resort development in Arizona and Hawaii for the past few years."

"Resort development is Asgard's specialty." Trent's voice was strictly neutral.

Brady summoned up his best business smile. "Local gossip says Asgard has sent you here to look us over."

"Is that right? Well, you know what they say about gossip," Trent said casually.

"I know what they say about smoke," Brady shot back bluntly.

Trent looked at him. "If I were you, I wouldn't waste any time looking for the fire. Not in this case. I'm here for a vacation, not business."

Brady chuckled and held up a hand. "Say no more. I get the picture. In your business I know you have to watch your tongue. But if I can be of any help in familiarizing you with the area, just let me know. I've lived here all my life, and I've got a lot of contacts. I know everyone who's anyone in business around this neck of the woods. Done some real estate investment myself, you know. I've got a feel for the area.''

"Thank you," Trent said with grave politeness. "I'll keep that in mind."

Brady turned back to Filomena. "Hey, little buddy, we'll have to get together while you're in town. Catch up on old times. We've got a lot to talk about, you and I. Have you told Trent that we were once engaged?" Behind him, Gloria looked more resentful than ever.

Filomena was about to gently deny that she had anything to talk about with Brady, but she never got the chance. Trent stepped in to answer before Filomena could speak.

"I'm afraid Filomena's going to be very busy while she's here. And, yes, she's mentioned the engagement. As she said, it's easy to make mistakes when you're nineteen. But she seems to know her own mind now. She and I are discovering we have a lot in common."

"Oh, ho," Brady said, undaunted. A sly expression crossed his face. "So that's the way it is, huh?" He winked broadly at Filomena. "Never a dull moment for you these days, right?"

"Right." Filomena shot Trent a dark glance. "A few highly exasperating moments, but seldom any dull ones."

Trent smiled with arrogant complacency. "I aim to please."

Filomena gritted her teeth behind her sugary smile. "The question, of course, is how good is your aim?"

"Practice makes perfect. When I take you home tonight, I'll try to get in a little more practice. I'm sure I'll get it right one of these days."

Aunt Agnes nearly choked on her own giggles. Filomena felt herself turning a vivid pink as her aunt led everyone else at the table in a roar of delighted laughter. Brady Paxton tried for an amused expression, but it turned slightly sour. Gloria just glared at Filomena. The Paxtons excused themselves while the laughter still filled the air around the Cromwell table.

Filomena contented herself by giving Trent a cool, dismissing look. The man was going to prove difficult, it seemed. Well, two could play at that game. She smiled at him with cold challenge.

"I'm sure your qualifications are excellent when it comes to developing multimillion-dollar resorts, Trent, but I think this other job you seem to be trying to undertake is a little outside your area of expertise. I wouldn't want to see you bite off more than you can chew."

He grinned at her. "Don't worry about me, Filomena. I've got staying power."

Aunt Agnes toasted him with her martini glass. "You listen to him, gal. Lot to be said for staying power in a man. The Brady Paxtons of this world haven't got it. I should know. Had that Paxton boy in my sixth-grade class. I knew the day you got engaged to him you'd made a big mistake. Didn't George and I tell you so? Damn glad to see it end, I can tell you."

"Now, Agnes," George interrupted, "there's no need to go over that old business."

"That's right," Meg decreed smoothly. She gave Filomena a direct look. "That's all in the past. I'm sure Filomena has no intention of raking over old ashes, do you, Fil?"

"Who, me?"

Shari gave her sister a perceptive glance. "Filomena would have to be out of her mind to want Paxton back, but you couldn't really blame her if she decided to exact a bit of revenge while she's here. I mean, it wouldn't be hard. It's as plain as the nose on his face that Brady is drooling already. And poor Gloria is an easy target."

"It would be like shooting fish in a barrel," Trent stated bluntly. "Which is one very good reason why Filomena isn't going to bother with revenge. It would be too easy, and she doesn't need it."

Filomena leaned back in her chair and toyed with her wineglass. The man was really beginning to annoy her. "How would you know what I need, Trent?"

Amery coughed loudly. "Uh, it's getting late, isn't it? Got to be up early tomorrow morning if we want to get in some good fishing, Trent. Meg, Agnes, George, come on, let's head for home. Shari and Jim probably want to stay and dance a while longer, but the rest of us need our beauty sleep.''

Filomena laughed at her father as he made a production out of the departure. "Trying to get me out of public view, Dad? Relax. I'm having a good time. I think I'll stay here with Shari and Jim. They won't mind.''

"Of course we won't mind," Jim Devore said gallantly. "We'll take you home, Fil.''

But Trent was already on his feet. "Amery's right. It's time for the rest of us to leave, and that includes the potential troublemaker in the crowd. Come along, Filomena. I'll drive you back to the lodge.''

"Thanks, but no thanks." Filomena made no move to get to her feet along with everyone else. "I think I'd like to dance some more.''

"Is that right?" Trent put a hand on her shoulder as she sat firmly in her chair. "Just who are you planning to dance with?''

"Oh, there's a whole roomful of people here tonight, see?" She waved a blithe hand at the crowd around them. "I'm sure there must be someone my height in here. What about Derek Overton, Shari? He was only about five-six or seven. The perfect size for me. Is he still in town?''

Shari grinned. "Afraid not. Derek announced he was gay, became a lawyer and moved to Portland a few years ago.''

"Ah, well, there must be someone else." Filomena wriggled her fingers in a goodbye gesture at Trent. "Run along, Trent. I'll be just fine. I'm very good at taking care of myself these days, in spite of what my family thinks.''

Trent responded by putting both of his large, strong hands on her shoulders. He lifted her to her feet as easily as if she were made of feathers. "I'm not so fortunate. I have the distinct feeling I might get lost on the way back to the lodge tonight if I don't have you along as a navigator. Say good night, Filomena.''

Aware that her family was watching anxiously and that several people at nearby tables were displaying an open, avid curiosity,

Filomena decided to give in gracefully. She really had no desire to cause a scene that would embarrass everyone concerned.

"Good night, Shari, Jim. Enjoy yourselves. Wish I could do the same." Filomena knew Shari and Jim could barely contain their amusement as she was led away.

"Don't try to sound so pathetic and woebegone," Trent advised as he prodded her toward the door. Amery was already shepherding the rest of the family through the crowd. "It doesn't work. Somehow it's tough to summon up a lot of sympathy for you tonight. You've been having a great time terrorizing everyone, haven't you?"

"I don't know why everyone insists on thinking I'm here to make trouble," Filomena complained. "I'm in town for a well-earned vacation and my sister's wedding. That's all."

"Uh-huh. You're swimming through these waters like a sleek, little barracuda, trying to look harmless and innocent."

"I am harmless and innocent."

"The hell you are. I saw that gleam in your eye when the Paxtons came over to the table."

"You said yourself that trying for revenge against those two would be like shooting fish in a barrel. You were right. And if you're fair, you'll admit I behaved myself very well tonight."

Trent's mouth curved faintly. "Okay, I'll admit you managed to resist a few of the obvious temptations that were put in your path. You didn't flirt with Paxton and you didn't get too nasty with his wife, although it was close there for a while."

"I was provoked."

"True." He pushed open the glass doors and ushered her outside into the velvet darkness of an Oregon summer night. "But I can't help wondering how far things would have gone if the rest of us hadn't been around to pull on the reins."

"Not far." Filomena waved to her father who had just finished helping her mother into the family car. "Baiting Paxton would have gotten very boring very quickly, I think. Who wants to be bored?"

"I'll try not to bore you, Filomena," Trent said coolly as he opened the door of his gray Mercedes and put her into the front seat. He shut the door deliberately on her answering comment.

Filomena glared at him through the windshield as he came around the front of the car, but by the time he was sliding into the seat beside her, she had stopped glaring. She was suddenly aware of just how much space he seemed to occupy in the vehicle. He really was a big man. Automatically she edged a little closer into her own corner as she fastened the seat belt. She watched Trent shrug out of his expensive jacket and toss it carelessly onto the back seat. "This whole thing is really very funny, isn't it?"

Trent switched on the ignition and put his arm along the back of the seat as he glanced over his shoulder. He backed the Mercedes neatly out of its slot in the parking lot. "You seem to find it all amusing. If you thought it was going to be fun to return to the old hometown and show everyone how much you've changed, why haven't you done it before now?"

Filomena shrugged. "There hasn't been much opportunity. I haven't gotten where I am by taking vacations. This is my first real one in ages. Usually I just grab a weekend here and there, and frankly there are more exciting places to spend a weekend than Gallant Lake. You're in a high-pressure business. You must know how it is."

"I know," he said with unexpected empathy. He guided the car out onto the narrow road that led back along the lake toward the lodge. "Sometimes we need to slow down and take the time to sort out priorities. I'm here on vacation, too, remember?"

"That's not what Brady Paxton thinks."

"I'm not interested in what Paxton thinks. I'm interested in what you think."

"Is that right?" She slanted him a covert glance. His face looked hard and unyielding in the shadowed confines of the car. But that didn't surprise her. Trent's face looked hard and unyielding most of the time except when he flashed his brief rather wicked smiles. "Why would you care what I think, Trent?"

"Seriously?"

She nodded. "Seriously. I know that you were doing my family a favor tonight by acting as an escort for me, but I figure that's about all it amounts to—a favor. Why should you care what I think about you?"

"If you have to ask that, then you haven't learned as much as you think you have during the past few years. Maybe we should talk about the gap in your education."

Before Filomena could answer, he slowed the car unexpectedly, turning off onto a tiny side road that led down to the lakefront.

Filomena straightened in her seat, her curiosity and desire to bait Trent fading rapidly as a new kind of tension rippled through her. "Where are we going, Trent?"

"To the fishing spot your father took me to yesterday morning." He reduced his speed even more to compensate for the unpaved surface. The narrow track wound down toward the lake through a thick stand of pine and fir.

Filomena told herself she ought to make a firm and forceful protest before they reached the water's edge. She was almost positive Trent would turn back if she made a fuss. He was, after all, a friend of the family. Her father certainly liked and trusted him, and Trent appeared to return the respect Amery showed him. Such a man would not abuse that trust. If she demanded to be driven straight home, Trent would do it. Filomena was sure of it.

Perhaps it was because she was so certain of it that she she refrained from making the demand. Trent probably intended to kiss her, but that hardly constituted an earthshaking event. She could handle him.

Filomena relaxed in her seat as Trent brought the Mercedes to a halt at the edge of the lake. He turned off the engine and rolled down his window. The whisper of the wind in the treetops made its way into the car. Moonlight glittered faintly on the surface of the dark lake. On the far side an occasional pinpoint of light marked the location of a house or a car driving along the shore. The evidence of human habitation was sparse and distant, however. Filomena was suddenly aware of how very much alone she and Trent were.

Trent unfastened his seat belt and turned slightly, draping one arm over the wheel as he lounged back into his corner. He definitely filled up more than his fair share of the car, Filomena thought. And she couldn't help noticing the faint gleam in his gaze.

"We made a good catch here just at dawn yesterday," Trent murmured. "The lake was like glass, and you could see every tiny ripple the fish made. Watching you is a similar experience. Did you know that? You've got a smooth, glossy surface, but it's easily disturbed by whatever emotion you're feeling. I like that. The laughter moves through your eyes and across your mouth the way the ripples move on the lake. So do irritation and sympathy and friendliness and anger."

"Did you bring me here to tell me I'm easy to read?"

"No." He reached over and unbuckled her seat belt. "I brought you here to see if passion moves through you the way all your other emotions do. I want to see if I can feel the ripples."

Filomena tensed as she found herself being enfolded in Trent's arms, her soft, slender frame cradled against his hard body. She felt the heat in him and inhaled the faint tang of soap and aftershave and an indefinable male essence that threatened to swamp her senses.

"So you're running an experiment on me, is that it?" she asked.

"Call it what you want." He looked down into her face as his hand moved through her hair and found the triangle of flesh exposed by the deep V in the back of the gown.

Filomena shivered a little as his warm fingers made contact with her bare skin. "Just remember you're not the only one who can run an experiment."

He traced the graceful line of her spine with a blunt-tipped finger. "I'll share the results I get with you if you'll share the results you get with me."

Filomena was torn between a deep, sensual curiosity and an abrupt burst of uncertainty. She wasn't really afraid of Trent, but she was suddenly afraid of the situation. For two weeks she had adroitly managed to prevent anything from occurring. Now the decision had been taken out of her hands. This wasn't going to be just a casual experiment, and she knew it. Her nervousness, she realized, stemmed from the fact that she was fairly certain Trent knew it, too.

But it was too late to call a halt now. Filomena felt both trapped and oddly comforted in the strong arms that were holding her. Her hands moved upward to brace herself against Trent's broad shoulders. She lifted her face to find the truth in his eyes, but his mouth came down on hers before she could see anything clearly.

Filomena's coral-colored nails sank reflexively into the fabric of Trent's white shirt, biting into the hard, muscled skin underneath as she endured the first impact of his kiss. Somehow, she thought dazedly, it just wasn't what she had been expecting. But she also realized she couldn't have described just exactly what she had been expecting.

Perhaps she had been anticipating more of a tentative, exploratory approach. Perhaps she had assumed there would be a little more initial hesitation. She should have known better, she told herself.

She should have realized that with this man everything would be deliberate, bold and inevitable. She ought to have expected this heat and this fierce, unleashed demand. He was not the kind of man who would do anything in a halfhearted or hesitant way. Most especially he would not make love to a woman with anything other than full power.

Trent's kiss was a deep, ravening thing that engulfed Filomena even as it compelled her response. Her mouth opened of its own volition, granting him an even more intimate access. When she felt the probing touch of his tongue, she shuddered.

Trent's response was a groan of hungry desire that she could feel deep in his chest. His hand moved across her bare shoulders to the narrow sleeve of her dress. "I knew it," he muttered against her mouth. "I knew I'd be able to feel the ripples go through you."

"Trent..."

But his fingers were already sliding beneath the fabric of her dress at the shoulders. With a smooth, easy movement, he tugged the front of the gown downward, sliding the jersey sleeves to her wrists and the once demure neckline almost to her waist.

Filomena gasped in startled dismay. It had happened too quickly, leaving her exposed and vulnerable long before she had made the decision herself. She pulled back but discovered she was bound, her hands trapped in her dress sleeves. Her widening eyes flew to his.

"Take it easy, honey. You know I'm not going to hurt you." Trent caught her wrists and began easing her hands free. His eyes roved over her bared breasts, and just before he released her wrists, he bent his head to drop a featherlight kiss on one budding nipple.

Another shiver of desire went through Filomena. Nervous tension followed in its wake. "Trent, this has gone far enough," she began in a soft, throaty voice that she knew betrayed her clouded emotions.

"I just want to touch you."

His tone was heavy with desire, but Filomena could feel the control he had on himself. She was as safe as she wanted to be. The knowledge only added to the sensation of walking a high wire. When his fingertips cupped her small, rounded breasts and grazed lightly across the nipples, she moaned.

And then her hands were free, and instead of pushing herself away and recovering her dress, Filomena found herself clinging to Trent. She buried her hot face against his shoulder and closed her eyes as excitement rippled through her.

"I knew it would be like this," Trent whispered roughly. "Ever since you arrived two weeks ago, I've known. Every time I've looked at you, I've ached because I realized what it would be like. I don't know how I waited this long."

"Oh, Trent..."

"Hush. Just relax and let it happen. It's going to happen, you know."

"Not tonight."

"If not tonight, then another night. It might as well be now."

Desperately she struggled to resist the compelling quality of his voice. She summoned up an image of her parents who would be slyly watching the clock to see how long it took Trent and their daughter to get home. "My family. They saw us leave right behind them. If we're not home soon, they'll know—"

"They'll know what? That we stopped off along the way? Why should they be surprised? They realize we don't have much privacy at the lodge. They'll understand." His big hands were moving luxuriously over her, savoring the shape of her.

"Trent, I am not going to have everyone thinking that the first time I was alone with you I let you seduce me!"

"Why should you care what they think?" He was running his fingers around her waist now, moving lower until he found the curve of her buttocks. He cupped her and squeezed gently. "You're twenty-eight years old, and you've made certain everyone knows you're a big girl now. You can do what you want."

"Exactly," she managed, struggling for a measure of common sense. "And what I want is not to have everyone leering at me around the breakfast table tomor row morning. I hardly know you, and I am not about to let you seduce me tonight in the front seat of a car."

"How about the back seat?" He nuzzled her ear beneath a fall of thick red hair. "God, you smell good."

"Trent, stop it." But she could already feel the change in him. There was a thread of good-humored resignation in his voice now. He wasn't going to push her any harder tonight.

"You're only postponing the inevitable, and I think you know it," he told her softly as he released her and assisted her back into her dress.

"No, I do not know that," she said tartly as she adjusted her clothing. "I don't know that at all. I didn't come home to have a summer fling with one of my parents' paying guests."

"Is there someone in Seattle?"

"There are lots of someones in Seattle."

"But no particular man?"

Filomena fastened her seat belt with a no-nonsense efficiency. "I don't think that's any business of yours. Take me home, Trent. It's getting late."

"If that's what you really want."

"It's what I want."

He turned the key in the ignition and drove silently back toward the main lake road. It wasn't until they were pulling into the lodge parking lot that he spoke.

"I was right," he said as if he were taking a great deal of satisfaction in something.

"Right about what?" Filomena gave him a suspicious glance.

"I could feel the passion in you just as easily as I can see ripples on a lake at dawn. It felt good, elf, even if it did leave me with an ache that's going to keep me awake half the night."

Filomena climbed out of the car and hurried toward the front door of her parents' home, which was just behind the main lodge.

As she fled up the steps she decided the evening hadn't turned out to be quite as amusing as she had anticipated, after all.

Chapter Three

FILOMENA ENJOYED THE DRIVE from the lakeside lodge into the town of Gallant Lake the next morning. The day was fresh and clean and already turning very warm. The forest that edged the road sent wave after wave of glorious pine scent through the open window of the Porsche, and the car felt good, as it always did, under her hands.

Alone at last, she thought with a smile. True, she was on a mission for her mother, but that was all right. She didn't mind making herself useful by picking up more supplies for Shari's wedding. Besides, it was a great excuse to get away for a while.

She had faced the expected inquisition at breakfast, but she thought she had handled it well. Fortunately breakfast wasn't a very private affair when the family ate in the lodge dining room. Chatting with guests and making sure everyone was enjoying himself or herself was the primary goal at such times.

Amery and Trent had both been absent. They had left to go fishing before dawn and hadn't returned by seven-thirty. That had left Shari and Filomena's mother to conduct the investigation.

"Did you have a good time last night?" Shari had asked her older sister brightly as she'd poured herself a cup of coffee. Shari had her own cottage near the lake, but she frequently showed up for breakfast in the lodge dining room.

"I had a great time," Filomena had replied. When she hadn't volunteered anything further, her mother had entered the conversation.

"Isn't Trent Ravinder a nice man? We've so enjoyed having him at the lodge this summer. He's rapidly becoming one of the family. Your father says he's an excellent fishing partner. Amery finds him quite interesting."

"He's interesting, I'll grant you that," Filomena had responded. "But I'm not so sure I'd label him 'nice.'"

"Don't keep us in suspense. Get to the good stuff," Shari had said with a grin. "Did he finally make a pass on the way home last night? Mom says you were about twenty minutes later than she and Dad were getting home."

Filomena had smiled benignly. "I'm afraid Trent took a wrong turn. It delayed us somewhat."

Shari had doubled over with laughter. "Oh, no, I don't believe it."

"What? That he made a wrong turn? It's understandable. You know how many little side roads there are around these hills. Very easy to get off on the wrong track if you don't know where you're going."

"Hah. A wrong turn? When he had you along? Come off it, Fil. You were raised around here. You know all the back roads. He *did* make a pass, didn't he?" Shari's eyes had danced as she'd turned to her mother. "See? I told you. No need to fret about Fil making mischief with Brady Paxton. Trent's going to keep her out of trouble for us."

"Such a nice man," Meg Cromwell had repeated in heartfelt tones. "You know, Fil, lately I've been worrying that you might be getting a little too picky about your men these days. You're not getting any younger, you know, and the latest statistics claim it's getting harder and harder for women in your age group to find a husband."

Filomena had laughed. "For your information, Mom, I could get married any time I choose. You'd be amazed how many men become interested in matrimony when they find out how much money I'm making these days." Filomena's mouth had twisted wryly. "Believe me, the income from Cromwell &

Sterling, Inc., is more than enough to compensate for all those dire statistics.''

"Well, you wouldn't have to worry about Trent Ravinder marrying you just to get a share of Cromwell & Sterling," Meg had retorted. "The man gets paid a fortune by Asgard Development. In addition, he's done extremely well on his own in real estate. Your Uncle George says Trent has an instinct for land and how to make money with it. George should know. According to George, Trent could probably buy and sell Cromwell & Sterling if he wanted to do so.''

"Somehow," Filomena had said thoughtfully, "that is not terribly reassuring.''

"You're just being difficult," Shari had declared. "But be warned: Trent is closing in on you, and by the time you realize what's happening, it's going to be too late to run. Wait and see.''

Filomena had sputtered slightly over her coffee, but the sputter had turned to laughter, and that had been the end of that topic of conversation.

Thinking about it now as she drove the curving road toward town, Filomena decided the morning inquisition could have been a lot worse. There was no doubt her parents and everyone else were quite taken with Trent Ravinder. Given the fact that they were also uneasy about any possible plans Filomena might have regarding Brady Paxton, it was understandable that they would all cheerfully conspire to push her and Trent together.

The only real mystery in the whole matter had been why Trent was allowing himself to be manipulated so easily. But perhaps that mystery had been cleared up last night when he had made that pass in the car.

He wanted her, and he was not averse to having her steered in his direction.

It made sense, Filomena thought, trying to be objective. Here he was spending several weeks in a relatively isolated location with only a small town nearby to provide entertainment. The possibility of a little dalliance with the innkeeper's daughter was probably not such an uninteresting proposition, especially since the innkeeper's daughter appeared old enough and savvy enough to know what she was doing. It was an added bonus that the innkeeper and his family were willing to aid and abet the affair.

There was only one drawback as far as Filomena could see and that was that, while she might be old enough to handle an affair with Trent Ravinder, she wasn't at all certain she was sufficiently savvy.

The truth was that Filomena's self-assurance had come from her business success and not from conducting a rousing love life. When one worked as hard as she had worked for the past nine years, there wasn't much time left over for an active love life, even if one had been interested in conducting affairs.

On top of that plain fact, there had been an added complication for Filomena. She knew deep inside she wasn't really cut out for a series of light and scintillating affairs. Perhaps she was too much of a small-town girl at heart, or perhaps she knew she was inclined to care too much when she allowed herself to care at all. Whatever the reason, she wasn't interested in a summer fling with Trent Ravinder or anyone else.

But as she pondered the matter of dealing with Trent, Filomena admitted to herself it wasn't going to be simple to keep him at a distance. That kiss in the front seat of the Mercedes had told her that much. It had forced her to confront the fact that she was attracted to the man, and she knew now he definitely wanted her. They were going to be spending the next few weeks in close proximity. That was a dangerous mixture. As far as she was concerned it was much more dangerous than anything that could possibly happen with Brady Paxton. She wondered why her family didn't see that as clearly as she did.

Probably because they seemed to have a sort of blind faith and trust in Trent. She could not really blame them. Ravinder had a way of commanding respect and trust.

Filomena parked the Porsche in front of the bank with a flourish. She knew she had an audience, and she didn't want to disappoint them. Bounding out of the car, she waved cheerfully at several people who recognized her and the vehicle. She grinned to herself when she saw them stare appreciatively at the Porsche and then at the slick little white summer dress with the wide, gutsy belt she was wearing. She knew the outfit fitted perfectly and that it had a definite rakish charm.

. The mission for her mother was soon accomplished, but when she had stashed the supplies in the back of the Porsche, Filomena decided she wasn't ready to head back to the lodge immediately. Trent would be there by now, and she still hadn't made up her mind about how to handle him.

A cup of coffee in the small restaurant next to the bank was an appealing option. She walked through the door and was immediately hailed by the middle-aged woman behind the counter.

"Well, as I live and breathe, it really is you, isn't it, Fil? Someone told me that was your hot little car out front, and I couldn't believe it. Haven't seen you in a month of Sundays. Let's have a look at you, girl. That is some outfit you've got on. Turn around and let's see the back."

Filomena obediently twirled around and showed off the triangle cutout that revealed a tantalizing glimpse of skin and the black buttons that marked the open slit at the hemline of the skirt. "Well? What do you think, Muriel? We're putting this into our resort collection this winter."

"You want my opinion?" Muriel chuckled with disbelief. "It's as cute as a bug's ear, but I'm no fashion expert, and you know it. Sure looks good on you, though. You've changed some, haven't you? Heard you wowed a few people at the country club last night."

Filomena winced. "You mean you've already had a report on what happened at the club last night?"

"You know how fast gossip travels around here. I also heard about that nice talk you gave to the local girls' club a few days ago. You really dazzled 'em."

"Girls that age are always fascinated with fashion and style." Filomena smiled slightly, remembering the amused tolerance in Trent's eyes when word had gotten back to the lodge about Filomena's highly successful talk. He hadn't said a word, but she had known exactly what he was thinking. *Another show for the hometown crowd.*

Muriel chuckled. "From what I hear, it wasn't just the talk on fashion you gave that interested them. You made a big point of letting them know that, if they were willing to work, they could grow up to be as successful as you've been. Good for young girls to hear that. I could have used a few lectures like that when I was growing up. Young girls need to know there's something out there besides boys."

"I gave them my opinion on boys while I was giving them the lecture on success," Filomena said.

"I heard." Muriel winked. "Something about treating boys like candy, wasn't it? Too much will rot your teeth."

"I hope they got the point," Filomena said with an answering smile.

"Even if they didn't, the volunteers who run that club sure appreciated the donation you made. Heaven knows they can use the money. They do a good job with those kids. Sit down and tell me what you've been doing with yourself."

Muriel reached for the coffeepot and took a seat in the booth across from Filomena. They chatted for fifteen or twenty minutes until the small café began to fill up with a late-morning coffee crowd. Muriel finally excused herself reluctantly.

"Sorry, but it looks like I'm going to have to get to work. You sit still and finish your coffee, Fil. I hear you're going to be around a while this summer, so maybe we'll get another chance to chat, hmm?"

"Don't worry, I plan to be here a while. I'll stop in again."

"You do that. Say hello to your mother for me."

"I will, Muriel."

Muriel went back around behind the counter, and Filomena picked up her coffee mug. She was sipping slowly, gazing pensively out the window at a street of shops that had changed very little since she had left town, when she sensed someone near her shoulder. Filomena stifled a groan and looked up.

"Hello, Brady."

"Hi, Fil. Someone said that was your green Porsche outside, so I decided to see if you were in here having a cup of coffee. I could use one myself." He sat down without waiting for an invitation and signaled Muriel for coffee. "That's quite a car, Fil. A real honey." He leaned forward, folded his arms on the counter and smiled.

Filomena remembered that smile. It had once seemed boyish and intimate and sexy. Now, after nine years in the hard world of business, she recognized the expression for what it was, a salesman's smile. Her mouth tilted in private amusement as she thought about just how naive she had been when she was nineteen. "I'm rather fond of that car myself."

"Did you have a good time last night, Fil?" Brady asked as Muriel poured the coffee.

Filomena caught the faint disapproval in Muriel's gaze before the older woman bustled back to the counter. "Terrific. What about you?"

Brady shrugged. "The usual. Gloria and I have been going out to the country club almost every Saturday night for nine years. Talk about being in a rut."

Filomena wondered where the conversation was going. "It's a nice place," she commented neutrally.

"It must seem pretty tame to you after all the world travel and city living you've been doing for the past few years." Brady's gaze became intent and curious. "You've really changed, haven't you, Fil? That car, those clothes and—" he made an all-encompassing movement with one hand "—and everything."

Filomena knew the "and everything" was Brady's attempt to describe the self-confidence she hadn't had at nineteen. She smiled slightly. "Time doesn't stand still, Brady. I've been busy during the past few years."

"So I've heard." He leaned forward even more, striving for

an air of greater intimacy. "Do you ever think about the old days, Fil? About us?"

"Nope," she said cheerfully.

"I do," he said bluntly.

"Waste of time, Brady."

"But you must wonder sometimes what we missed together, you and me," he murmured.

"I don't have much time for that kind of wondering. I've got too much going on in my life."

"I think about it a lot." He looked down at his coffee and then raised his eyes. "Gloria and me, well, it didn't quite turn out the way I thought it would."

"Things rarely do turn out the way we think they will. But in my case, they definitely turned out better than anything I could have imagined when I was nineteen. Sorry about your situation, but that's the way it goes, I guess."

"You've never married," Brady pointed out, as if the fact was evidence of her lingering heartache.

"Haven't had time for that, either."

"I burned you pretty bad, huh?"

Filoména grinned. "You want the truth, Brady? Finding you and Gloria in bed together that day was the best thing that ever happened to me. I've been profoundly grateful to both of you ever since. When I think of what I would have missed if I'd married you..." She let the sentence trail off and shook her head. "I get cold chills down my spine. Believe me, Brady, I can't thank you enough for ending our engagement."

A flash of anger appeared in Brady's eyes, and his mouth tightened briefly. Then he said coldly, "I suppose you've been through a lot of men in the past few years. Is this Ravinder guy going to be another scalp on your belt?"

Filomena felt her temper start to rise, and then she was laughing softly instead. "That's an interesting image." She wondered what Ravinder would say to becoming a scalp on her belt. The truth was, she was far more likely to become one on his if she wasn't careful.

"What's so funny?" Brady's voice turned belligerent.

"Never mind." She finished her coffee and reached for her purse. "Well, Brady, I hate to rush off, but Mom's waiting for me. I'd better be on my way."

"Fil, wait." He put out a placating hand. "I want to talk to you."

"I don't think we have much to say to each other, Brady."

"Damn it, this is important, Fil. It's business."

She eyed him warily. "What kind of business?"

"Real estate business." Brady hunched closer yet and lowered his voice. "Fil, I know Ravinder's in town to check out lakefront property for Asgard."

"He says he's not."

"What do you expect him to do? Blurt it out? Take my word for it, he's here on business. You know, you can do me and some other folks a big favor, Fil."

"I doubt it," she retorted lightly, knowing now exactly where the conversation was going.

"There's a cut in it for you," Brady said slyly. "I hear you're a hotshot business lady these days. Well, this should definitely interest you. Growing businesses always need capital. Don't try to tell me your company couldn't use some."

Filomena didn't bother. The truth was, Brady was right. Cromwell & Sterling was actively searching for capital at that very moment. She decided it was probably better if Brady didn't know that, however, so she kept her mouth shut.

"There's money in this, Fil. I guarantee it. All you have to do is use your influence on Ravinder to find out exactly what area of the lake he's interested in picking up for Asgard. I've got options on a lot of property around here. I've formed a real estate partnership operation that's been picking land up over the years just on the chance that something like this would happen. Find out which way Ravinder's going to move, and I can exercise my options on the right parcel. Then we can turn around and sell the land to Asgard."

"At about triple the value?" Filomena asked politely.

"That's what business is all about, Fil." Brady gave her an impatient look. "This could be our big chance. There's a fortune in this if we play our cards right."

"And I'm the card you want to play, is that it?"

"Look, you've got the inside track. Ravinder's interested in you. Any fool can see that. All you have to do is play up to him, get him to talk, feel him out. Finding out what he's going to recommend to Asgard should be easy for you. My partners and I would pay you a commission if the deal goes through, say five percent."

"Your generosity overwhelms me." Filomena made another move to get out of the booth.

"All right, eight percent. Fil, what's the big problem? You're probably sleeping with him already, right?"

"Wrong." Filomena realized with a sense of amazement that she was suddenly on the verge of losing her temper, really losing it. It took a lot these days, but it could still happen. Her eyes chilled as she met Brady's gaze across the table. "I am not sleeping with him, and for your information, I resent the implication that I am. I am a businesswoman, not a prostitute, and if you imply otherwise once more I will announce to the entire town exactly what you're asking me to do. I will also tell Trent Ravinder, which should put paid to your ideas of making a killing on your land options. Do we understand each other, Brady?"

"Calm down, Fil. What the hell's the matter with you? If you're a businesswoman, then you know damn well I'm only talking common sense. You're in a position to help an old friend and make a nice little commission yourself on the side. It's not like I'm asking you to seduce the guy. It's obvious you two already have something going. Think about it, Fil, that's all I'm saying. Just think about it."

Filomena smiled dangerously. "Brady, *old friend*, I learned everything I needed to know about you nine years ago, and the most important thing I learned was that you can't be trusted. I never get involved in business arrangements with people I can't trust. I'm sure you can understand that. It's just common sense. Goodbye, Brady. Go home to your wife. You wanted her badly enough nine years ago.'' She started to slide out of the booth.

Brady looked at her knowingly. "You still haven't gotten over it, have you, Fil? You're still hurting because of what happened back then. That's why you've never married, isn't it? That's why you're so upset. But things are different now. I've changed and you've changed. You're a much more interesting woman these days. This time around we could really have something together, you and I.''

"Don't hold your breath, Brady," Filomena said bluntly, and turned to walk out of the restaurant. She was aware of the interested glances from Muriel and the other customers, but she was too angry to pay much attention. Brady Paxton hadn't changed much over the years. He was still a snake. She felt sorry for Gloria, who by now had probably discovered that for herself.

Filomena tossed her purse onto the passenger seat of the Porsche and slipped behind the wheel. As soon as she felt the familiar confines of the car, she began to relax. She shouldn't have let Brady get to her. She wouldn't have if he hadn't thrown her relationship with Trent Ravinder in her face and asked her to spy on the man.

Being asked to betray Ravinder really did something to her normally placid temper. She shuddered to think what Trent himself would have to say if he knew what had just happened.

Better to let sleeping dogs lie, Filomena thought as she put the Porsche in gear and pulled out onto the main road. Trent claimed he was here for a vacation, and she was inclined to believe him. Whatever else you could say about the man, he appeared to be rigid on the subject of honesty and his own integrity. He wouldn't lie, and he wouldn't take kindly to the idea that someone was plotting to use Filomena against him. No sense risking his temper. It was probably a heck of a lot worse than her own.

By the time she was pulling into the parking lot of the Gallant

Lake Lodge, Filomena's mood was back to normal. She got out of the car and began retrieving the packages she had stashed in the back.

"I'll give you a hand," Trent said behind her.

Filomena straightened abruptly, startled by the sound of his voice. She blinked as she looked at him in the sunlight. He seemed very large standing there in his faded denims, plaid shirt and scuffed boots. Very large and very much at home in the setting of lake and trees and sky. He didn't look at all like a high-powered businessman today. He looked more like a man who made his living working outdoors with his hands.

"Hi, Trent," Filomena said politely, automatically edging a couple of steps away from him. It was a habit she had around large males. "How was the fishing?"

"The fishing was fine. It usually is with your father along." He took one of the packages out of her arms and eyed her assessingly. "Why do you do that?"

"Do what?"

"Move away from me whenever I get close."

Filomena shrugged as she started up the path toward her parents' quarters. "I just don't like people looming over me, that's all."

"Especially men?" he asked politely as he followed her up the path.

"Especially men," she agreed sweetly. "They tend to block the light. Are we eating the fish you caught for lunch today?"

"I don't know what the others are eating, but you and I are going to have tuna fish sandwiches, dill pickles and chips."

She stopped and swung around in surprise. "We are?"

"Uh-huh." Trent looked pleased with himself. "You and I are going on a picnic. Your mother had the chef pack us a lunch. How long has it been since you've been on a picnic, Filomena?"

"Ages," she admitted, continuing to stare at him uncertainly. A picnic meant being alone with Trent. She wasn't sure that was such a good idea.

"Relax," he said softly, as if he'd read her mind. "I'll try not to block out too much of the light."

Filomena found herself responding to the invitation and the reassurance in his eyes. There was no need to let him know she was wary of him. It was embarrassing and annoying. After all, she wasn't a nervous, unsophisticated teenager. "Well," she said thoughtfully, "it is a lovely day for a picnic, isn't it?"

His grin was slow and compelling. "Yes," he said. "It is."

FORTY MINUTES LATER Trent finally pronounced himself satisfied with the picnic location Filomena had suggested. She'd chosen a pebbly beach near the lake. There were several convenient boulders to provide seating, and in the trees behind them was a cool, shaded forest floor covered with pine needles. Best of all there was plenty of privacy. Trent speculated on how difficult it might be to get Filomena down onto that bed of pine.

It would probably be extremely difficult initially, but once he had her down there he was fairly certain he could convince her to stay. He knew now he could make her want him. Probably not as much as he wanted her, but he was willing to work on that part. It was just a matter of time, and he had the next few weeks ahead of him.

He watched as she unpacked the picnic basket. Her red hair shone in the sunlight that filtered through the trees. She had changed into a pair of jeans and a teal-blue shirt that was cut in a man's style yet somehow seemed to emphasize her femininity.

Trent tormented himself with visions of shaping Filomena's nicely rounded buttocks in his hands and lifting her up against his chest so that he could feel her soft, pert breasts. The images burned in his mind until he felt the sudden tightness of the denim below his waist. His body was already reacting strongly to the fantasy.

Trent stifled a rueful curse and unobtrusively shifted his position slightly as he lounged back against a boulder. Filomena's effect on him could be embarrassing at times. He didn't know whether to be relieved or annoyed that she seemed totally unaware of it.

"How was the drive into town?" Trent made himself ask conversationally. He had already decided to keep this picnic scene as casual and unthreatening as possible. Last night he had confirmed the physical attraction between them. For a few minutes there in the front seat of the Mercedes, she had practically melted in his arms. Now that he knew for certain that she would respond to him when the time came, he could afford to take it easy.

"Fine. I was just on an errand for my mother."

"Your dad says you drive that Porsche as if you were practicing for the Indianapolis 500. I'm inclined to agree with him."

Filomena chuckled. "Does that bother you, too? Poor Trent. You've taken on a terrible responsibility if you're going to start worrying about everything from my clothes to my driving. You'll be gray in no time."

"I can see why Amery worries about you."

Filomena took a sizable chunk out of her sandwich and chewed enthusiastically. "My parents have always worried about me. They used to worry because I didn't have a social life in high school. Shari, who's nearly two years younger than me, had all the dates she wanted from the moment my father allowed her out of the house at night. I always sat home and read or baby-sat. Shari was on the cheerleading squad. I never even went to the games. Then I started seeing Brady during my first year of college, and they really panicked."

"They didn't like him?"

"They thought he was taking advantage of me, just toying with me," Filomena said smoothly. "They weren't alone. Everyone wondered what Brady saw in me. That did a lot for my ego, as you can imagine. When it turned out everyone was right about Brady, my family worried about me again. They knew how humiliated I'd been. When I went back to college in the fall, they were all relieved for a while until I entered a fine arts program instead of taking more useful classes. When

Glenna and I opened our own business three years ago, Mom and Dad panicked again. They just knew it would fail because I didn't have the vaguest notion of how to run a business. But they forgot that I'm a fast learner.'' Filomena laughed at him with her eyes. "Shall I go on?''

"I think I get the picture. So now you're back in town and the family has something new to worry about.''

"Lots of new things to worry about apparently. It isn't just this business about whether or not I'm going to cause a scandal with Brady. Now Mom has started to get nervous about the fact that I'm twenty-eight years old and not married. She's been reading too many statistics, it seems. When I tell her I'm not particularly interested in marriage, she really frets.''

"Is that true? You're really not interested in marriage?'' That bothered him. She was an independent little thing. He was glad she hadn't married Paxton when she was nineteen, but it annoyed him to think she might still be off marriage.

"Frankly, I've got other, more important things going on in my life at the moment.''

"Such as?''

"It's a business matter.'' She looked at him. "Do you really want to hear about it?''

"Sure.'' He told himself he needed to know as much about her as possible. "I'm a businessman myself, remember?''

"When I see you dressed like that, it's easy to forget.''

"It's a mistake to let one segment of your life dominate all the others,'' Trent said seriously. "I've been learning that lesson lately.''

"Is that why you're taking a long vacation this summer? Trying to get some balance in your life?''

Her unexpected insight astonished him. His eyes met hers. "How did you guess?''

"I don't know,'' she confessed. "But most high-powered business people don't take six weeks off at a time. The pressure is too great. If, as you claim, you're not here to scout for Asgard, then you really must be on an extended vacation. It just struck me that maybe you're here to, well, look for something. Something personal.''

"You are a shrewd woman, Filomena. You're right. I am here to look for something. I'm thirty-six years old, and there are some things missing in my life. I came here to sort through my priorities and decide what I really want.''

Her eyes were warm with understanding. "You're a smart man and a brave one. Not everyone has the courage to assess his life and make major decisions about it. Most people find it easier to drift.''

"I think I'm in the middle of a mid-life crisis.''

She shook her head. "No, it's not a crisis. Not when you control the situation and handle it rationally the way you're doing.''

Trent began to feel uneasy. He had brought her here to learn more about her. Instead she was the one conducting the psychological probe. It was time to get things back on track. "Tell me about the business matter that's more important to you than marriage.''

She laughed. "Just a normal business decision. My partner and I have decided to expand. We're thinking about opening our own shops instead of selling just through the major department store chains. It would allow us a lot more flexibility.'' Her voice reflected her enthusiasm for the project as she spoke. "We're also considering adding a line of sports clothes for larger women, the ones who are on the other side of the average scale. They've been as overlooked by the designers as we shorter types have been.''

Trent nodded, the business side of his nature momentarily coming to the fore. "Where are you going to get the capital for that kind of expansion?''

"That's part of the problem,'' she admitted. "But Glenna and I are working on it. We've got a loan application into a bank that financed us three years ago. They were reasonably supportive in the past, and I think they will be again.''

"Maybe you shouldn't try to do both projects at once," Trent suggested. "Opening your own shops is going to be a very expensive proposition, and so is starting a new line of clothing. Pick the one you think you can handle and let the other idea ride for a while."

She flashed him a piercing look. "You're hardly an expert on the fashion business."

"True, but I am an expert on such basics as the dangers of overexpansion and the problems of finding financial resources. Maybe you and your partner should get a financial consultant in to look over your situation before you go off in a direction that could sink you and your firm. I know a good man in Seattle named Handel. He's made a specialty out of advising growing businesses like yours. He knows how critical these expansion stages are. A lot of companies collapse at this point in their development."

"If I want your advice," she said dryly, "I'll ask for it."

"I doubt it. You've probably decided I'm not qualified to advise you on the grounds that I'm too large."

She stared at him for a second and then burst into laughter.

Trent began to relax. It was going to be all right, he told himself. He could handle her. She was a challenge, but he was good at responding to challenges. All he needed was time.

Time and opportunity.

He would have time this summer, but he began to worry about opportunity. It wasn't going to be easy enticing Filomena Cromwell into a love affair when her whole family and a good portion of the local residents would be watching with avid interest. Filomena herself was too busy putting on her flashy show for the hometown folks. She was having too much fun being a big fish in a small pond. It wasn't going to be simple to distract her long enough to lure her into his arms.

He watched her eat a dill pickle and told himself that somehow, some way, he had to get her into bed. He had to find a way to overcome her wariness, a way past that slick, polished facade. Above all, he wanted to teach her that she could trust him. But he was going to have to get her full attention first.

Based on what he had learned last night when he'd held her in his arms, he had a hunch the fastest way to accomplish his goal was to awaken the passion she kept leashed inside her.

Opportunity, he told himself again. That was what he needed. He had been in the business world long enough to know that sometimes a man had to create his own opportunities. He let the conversation wander off into a variety of pleasant byways while he considered his problem.

Two hours after they had left the lodge, Trent and Filomena returned. They walked across the wide lawn toward the terrace of her parents' home, where Amery, Meg and Shari were sitting with glasses of iced tea. Trent had just decided that the afternoon had been a reasonable success and was congratulating himself on his clever handling of Filomena when the tension of the three people seated around the table finally got through to him.

It seemed to get through to Filomena at the same time.

"Hey, what's up? You three look as if you just got advance word of an earthquake," she remarked cheerfully.

Amery glanced at Trent and then at his daughter. "I don't think it's quite that serious. But you managed to shake Meg and Shari up a bit along with a fair number of neighbors."

Filomena's eyebrows rose. "Is that right? How did I do that?"

Meg Cromwell sighed. "I know there's nothing to the tale, dear, but you know how rumors fly around here. We heard you met Brady Paxton in town this morning. Someone said you'd been seen sharing coffee with him at Muriel's café. And if we've heard it, you can bet everyone else in Gallant Lake has, too, including Gloria."

Trent felt all his good resolutions about taking his time with Filomena go up in a cloud of smoke. This, he decided, was what came of giving a woman too much time, especially a woman who was endowed with a bent toward mischief and who had an old score to settle.

"Apparently I'm not doing my job properly," he remarked coolly.

Filomena whirled on him. "What's that supposed to mean?" she demanded in ominous tones.

Chapter Four

"IT LOOKS LIKE I'll have to pay more attention to the task of keeping an eye on you," Trent said a little too casually.

Filomena stiffened at the implied accusation. She saw the anxiety in her mother's eyes and was furious with whoever had relayed the story of her unwelcome chat with Brady Paxton. Shari and her father didn't appear as upset as her mother, but there was no doubt that the news had made them uneasy. Most of all, Filomena was aware of the cool, possessive watchfulness in Trent.

"You've assured me you're not here to work this summer, Trent, so don't start worrying about the job of keeping me out of trouble," she said icily.

"Hey," Shari put in quickly, "he was just teasing you, Fil."

"No, I wasn't," Trent said calmly. He reached for the pitcher of iced tea and poured himself a glass. "I was dead serious. No more unsupervised trips into town for you, Filomena. You're obviously incapable of steering clear of trouble. You can't resist putting on your show for the locals, can you? Fortunately for you I'm willing to keep an eye on you."

"Oh, gee, thanks." A flash of recklessness went through her. She put her hands on her hips and regarded Trent and her family with narrowed eyes. "Would you all like to know exactly what happened this morning at Muriel's? I'll tell you. I was sitting there alone, enjoying a quiet cup of coffee, when Brady came in and sat down across from me. Guess what he wanted."

"Uh, I think we can all guess what he wanted," Amery said uncomfortably.

"Sure," said Shari. "Everyone knows he'd jump at the chance to have a fling with you this summer. He's restless and bored and everybody in town knows it."

"Is that right? Well, I've got news for you. What he wanted was for me to pump Trent for information on Asgard Development's plans for a resort here on the lake. He's convinced Trent's here to scout the territory for Asgard. Furthermore, Brady offered me a nice little commission if I'd get the information for him and his real estate partnership cronies. There. Does that answer all your questions?" Filomena lifted her chin in triumphant challenge.

"Oh, dear," Meg said. "How awkward."

Shari was grinning. "Trust old Brady to put business before pleasure."

Amery groaned. "I should have known. I've heard Paxton's got options on some prime land around the lake."

It was Trent who put the next question to Filomena. He grinned at her over the rim of his tea glass. "You haven't told us yet whether or not you're going to do it."

"Do what?" Filomena demanded.

"Pump me for the information about Asgard's development plans."

"You don't look particularly worried," she muttered. The rush of recklessness faded as she realized Trent wasn't going to rise to the bait.

"Probably because I've already told you Asgard doesn't have any plans for Gallant Lake, and I think you believe me. But I won't mind if you try to worm the details of our lack of plans out of me."

He looked so expectant that Filomena felt her annoyance begin to melt. Her sense of humor resurfaced. "Too late. I already told Brady you didn't have any plans, and he didn't give me a dime for the information."

"Probably because he didn't believe you," Trent said.

"Probably," she agreed, remembering the depth of Brady's conviction on the subject. She smiled faintly. "That's his problem."

"Yes," he agreed blandly, "it is."

Shari spoke up. "That reminds me," she said quickly, "you may have some problems of your own, Trent. There was a call for you from Portland an hour ago. You're to contact a Mr. Reece as soon as possible."

Trent's good humor vanished. "Reece called?"

Shari nodded. "The front desk took the call and gave the message to me. They figured one of the family would see you first. Bad news?"

"No, not really." Trent finished his iced tea. "Reece is my assistant. He had instructions not to bother me here unless it was important. I guess something's come up. Excuse me while I return that call."

Amery got to his feet. "I'd better get back to the office. I've still got a lot of work ahead of me this afternoon."

Meg nodded and put down her half-finished iced tea. "And I've got to have a chat with the chef. I'll see you all at dinner."

"I'll come with you, Mom," Shari said. "I want to talk to Henry about my wedding cake. He's got to understand that I want a decent tasting frosting, not one that's just designed to hold pretty shapes."

When Filomena looked around a moment later, she had the patio to herself. With a relieved sigh, she flopped down in one of the lounge chairs and poured herself the last of the iced tea. Life could be stressful at times.

IT WASN'T UNTIL he finished the terse call with Hal Reece that Trent finally realized the potential of the opportunity that had just been dangled in front of him.

He was a man who knew how to grab opportunities when they appeared. He couldn't afford to ignore this one, especially now that Filomena was showing signs of needing a firmer hand.

He sat on the edge of his bed, elbows resting on his thighs, his big hands clasped loosely between his knees as he stared thoughtfully into space. Mentally he looked at this golden opportunity from every angle, searching for flaws, dangers and possible explosive points. It was risky, but it just might work. If it did work, he would have solved the problem of finding both time and opportunity to forge a way through Filomena's slick facade.

He sat very quietly for another ten minutes, planning for as many unknowns as he could. Then he got to his feet and went in search of Filomena.

FILOMENA WAS STILL ENJOYING her solitude on the patio after everyone else's departure when she heard her parents' private phone ring through the open sliding glass doors behind her.

Reluctantly she put down the copy of *Vogue* she had been scanning and went inside to answer the summons. It would probably be a friend of her mother's, inquiring about shower-gift ideas for Shari. That was all right, Filomena thought. She was equipped to answer any question in that line. She had lots of gift ideas in mind for Shari.

"Cromwell residence," she said cheerfully as she snatched the receiver out of its cradle.

"You think you're so damn smart, don't you?" a woman's voice snapped. Whoever it was sounded wretched with fury. There was a choking sob before she continued. "You think you can just come back after all this time and take him away from me, but you're wrong. You're nothing but a little tramp, and I'm going to make sure everyone knows it. You think it's a lot of fun to make a spectacle of yourself? Are you getting a kick out of racing around in that expensive car and showing off your fancy clothes while you dangle yourself in front of every man in town?"

"Gloria?" Filomena was stunned by the venom in the woman's voice. "Hold on a second. You've got no reason to yell at me. Just calm down—"

"Calm down!" Gloria's voice rose to an agonized shriek. "Calm down while you seduce my husband? Calm down while you wiggle your tail in front of him every time you get near him? You were a silly, unsophisticated, ugly little fool nine years ago, Filomena Cromwell. But you haven't changed for the better. You've just succeeded in turning yourself into a rich, flashy little bitch. But I won't let you get your hands on my husband. Do you hear me? I know you're after revenge, but you're not going to get it!''

"Believe me, Gloria, I don't have any desire to get my hands on Brady. He's all yours, and you're welcome to him.'' Filomena tried to keep her tones soothing, but she had a sick feeling she was only stoking the fires of resentment and anger that were burning in Gloria Paxton.

"Don't lie to me,'' Gloria raged. "I saw you looking at him last night. You want to prove you can get him back, don't you? It's not as though you still love him. You just want to prove something!''

Filomena held the phone away from her ear. Gloria's words were coming through so loudly that they were audible at some distance. "Gloria, listen to me, you've got it all wrong.''

"No, you listen to me, you little tramp. I heard you met Brady in town this morning. I know all about your private meeting at Muriel's.''

"Private! Everyone in town has coffee there.''

"And you knew I'd find out, didn't you? You're trying to punish me as well as seduce my husband. But it won't work. I won't let you. He didn't want you when you were nineteen, you fool. He was just bored that year, and you were available. He was just playing with you. He told me so. He used to laugh about what a little twit you were, and I used to laugh with him. Do you hear me?''

Before Filomena could respond, the phone on the other end was slammed down with such force that she flinched. She stood very still for several seconds, listening to the loud dial tone.

"What's the matter, Filomena?'' Trent asked quietly behind her. "Finding out there are a few perils and pitfalls in this game of coming back to the old hometown and showing everyone how you've changed?''

Filomena jumped, whirling around in surprise. For an instant she knew the chagrin she was feeling was visible in her eyes. She realized it because of the way Trent was studying her so intently. He leaned against the jamb in the open doorway, his arms folded across his broad chest. He was a perceptive man, she thought distractedly. Too perceptive by far.

"I'm not playing games, Trent. I'm simply here to enjoy a few weeks of vacation. But I seem to be having a hard time convincing anyone of that fact."

"Especially Gloria Paxton, I'll bet. That was her on the phone just now, I take it? Warning you off her husband?"

Slowly Filomena replaced the instrument. "I told her there was no need."

"Uh-huh. Do you honestly expect her to believe you? She's scared of being put through the same kind of humiliation she and Brady put you through nine years ago. As far as she's concerned, you're the enemy. People don't always react rationally when they're frightened. Especially if they've got good reason to be nervous in the first place."

"She's got no reason to worry about me running off with Brady!" Filomena snapped. She swung around and stalked to the huge picture window that overlooked the lake.

"She thinks she has. And so does just about everyone else in town apparently."

"Well, they can just chew their fingernails down to the quick worrying about it as far as I'm concerned."

"The people who are watching you this time are the same ones who watched you when you were nineteen, aren't they? It must be satisfying to show them you're not the one to be pitied this time around."

"I am *not* here to prove I can take Brady Paxton back. I don't want him. I'll admit it's fun to let everyone know I've made a success of myself, but that's all I'm interested in doing," Filomena said in a grim whisper. "No one seems willing to believe that."

"I believe it," Trent said coolly.

Filomena experienced a rush of relief that was almost startling. Someone believed her. She clamped down on the sensation and nodded politely. ''Thank you.''

''You're welcome,'' he said dryly. ''I know what it's like not to have anyone believe you. It gets to the point where you feel like you're beating your head against a stone wall.''

His words surprised her. Filomena glanced at him over her shoulder. ''Is that right?''

He didn't move, just stood there watching her with that curious intensity. ''Yes. But my understanding isn't going to do much good. You're a walking keg of dynamite as far as everyone else is concerned.''

Filomena made a face. ''Not a pleasant thought, is it?''

''If you're interested, I have a suggestion to make, one that might relieve some of the tension that seems to be building up around you.''

She glanced at him quickly. ''What kind of suggestion?''

''A practical one. It would give everyone something else to talk about besides you and Paxton.''

''And how am I supposed to do that?''

''I have to drive to Portland this afternoon. Business. I'll be staying the night and returning in the morning. Come with me, Filomena.''

Filomena caught her breath, unable to look away from his jade gaze. ''With you?'' she echoed faintly.

''You can spend the night with Reece and his wife. We'll have dinner with them and then you can go back to their place, if that's what you want.''

''I don't like to impose on strangers.'' Her voice sounded weak and breathless, even to her own ears.

''Then you can stay in a hotel, or...'' He let the sentence trail off.

''Or what?''

''Or you can stay with me at my apartment,'' he finished bluntly. ''The choice will be yours, I promise.''

Filomena couldn't seem to organize the chaotic thoughts that were suddenly filling her brain. She could hear Gloria Paxton's voice screaming in her ears, could still see the concern and anxiety in her mother's eyes. Filomena thought of the shower she was supposed to attend tonight, and the realization that every other guest would be speculating about her and Brady was more than she wanted to face. It might be nice to get away for a while.

Going to Portland with Trent suddenly looked like a reasonable escape. She made up her mind with the quick, firm resolve she was accustomed to exercising in business. "All right, Trent. Thank you for the invitation. Maybe a day or two away from here is just what the situation calls for. I'll go pack."

"It's nearly a three-hour drive," Trent said. "I want to leave as soon as possible."

Filomena nodded and turned to go to her room. "I won't keep you waiting."

THE DRIVE TO PORTLAND turned out to be a surprisingly pleasant experience. The farther she got from Gallant Lake, the more Filomena began to relax. It made her realize just how tense she had been after Gloria's phone call.

Her family had been temporarily astonished when she had informed them of her decision, but there had been no doubt about the relief that had followed. No one had asked where she would be staying, and that had annoyed Filomena for some reason. Her family didn't seem to have any objections to the possibility of her running off to Portland for a one-night stand with Trent Ravinder if it meant she wouldn't be around to cause any trouble with the Paxtons back in Gallant Lake. That rankled.

"What's the matter?" Trent asked casually at one point during the trip.

"I was just thinking that no one asked where I would be staying tonight. All that fuss about having a little cup of coffee with Brady, yet no one says a word about me dashing off to Portland with you for a whole night."

Trent slid her a quick, assessing glance. "You're an adult. As long as you aren't causing anyone any trouble, your family is content to let you make your own decisions."

"It doesn't strike you as slightly hypocritical?"

"No. You going with me to Portland is an entirely different situation than you driving Gloria Paxton crazy with jealousy."

"Oh, I see," Filomena said too brightly. "Well, that explains it, of course. No one minds if I sleep with you, so long as I don't show any signs of wanting to seduce Brady. Is that it?"

"That's it," he said in a mock-congratulatory tone. "No wonder you've done so well in the business world, Filomena. You're very good at putting two and two together."

A slow, unwilling smile tugged at her mouth. "It's a wonder you've survived at all. I would have thought by now that someone might have clobbered you on general principles."

"It's been tried a time or two." He shrugged. "But when it comes to defending principles, I always win."

"Because you don't give an inch?"

"Right."

"Just what is this all-important business that's forcing you to return to Portland on the spur of the moment?"

He gave her a sharp glance. "The business is for real," he said crisply. "I didn't invent it as an excuse to lure you to Portland."

She heard the familiar arrogance in his voice and put up a hand. "Okay, I believe you. What is it?"

He seemed to relax slightly. "Asgard's been trying to close a deal for some property over on the coast for three months. The old man who owns the land has been unwilling to sell because he was afraid of what would happen to the place afterward. He needs the money, but he doesn't want to see his family land covered with a bunch of ugly condos and shopping centers. I've shown him the plans Asgard has for the place and assured him that the architect's rendering is accurate and will be adhered to. Asgard wants to put in a quiet luxury resort and will spend a lot of money making sure the land retains its original appeal. It won't be ruined with parking lots and shopping malls. Apparently the owner is finally ready to sign."

"And you have to be there when he does?"

"The old man doesn't trust development companies," Trent explained wryly.

"But he trusts you?"

"Yes."

They reached Portland shortly before five, and Trent drove immediately to the downtown offices of Asgard Development. A harried-looking man in his early thirties with thinning hair and a quick smile was waiting for Trent in an eighth-floor office that had a view of the Willamette River. He got to his feet as Trent walked through the door.

"About time you got here, Trent. Baldwin has been sticking to his guns, just as I told you on the phone. Won't sign a damn thing until you shake hands with him on the deal and assure him everything's going to be just as stipulated in the plans." The man broke off as he caught sight of Filomena. "Excuse me, ma'am. I didn't see you. Please come in."

"Filomena, this is Hal Reece. Reece, this is Filomena Cromwell, a friend of mine." Trent made the introductions quickly, his attention obviously on the business at hand.

"Pleased to meet you, Filomena. Trent said he might be bringing someone with him. You'll join us for dinner?"

"Thank you," Filomena murmured.

"Where's Baldwin and the paperwork?" Trent interrupted to ask.

"I've got him waiting down the hall in a conference room. Asgard is there, too, but Baldwin won't take his word for anything. The guy is only willing to trust you."

"Doesn't he realize he's got a solid legal contract that stipulates how the land can be developed?"

"Asgard has explained it to him several times. But Baldwin wants to see you before he signs. He's got a point, Trent. Once that land officially belongs to Asgard, we can do anything we want with it. Baldwin knows that and doesn't want to take any chances. You ready?"

"Sure." Trent turned to Filomena. "You can wait in the outer office, if you like. We'll be through in a half hour or so. Then we'll go have a drink and some dinner with Reece and his wife.''

Filomena nodded, glancing around the office in open curiosity. "Don't worry about me. I'll be fine.''

Reece saw her appraising glance and chuckled. "Trent's offices are upstairs, if you're interested. His secretary's gone home for the day, but you're welcome to snoop around, if you like. He's got a much wider view of the river than I do.''

Filomena smiled. "Thank you, that sounds like an interesting way to pass the time.''

Trent frowned. "Why on earth do you want to see my offices?''

"Sheer, unadulterated curiosity, Trent," she explained. "Run along and shake hands with Mr. Baldwin.'' She swung around and walked out of the office. As she did so, Hal Reece's voice trailed clearly after her.

"I thought you were supposed to be on vacation, pal. Where in the world did you find her?''

"Out in the woods, living under a mushroom," Trent replied blandly.

"Never can tell what you'll find in those Oregon woods, can you?'' Reece mused pleasantly.

Filomena wrinkled her nose and kept walking.

DINNER PROVED VERY ENJOYABLE. They ate in a posh downtown restaurant that featured seafood and pasta. Evelyn Reece was a charming, attractive woman in her early thirties who delighted in talking about her two young children. She and her husband were obviously very much in love, and they both seemed pleased to meet Filomena.

"I'm so happy you could come along, Fil," Evelyn said at one point, leaning confidentially across the table. "Trent doesn't get out nearly often enough these days. I'm always telling him he's never going to meet the woman of his dreams while he's sitting alone in his apartment working every night. Honestly, I thought it was women who needed to be encouraged to get out and meet their prospective mates, but I've learned men can be just as stubborn and reclusive.''

"I resent that," Trent said mildly, his gaze on Filomena. "I am neither stubborn nor reclusive."

"Just picky, is that it?" Evelyn laughed. "Well, congratulations on finding yourself such a nice date for tonight. Does this mean I should give up my matchmaking efforts?''

"Yes, thank you, Evelyn. I would very much appreciate that." Trent spoke with so much depth of feeling that everyone, including Filomena, laughed.

Evelyn groaned and turned to Filomena for understanding. "I've tried, Fil, Lord knows I've tried. The man wants to get married. He needs to get married. It's written all over his face. But no luck."

"Uh, Evelyn," her husband said uneasily, his gaze flicking to Trent's impassive expression. "Fil probably isn't terribly interested in your past failures as a matchmaker. And neither is Trent."

"Nonsense," Evelyn said deliberately. "Fil ought to know what she's up against."

"I'm not up against anything, am I, Trent?" Filomena toyed with her wineglass and smiled at Trent, who regarded her with steady green eyes. "I'm just here to spend an evening away from all the peace and quiet of Gallant Lake."

"If you say so," he replied calmly, lifting his own wineglass.

She remembered what he had said about it being her decision where she would spend the night. So far she hadn't checked into a hotel; there hadn't been any time. She had changed for dinner in the ladies' room at the offices of Asgard Development. Trent had worn the same jacket and tie he had worn to the meeting with Baldwin. And with Hal Reece they had gone straight from Asgard to the restaurant, where Evelyn had been waiting.

But soon dinner would be over and then the decision could be delayed no longer. Filomena met Trent's eyes and felt herself drowning in the jade depths. The wineglass in her hand trembled.

"If you'll excuse me," Evelyn Reece announced lightly, "I'm

going to take a trip to the ladies' room for a few emergency repairs. I'll be right back.''

"I'll come with you,'' Filomena said, jumping to participate in the age-old feminine ritual of going in pairs to the rest room. She grabbed her purse.

Evelyn smiled and led the way through the crowded dining room. When they reached the marbled facilities, she grinned broadly and opened her bag to find her lipstick. She leaned toward the mirror to apply the lip color.

"I can't believe that after all my efforts Trent has finally found someone on his own. And in Gallant Lake, Oregon, no less. Although I must admit you don't look like you come from somewhere called Gallant Lake.''

"You should have seen me nine years ago when I left the place,'' Filomena said with a chuckle as she ran a brush through her long hair.

"You said your business is headquartered in Seattle?''

"That's right.''

"Will you be able to move your business down here to Portland, or is Trent going to have to move to Seattle?'' Evelyn asked casually.

"What?'' Filomena stared at her new friend in the mirror, stunned. "Why should either of us move?''

"Because I strongly suspect you're going to find yourselves married soon, and frankly, I can't see Trent in a commuting marriage. He's the kind of man who's going to want a strong, stable home life. He's waited for it long enough, and he deserves it. He was married once, you know, when he was in his early twenties. It was a disaster from what I understand. She left him for someone much older and much richer. Apparently she didn't realize just how successful Trent was going to become.''

Filomena felt a wave of panic. "Please, no offense, Evelyn, but I assure you, you're jumping to conclusions. Trent and I have absolutely no permanent plans. We're simply friends.''

"Sure, and if I believe that, you've got a bridge you can sell me, right?'' Evelyn's eyes danced. "Come on, Fil, I've seen the way he looks at you. What's more, I'm in a position to compare that look with the way he's looked at half a dozen other women in the past year, and believe me, there's no comparison.''

"Evelyn, please, I know you mean well but—''

"What I mean isn't nearly as important as what Trent means,'' Evelyn said bluntly. "The man wants to get married. Oh, he won't come right out and admit it, but I've watched him. He's been circling the available herd of females for eighteen months, looking for one to pair off with.''

"You make him sound like a stag ready to mate.''

"That's a pretty accurate description. For a while the hunt was fairly intense. He was dating a different woman every week. Then a few months ago he seemed to just give up. He stopped the heavy dating routine and started staying home more and more. I tried to fix him up a few times, but nothing ever clicked. Then he announced he was going to take off most of the summer and do some serious vacationing. Claimed he needed to get away for a while. The next thing we know he shows up with you and a look in his eyes that tells me the hunt is finally finished. What's this about him finding you under a mushroom?''

Filomena shivered slightly but struggled to keep her composure. She shook her head as she dropped her brush back into her bag. She decided to ignore the mushroom joke. "You're reading far too much into this, Evelyn, believe me.''

"We'll see.'' Then she smiled reassuringly. "You don't have to be nervous, you know. Trent is one hundred percent for real. There's not a drop of falseness in the man. You can trust him to the ends of the earth. If he's serious about you, he'll make his intentions clear soon enough, and he'll stand by them.''

Filomena's uneasiness grew. First her family had taken the attitude that she and Trent made an ideal couple. Now the Reeces appeared to have come to the same conclusion. As far as Filomena could tell, Trent wasn't doing anything to discourage the notion.

"Evelyn, I hate to disillusion you, but Trent has said nothing about marriage. He's said nothing about next week or next

month, for that matter. To put it bluntly, I expect he's only looking for someone to entertain him while he stays at my parents'
lodge. I landed on the doorstep a couple of weeks ago, and
everyone, including Trent, seems to have decided it would be a
good idea if he and I paired off together. It's difficult to explain,
but there are reasons why everyone thinks it's such a nifty notion. And those reasons have nothing to do with a permanent
relationship.''

"I think you may be the one who's laboring under an illusion," Evelyn said lightly. "But don't worry about it. I expect
Trent will make everything clear in his own good time.''

There was no point in pursuing that topic, Filomena decided
with a resigned sigh. But since Evelyn seemed chatty on the
subject of Trent Ravinder, Filomena decided to try for an answer
to a question that was beginning to bother her.

"Do you know why we drove all the way to Portland today,
Evelyn?''

"Sure. Hal told me Baldwin was finally willing to sign the
papers on that coast deal. Doesn't surprise me at all to learn he
wouldn't do it without Trent present. Baldwin doesn't trust land
developers.''

"But he trusted Trent Ravinder?''

Evelyn grinned. "Your Mr. Ravinder is one of Asgard's
greatest secret weapons. People trust him and will deal with him
when they won't deal with anyone else. The man's as honest as
the day is long, and his word is solid gold. Asgard uses him to
negotiate deals no one else can close.''

"What would happen if Trent made a promise on behalf of
Asgard that wasn't carried out?'' Filomena asked curiously.

"I doubt that could occur except by a genuine error. Old Asgard knows Trent would be gone in five minutes flat if something
like that happened. He'll only work for Asgard as long as he
knows Asgard will back him up. Asgard's biggest worry is that
Trent will decide to go into business for himself one of these
days, which is a distinct possibility.''

"But how did Trent get such a reputation in the first place?''

"He earned it, I suppose," Evelyn said matter-of-factly. "And he defends it. He takes pride in it."

"I know," Filomena said slowly. "He can be very arrogant at times."

"If you want my opinion, I think something must have happened a long time ago, something that made Trent decide people would take him at his word or else."

"Hmm." Filomena gazed thoughtfully into the mirror.

Evelyn smiled back at her. "Better watch your step, Fil, especially if you're not sure you want to have him serious about you. Trent is famous for keeping his word come hell or high water. There's a corollary to that kind of reputation."

"What's that?"

"He always does what he sets out to do. The same pride and arrogance that makes it impossible for him to break his word also makes it impossible for him to be deflected from his goals. That particular talent has also made him useful to Asgard."

"I'll bet," Filomena replied. She wondered if she ought to just take to her heels right now before she got any more mired in Trent Ravinder's slowly closing trap.

But she hadn't run from anything since she'd fled from the scene of her fiancé in bed with another woman, Filomena reminded herself. She smiled at Evelyn, turned around and led the way to the door of the ladies' room. "Fortunately I'm quite fast on my feet," she murmured.

"You'll have to be to outrun Trent."

Chapter Five

THE REMAINDER OF THE EVENING passed all too quickly. In no time at all, the Reeces were saying good-night on the sidewalk in front of the restaurant. They got into their car, waved and pulled away from the curb, leaving Filomena standing on the sidewalk next to Trent. He took her arm and started toward the Mercedes.

"Well, Filomena," Trent said a moment later as he slid into the driver's seat beside her, "have you made up your mind about where you want to spend the night?"

She felt her breath catch. It was supposed to be so easy. All she had to do was tell him he could take her to the nearest hotel and leave her there. Determinedly she cleared her throat. "It's been a lovely evening, Trent. I enjoyed meeting your friends. I think it would be best if you took me—"

"I'll take you to my apartment first," he interrupted smoothly, as though he'd figured out what she'd been about to say. "We can have a nightcap while you decide where you want to spend the night."

She blinked, recognizing defeat when she saw it. She knew what would happen if she went home with him. Still, she felt obligated to try to salvage some of her feminine independence.

"One nightcap," she said clearly. "And then you can take me to a hotel. I'll phone one from your apartment."

"If that's what you want." He spoke easily, apparently unconcerned with whatever she chose to do.

But Filomena knew otherwise. She could feel the tension in

him. He appeared relaxed and at ease as he piloted the Mercedes through the downtown streets, but she sensed the hungry anticipation in him. It was easy to understand Evelyn Reece's likening Trent to a prowling male animal circling the herd until he found the female of his choice. Filomena knew now that he had been stalking her for the past two weeks. It alarmed her to realize she hadn't understood just how intent and serious he was about the whole thing until tonight. She stirred slightly in her seat.

"You're not going to panic now, are you?" Trent asked conversationally as he guided the Mercedes into the underground parking garage of a modern high rise.

"Why should I panic?" Filomena asked aggressively. She wished he didn't find it so easy to read her mind.

"Because you're finally starting to focus on me, and you're realizing that you can't keep dancing just out of reach. It's time to stand still and face me."

"What's that supposed to mean?"

"For the past two weeks I've had to compete with everything from an old flame to a houseful of your relatives. On top of that, you've been only paying scant attention to me because you've been having so much fun causing a sensation in Gallant Lake. But tonight you're on your own, aren't you? No family to use as an excuse for going home early. No one around to be impressed by your flashy Porsche and your one-of-a-kind clothes. No outrageous parties to give. There simply aren't any more distractions to put in my path. Tonight it's just you and me."

"Is that a threat?" Filomena asked, trying to remain calm.

He smiled at her as he pulled into a parking space and switched off the ignition. The curve of his mouth was enigmatic, but the garage lighting revealed the watchful brilliance in his eyes. "No, Filomena, it's not a threat. Just a statement of fact. There's nowhere to run tonight. You have to deal with me. One way or another, you have to make some decisions about us."

Her chin came up with a touch of defiance. "And if I'm not ready to make any decisions?"

He regarded her in silence for a long moment and then he

opened his door. "You're ready. You just don't want to admit it." He got out of the car and came around to open her door. "Come on, honey. Let's go upstairs and decide where you're going to spend the night."

She got out of the car without a word, drawn by a magnetism that was too strong to resist. Filomena could feel the satisfaction in Trent. It radiated from him. He was sure that two weeks of patient hunting had finally paid off. All of the way up to the twenty-second floor in the elevator, Filomena reminded herself that she didn't have to stay unless she wanted to. She could have the promised drink and then leave. She could call a cab. She could insist Trent drive her to a hotel. In a pinch, she could walk.

She was still giving herself that reassuring pep talk when she walked through the door of his apartment. Curiosity took over immediately, banishing her uncertainties. This was the same sort of curiosity she had experienced that afternoon when she'd walked through his offices. There she had found cool, clean, utilitarian lines and shapes and forms, evidence of a man who worked hard and efficiently, a man who did not like his office environment cluttered up with frills and amenities.

"Well?" Trent asked in amusement as he watched her walk across the gray carpet, "is it what you were expecting?" He closed the door, locked it and then leaned against it as he followed her progress around the living room.

"I think so," Filomena said slowly as she examined the functional, comfortable furnishings. "Yes, it's exactly what I was expecting." It was a room that had been designed for a man's comfort and convenience, a *large* man's comfort and convenience. The furniture seemed oversized to her, rather like the furniture in her parents' house. The leather and wood were expensive but not flashy, modern but not high tech.

"I'll bet it's a lot different than your apartment," Trent observed. He came away from the door and headed toward the kitchen.

Filomena trailed after him, intrigued. "What do you think my place looks like?"

He shrugged as he opened a cupboard door and took down a bottle of brandy. "Oh, probably lots of delicate, sleek, modern stuff. Glossy, trendy, eye-catching. The sort of stuff that would probably collapse if anyone larger than a jockey sat in it. Not especially comfortable but definitely state of the art."

She smiled to herself at the accuracy of his description. "You sound disapproving."

He shook his head. "No. You have a strong interest in design. It makes sense you'd indulge that interest in your own apartment. Nothing wrong with that." He poured the brandy and handed her a glass.

Filomena took it, still smiling faintly. "You're wrong about one thing. My furniture is not uncomfortable. At least, not for me," she amended, glancing from the top of his head to the toes of his leather shoes. "It's possible that someone of your size and height might find it a bit cramped, though."

"You must be feeling desperate if you're resorting to cracks about my size." Trent took a sip of his brandy.

"I heard you making cracks about my height to your friend Hal Reece this afternoon."

"Such as?" Trent asked politely.

"Something about finding me living under a mushroom out in the woods, I believe."

He grinned, not the least abashed. "Ah, that. Well, I'll admit there's something about you that reminds me of an elf, and it isn't just your size."

"No?"

"No, it's the fact that you have a talent for creating mischief."

"I resent that," Filomena said lightly. "I do not go around causing mischief. I've got better things to do with my time."

"Perhaps when you're working in the offices of Cromwell & Sterling you do, but when you're on vacation I'm not so sure. If you want my opinion, your entire family was grateful to me this afternoon when I offered to get you out of town for a while.''

Filomena couldn't stifle the burst of laughter that rose within her. "Have I really succeeded in making everyone so nervous?"

"Yes, and you enjoyed every minute of it, didn't you?"

Filomena's laughter faded. "I didn't enjoy that phone call from Gloria Paxton this afternoon," she confessed with a sigh. She turned away, walking slowly back into the living room.

"I'm glad she called," Trent surprised her by saying as he followed her.

Filomena frowned at him over her shoulder. "You are?"

"Sure." He reached out and flicked a wall switch that turned off the lights. A soft, velvety darkness descended on the room. "If Gloria hadn't called when she did," he went on softly, "it might have been a lot harder to talk you into coming to Portland with me."

Filomena stood unmoving in the shadows. She tried to concentrate on the lights of the city below her, but the only thing she was really conscious of was the knowledge that Trent was almost upon her. He moved quietly, she thought, all silent grace and sleek male strength. A prowling male looking for a mate. And he wanted her.

"But you would have tried to talk me into the trip, anyway?" she asked in a whisper.

He stopped directly behind her. His hand touched her shoulder, his palm warm and large and strong. The feel of him burned through the turquoise silk of her dress. "Would it have been so hard to convince you to come with me?"

She hesitated and then turned slowly to face him. "I don't know," she admitted honestly.

Trent gently removed the glass from her hand and set it down beside his own on a nearby table. Then he slowly pushed his fingers into the depths of her fiery hair. "Are you sure?" He lowered his head until his forehead was resting against hers. "Are you sure you don't know the answer, Filomena?"

"Is it important?"

"I want to be sure you know what you're doing."

She trembled as his fingers traced small, random circles on the nape of her neck. "I seem to be doing what you want me to do. Isn't that enough?" she demanded softly.

"No."

"What do you want from me?" She felt slightly desperate.

He tilted her chin with his thumbs and brushed his mouth against hers. "I need to hear you say you want me. I've seen hints of it in your eyes, in the way you tease me by staying just out of reach, in the way you kissed me last night. But I want to hear the words. Is that simple and straightforward enough for you, Filomena?"

"Yes."

"Then tell me," he ordered softly, his thumbs stroking her jaw in a slow, deliciously hypnotic manner. His eyes had been made colorless by the absence of light, but no shadow could dim the gleam of masculine desire in his gaze as he looked down at her.

"I...I want you, Trent." The words came out in a rush before Filomena could stop them. She bit her lip, wishing she could have called back the confession, but it was too late. And it wouldn't have made much difference anyway, she thought with a flash of unnerving insight. He already *knew*. He was only making her say the words so that they would both know.

"Thank you, Filomena. I swear you won't regret it." He covered her mouth with his own, his breath a sighing groan of need and rising desire.

Filomena felt his hands slide down her shoulders, and then his arms were around her, locking her to him as he kissed her with slow, drugging thoroughness. The strength and heat of him reached out to engulf her. She was trapped, not just by his physical size and power, but by something far more insidious. Filomena couldn't put a name to the emotion that held her in a grip as unshakable as Trent's arms, but it made her wary. For a moment or two she experienced a flare of panic. It warred with the flames of passion that were uncurling inside her, and Trent seemed to sense it.

"You're not afraid of me," he said against her soft mouth.

"No." Her nails sank into his shirt.

"Are you afraid of yourself?" It was a challenge.

"No!"

"Then stop fighting both of us. I'm going to make love to you tonight, and I don't want you thinking about anything else but that. Most of all I don't want you thinking of escape."

She tipped her head back and met his gaze. He was filling her senses and her mind tonight. All of the excuses and distractions she had been using for the past two weeks to avoid this moment had dissolved into mist. Tonight there was nothing else to cling to except Trent. She couldn't think of anything else except him, didn't want anything else except him.

For a moment they stared at each other and then, with a soft murmur of surrender, Filomena rested her head on Trent's shoulder. She trembled as he lifted his hand to stroke her hair.

Filomena never knew how long they stood there in the shadows. She realized that Trent was deliberately not rushing her now that he had won her acceptance of the attraction that existed between them.

"I want you to get used to this," he said quietly as he continued to hold her close. "I want you to learn the feel of me, the feel of being in my arms. I want you to know this is where you belong."

Filomena stirred against him, putting her hand on his chest. He smelled good, she thought. Very male and very sexy. She opened her eyes and found herself staring at the buttons on his shirt. Without even thinking about it, she slid her fingers to the first one and pried it free. Trent drew in his breath but said nothing.

When he didn't move or try to push matters along any more swiftly, Filomena grew bolder. She undid another of his shirt buttons and slipped her fingers inside the opening to find the rough, curling hair on his chest.

Trent's hand twisted urgently in her hair and then Filomena felt him force himself to relax. The realization that he was deliberately restraining himself warmed her. She pushed aside the fabric of his shirt and dropped a tiny kiss on his chest.

"Sweetheart," he muttered in a dark voice filled with gathering passion. "I want you so badly it's eating me alive." He groaned as he lowered his mouth to hers once more.

Filomena sighed deeply and opened herself to him both physically and mentally. This was what she wanted tonight. She was through with the game of hide-and-seek she had been consciously and unconsciously playing for the past two weeks. Tonight she longed to explore the emotions and the passions she had been deliberately keeping at bay.

She murmured his name, heard him groan again and then she felt the exciting slide of his tongue along the edge of her lips. A second later he was inside, claiming her mouth with an intimacy and aggression that foreshadowed the other claim he would soon make.

When Trent broke the heavy kiss at last, it was to find the gentle curve of her shoulder. Filomena closed her eyes as he tasted her skin with the tantalizing edge of his tongue. She leaned into his warmth, no longer shying from the size and strength of him. Tonight that size and strength promised passion and excitement, unlike anything she had ever known. She pushed herself closer to him, her hands circling his neck, her breasts crushed against his chest.

"This is the way I've wanted you," Trent muttered. "For days I've been torturing myself with thoughts of you clinging like this."

"I want you," she whispered, unable to say anything else. She felt dazed with the need for him.

"I know, darling," Trent said with soft satisfaction. "I know." He found the buttons at the back of her dress and undid them with slow, deliberate movements. A moment later the turquoise silk slid from her shoulders, down to her hips and then crumpled into a soft pool on the carpet. When she stepped out of it, she also stepped out of her shoes.

Filomena felt suddenly very vulnerable in Trent's arms. She had on only a lacy scrap of bra, a pair of panty hose and tiny silken panties. She buried her face against his shirt when his fingers freed the snaps of the small bra. When it fell to the floor at his feet, Filomena couldn't stifle a small cry that was part anticipation, part wariness.

"You want this, honey," he whispered as he slid his palms down over the curve of her breasts. "You want it as much as I do."

She felt her nipples tightening into hard buds of desire under his hands. "I know," she admitted.

"Prove it," he said with a slight smile. "Show me how much you want me tonight."

She saw the challenge in the smile, but she also saw something else. Beneath the masculine provocation there was another, deeper message. He needed to know how much she wanted him tonight. Filomena couldn't deny him the proof he sought.

Slowly, with fingers that shook slightly, she began undoing the rest of the buttons on his shirt. When the last had been freed, she pushed the garment from his shoulders. It fell to the carpet alongside her dress.

"Come here," Trent said thickly. His hands slid down her back and curved under her bottom. He lifted her easily until her breasts were on a level with his mouth. Filomena's fingernails dug into his shoulders as he tasted first one throbbing peak and then the other. She gasped as he let her slide slowly back down the length of him. The hair on his chest teased her nipples as she was lowered slowly to her feet.

She looked up at him from under her lashes. "I suppose there are some advantages to your size."

His smile was brief, sexy and wicked. "I've been wanting to do that for a long time. There are definitely some advantages to your size. Very convenient."

"Such as?" she demanded.

"Well, for example, I can pick you up in one hand."

"I'm not that small or that light!"

"Want to bet?" He slid one arm around her waist and lifted her easily up against him again. With his free hand he drew a circle around one of her nipples.

Filomena gave him a rueful grimace and then she laughed softly. She thrust her fingers into his hair and pressed herself closer. "You win," she said huskily.

"Do I?" There was an unexpected seriousness in his eyes as he set her back down on her feet.

She wanted to ask him what he meant by that, but he wasn't waiting for an answer to the enigmatic question. Instead he slid his fingers under the waistband of her panty hose and pushed the hose and her panties quickly down over her hips. An instant later Filomena was completely naked. She stood in the circle of his arms and looked up at him.

"You're so small and graceful," he murmured wonderingly. "So light and soft and delicate." He shook his head slowly and ran his hands down her waist to her hips. "And you've kept me dangling so long."

"No, not deliberately. I just wasn't sure." Anxiously she tried to explain. "And it hasn't been a long time. Only two weeks."

"The longest two weeks of my life," he assured her. "But now the waiting is over." He moved, lowering her to the carpet. Then he knelt on one knee beside her, his hands impatiently at work on his belt buckle.

When he shoved aside his slacks and briefs, Filomena stared at him, drinking in the solid planes of his body. She put out a hand and touched his muscled thigh. Her eyes lifted to his. "No one could ever accuse you of being elf size," she whispered tremulously.

"I'll assume that's a compliment," he said with a soft chuckle.

Then he was lowering himself alongside her on the carpet, exploring her with his hands and his mouth and occasionally, excitingly, with his teeth. His leg moved over hers, sliding between her thighs and forcing them gently apart.

Filomena felt as if she were being inundated by a huge, breaking wave. She no longer had any thoughts of resistance or caution or even of the future. All she wanted, all she longed for in this moment was Trent's touch. She could no longer even imagine why she had been trying to stay clear of such exquisite involvement. She clutched at him, urging his mouth back to hers when he would have spent more time in the vicinity of her belly button.

"What is it, Filomena?" he asked. But there was a knowing look in his eyes as he stretched out alongside her again.

"I was just wondering why I waited so long," she said honestly. Her palms moved over his shoulders, enjoying the hard feel of contoured muscle and bone. She twisted against him and felt the throbbing heat of his manhood brush along her thigh.

"That's a good question. Unfortunately it doesn't have a good answer." Trent flattened his palm on her stomach and drew his hand lower. His fingers clenched briefly in the small, soft triangle at the apex of her legs and then he was exploring even lower. His touch became excruciatingly intimate.

Filomena sucked in her breath, dizzy with sensation as Trent found the liquid warmth between her thighs. She heard his groan of desire and shivered in his grasp. He held her more tightly.

"The waiting is over, for both of us," he muttered as he widened the space between her legs with his hand.

She had no response to that. She doubted if she could have said anything very coherent at all in that moment. She felt him moving, lifting himself and then coming down on top of her. His arms went around her, cradling her as he began to crush her into the carpet.

"Look at me, Filomena," Trent ordered in a thick, hoarse voice as he positioned himself. "I want to see your eyes when I make you mine this first time."

She obeyed, unable to look away as he pressed himself against her. She felt the hard, thrusting pressure between her legs and instinctively lifted her hips to receive him.

"Trent."

He responded by pushing forward relentlessly. His fingers tightened on her skin. Slowly, inevitably, he filled her with himself.

Filomena's eyes did close then, squeezing shut as Trent entered her. The moment of union was almost overwhelming. Her whole body tightened to a point just short of pain in response to the intrusion. Trent was a large man, and she'd had very little experience with men in a physical sense.

But a glittering, intoxicating excitement followed rapidly on the heels of the initial reaction.

It was unlike anything Filomena had ever experienced. When she opened her eyes again, Trent was looking down at her. He didn't move for a long moment, giving her a chance to adjust to the feel of him deep inside her.

"I've never felt anything like this before in my life." Trent flexed his hips slowly, withdrawing an inch or so and then carefully retracing his path so that he was once again deep inside her.

"No," Filomena managed, dimly aware that she was clutching at him. "Neither have I."

"Don't you think I can tell? I can see it in your eyes, feel it in your body. I knew we were going to be good together. I knew it the moment I met you." He buried his face in the curve of her neck and began to move again, this time establishing a slow, sensual rhythm that sent tremors of excitement through Filomena.

"Oh, Trent…"

"Hold on to me, sweetheart. Hold on to me and never let go. We'll find it together, I promise."

He was right. That was the thing about Trent Ravinder, Filomena told herself, you could count on him. He knew where he was taking her. He led the way, making sure she kept up with him all along the route.

The pattern of excitement swirled outward, encompassing both of them. Filomena had never explored this kind of sensation before in her life. She was old enough and sophisticated enough to know she had missed out on something, but there had been too many other things going on in her world to let it worry her. Or perhaps there had simply never been a man in her life who could make it worthwhile to worry about such matters. Whatever the reason, the explosive climax that was the final culmination in lovemaking burst upon her with unexpected force.

"Yes, sweetheart, *yes*. Take it. Hold on to it. Hold on to me." He drove himself into her one last time as her satisfaction pulled him over the edge. His hoarse shout of triumph and pleasure echoed in the dark room, mingling with Filomena's panting, breathless cries.

And then they were falling together through the slackening currents, collapsing in a tangle of perspiration-dampened arms and legs.

"Trent, I didn't know..." Filomena tried to find the words through a languid haze. "I didn't realize it could be like this."

"I know," he soothed, stroking long strands of her hair back from her face. "I didn't realize it, either."

"I thought you said you knew." She lifted her lashes and smiled dreamily up at him.

He grinned faintly. "I said I knew it would be good. I didn't know how good."

"Hah. I thought you knew everything."

"Not quite. Not about you."

"Well, thank goodness for that," she said decisively. She curled into his arms and planted a small kiss on his chest. "A woman is entitled to a few secrets."

His eyes grew serious again as he looked down at her. "I don't want there to be any secrets between us, Filomena. I want us to know each other so well that we have no secrets. Do you understand?"

Her fingers drifted across his chest as a sudden thought occurred to her. "Do you want to tell me your secrets?"

"What do you want to know?"

She drew a deep breath and took the plunge. "Well, for starters, I'd like to know why you have this thing about trust."

He frowned. "What thing?"

"You know what I mean," she said slowly. "You're very arrogant about your...your sense of honor, the fact that your word is your bond and all that. Why is it such a big deal with you, Trent?"

"Most people want others to respect them. I don't see what's so strange about my feelings on the subject."

She smiled gently. "You said no secrets, remember? But you've got a few, don't you?"

He lay on his back, one arm folded under his head, looking up at the ceiling for a long time. One knee was drawn up as he absently stroked her hair and shoulder. "I guess it has something to do with the way I was raised," he said finally.

"Your parents were strict?" she ventured.

He laughed shortly. "No, it wasn't that. My father died when I was a baby. My mother remarried before I was two, and I grew up thinking of my mother's second husband as my father."

"Was he a good man?" Filomena asked hesitantly, beginning to wonder if she'd had any right to pry. It was obviously a difficult subject for Trent.

"I thought so until I was eight."

"What happened then?"

"He was arrested for embezzlement at the bank where he worked. They sent him to prison for a couple of years."

"How awful for you and your mother."

"It was bad because we lived in a small town. Everyone knew what had happened, and no one let my mother or me forget it for a single moment." Trent's voice hardened. "Whenever anything was missing out of someone's desk at school, the finger usually got pointed at me. Storekeepers kept a sharp eye on me whenever I came through the doors in case I had inherited any of Dad's light-fingered tendencies. Whenever I got into trouble there was almost always someone around to say, 'Like father, like son.'"

"I think I get the picture," Filomena said unhappily.

"When Dad got out of prison, things didn't get much better. We finally had to move. It was difficult for him to get a job and harder for him to keep it. Sooner or later someone would find out about his past, and the next thing I knew I was in a fight at school or out in a parking lot trying to shut someone's mouth the hard way."

"I'll bet you won most of those fights." Filomena's heart went out to an embattled boy struggling desperately to defend the family honor.

He shrugged. "Winning didn't change anyone's opinion or make them stop talking."

"So you grew up determined to compensate for your father's weakness, is that it? You made sure everyone knew you weren't the same kind of man he was. Whatever happens, you can be trusted and everyone else had damn well better be honest with you or you'll demolish them, right?"

His mouth curved slightly as he raised himself on his elbow and regarded her with a thoughtful expression. "Something like that."

She searched his face. "Aren't you afraid at times that you might be a little too, well, rigid about it? I mean it's all well and good to be noble about this sort of thing, but not everyone can live up to your standards, Trent."

"Honesty is a clear-cut, black-and-white issue, Filomena. There's no room for gray areas."

"That's a harsh way to view things."

He shrugged. "I'm not gullible. I won't be played for a fool, and I definitely won't let someone get away with taking advantage of me. If that strikes you as overly rigid and harsh, well, that's too bad. It's the way I am."

Filomena gnawed on her lower lip as she considered that. "Does it happen often? Someone trying to take advantage of you, I mean."

His expression turned sardonic. "What do you think?"

She shook her head. "I don't think it does."

"Maybe that only goes to prove that if you treat people fairly, they'll treat you that way in return."

"I doubt it," Filomena said. "I think what it proves is that people are probably scared to death to mess with you."

"Either way, it works," he said equably. "Very few people try to cheat me or play me for a fool."

"I'll bet," Filomena said with great depth of feeling.

Chapter Six

FILOMENA OPENED HER EYES to sunlight and a strange room. She lay perfectly still for a moment, clinging to the very edge of the wide bed. Without turning to look she knew Trent was lying beside her. There was nothing magic about the realization; she could feel his weight putting a definite dent in the center of the king-size mattress. She could also feel the warmth of him under the covers. Sleeping with a man of Trent's size, she discovered, was like sleeping with a large bear. He provided enough heat for both of them. The thought made her smile.

"Do you always wake up smiling?" Trent asked through a hearty yawn.

"Nope."

"Good. A little of that kind of thing goes a long way in the mornings." He chuckled lazily and reached out to tumble her back across the mattress until she was curled next to him. "What are you doing over on that side of the bed? How did you get away from me in the middle of the night, anyway? When I went to sleep I had you right here by my side."

"I was afraid I'd get crushed," she said half-seriously.

"The hell you were. You just aren't used to sleeping with someone." He patted her rear with a casual, proprietary gesture. "But that's all right. You'll get accustomed to it."

"I take it you are accustomed to it?" she asked before she could stop herself.

She sensed rather than saw his slow grin. "Are we at the stage where you start asking pointed questions about my past relation-ships?''

Filomena cleared her throat. ''Uh, I don't think I want to hear about your past relationships.''

''Coward.''

''I prefer to think of myself as discreet.''

He pretended to give that considerable thought. ''Okay, I'll go along with that. Discreet, it is. You're a surprisingly rational, pragmatic, levelheaded, intelligent female, for an elf.''

Filomena was silent for a long moment and then she asked very cautiously, ''Have you had a lot of relationships?''

Trent roared with laughter, moving abruptly to pin her beneath him. ''So much for discreet, rational, pragmatic, levelheaded and intelligent, huh?''

''I resent that. I am definitely intelligent.''

''All right, I'll give you that. The answer to your idiotic ques-tion, Filomena Cromwell, is no, there haven't been a lot of re-lationships in my past. And certainly none that were anywhere near as important as the one I have with you.'' He paused and then went on more seriously. ''I was married once. It didn't last very long. She didn't want to wait for me to make it to the top. Found someone else who was already there. End of story.'' His expression relaxed once more. ''Well? How's that for discre-tion?''

''I'm glad you don't apply your honesty-is-the-best-policy to every little thing,'' she murmured. She really didn't want to know too much about the women in his past, especially the one he had married.

To her surprise, he took the comment seriously. ''I swear I will always be honest with you, sweetheart, but there are some things that don't concern us. I'm an advocate of the truth, but that doesn't mean I believe that everything has to be dredged up out of the past and rehashed. Satisfied?''

She nodded. ''I'm satisfied.''

He drew his hand over her hip and squeezed gently, clearly enjoying the feel of her. ''Now that we've agreed the past can be more or less consigned to oblivion, let's talk about the future.''

For some reason his words sent a wave of uneasiness through her, the first she had experienced since surrendering to his love-making last night. Filomena pushed the trickle of alarm aside and smiled boldly up at him. "What about the future?"

"On second thought," he murmured, pausing to drop a kiss in the hollow of her throat, "I don't think there's any need to rush that discussion. We've got plenty of time." He dropped another teasing kiss, this time on the upper swell of her breast.

Filomena relaxed. "I agree. No need to rush into that particular conversation."

He lifted his head and eyed her quizzically. "You sound as if someone just granted you a reprieve. I thought women were very big on discussions of the future."

"We have a lot to learn about each other, Trent," she pointed out. "The future will take care of itself. It always does."

"No," he said with a faint edge to his voice, "the future doesn't always take care of itself. But in this case, you don't have to worry about it too much."

"Why?"

"Because I'll be taking care of it for you."

Her sense of uneasiness returned in a rush. "Trent, maybe we should have that discussion now. I think we ought to get things clear between us, don't you? I mean, we hardly know each other, and I wouldn't want either of us to get any false impressions or wrong ideas or—"

He silenced her with a brief, possessive kiss. When he raised his head, his eyes were very green in the morning light. "Don't panic, elf. You're in good hands."

She felt those hands moving on her, parting her legs and exploring the sensitive skin of her inner thigh. Her arms went around his neck, and the future receded. "Yes," she whispered, tugging his head back down to hers, "I'm very definitely in good hands."

TRENT COULD SENSE the difference in the atmosphere between himself and Filomena from the moment they awoke that morning. Her awareness of him had exploded into full bloom at last. He could see it in her eyes and feel it in her touch. She was finally within reach, he thought. He'd managed to lure her close enough to the flame to ensure she felt its compelling pull.

The task was far from over, though, he reminded himself during the drive to Gallant Lake. But the hard part, the trickiest part, had been accomplished. He could afford to relax a little now and watch Filomena explore her new feelings toward him.

She was still nervous, still uncertain, but already the barriers were tumbling. Trent could tell that at odd moments she would realize that things were changing quickly for her, and the knowledge worried her. He could also see the occasional bemusement in her eyes.

But most of the time she ignored her fears and concentrated on the intriguing pleasure she was learning to enjoy around him. Filomena Cromwell, Trent thought, was discovering what falling in love was all about. At least, he added, mentally crossing his fingers, he hoped that was what she was discovering.

"What are you thinking about?" Filomena asked cheerfully at one point on the drive back to Gallant Lake.

He smiled faintly, his eyes on the traffic ahead. "I'm thinking that I've finally got your attention."

For some reason she seemed to find that hilariously amusing. She laughed for the next mile.

Trent wasn't the only one who noticed the difference in Filomena. When they arrived in Gallant Lake, her whole family sensed the change in the relationship almost immediately. Trent saw the warm humor and the undeniable expression of relief in their eyes. At dinner that night the conversation inevitably got around to the trip to Portland. Filomena was surprisingly vocal on the subject.

"Hal Reece and his wife were quite charming," she said chattily as she helped herself to salad. "We had a lovely dinner after Trent finished his business. Evelyn Reece apologized to me for her husband having to drag Trent away from his vacation, but there was obviously no alternative. Mr. Baldwin refused to sign on the dotted line until he had shaken Trent's hand over the deal. Evelyn told me that happens a lot. Asgard uses Trent to wrap up the big ones because people trust him. They'll deal with him when they won't deal with anyone else.''

"I see,'' Amery said, his half amused, half speculative gaze on Trent who was calmly making his way through a thick chunk of sourdough bread. "Is that your main job with Asgard? Closing the tough ones?''

Trent shook his head. "No, that's just part of it. I do a lot of what I guess you'd call troubleshooting. I'm the one who gets sent out when things start going wrong on a deal or a job site. I think Asgard sees me as a sort of handyman.''

"Don't let him give you any false impressions,'' Filomena declared. "He's got an office three times the size of mine. It's got a spectacular view and wall-to-wall carpeting. He's even got his own secretary. Companies such as Asgard don't reward their handymen with huge corner offices and private secretaries unless they are very, *very* handy.''

Trent realized that Filomena was the only one at the table who seemed unaware of the pride in her voice. He was shocked to feel a faint warmth in his face as she continued singing his praises to her family. He was also acutely aware of the fact that it was all everyone could do to stifle smiles. He didn't know whether to laugh or groan, but he decided he'd better find a way to change the subject before she managed to thoroughly embarrass him.

"Filomena,'' he began gently when he found a slight pause in her monologue.

"...and Evenlyn Reece also told me that Asgard is willing to back up any promise Trent makes to a client because the company doesn't dare take the risk of losing him...''

"Filomena...''

"I met Mr. Asgard himself after the meeting. He told Trent he 'owed him one.' Wasn't that how he put it, Trent? Said he couldn't have closed the deal without you, and he wanted that land very much.''

Trent cleared his throat. "Filomena, would you please pass me the potatoes?''

"Of course.'' She reached for the potatoes and started to tell her family about the view from Trent's office windows. "You can see the river and most of the bridges.''

"Filomena,'' Trent tried again, putting more force into his voice. "How about another helping of vegetables?''

"Oh, no thanks, I've had enough.'' She smiled brilliantly at him and went off on another tangent. "Evelyn and Hal Reece hinted that Trent is probably going to become a partner in the firm one of these days unless he decides to leave and start his own company. Reece said Asgard is terrified of that possibility and will probably do anything to keep him.''

"Filomena."

She broke off expectantly. "Yes, Trent?''

"I think,'' he said firmly, "your family might appreciate a change of topic. I know I would.''

She blinked at him and then comprehension flooded her expression. Her cheeks turned a light pink. "Oh, dear, was I embarrassing you, Trent?''

"That's putting it mildly.''

She grinned. "You should have kicked me under the table.''

"I was considering it,'' he admitted.

"Afraid I might have kicked you back?''

"The thought occurred to me, but I was getting desperate.''

"Poor man. All right, the field is yours,'' she declared, waving a hand to include the entire spectrum of human conversation. "Pick a subject, any subject.''

"Fishing,'' Trent said, turning to Amery with a sense of relief.

His host accommodated him immediately, but not before Trent had seen the amused satisfaction in Amery's eyes. Meg and Shari were eyeing Filomena with the same expression. Only Filomena seemed blissfully unaware of how much she had just revealed about her feelings for Trent.

Trent decided he could put up with some dinner-table embarrassment in exchange for those revelations. When Filomena finally started falling in love, she did so with considerable enthusiasm.

During the next three days, Trent basked in Filomena's awakening emotions. Her newfound awareness of him was expressed in a variety of ways. For example, two days after the return from Portland he came back from a morning's fishing expedition with two beautiful trout. Amery had been unable to accompany him that morning, so Trent had gone alone. It was Filomena who jumped up from the breakfast table where she had been lingering over her coffee with her sister and offered to fry the catch.

"The kitchen is very busy this morning," she explained, taking the fish from him. She headed toward the swinging doors that divided the kitchen from the dining area. "I'll take care of these for you."

Trent caught Shari's astonished look as he sat down across from her and reached for the coffee. He smiled blandly in return. "Something wrong, Shari?"

"I can't believe it," Shari murmured dryly. "I think she wants to show you she can cook."

Trent grinned. "Can she?"

"Oh, yes. Mother made sure we both learned how to do a decent job in the kitchen. She has old-fashioned ideas about what makes a woman marriageable. Not that those ideas have done Fil much good. Lately we'd all begun to wonder if Fil might have actually meant what she said nine years ago when she left town."

Trent sipped his coffee. "What did she say nine years ago?"

Shari lifted one shoulder. "A lot of things we didn't think she meant at the time."

"Things about not ever getting married?"

Shari smiled slightly. "Something like that. She would never admit it, but the truth is, she was badly shaken by the way her engagement ended. If Brady had just told her he wanted out of the arrangement, it wouldn't have been so bad. Fil could have handled that with a few tears and some sighs. Instead, she had to walk in and find him in bed with Gloria Halsey. Gloria was Fil's nemesis all through high school. She was the opposite of Fil in so many ways. Homecoming Queen, cheerleader, most popular girl in the class. You know the type. And she wasn't an especially nice person. She had a tendency to make fun of Fil.''

"Do you think Filomena was in love with Brady?"

"Filomena was infatuated with him, but I don't think she was really in love with him. She was too young and too naive in many ways for that. She'd never even had a real boyfriend before Brady. He was the first man who had ever paid much attention to her, and she was starved for masculine attention. When Brady started courting her, she was thrilled."

"Why did Brady start chasing her if he preferred the Gloria Halsey type?"

Shari considered that carefully. "I've wondered about that myself a few times. It might have had something to do with the fact that Fil was finally starting to come out of her cocoon that first year in college. She began losing weight and became more sociable. She developed a lot of new interests in school and began to gain some confidence. She came home on weekends and vacations that first year, and Brady had just returned to town after graduating from college. He probably noticed the changes. Or maybe he was just bored. There weren't a lot of single women around, and Gloria was involved with someone else at the time and rarely came home from school. It's a small town. Brady didn't have a lot to choose from on Saturday night."

"So he just started hanging around with Filomena, is that it?"

"Yes. I'm sure his ego got a boost out of the association. She adored him, and it showed. And then, before anyone had quite realized how serious it all was, they announced their engagement. Filomena was on cloud nine. Meanwhile, Gloria came back for the summer. She was free and bored, and she decided she wanted Brady. Brady decided he wanted Gloria and a partnership in her father's insurance business. But I guess he had a little trouble figuring out how to break the news to my sister."

"So he let her find out the hard way." Trent heard the rough edge in his voice and deliberately tried to blunt it.

Shari nodded. "Poor kid. It was a terrible way to learn that a lot of men can't be trusted. I'm afraid she took the lesson to heart. She has no feeling left for Brady, but she never quite got over the lesson he taught her. She left town swearing she would never marry." Shari's mouth curved slightly. "My mother has been waiting nine years for her to change her mind."

"But instead of changing her mind about marriage and men, Filomena has devoted herself to founding Cromwell & Sterling," Trent concluded.

"Not entirely," Shari said slowly. "She does seem to have a very active social life in Seattle."

"I was afraid of that," Trent said with a groan. "She's got money of her own, style and flash. That would buy anyone an active social life."

"True, but she's never gotten involved enough with any man to consider a permanent relationship. These days she has to worry about fortune hunters, you know. Cromwell & Sterling is growing by leaps and bounds. There are plenty of men out there who wouldn't mind having a piece of the action. So, what with one thing and another, Fil has learned to keep men at a distance. I don't think she's even aware of doing it most of the time."

"I know." Trent wasn't aware of how much feeling he'd put into the words until he saw Shari smiling. "What's so funny?"

"Nothing, really. It's just that, as I suspected all along, when Fil's barriers started to collapse, they did so in a big way. She's a changed woman since you brought her back from Portland, Trent. I've never seen her like this with anyone. If she isn't in love with you yet, she's getting there in a hurry."

Trent kept his smile noncommittal even though his body was growing tight with a combination of desire and fierce satisfaction. "Do you think so?"

"Oh, yes," Shari said quietly, "I think so. Is that what you really want, Trent? Because if it's not, please don't take this any farther. It wouldn't be fair to Fil, and frankly, I think the family would be awfully upset if you hurt her badly.''

Trent gave Shari a level look. "You have my word of honor I have no intention of hurting your sister. I want her. My main goal right now is to make her want me.''

Shari held his gaze for a long while and then she nodded, satisfied. "I believe you." Her expression lightened. "I think you're well on your way to accomplishing your goal.''

Trent raised his eyebrows as he took another sip of coffee. "Knowing Filomena, it won't be that easy.''

"You're probably right." Shari leaned back in her chair, contemplating him with sisterly concern. "Right now everything is peaches and cream, isn't it? But what's going to happen the first time you two argue? I'd better warn you that Fil doesn't take orders from any man, and she usually gets her own way when the chips are down.''

"I'm not surprised," Trent said equably.

"So what happens the first time you put your foot down?" Shari asked with great interest. "She's become very independent during these past few years. She's her own woman. And even though she keeps it under control these days, she has a temper to go with that red hair. No matter how much you want her, I don't see you letting her run roughshod over you.''

Trent chuckled. "That's a funny image. A redheaded elf running roughshod over me. She'd probably wear cleated boots to do the job right.''

"Probably. So?''

Trent sighed. "So what will happen the first time I put my foot down? I'm not sure. But there's one thing in my favor.''

"What's that?''

"I have very big feet.''

AT THE BEGINNING of the third day back after the fateful trip to Portland, Filomena began to get impatient. She'd had almost no time at all alone with Trent. Even more annoying was the fact that he didn't seem to be going out of his way to create any time for the two of them to be together.

It didn't make sense. For the first couple of weeks of their relationship he had concentrated on finding ways to get her alone. She had had her hands full trying to avoid such encounters. Now Trent appeared to be content to share her with her family.

She had a few anxious moments when it had occurred to her that, having gotten her into bed once, he'd lost all interest in repeating the experience. Whenever these doubts struck, however, she would invariably look up to find him watching her with those jade eyes of his, and she'd know in her bones that he still wanted her.

So why wasn't he making more of an effort to find a time and place to make love to her? she wondered in growing annoyance. It would be simple enough. He could take her for a drive in the evening, or invite her on a walk down by the lake at dusk, or have Henry, the lodge chef, pack another picnic basket.

A picnic. Filomena smiled to herself. It was the perfect answer. She owed him a picnic, she decided. After all, he'd once invited her on one. But this time she wouldn't let the conversation degenerate into business subjects the way it had last time. With her mind made up, she headed for the lodge kitchen. Henry always had plenty of picnic food available. She would pick her favorite items and pinch a bottle of fumé blanc from the cellar. Her father wouldn't care.

Half an hour later, basket slung on her arm, she went in search of Trent. She found him reading a book on the patio overlooking the lake. He looked up as she strode toward him. His eyes moved over her appreciatively, taking in the yellow band holding back her red mane, and yellow tie-front shirt that exposed her flat midriff and the white, hip-riding pants that lovingly shaped her thighs and tapered narrowly down to her ankles. Filomena saw the sensual awareness in his gaze just before he masked it with an expression of polite interest.

"Going somewhere?" he asked casually, closing the book.

"Uh-huh. Want to come along?" She realized this was the

first time she had ever invited him anywhere, and for some reason she felt vaguely nervous.

"That depends," he said teasingly.

"On what?" She kept her smile bright and breezy, but she still wasn't sure of what would happen next.

"On what you've got in the basket," Trent explained, folding his hands behind his head as he watched her from the depths of the lounger.

"A bottle of Dad's best fumé blanc, chicken salad sandwiches, a huge bag of potato chips and two slices of chocolate cake."

Trent came out of the chair at once. "Hell, why didn't you say so right off? Let's go."

"My mother always did say that the way to a man's heart was through his stomach. But I never really believed her. I always gave men credit for being a little smarter than that."

"You should listen to your mother more." Trent draped an arm around her shoulders. "Where are we going to eat this feast?"

Filomena hesitated and glanced up at him out of the corner of her eye. "I was thinking about going back to the place where we had the last picnic."

"Lead on."

Filomena's smile became a shade more brilliant. This wasn't going to be so hard, after all. All she had to do was get Trent alone somewhere, feed him some good food and wine and he was sure to take matters into his own hands, just as he had in Portland.

Unfortunately things didn't go quite as smoothly as she had planned. They found the isolated picnic spot, spread out the blanket Filomena had packed in the basket and munched their way through the food and wine. But matters ground to a halt right there. Trent showed no interest in taking over the seduction.

This was ridiculous, Filomena thought as she ate the last pickle and wondered frantically how to extend the picnic now that the food was gone. They had talked about everything from business to fishing, but they hadn't touched on the subject of

Filomena Cromwell and Trent Ravinder. Filomena got the impression that if she wanted the subject brought up, she was going to have to do it herself.

It surprised and annoyed her to discover that she had such an aversion to risking rejection. She had never thought of herself as a coward before. But, then, she had never pursued a man since that awful year with Brady Paxton. It was easier and safer to let the men do the running. Unfortunately, although he'd gotten off to a flying start, Trent seemed to have slowed down considerably.

"I'd like to pick up a case of that wine when I return to Portland," Trent said conversationally as he packed the empty bottle back into the basket. "Your dad has excellent taste."

"Yes," Filomena agreed, propping herself on one elbow while she watched him replace the rest of the picnic things. "He likes everything first class at the lodge."

"It shows. He's a good businessman."

"I know." Filomena frowned. "Trent?"

"Hmm?"

"Did you want to rush back to the lodge right away?"

"Not particularly." He looked at her.

"Good." She smiled. "I was thinking we could stay here a while. There's plenty of privacy, and no one's expecting us or anything."

"I know. I should have brought my book along. Great place to sit and read. Maybe I'll take a nap instead."

"Oh." Filomena was slightly disconcerted. She hadn't been expecting that. "You don't look tired."

"I'm not, but I'm on vacation. I'm supposed to do things like take naps and read in the shade after a picnic," he explained with a smile as he settled down with his back braced against the tree. He looked out over the lake. "This is a beautiful place, isn't it?"

"Having grown up here, I guess I take it for granted," she admitted absently. "Trent?"

"Hmm?" He was watching the sunlight on the water, apparently mesmerized by it.

"I was thinking about…about us."

"Were you?"

"And about the other night in Portland," she went on with dogged determination. "It was special, wasn't it?" She held her breath.

"Yes," he said quietly, "it was."

She began to breathe again. "I'm glad you think so. I mean, I was beginning to wonder if…"

"If what, Filomena?"

She studied his profile, unable to tell what he was thinking. "Nothing. It's just that you haven't said much about it since we got back."

"Neither have you," he pointed out.

She winced. That was true. Changing position on the blanket, she edged her way closer to where he was sitting. One leg was drawn up in front of him, and he had his arm across his knee. His attention was still on the sunlight dancing on the lake. "Well, I'm bringing the subject up now," she told him with a touch of aggression.

"So you are." He didn't move. "What exactly did you want to discuss?"

Filomena felt her patience snap. She sat up and leaned toward him, her brows coming together in a fierce line across her nose. "I don't exactly want to discuss anything at all!"

He gave her a politely inquiring glance. "Then why bring up the subject in the first place?"

"I thought it might be a good excuse to kiss you," she declared rashly and threw herself into his arms. Automatically he caught her, cradling her across his thighs. "You haven't done any more than give me a couple of good-night pecks on the cheek since we got back from Portland." She put her arms around his neck and pulled his head down to hers. She kissed him with all the passion and need she'd discovered that night in

Portland and which she'd been bottling up inside herself ever since.

Trent didn't even try to resist. His mouth parted under the pressure of her lips, and he willingly returned the hungry embrace. When Filomena realized that his desire was as strong as it had ever been, she breathed a sigh of relief and nestled closer. Her hand rested possessively on the front of his shirt.

When she broke the kiss at last, she was breathless and flushed. Her eyes sparkled as she looked up at him. "Why?" she demanded.

He smiled. "Why what?"

"Why haven't you kissed me like that since we got back from Portland?"

His big hand slowly stroked her breast. "I wanted you to realize just how much you trust me."

"What's that supposed to mean?"

He caught a strand of her hair and wrapped it around his finger. "You needed to prove to yourself that you don't have to be afraid of rejection. Not with me."

Filomena stiffened in his arms. "I'm not sure I like being manipulated like that."

His face gentled. "There was more to it than just forcing you to take the chance of making the first move."

"What else was there?" she asked suspiciously.

"Has it occurred to you that I might have wanted a little reassurance that you hadn't forgotten what happened in Portland, either?"

Instantly Filomena was contrite. A warm rush of feeling welled up in her. "Trent, I'm so sorry. I didn't think of it that way."

"I know. You're used to being the one who hovers just out of reach. But sometimes a man likes to know he's wanted, too."

Her eyes were luminous. "I want you, Trent."

"I know, sweetheart. You're convincing me." He lowered his head to hers, and this time the kiss was a sweet mingling of desire and trust.

When Trent's hands went to the knot of Filomena's shirt, she tightened her arms around his neck and whispered shyly to him of her eagerness for his lovemaking.

"Sweetheart, you don't know what you do to me," he accused with a thick groan as he carefully settled her on the blanket and came down beside her.

Her fingers trailed teasingly down the front of his shirt to his waist. Then she let her palms wander lower, seeking the hard evidence of his desire. "I'm learning," she said softly. She undid the buckle of his belt.

THEY DIDN'T GET BACK to the lodge until nearly three-thirty. Hand in hand, Filomena and Trent strolled past the front desk in the main lobby. Meg Cromwell glanced up from some work she was doing behind the counter and smiled fondly.

"There you are, Fil. I was wondering where you'd gone. Don't forget the cocktail party for Shari and Jim tonight. By the way, there was a call for you an hour ago."

"Really? Who?"

"Glenna Sterling."

Filomena's eyes widened. "The bank. She must have heard from the bank." She dropped Trent's hand and grabbed the phone, dialing rapidly.

The instant Glenna came on the line, Filomena knew the news was not good. Her heart sank.

"No luck, Fil. They said we're expanding too fast. They suggested we reapply when we've got a broader distribution base."

"But we need the capital to extend the distribution base in order to broaden it in the first place," Filomena snapped. "That's the whole point." She caught Trent's thoughtful gaze on her.

"I know, Fil. And I had so many ideas for the new line. Look, we knew this was a possibility. We'll just have to start over at another bank. Maybe one that's got a better reputation for loaning money to women entrepreneurs. I'll do some research on that end of things while you're on vacation."

"Maybe I should come back," Filomena said uneasily.

"What's the point? It will take me a while to check out other bank possibilities. You can't accomplish anything here by coming back early. Enjoy your sister's wedding, and I'll see you at the end of the month. This is only a setback, Fil. We've battled through worse."

"True." Filomena hung up the phone and leaned dejectedly back against the counter. She folded her arms across her chest and moodily regarded the tip of her sandal.

"The loan fell through?" Trent asked gently.

"They turned us down cold."

"Maybe now's the time to get hold of a good financial consultant," Trent suggested.

"Maybe. What I'd really like to get hold of is that loan officer's neck. We were counting on that money."

"Never count your chickens before they're hatched, Fil," Meg said with that bracing quality all mothers seem to have in times of trial.

Filomena smiled wryly. "Yes, Mother."

Trent chuckled at her expression and put his arm around her shoulders to lead her toward the patio. "Listen to your mother, Filomena. Better yet, listen to me."

She eyed him warily. "What's your advice?"

"Never count your chickens before they're hatched."

Chapter Seven

"WHAT DO YOU THINK of this, Shari?" Filomena spun around in a neat pirouette, showing off the sleek, bare, body-hugging white knit dress she had chosen for the cocktail party that evening.

Shari, dressed in a demure red silk dress that highlighted her shining blond hair, leaned in the doorway and stared in mingled admiration and astonishment.

The white dress left very little of Filomena to the imagination. The front plunged nearly to the navel, and the back dipped almost to the waist. The skirt was short, exposing a considerable amount of leg, which Filomena had emphasized with a pair of impossibly high heels. There was an innocent gold necklace around the throat, which somehow only served to heighten the outrageousness of the rest of the dress.

"Every time you dress for a party around here, the outfit gets wilder and wilder. There was that little blue number with the tight bodice you wore for the replay of the prom party that exposed half your bosom. The splashy little red-and-yellow number you wore to my 'farewell to singlehood' party raised even the caterer's eyebrows. And then there was the green jersey, which, as Aunt Agnes observed, exposed half your backside. Now this. What are you trying to do? Prepare us for a bridesmaid dress made out of clear plastic food wrap? I'm traumatized at the thought of what you're actually going to wear to my wedding."

Filomena made a face at her sister. "Don't be a prude, Shari. You may have decided to come back to live in Gallant Lake, but your tastes are no more small-town than mine are these days. This dress is considered very hot this season.''

''It shows an awful lot of skin, Fil,'' Shari said dubiously. ''It's cute on you, I'll grant you that, but I'm not sure it's right for a Gallant Lake cocktail party. That green jersey thing was about as much as this town can take in the way of high style.''

''Nonsense.'' Filomena paused in front of the mirror to check her hair. She had caught it up in a deceptively casual little twist on the top of her head. Several curling red tendrils trailed down her throat. ''I'm sure Gallant Lake society will be able to handle the impact.''

''What about Trent?''

''Hmm?'' Filomena clipped on dangling, glittery earrings. ''What about him?''

''Is he going to be able to handle the impact?''

Filomena frowned at her sister in the mirror. ''You don't think he'll like the dress?''

''I think that man is rapidly developing a streak of possessiveness where you're concerned. I'm not so sure he's going to want Brady Paxton and everyone else ogling you tonight.''

Filomena paused in the act of applying her lipstick. ''I haven't made a habit of letting any man tell me what I can and can't wear for the past nine years, Shari. I'm not about to start now. Besides, Trent isn't a small-town type, either. He isn't going to be upset about this dress.''

Shari smiled knowingly. ''We'll see.''

Filomena narrowed her eyes. ''What could he do except mumble about it, anyway?'' she asked, remembering his grumbling remarks about the green jersey she had worn to the country club.

''Put his foot down?'' Shari suggested helpfully.

Filomena giggled. ''Not likely. What good would it do him? He's smart enough not to try anything like that.''

''If you say so.'' Shari looked her sister over again. ''It is a darling dress on you, even if it does cover less than a swimsuit. Gallant Lake won't forget it soon, that's for sure. Enjoying your vacation, Fil?''

Filomena met her sister's perceptive gaze. "I was enjoying it a lot more before I heard the bad news from Glenna this afternoon."

"Mom told me," Shari said sympathetically. "But she said Trent hinted at being able to get you and Glenna some professional advice from a hotshot financial consultant?"

"That's what he said. He thinks it might be helpful. He says Glenna and I are at a very precarious point in our business. We've got to make some decisions and plans instead of just growing willy-nilly as fast as we can."

"Mom and Dad are extremely pleased with themselves, you know."

"Because they sicced Trent on to me and things seem to be working out?"

"Uh-huh."

"Well, what can I say?" Filomena asked with a grin. "They deserve to take some credit."

"Mom says Trent has the same look in his eyes as Jim did when he first started dating me. Lean and hungry."

Filomena dabbed on some perfume and headed for the door. She looked at her sister. "Lean and hungry, huh? Well, what do you say we go downstairs and confront the lions?"

Shari laughed. "You go first. I want to watch Trent's face when he sees that dress."

Filomena shrugged and walked toward the staircase. She was looking forward to the evening. It was the first time she had been out with Trent on anything resembling a real date since they had returned from Portland.

Trent was standing in the hall along with her parents and Jim Devore. He looked up from something he was saying to Amery and saw Filomena as she flitted lightly down the stairs. She smiled happily at him, aware that her parents and Jim were all staring at the white dress.

Trent was the only one who didn't appear shocked. His jade eyes moved over the dress with cool deliberation and then went back to Filomena's face. He didn't say a word.

"Fil, dear," Meg Cromwell began in a worried tone, "isn't that dress a bit...a bit...?" Her voice trailed off.

"I warned her," Shari said blithely as she stepped forward to accept Jim's kiss. "But she thinks Gallant Lake can handle it."

Jim grinned at Trent. "The question is, can Trent handle it? Good luck, pal. I warned you about the perils of trying to manage a female from this household."

"I see your point," Trent murmured, his eyes still on Filomena, who was smiling far too sweetly.

Amery Cromwell cleared his throat and made a production out of looking at his watch. "Uh, maybe we'd better be on our way, Meg. Shari's going to go with Jim, and Trent says he'll bring Filomena in his own car." He took his wife's arm and started determinedly toward the door. Meg glanced back doubtfully at Filomena and allowed herself to be led out of sight.

"We'd better be going, too, love," Jim said smoothly, reaching for Shari's hand. "I have a weak stomach. Can't stand the sight of blood."

"You're a doctor!" Shari reminded him as he hurried her outside.

"That's why I know I can't stand the sight of blood." Jim shut the door, leaving Filomena and Trent in the hall.

Filomena stood on the bottom step and looked at Trent expectantly. "Well? Shall we be on our way? Let's take my car."

He walked forward slowly, something between amusement and determination showing in his eyes. His mouth edged upward in a faint smile. "You couldn't resist, could you?"

"Resist what?" she asked innocently.

"Filomena, my sweet, I think you have developed a nasty habit of equating large size with stupidity. Just because I seem larger than the average dinosaur to you, it doesn't automatically follow that I have the brain of one."

She laughed at him with her eyes, enjoying the fact that because she was standing on the bottom step and had on a pair of high heels she was actually looking down on him. "Are you trying to tell me you're smarter than the average dinosaur?"

"I'd like to think so. But even if I'm not, I still have size on my side. Go and change the dress, sweetheart," he ordered gently.

Filomena blinked. "You don't like the dress?"

"The dress," he said evenly, "is designed to make a man want to pick you up and carry you off to bed. Unfortunately we are going to a cocktail party, not bed."

She reached out and patted him on the head, smiling with womanly assurance. "So that's the trouble. Shari was right. You're feeling a little possessive. Well, don't worry about a thing, Trent. This is very definitely a look-but-don't-touch sort of dress. No one at the cocktail party is going to pick me up and haul me off to bed." She paused, grinning wickedly. "Unless, of course, you get carried away and do something rash."

He ignored the reassuring pat on the head. His faint smile didn't waver. "Shari was wrong. I am not feeling a little possessive. I am feeling very possessive. You've teased and tormented Gallant Lake often enough since you've been here. You don't need to consolidate your victory tonight. Run along and change, honey. It's getting late."

Filomena studied his expression and came to the conclusion that beneath the slight smile and the flicker of amusement in his eyes, Trent was serious. She drew a deep breath and let it out slowly. "Why do I get the feeling this is a turning point in our relationship?"

"It's not a turning point in our relationship. It's a turning point for you. You've had your fun with the good folks of Gallant Lake. Change the dress, Filomena."

She drummed her fingers on the banister. "Or what?"

"Or I'll use my size and small brain power to help you change it."

Filomena smiled grimly. "Threats, Trent?"

"Promises, sweetheart."

There was a long pause. The hall clock ticked loudly in the silence as Filomena assessed Trent's mood and determination.

"Let's consider this from a mature, rational viewpoint,

Trent,'' she finally said carefully. "There are several potential problems here. If I allow you to intimidate me into changing my clothes, my entire family will know I am basically a female wimp as soon as I walk into the party."

"If you don't change your clothes, your entire family will be forced to the conclusion that I'm the wimp," Trent pointed out blandly.

"Not likely," she said, airily dismissing his claim. "No one would ever think of you as a wimp. Another problem with me changing my dress is that you might be left with the impression that you can order me around whenever the mood takes you. It's an attitude a lot of large people have toward those who are shorter and smaller. It's one of the fundamental reasons, I think, why men in general have always assumed they have the right to dominate women. The world would be a much different place if women were taller and stronger than men. All the attitudes between the sexes would be reversed."

Trent glanced at the stainless-steel watch on his wrist. "I'm not sure we have time for anthropological speculation."

But Filomena was warming to her subject now. "Just think how different everything would be, Trent. If women were taller and bigger and stronger, they would be the ones who made the decisions and gave the orders. They would be the ones who felt possessive and protective and dominant."

"I think we're wandering from the main point here."

She waved that aside, her eyes lighting with enthusiasm for her new subject. "Everyone would assume it was natural for men to stay home and take care of the children and dress in frilly little dresses. After all, they would be the weaker sex, right? Our whole family structure would be different. What's more, women wouldn't be victimized so much. They wouldn't have to walk around in fear of rape or domestic violence. They wouldn't have to pretend they weren't as bright as men. They wouldn't have to play games—"

"Filomena," Trent broke in with the first hint of diminishing patience, "I have the distinct impression you are trying to play games with me right now and I think I'd better warn you I am not in the mood. Go and change the dress.''

"Why should I?" she challenged. "Give me one good reason why I shouldn't wear exactly what I want to wear tonight!''

Trent shoved back the edges of his light-colored linen jacket and planted his hands on his hips. His eyes narrowed coolly, and the last of the indulgent smile faded from his mouth. He looked up at Filomena. "You want one good reason? I'll give you one good reason. We are not living in your dreamworld. We are living in a world where you happen to be a lot smaller than I am. *Go upstairs and change the dress.*''

Filomena stood still for an instant longer. Trent's voice hadn't risen, but, then, he didn't have to raise it in order to make his point.

"Might does not make right," she proclaimed.

"No, but it has a hell of an influence on the final outcome, doesn't it?''

Filomena knew when she was beaten. She lifted her chin and gave him a disdainful smile. "Just remember what happened to the dinosaurs." She swung around and walked back up the stairs as Trent's laughter filled the hall.

When she reached her bedroom, she caught sight of herself in the mirror and smiled suddenly. The white dress did, indeed, expose a great deal of skin. Shocking Gallant Lake no longer mattered. What mattered was that Trent was showing every sign of being possessive and jealous. The man was falling in love with her, she thought happily. Given that delightful assurance, she was in the mood to make a few concessions.

Ten minutes later she came back down the stairs wearing a close-fitting, off-the-shoulder dress fashioned in warm peach tones. There was a flounce at the knee to give the dress some sophisticated playfulness, but there was nothing in the design that could give Trent anything to complain about. She paused once more on the bottom step.

"Satisfied?" she asked with a haughty smile.

He grinned. "It'll do." He reached for her hand. "Thank you, Filomena."

"For what?"

"For not making me look like a wimpy dinosaur in front of your family."

She slanted him a sardonic glance. "You owe me one."

He laughed as he opened the front door and shut it behind them. "Trust you to find a way to salvage something from the situation. Okay, I owe you one." He paused on the front step, leaned down and brushed his mouth lingeringly against hers. "When are you going to collect?" he murmured.

"Probably when you least expect it." She started down the path to where the cars were parked. "Let's take the Porsche."

"There's no need. I think everyone in Gallant Lake has already seen it."

"That's not why I want to take it," she explained, digging her keys out of her purse. "I want to take it so that I can do the driving."

Trent groaned as he reluctantly slid into the passenger seat beside her. "Is this going to be my punishment for having won the battle over the dress?"

"You sound nervous," she taunted as she turned the key in the ignition and slipped the car into gear.

"You drive like a bat out of hell. Naturally I'm nervous."

"I," declared Filomena as gravel hissed under the wheels, "am an excellent driver." The Porsche shot out of the parking area like a Thoroughbred out of a racing gate. By the time the vehicle hit the main road around the lake, it was moving at a very brisk clip. Filomena drove with both hands on the wheel and a great deal of attention. She loved the feel of the car as it responded to her lightest touch. Deliberately she put it through its paces on the curves.

Trent endured the situation in absolute silence for nearly ten minutes and then he said quietly, "All right, that's enough."

"Enough what?" she asked politely.

"You've gotten even for the battle over the dress. Now slow down and show some common sense."

There was an edge to his voice that hadn't been present when he'd ordered her to change her clothes. Filomena realized Trent had had enough of the Porsche's gymnastics. Obediently she slowed the car to a more sedate pace. There was a long silence.

"I'm not used to it, you know," she finally said.

"Not used to having to adjust your life to accommodate a man? I know. It works both ways. I'm not accustomed to feeling this possessive about a woman. But I think we'll both learn to handle it."

There was another long silence, this time a thoughtful one that lasted until Filomena parked the Porsche in the driveway of the Aikens's lakeside home. She turned off the ignition and sat quietly surveying the cars that were parked up and down the street.

"Just remember you still owe me a favor."

"I'll remember," he said.

Filomena was quiet for another moment. "It looks like the Aikens have invited everyone in Gallant Lake tonight."

Trent opened his door and got out. "Don't worry, that dress is going to make an even bigger impression than the white one would have."

She looked down at the peach-colored dress and grimaced as she climbed out of the car. "Why do you say that?"

He grinned at her in the street light. "Just a guess, but I have a hunch most of your old high school girlfriends have been hearing about your clothes for days. They've probably all gone out and bought themselves the most outrageous outfits they could find in an effort to compete tonight. When you show up in something respectable and modest, they're all going to feel terribly overdressed."

Filomena burst out laughing. "Since when did you become such an expert on the female psyche?"

"I'm a fast learner." He took her arm and led her toward the open doors of the house.

It didn't take Filomena long to decide she had been right when she guessed that just about everyone in town had been invited to the Aikens's party. The crowd filled the living room, den and kitchen and spilled out onto the patio. There was food everywhere, and Todd Aiken had set up a generous bar near the door. Few people noticed the new arrivals at first. In the crush it was difficult to see who was coming and going.

"I'll get us a drink," Trent said. "Don't move."

Filomena nodded, watching him head for the bar. His height made it easy to keep track of him in the crowd.

"Fil! There you are. What in the world took you and Trent so long to get here? I was just about to phone home and see what was going on." Shari emerged from the throng, smiling down at her sister. Her eyes went over the demure peach-colored outfit. "Aha. I was right. He made you change your dress."

"Trent did not *make* me change my dress," Filomena informed her. "We had a discussion on the subject, and after some rational arguments on both sides, I decided not to make him look like a wimp."

Shari gave a shout of laughter that caused several nearby heads to turn. "As if you could." At that moment Trent appeared with a glass of wine for Filomena and a mug of beer for himself.

"Hello, Shari," he said easily. "Where's Jim?"

"Talking about the merits of flu shots with the mother of one of his patients. I was just asking Filomena what took you both so long to get here and then I realized she had on a different dress."

Filomena had had enough. "If anyone says one more word about the fact that I changed clothes this evening, I swear I will strip naked right here in the Aikens's living room and give you all something to really talk about. Do I make myself clear?"

"Don't say another word, Shari," Trent advised. "I, for one, believe her."

"Oh, so do I," Shari said quickly. "You can only push Fil so far and then she goes up in flames."

Another voice interrupted before anyone could comment on that. An attractive dark-haired woman of Filomena's age and height pushed her way through the crowd. "Fil! There you are. I heard you were going to be here tonight. Long time, no see. Geez, you look good. Just like everyone says."

"Hi, Liz. I almost didn't recognize you." Filomena laughed at her old acquaintance. "You're looking very good yourself." She hadn't seen Liz Sawyer since high school. Liz had been two years ahead of her. She was about Filomena's height.

"I'll bet you recognized the dress, though, didn't you?" Liz spun around, displaying the brightly patterned knit sweater and silk skirt she was wearing. "It's a Cromwell & Sterling, naturally. I love it. My wardrobe is filled with your things. They fit so beautifully."

Pleased, Filomena thanked her and made introductions. It wasn't long before a lively group of young women had formed, and Filomena became involved in a discussion of her travels in Tahiti and India in search of patterns and exotic materials. She looked up briefly when Trent touched her arm and said he was going to find her father.

"Okay," she said with a smile. "I'll see you later."

He kissed her forehead with casual possessiveness and walked away in search of his fishing buddy. Liz and the others stared after him with speculative expressions, then they turned back to Filomena and demanded to know what the fashion forecasts were for the coming season.

After a while it dawned on Filomena that she was enjoying herself. For the first time since she had returned to Gallant Lake she wasn't thinking about causing a sensation or making certain everyone knew just how different life was for her now. Instead, she relaxed and renewed old acquaintances.

Life in Gallant Lake in her younger days hadn't been all that bad, she thought. There had been a lot of young women besides herself who hadn't made the cheerleading squad or who had lacked a date for the homecoming dance. Most of them had survived quite well, just as she had.

When the cigarette smoke and the heat became a little overwhelming, Filomena excused herself to get another glass of cool wine. She spoke to her host for a few minutes as he wielded bottles behind the small bar and then she decided to get a breath of fresh air out on the terrace.

She glanced around to see if she could spot Trent before she went outside and saw him standing across the room talking with her father and two other men. From their serious expressions, Filomena assumed they were either discussing the possibilities for a third world war or the merits of certain fishing locations on the lake. Men sometimes lacked a sense of proportion about life, she thought with an inner smile.

A balmy breeze greeted her as she walked through the open sliding glass doors. She was pleased to see she had the terrace to herself, at least for a while. She needed a few minutes to recover from the cheerful noise and confusion inside. Glass in hand, she moved to the far side of the terrace and leaned against the rail to contemplate the moonlit lake.

It was the first time all evening that she'd had a few minutes to herself. She used them to think about Trent Ravinder.

She wouldn't have changed that white dress for any other man on the face of the earth. It was a sobering thought. Strange how the little things sometimes held so much importance and meaning.

"Fil?"

Brady Paxton's voice interrupted her reflections.

"Hello, Brady," Filomena said without much enthusiasm. She didn't bother to turn around. Instead, she continued to lean on the railing, her drink cradled loosely in one hand.

"I've been looking for you," he said earnestly, moving toward her. "We need to talk."

"I don't think so, Brady."

He came to a halt beside her and joined her in leaning on the railing. The breeze ruffled his tawny hair and brought the scent of his cologne to Filomena's nostrils. She wrinkled her nose and decided she didn't like the fragrance.

Brady let out a long sigh. "All right, I was a little slow in the beginning, but I've got it figured out now. You're really slick,

Fil. I'll give you that. I never would have believed you could pull it off.''

Filomena tapped one long nail on the cedar railing. ''Pull what off, Brady?''

''No wonder you didn't want to do a deal with me when I offered you a commission the other day. You had your own plans, didn't you? You must have laughed all the way home about my offer of a five percent commission.''

''Not exactly,'' she said dryly, wondering where this was going. ''How's your wife? Is she here tonight? Maybe she'd like to join us.''

''Forget Gloria,'' Brady snapped. ''We're talking business, you and I.''

''I'm not talking business. I'm out here to get some fresh air.''

''You are one tough lady these days, aren't you, Fil? Who'd have thought you, of all people, would turn out like this? You were so sweet nine years ago.''

''You mean I was so stupid nine years ago. I actually trusted you, Brady. Talk about dumb. Ah, well, it takes some of us longer to grow up than it does others, I guess. But I did eventually grow up.''

He looked down at her with hot, intent eyes. ''You haven't forgotten, have you? You still want me. I can tell. Beneath all that bravado, you still want me.''

A slow, mocking smile shaped her mouth as she turned to him. ''If you think that, you're a bigger fool now than I was at nineteen. I wouldn't have you if you came served on a silver platter.''

His mood shifted abruptly. Anger appeared in his eyes and in the twist of his mouth. ''Because you think you can do better, is that it? You think now that you've got your hooks into Ravinder, you've got it made? Think again, lady. He's big time. You're nothing more than a summer fling to him. If you've got any sense you know that and you'll use it to get the information we both want. But you won't fool yourself into believing he's serious about you.''

"The way I once fooled myself into thinking you were serious about me?" she asked with a dangerous lightness.

Even in the shadows, the flush was evident on Brady's cheeks. His gaze grew more intense. "Nine years ago I had to make a decision. If it's any consolation to you, I've paid for that decision. I am not a happily married man, Fil. There have been a lot of nights when I've lain awake wondering what would have happened if you and I had stayed together. The only reason I haven't divorced Gloria is because her father would dissolve the insurance partnership."

"How about the fact that you've got two children? Isn't that a factor in your decision not to get a divorce? Or don't they count, Brady? You don't have any qualms about hurting people, do you? But heaven forbid you should jeopardize a business arrangement. Well, you made the right decision nine years ago. I am very, very glad you didn't marry me. Your wife and children have my deepest sympathy."

"Don't give me that garbage, Fil," he said hoarsely. "You don't feel sorry for them or anyone else because you're too busy looking out for number one these days. I've figured out what you're up to, you know. You don't fool me."

"Is that right?" she taunted. "Just what am I up to?"

"You're having an affair with Ravinder. The whole town knows it."

"No kidding?"

"We all know you went to Portland with him for the night a few days ago. Hell, Gloria practically hit me over the head with the news when I got home from work that day. She couldn't wait to tell me. Wanted me to know what a little tramp you are and how you weren't exactly hanging around Gallant Lake to seduce me. She said you had bigger fish to fry. That's when I realized what you were up to."

"I think it would be best if you didn't say anything more, Brady."

He ignored that. "You think you know what you're doing, but you're going to land in real trouble if you don't listen to me.

I know you've started the affair with Ravinder in order to find out what Asgard's intentions are. But you can't do a thing with the information unless you deal with me. I have options on just about every decent piece of land on the lake. Sooner or later you're going to have to work with me. Now, I'm willing to raise your commission a bit.''

''Forget it, Brady.''

''All right, we can form a partnership, if that's what you want.''

''I said forget it, Brady.''

He was infuriated by her quiet refusal. ''Who do you think you're going to sell the information to, if not to me? You don't have any choice, damn it!''

Filomena finally lost what remained of her patience. She whirled around to confront him face-to-face. ''Brady Paxton, you are a fool, even if you do own most of the good land around Gallant Lake. Number one, Asgard is not interested in putting in a resort development around here. Number two, even if the company was interested and even if I knew which tracts of land it wanted to buy, I wouldn't tell you, no matter how much money you offered for the information. Want to know why?''

''Because you think Ravinder's in love with you? Is that it?''

''Because I know I am in love with him,'' Filomena corrected bluntly. ''And what's more I'm going to marry him. If you think I'd betray the man I'm going to marry for the sake of a lousy real estate deal, then I think it's safe to say you never did know me very well. Now why don't you trot back inside and find your wife. I'm sure she's looking for you.''

''Why, you little bitch!''

Brady's hand came up as he loomed over Filomena. She held her ground, the wineglass clenched in her hand in case she had to hurl it in self-defense. But the confrontation never got a chance to explode into violence. Trent spoke from the doorway, his voice slicing like cold fire through the shadows.

''If you so much as touch her, Paxton, I'll take you apart so thoroughly they won't ever get all the pieces back together again.''

Chapter Eight

FILOMENA WHIRLED AROUND and saw Trent striding swiftly across the terrace. With a little gasp of relief, she set her glass down on the railing and ran forward to throw herself against his chest. His right arm went out to grasp her and hold her close. She was swallowed up immediately in the confines of his embrace. He felt very large and sturdy and safe, she reflected. There were times when size was comforting.

"I'm sorry about this," she mumbled into his jacket.

He crushed her gently. "I'm not." Then he raised his voice slightly. "I think you'd better go back inside, Paxton. There's no point in pestering my fiancée anymore. She wouldn't sell you the information you want, even if she had it, which she doesn't. And by now you've probably figured out for yourself she has no intention of letting herself get dragged into an affair with you. But if you can't grasp that simple concept, then take my word for it that if you come near her again, I'll slaughter you. Do we have an understanding?"

Brady edged around him, his face set in bitter, resentful lines as he started back toward the sliding glass doors. "She's playing games, Ravinder. If you're as smart as people seem to think, you won't be fooled by them. I'll admit she's turned into a hot little piece of tail, but she's definitely got her eye on the main chance. She's a real businesswoman these days. Better keep that in mind if you know what's good—"

Brady never finished the sentence. Filomena felt Trent's body tighten briefly and then uncoil with the speed and power of a natural predator. She barely had time to realize she was free from his comforting grasp when she heard the ominous thud and the sound of air whooshing from Brady's chest.

"Oh, my God," she breathed, shocked by the swiftness with which it had all happened as much as by the violence itself. She found herself staring down at Brady's crumpled body. He raised himself on one elbow, gasping for air and glared at Trent who was standing over him.

"*Now* do we understand each other?" Trent asked.

"You bastard, you're welcome to her!" Brady scrambled to his feet, brushed furiously at his clothing and stalked painfully back into the house.

"What if he sues?" Filomena asked faintly, voicing the first fear that came to mind.

"Trust me, he won't." Trent looked at her and shook his head slightly when he saw the anxious expression on her face. "He won't want to have to explain how it happened," he elaborated. "Too embarrassing."

"Oh." Filomena chewed on her lower lip, considering that. "It would be, wouldn't it? Brady would hate to humiliate himself like that."

"Yes."

She eyed him with a sense of trepidation. "Well, don't keep me in suspense. How much did you hear?"

There was a short pause. "Enough. But the only part that mattered was the bit about marrying me."

"I was afraid of that." Filomena sighed and went to lean against the railing again. "I'm sorry, Trent. It just sort of slipped out. I wasn't thinking, really. I wanted to convince Brady I had absolutely no interest in him, and he said something about having an affair with you and I just sort of took it from there." She picked up her wineglass and took a shaky sip for courage. "Sometimes I do things on impulse. An old habit."

"I know the feeling." Absently he rubbed his knuckles as he moved toward her. His eyes were very brilliant in the moonlight.

"Occasionally I do a few things on impulse, too. But that doesn't mean I always regret them. How about you?"

Her fingers tightened on the glass in her hand as she looked up at him with a clear, honest longing in her eyes. "I don't usually regret the things I do on impulse, either. I figure that...that fundamentally they're really not all that impulsive. Sometimes they're just things my subconscious has been mulling over for a while, and suddenly the truth jumps out without any warning."

Trent's eyes softened but lost none of their brilliance. He lifted a hand and stroked the side of her cheek. "Tell me this great truth that just jumped out at you without any warning," he urged.

"I...I just realized as I was talking to Brady that I've fallen in love with you."

Trent buried his lips in her hair. "I can hardly believe it."

"I know I've taken you by surprise," she said hurriedly, "but, you see, I—"

He hushed her with a tender finger on her lips. "It's all right, sweetheart. It's all right. I'm not complaining, believe me. It's just that it all happened so quickly. I think I'm in shock."

"So quickly?"

He smiled. "I fell in love with you within a few hours of meeting you, elf."

"Oh, Trent, really?"

"Really. I've known where I was headed for a long time now, and I told myself I was succeeding in coaxing you along in the same direction. But to be honest, I thought it was going to take you a lot longer to arrive at the same destination. You've been so uninterested in love and marriage that I figured it would take a lot more effort than this on my part to get you to the altar."

She smiled up at him. "Disappointed at an easy victory?"

"Are you kidding? I'm just grateful you came to your senses so quickly. Saves me a lot of work. I'm not about to question my luck."

She wrapped her arms around him with fierce longing. "Oh,

Trent, I'm so glad. I can't believe it," she rushed on as happiness overtook her. "I never realized where it was all leading. I must have been blind. My God, I've never felt like this about anyone. Why didn't I understand sooner?"

He laughed softly, his fingers urgent on her skin as he held her close. "You were too busy staying out of my reach while you showed Gallant Lake you've gone big time. You didn't see the tree because you were looking at the whole forest."

She laughed against his shirt. "Such a big tree, too. So you took me to Portland and made sure you got my full attention for a while, is that it?"

"After that, everything fell into place very nicely."

"You're a very clever man," she said.

"I know."

"And modest, too."

"It's tough to be modest when you're this clever, but I try," he agreed modestly.

Her eyes were filled with joy as she raised her head to meet his gaze. "Making me fall in love with you is one thing, but I told Brady that I was going to marry you. That's another matter altogether. Are you clever enough to keep me dangling while you steer clear of marriage?"

"I'm not even going to try to avoid marriage," he told her with rough passion, and then he kissed her thoroughly. When he finally lifted his mouth from hers, she was trembling. He looked down at her with satisfaction and smiled. "You're committed, you know. You've told Brady, and that means everyone at the party will have heard by now."

"A daunting thought."

"Uh-huh. In another few minutes I expect to see your family stampeding out here to demand confirmation."

"You don't look nervous."

"I'm not," he said. "Are you?"

Filomena shook her head with grave certainty. "No," she whispered. "It's what I want. I never would have guessed it, but it's what I want. Trent, there's so much to talk about. So much we have to discuss. I want to know—''

"Filomena! Trent! What the devil is going on?" Amery Cromwell's voice bellowed across the terrace.

Trent turned with Filomena in his arms as Amery led the charge. He was followed by Meg and Shari and a grinning Jim Devore. Uncle George and Aunt Agnes brought up the rear. George was waving a bottle of champagne and calling for glasses. Several other people trickled out onto the terrace behind them, wearing curious expressions.

Trent surveyed the assembled crowd of interested faces. "It's tough to keep things quiet in a small town, isn't it?" he observed.

THE FOLLOWING AFTERNOON Filomena lounged comfortably against Trent who had his back braced against a tree near the water's edge. He had one arm wrapped around her, and with his free hand he was tossing occasional pebbles into the lake.

"Are you sure we know what we're doing?" Filomena asked with lazy amusement.

"Relax. I'll take care of everything."

"Maybe we should have waited until after Shari's wedding to announce our engagement. I don't want to steal any of her thunder. This is her special time."

Trent grinned. "Don't worry about it. Shari was thrilled, just as everyone else in the family was. It might have been tacky to get married ahead of her, but no one's going to hold the engagement announcement against us."

"You're sure?"

"I'm positive. I had a long talk with your father about it," he informed her.

"You *what*?" She pulled away from him to peer up into his face. "What do you mean you had a long talk with him? What sort of long talk? And why wasn't I present?"

"You weren't present because you didn't get up at five-thirty to go fishing with us this morning."

"If I'd known you were going to discuss something important, I might have made the effort," Filomena grumbled.

"It was men's talk," Trent explained condescendingly.

"Is that right? And what precisely got said between you two men?"

"Mostly we talked about how glad everyone is that I'm going to marry you. The rest of the family can stop worrying about you now. You're not getting any younger, you know. It's all well and good to be a successful career woman, but your family is convinced you need a man to love. They appreciate the fact that I've volunteered. I detected more than appreciation, to be honest. I got the feeling that a vast sense of relief was felt by all concerned."

Filomena collapsed in outraged laughter and began pummeling him mercilessly. "Arrogant, overbearing, egotistical male." Her small blows rained over him like popcorn.

He grinned, catching hold of her wrists. "Hey, is that any way to treat the man who is going to be your lord and master?"

"You're really getting into this, aren't you?" she accused with gleaming eyes. "I had no idea you were so eager to become a husband."

His expression sobered. "I had no idea you were so eager to become a wife."

"I wasn't," she admitted, growing more serious. "My life has been full. I thought I had everything I wanted or needed."

"And when you thought of marriage, you thought of walking in on Paxton and Gloria nine years ago," he finished for her.

Filomena nodded. "I suppose so. It wasn't just walking in on them, you understand. That was bad enough. But the whole town found out about it within twenty-four hours. When Brady broke the engagement and announced he was marrying Gloria, I thought I was going to die of humiliation. I wanted to run and hide and never show my face around here again." She paused. "I was very young in many ways."

"That kind of scene would traumatize anyone." Trent tangled

his fingers in her hair. "Especially someone like you, sweet-heart."

"What do you mean?"

He smiled. "You can put on a good act these days with those showy clothes and that confident chatter, but deep inside you're still soft and innocent in a lot of ways." She started to protest, but he held up his hand. "It's built into you, and you're going to be that way the rest of your life, so don't bother arguing about it."

"How do you know?" she demanded.

"I know every time I take you in my arms."

"I sense a touch of chauvinism here," Filomena said warn-ingly. "Typical of a man to think he knows all there is to know about a woman simply because he's made love to her a few times."

Trent was unfazed. "I don't know all there is to know about you, but I know the important things."

"Such as?"

His eyes softened as he looked down into her face. He touched her breast lightly, cupping it until the nipple stirred eagerly and began to grow taut beneath the fabric of the tropical flower print jumpsuit she was wearing. "I know you've been wary of giving yourself to any man for the past few years, but when you finally gave yourself to me you did it completely. You surrendered to-tally and honestly. You made me feel more wanted than I've ever felt in my life. You couldn't have done that if you were basically selfish or hard or emotionally brittle."

Filomena drew in her breath, trembling under the warmth of his gaze. "I know a few things about you, too," she managed to say with light challenge.

His mouth crooked. "Is that right?"

She nodded quickly. "You're a good man, an honest man, a man I can trust. I think you're hard in some ways, maybe too rigid about some things, but I expect marriage will soften you up some."

"Think so?"

"Umm." She paused thoughtfully. "The only thing I'm not sure of is why you want to marry me."

He brushed his mouth across her lips. "That's your streak of insecurity showing. Shari was right, you never completely got over what Paxton did to you when you were nineteen. And for the past couple of years you've been running into men who are attracted to Cromwell & Sterling as much as they are to you. No wonder you're a little insecure when it comes to men. But I can fix that."

Filomena rolled her eyes. "For crying out loud. You've been discussing me with my sister, too?"

"I believe in thoroughly researching a project."

"Well, next time you have any questions about me, ask me, understand?"

"Got it."

"All right, tell me why you want to marry me," she persisted.

"You're smart, sexy and lovable. What other reasons do I need?"

"Evelyn Reece said you spent the past year looking for a wife the way you look for choice land for Asgard. She had the impression you had just abandoned the project until you finally ran into me."

Trent's indulgent smile faded, and his eyebrows rose in mild disapproval. "You and Evelyn appear to have had quite a conversation in the ladies' room of that restaurant."

Filomena gave him a complacent look. "Now you know what it's like to be discussed with third parties."

"I'll keep it in mind." It was obvious Trent was not pleased by what Filomena had learned about him behind his back.

"Well?"

"Well, what?" he retorted.

"Have you spent the past year shopping for a wife?"

His displeasure flared in his eyes, but he didn't try to prevaricate. "You want to know what I was doing this past year? All right, I'll tell you. I decided it was time."

"Time to get married? Just like that you decided?" she asked, torn between disbelief and laughter. "I can see it now. The big honcho executive decides he wants to get married, so he sets out to negotiate a wedding the same way he would a land deal. It's wonderful. I love it."

He growled something about her sense of humor and then went doggedly on with his explanation. "I'm thirty-six years old, honey. Until now I've devoted everything to my career. After the disaster of my first marriage, I wasn't all that eager to take the plunge again. I thought there was plenty of time to worry about finding another wife and having a family, but one day I woke up and looked around and realized the important things in life were slipping rapidly out of reach. There wasn't as much time as I had thought. I guess there never is. My career is important to me, but there are other things that are important also. I wanted someone else in my life. I wanted a woman who loved me in my home and in my bed. I wanted a woman to come home to at night, someone to share the highs and the lows with. Does that sound so strange?"

"Nope."

"Then why are you struggling to keep from laughing out loud?" he demanded wryly.

"It's just the thought of you setting out to find a wife in such a methodical fashion." She smiled up at him. "Actually, it's very sweet in a way."

"Sweet, huh?"

"Sweet," she repeated firmly. "Rather touchingly innocent. Go on, tell me what went wrong. Evelyn said you seemed to have abandoned the search."

"When I get back to Portland, I'm going to have a talk with Reece about his wife's tendency to gossip."

"Don't be an idiot," Filomena said fondly. "Evelyn was just being helpful. Now tell me what went wrong during the big search."

Trent shrugged. "I didn't find anyone I wanted to marry. Maybe I was looking too hard. I don't know. Maybe I worried too much about finding someone who wanted me for myself and

not my position at Asgard. Whatever the reason, nothing seemed
to click. I gave up and went back to my normal routine. Then I
decided that what I really needed was a long vacation. I came
up here, you arrived at the speed of light in that Porsche and
presto, everything fell into place.''

He looked so pleased with himself that Filomena began to
laugh again. His hand moved on her breast, and her laughter
turned into a soft little moan of pleasure. Trent eased her down
onto the bed of pine needles.

''Trent?''

''Hmm?'' He was busy unbuttoning the front of the jumpsuit.

''When do you want to get married?'' Filomena asked hesitantly.

''As soon as possible.'' He had the top open now and was
unbuckling the wide belt. Frowning slightly, he looked down
into her face. ''Why? Did you want a big wedding like Shari's?''

''No.''

''Good. Then there's no reason we can't arrange something
small in a few weeks, is there?''

She smiled, shaking her head. ''No.''

''I think you're going to make me an excellent wife, Filomena
Cromwell.''

''What makes you say that?''

''You know when to say no and you know when to say yes.''
He bent to take one budding nipple into his mouth.

Filomena thrust her fingers urgently into his hair, lifting herself into his kiss. ''Yes,'' she whispered in a soft, throaty voice.
''Oh, yes, Trent.''

He loved the sound of the word ''yes'' on her lips, Trent
decided as he quickly began to lose himself in the warmth and
sweetness of Filomena's body. He could never hear it often
enough, no matter how long he lived.

A part of him still couldn't believe his good luck. The relationship between himself and Filomena seemed to have been
finalized with an unexpected suddenness that left him feeling
slightly dazed. When Filomena made up her mind, she acted

quickly. But she had been staying just out of reach for so long he was almost wary of accepting the reality of her surrender.

But a smart man didn't question good fortune when it came his way, Trent told himself. Filomena was here in his arms, and she was going to marry him. Surely that was all that mattered.

TWO DAYS LATER Shari's wedding went off like clockwork, which didn't surprise anyone who knew Meg Cromwell's talent for organization. Virtually everyone in town was invited and virtually everyone came. The reception was held at the country club, and the lavish buffet was replenished frequently to keep up with the throng of hungry guests.

An hour into the celebration, Filomena found a moment or two alone with her mother, who had been bustling about with tireless energy.

"Everything's perfect, Mom. You pulled it off beautifully. Don't Shari and Jim look terrific together?"

Meg nodded in maternal satisfaction as she gazed fondly at her statuesque blond daughter who was in the middle of a crowd. "Perfect. A lovely couple. And they're so happy. Jim's going to make Shari an excellent husband."

Filomena sipped her champagne. "I think you're right."

"Trent is going to make you an excellent husband, too, my dear. I'm so pleased things worked out between the two of you. I don't mind telling you I was a little nervous there for a while."

"Afraid I'd blow it, huh?" Filomena smiled over the rim of her glass.

"Well," Meg said bluntly, "you seemed to be doing your best to keep him at arm's length."

"He made me nervous," Filomena explained.

"Nervous! How on earth did he do that?" Meg looked and sounded shocked.

"I'm not sure. Maybe because deep down I knew I wouldn't be able to keep him at arm's length for very long, not if he decided to close the gap."

"Which he did, thank goodness," Meg concluded. "I just wish the two of you weren't going to rush the ceremony. Just think what a terrific job I could do on a second wedding now that I've had an opportunity to practice.''

Filomena laughed. "Talk to Trent. He's the one who doesn't want to wait.''

"Well, I suppose I can see his reasoning. He's waited long enough, hasn't he? And so have you, for that matter. High time both of you made a commitment. Life goes by so quickly, and sometimes we forget the important things, thinking there's going to be plenty of time.''

"Trent said something about that, too.''

"Well, it's the truth. The older you get, the more you realize it. Trent is a good man, Fil. You couldn't have found anyone better.''

"I know.'' She paused and then said cautiously, "He's got a thing about honesty. Did you know that? He's rather unbending in some ways.''

"So? Do you want a man who doesn't have a strong sense of integrity? Someone like Brady Paxton?'' Meg demanded bracingly.

"Of course not.'' Filomena decided to change the topic. "Looks like everyone's here. Even Brady and his wife. I'm surprised they showed up.''

Meg was mildly astonished. "Why wouldn't they show up? It would have looked very awkward if they hadn't. People would have talked, and I'm sure the Paxtons knew it.''

"People were already talking about Brady and me, apparently.''

"Don't be ridiculous. That sort of gossip came to a quick halt when you and Trent announced your engagement. Actually, I think it stopped before that. I didn't hear another word about you and Brady after you went to Portland with Trent. Thank goodness that man took the reins into his own hands. As I said, I was getting very worried.''

"If I were you, I'd start worrying about Uncle George and Aunt Agnes.'' Filomena nodded meaningfully toward her relatives who were regaling a large group across the room with increasingly loud conversation. Gloria Paxton, dressed in an overly snug knit dress, was standing in the group. So was Trent. He seemed to be amused by whatever George was saying.

Instantly alarmed, Meg snapped her head around to pin down George and Agnes in the crowd. "What are those two up to now? I swear, Fil, if they make a scene this afternoon, I will personally murder both of them."

"They do seem to be getting a little loud. They're obviously having a good time."

"Oh, heavens, I'd better go put the lid on George before he gets up on a table or something. I must speak to your father about cutting off their champagne." Meg dashed into the crowd, the skirts of her mauve mother-of-the-bride dress swirling out behind her.

Filomena watched her mother for a moment and then turned with a small, private smile to help herself to another round of goodies from the buffet table. Uncle George's laughter sailed across the room. It faded a bit as Meg Cromwell joined the group. Filomena didn't envy her mother the task of keeping a lid on Uncle George. He was a big, boisterous man, and when he was in an expansive mood everyone around him knew it.

Filomena was taking a bite out of a cream cheese and shrimp canapé when she heard her uncle say something about a dowry. She paused, the cracker halfway into her mouth, and listened with a sense of startled surprise that rapidly turned into shock.

"Don't want anyone here to think we'd send our two nieces into marriage without a proper wedding gift," Uncle George declared loudly. He grinned first at Shari's new husband and then at Trent. "Agnes and I've been saving this announcement until now because we wanted it to be a surprise. Fact is, I bought some good land along the coast a few years back. Picked up two nice-sized tracts for a song. I told Agnes they'd be a heck of an investment, and I was right. As usual. I don't mind telling you all that both parcels are worth a tidy sum now. And Agnes and I are going to give each of our nieces a tract as wedding gifts.

What do you think about that?'' George and Agnes gazed around at the crowd with an expectant air.

They weren't disappointed. Everyone broke into hearty congratulations. The room was full of delighted comments and good wishes. Filomena could hear Shari exclaiming in amazement. Her husband looked startled but pleased. Filomena's parents were shaking their heads in wry, amused wonder.

But Filomena's gaze collided with Trent's in that moment, and she went cold inside.

He looked at her across the heads of the people separating them. There was no amusement in his eyes, no look of cheerful congratulations or delight in Shari's and Filomena's good fortune. There was, instead, a strange, forbidding anger. It was an expression unlike anything Filomena had ever seen in his gaze. It frightened her as nothing had frightened her in a very long time.

Filomena was filled with a sudden, sickening foreboding.

Trent glanced toward the patio and then back at her. The message was unmistakable. *Message, nothing,* she thought. It was an order. He wanted to talk to her out on the patio. She gave him a small, almost imperceptible nod and slowly started to make her way through the crowd.

But it wasn't Trent who was waiting for her near the open door. It was Gloria Paxton. Her face was flushed, and it was obvious she'd had a considerable amount of champagne. Her eyes were dangerously bright.

"Hello, Gloria, I hope you're enjoying yourself."

"Oh, I'm enjoying myself tremendously now that some very interesting questions have been answered."

"Good. Excuse me. I thought I'd get away from the noise for a while." Filomena tried to step around the other woman. Gloria allowed her to slip outside, but she followed hard on Filomena's heels.

"I see you didn't wear one of those tarty dresses you and your friend design." Gloria ran a disparaging eye over the discreetly cut, patterned yellow silk dress Filomena was wearing. "Decent of you not to cause a scene at your sister's wedding. I half expected you to show up in a harem outfit or a string bikini. But I guess your *fiancé* wouldn't approve of that, would he?''

Filomena counted slowly to ten and promised herself she wouldn't shove Gloria Paxton into the pool, at least not until Shari and Jim had left the reception. She owed her sister that much consideration. "If you don't mind, Gloria, I'd like a few minutes alone. It's been a hectic afternoon.''

"Not just a hectic afternoon, a hectic vacation, right, Fil?'' Gloria asked maliciously. "You certainly had your work cut out for you, didn't you? First you made a try for Brady. But that didn't get far, did it? He never did want you, Fil. It was me he wanted, right from the start. He was just killing time with you nine years ago.''

"Gloria, I think we'd better put paid to this conversation before it gets any more embarrassing.''

"Are you embarrassed, Fil? That's hard to believe. The last time you looked really embarrassed was when you walked in on Brady and me. I never told you I planned that little scene, did I? I knew you were on your way over to see Brady. I'd phoned your house to check. But I got to his place first and staged a big bedroom scene for your benefit. It worked like a charm. Brady had been stalling about breaking off your engagement, but after you found us he had to act.''

Filomena sighed. "All that might have mattered once, but it doesn't anymore.''

"I'll never forget the expression on your face. You looked like someone's pet dog whose master had just kicked it in the teeth. But you've turned into a real tough cookie since then, haven't you? You're a lot smarter now than you were in the old days. You came back here to see if you could get your claws into my husband, but you pulled off an even bigger coup when you tricked Trent Ravinder into proposing, didn't you?''

"Gloria, you don't know what you're talking about. I suggest you cut back on the champagne.''

"Don't worry about me. Worry about yourself. Because this

time I think you've bitten off more than you can chew. Ravinder is no fool, and now that he's found out you've played him for one he's not going to be pleased. He'll probably wring your neck.''

Filomena, who had been on the point of turning away and walking back into the crowded room, stopped and stared at her, stunned. ''What on earth are you talking about?'' she asked. But she knew what Gloria was about to say.

''Don't look so stupid and innocent. That's the same dumb look you had on your face nine years ago. It won't wash, Fil. You're a big girl now and you know what you're doing. It's no secret any longer. We all heard what your generous Uncle George just said in there, didn't we? It's all clear now, Fil. I can see exactly what you've been planning.''

''Is that right?'' Filomena took a step toward Gloria. Her voice was too soft, but Gloria didn't seem to comprehend the significance of that. ''Just what is it you think I've been planning?''

''It's obvious.'' Gloria waved her arm, and some of the champagne in her glass spilled over the rim. ''You decided to find a way to collect that land your aunt and uncle planned to give you when you got married, didn't you? Your uncle's announcement explains everything. It was so touching to hear George and Agnes talk about their little 'surprise' wedding gifts for you and Shari, the two wonderful nieces who are almost like their own daughters.'' Gloria's mouth twisted savagely.

''You don't know what you're talking about.''

But Gloria ignored Filomena's fierce protest. Her bitter gaze moved past Filomena to the man who had appeared in the doorway. She smiled grimly at Trent. ''What about it, Trent? Weren't you amazed to learn that Filomena's going to receive that valuable land on the coast? And all she had to do to get it was get married. Lucky you came along, isn't it? I must admit, I'm glad you did. If you hadn't been available, she would have tried to take Brady. It's obvious she needed a man, any man, in order to get hold of that land.''

Gloria's face crumpled in a combination of rage and tears.

She flung aside her champagne glass and ran clumsily past Filomena and Trent. An instant later she disappeared into the crowded room.

Filomena turned slowly to confront a grim-faced Trent. She looked for amusement or indulgence or impatience in his expression and saw nothing. The jade-green eyes were totally unreadable. He was regarding her as if she were some new and unknown example of alien life form. A sick feeling washed over Filomena.

"Trent, please don't look at me that way," she begged.

"How should I look at you, Filomena?"

She shook her head frantically. "Why are you so upset about what my uncle just said?"

"How long have you known about the land, Fil?"

She looked at him helplessly. "I knew my aunt and uncle had a lot of real estate, but I didn't know they were going to use some of it as wedding gifts for Shari and me. What difference does it make, anyway? What's wrong? What are you thinking?"

"I'm thinking about how much you need a large chunk of cash to finance your ambitious expansion plans for Cromwell & Sterling, Inc. I'm remembering how disappointed you were when Glenna phoned the other day to tell you the bank had denied your application for a loan."

Filomena went pale. "Trent, you can't possibly think that I—"

"I'm remembering that it was right after you found out you weren't going to get the bank loan that you suddenly announced you were going to marry me. I'm thinking that there's a good explanation now for your sudden reversal of attitude on the subject of love and marriage. I wondered at the time why you changed your mind so quickly. I should have known my so-called victory came a little too easily."

"*Trent.*"

"So you tell me what's wrong, Filomena," he went on harshly. "Tell me all the reasons you suddenly changed your

mind about marriage after nine years of declaring you had no
interest in being a wife.''

She fought for air, feeling faint for the first time in her life.
This was worse than that horrible moment when she'd walked
in on Brady and Gloria. A frenzied fear shafted through her. Her
mind was already leaping ahead to the obvious conclusion to
this terrible scene. *This couldn't be happening.* Not between her
and Trent.

"You must know I can't prove anything," she said in a dry,
agonized whisper. "My aunt and uncle are always pulling surprises out of the hat. I've known about their real estate investments for years."

"For nine years you've been more interested in your career
than you have in marriage. Then one summer you suddenly need
a lot of money for your all-important business plans. The bank
loan falls through, but you're too damn proud and independent
to ask a man for money. But there's no reason you shouldn't
find a way to tap into your future, is there? Some day that land
on the coast was going to be yours, anyway. Why not collect it
now and sell it? Maybe you'd almost forgotten about that real
estate over the years because you didn't want to pay the price
of marriage to get it. But now you really could use the money.
And marriage to me might not be so bad. After all, we're good
in bed together, we have a lot in common and the family ap-
proves of me. And if it doesn't work out, what the hell? That's
what divorce is for, right?''

"Stop it, Trent. Stop it right now. Don't say another word."
Filomena clamped her hands over her ears in a futile effort to
halt the inevitable.

He stepped forward and caught hold of her wrists, yanking
her hands down to her sides. "Damn it, Filomena, what kind of
a fool do you think I am?''

Filomena's temper exploded as it hadn't done since childhood.
This time the result was far more cataclysmic because it contained the full power and fury of a woman, not just that of a
young girl.

"Let go of me!" she snapped, jerking herself free of his hold. Trent was so startled by the abrupt, violent maneuver that he released her. She backed away from him. "You've got a hell of a nerve, you arrogant bastard. You demand trust from everyone else, including me. You insist on everyone respecting your honor and your word. You're so damn proud of your shining integrity. But you're not willing to put a little faith in someone else's honor, are you? Not even that of the woman you claim you love. I'm supposed to trust you implicitly, but apparently you don't have to trust me when the chips are down. Oh, no. I have to give you proof that I'm on the level."

"Filomena…" He started forward but halted when she held up her hands.

"Stop right there, Trent. Don't come any closer. I know what you're going to say."

"You think so?" he shot back, looking furious.

She nodded proudly. "Oh, yes. I know what comes next. You're going to break off the engagement, naturally. A man of your magnificent integrity, a man with your kind of honesty and pride, couldn't possibly marry a scheming little hussy like me. I realize that. Don't worry, I won't make a scene. I've lived through one broken engagement and I'll live through another. But this time around it's going to be different. Do you hear me?"

"Filomena, will you shut up?" he said through gritted teeth. "I've got a few more things to say."

"I don't want to hear them. I already know what you're going to say. But you can damn well wait until after my sister's wedding. Do you understand?" She drew herself up with fierce pride. "In fact, you can wait until after I'm out of this town. I won't go through it again. I will not be humiliated in front of everyone in Gallant Lake tonight the way I was nine years ago. I went through it once and I refuse to let another man do it to me again. I know you're going to break off the engagement. *But you will keep quiet about it until I'm out of this town.*"

"Damn it, Filomena!"

"You owe me that much, Trent," she reminded him tightly.

"Remember? You owe me for the night I changed that dress. Since you're a man of such rock-hard integrity, I'm sure you wouldn't want to welsh on the deal. All I'm asking is for you to hold off breaking the engagement until I can get packed and leave for Seattle."

He reached for her then, but she was gone, slipping through his fingers before he could close them around her and hold her still.

Trent was left clutching a handful of air.

Chapter Nine

TRENT RAVINDER WAS TORN between hot fury and cold, clammy fear. He had never experienced such a volatile combination of emotions before in his life, and they left him feeling almost paralyzed. He stood at the edge of the crowd, his fingers locked in a death grip around a glass of champagne and watched Filomena dance with anyone who asked her.

She was never free for an instant. She flitted from one man to another, her eyes dangerously bright and her smile unnaturally brilliant. Her red hair swung free, a wave of fire down her back as she was whirled about the floor. The golden silk skirts of her dress whipped teasingly around her legs, and her silvery high-heeled sandals flashed in the light.

She was untouchable and unreachable even when one of her partners held her close in a slow dance. She was a glittering elfin queen, a creature of magic, a woman who shimmered and tantalized just beyond a man's reach.

For a little while he'd caught hold of her and kept her safe within the circle of his arms, Trent thought. But now she was trying to break free again. He sensed in the pit of his stomach that she was about to vanish in a puff of smoke.

It infuriated him that she assumed he was going to break off the engagement. The truth was he hadn't gotten that far in his thinking. He'd gone up in flames at the idea that she might have agreed to marry him just to get hold of that valuable land. But his anger hadn't taken him any farther than the immediate need to confront her and punish her in some way for trying to use him.

He was equally enraged to receive that lecture on trust and integrity. Who did she think she was to be lecturing him on the subject? She was the one whose ethics were in question here. She was the one who had apparently decided that after nine years of stating otherwise, marriage now would be financially convenient.

Trent's eyes narrowed as he watched another man swing Filomena out onto the dance floor. He wanted to shake her. He wanted to yell at her. He wanted her to learn that she couldn't use him, even if she did melt like warm honey in his arms. He wanted her desperately, but he wasn't about to let her get away with murder. Shari had warned him once that Filomena might try to run roughshod over him. Well, she was not going to succeed in treating him as a pleasant, useful toy. The elf had to learn the limits of the spells she cast over him.

But even while he told himself he was going to teach her a lesson, Ravinder wondered at the anguish and the sense of betrayal he had seen in her eyes when she had told him he must not break the engagement until she was out of town.

On top of everything else Trent was infuriated by the idea that Filomena thought he would humiliate her at her own sister's wedding. She should know him better than that. She should have trusted him. This business about the land was between the two of them; it didn't involve anyone else.

But the moment he had turned on her, angry and accusing, she'd immediately leaped to the conclusion that he was rejecting her. And she was sure he was going to do it right then and there in front of most of Gallant Lake, Oregon.

Just as Brady Paxton had rejected her so long ago.

The thought chilled Trent. He would never have hurt her like that. He loved her. And when she sorted out her priorities she would find out that she loved him, too. But damned if he was going to let her marry him just because it was financially convenient. He'd waited too long, searched too hard and fallen too much in love with Filomena Cromwell to allow her to do that to him.

Trent got a grip on his raging temper and made himself plan. He would marry Filomena, but it would be on his terms. She could kiss her aunt and uncle's wedding gift goodbye or put it in trust for the children. He didn't care what she did with it as long as she didn't use it to expand Cromwell & Sterling. Filomena was going to have to prove to him that she was marrying for love.

Out on the dance floor Filomena alighted like a butterfly on the arm of yet another man. Trent instinctively took a step forward, part of him wanting to snatch her away from her new partner. He hated to see another man's hands on her, even in the formal embrace of a dance. They had things to settle, he and Filomena. She wasn't going to get away with avoiding him like this.

He halted, frustrated and angry when the dance swept her out of reach. If he went after her now, he would cause a scene that would probably turn into a local legend. Filomena would never forgive him.

Seething with fury, Trent stayed where he was. The wedding reception couldn't last forever. He was spoiling for a fight, but he could wait until after the reception when he would be able to corner Filomena.

But half an hour later when the bride and bridegroom departed, Filomena did, too. By the time Trent realized she had left the country club, it was too late. By the time he got back to the lodge, she had left town.

He stormed into the bedroom she had been using and found it bare except for one silver high-heeled sandal that had apparently gotten pushed under the bed and overlooked in the hasty packing process.

Trent stood in the middle of the empty room holding the silver sandal and decided he didn't feel like Prince Charming after the ball.

THREE DAYS LATER Filomena returned from grocery shopping with an armful of packages bearing Pike Place Market labels.

The phone was ringing in her apartment as she juggled a long loaf of French bread, a sack containing fat, fresh peaches and plump blueberries and a package of freshly made ravioli.

Filomena listened with dread to the imperious ringing of the phone as she halted in front of her apartment door and fished out her keys. She wasn't eager to answer the summons. With a little luck the caller might give up before she got inside the door. Every time the phone had rung since her return from Gallant Lake, she had been certain it would be her mother and father calling to express their shock over the broken engagement.

Filomena didn't want to deal with the inevitable postmortems, though sooner or later she knew she would have to do so. She kept telling herself she just needed a little more time to regain her emotional equilibrium, but the truth was she didn't seem to be making much progress in that direction. Her moods swung wildly from a numb depression to a blazing fury that showed few signs of abating.

During the first twenty-four hours after she'd returned from Gallant Lake, Filomena hadn't answered the phone at all. She had huddled in the safety of her apartment the way a small animal huddles in its burrow while waiting for the shadow of the predator to pass.

The following day she had recovered enough to be angry with herself for her lack of spirit. She was no vulnerable, naive nineteen-year-old hovering on the brink of adulthood. She was a mature, successful, self-confident woman, and she would not let any man do this to her, least of all a hypocritical, arrogant bastard who had only wanted to marry her in the first place because he had decided it was time to find a wife.

She had blotted up the last of her tears and gone for a walk. It wasn't much, but it was a start. At least it had gotten her out of the apartment. When she returned, she found the courage to start answering the phone again. No one who knew anything about the Gallant Lake fiasco had called, however. She wondered at the silence from her parents but decided to be grateful for small favors. She didn't question the silence from Trent Ravinder. She assumed he had no wish to speak to her again.

The bastard.

The phone shrilled its summons as Filomena fumbled with the key and opened the door. It was still ringing by the time she had set down her packages and grabbed for the red instrument.

"Hello?" Filomena's voice was cautious but firm.

"Fil? Is that you? What's wrong? You sound strange."

Filomena relaxed. "Hi, Glenna. How did you know I was home?"

"I called your parents' place in Gallant Lake. Your mother said she thought you were here in Seattle. What's going on? I thought you were going to take another couple of weeks to unwind in bucolic splendor."

"Bucolic splendor gets boring after a while. How are things going?"

"Okay. I was just calling to tell you I've filled out a couple more loan applications, but I'll need your signature before I turn them into the bank. I was going to express-mail them to Gallant Lake, but since you're in town I guess it won't be a problem."

Filomena glanced at her watch. "It's too late to do anything about them today. I'll come by the office tomorrow and sign them. Thanks for doing all the paperwork, Glenna."

"No problem. That first loan form we did together was the hardest. I'm feeling more hopeful now than I was a few days ago when the first bank turned us down. I guess this is what being entrepreneurs is all about. Lots of highs and lows."

"I hate being dependent on banks," Filomena muttered.

"So do I. But since neither one of us has won the lottery recently, there's not much else we can do. How else can we get hold of the kind of money it takes to expand?"

"Good question," Filomena said wryly. She supposed Trent would have had a few nasty comments to make on that subject. "I'll see you bright and early in the morning."

"Right." Glenna hung up the phone.

Filomena did the same but more slowly. She stood gazing

unseeingly at the view of Mount Rainier that was framed in the angled window of her corner apartment and wondered how long it was going to be before she recovered her enthusiasm for Cromwell & Sterling's ambitious plans. Somehow it was hard to feel enthusiastic about anything today.

It wasn't until she turned to head back to the kitchen to unpack her groceries that she realized she wasn't alone in the apartment. Too late she remembered she had left the door open in her haste to get to the phone. A wave of cold terror raced through her as she whirled around to confront the intruder.

Trent Ravinder was lounging in the open doorway. He was wearing the kind of clothes he'd worn in Gallant Lake: a pair of jeans, a plaid shirt and low boots. His arms were folded across his chest, and he was watching her with an unwavering regard. The shock of seeing him held Filomena speechless for several seconds.

"You shouldn't leave the door open behind you when you come home, Filomena," he remarked coolly. "No telling who might decide to follow you inside."

"I can see the problem," she managed through dry lips. "What do you want, Trent?"

He came through the door, shutting it behind him. "That's obvious, isn't it? I came to finish the conversation we started at your sister's wedding reception. You skipped out on me before we could conclude it."

Tension ripped through her, driving out the misery and replacing it with a surge of white-hot anger. "There was nothing left to say. You said it all." She glanced down at her bare hands and then raised her eyes back to his. "We never got around to buying rings, so I don't have one to return."

"You're so sure I want to end the engagement, aren't you?" He shoved his hands into his back pockets and began stalking through her living room.

Filomena resented the way he eyed everything with deep curiosity, as if he had a right to investigate her secrets. He looked huge in the room, dwarfing her chic, trendy furnishings. "Of course I assumed you wanted to end the engagement,'' she snapped. ''Why would you want to marry a conniving, money-hungry woman like me? And why haven't you told my parents that we're through?''

He stopped to examine a whimsically designed one-legged counter stool that looked as if it would collapse if he were to sit on it. ''I haven't told your parents that we're through because we aren't through.''

She drew a deep steadying breath. ''I don't understand, Trent.''

''I know you don't. You're so busy worrying about how to handle the big rejection scene that you haven't given much thought to the fact that I haven't actually rejected you.''

''At least you didn't do it in front of all those people at my sister's wedding reception,'' she shot back bitterly. ''I guess I should thank you for that much.''

''I didn't do it then and I'm not doing it now because as far as I'm concerned we're still engaged.''

''That doesn't make any sense, Trent. Why would you want to marry me? You're convinced I was using you to get my hands on some convenient money.''

He looked at her from across the room, his green eyes brilliant and unrelenting. ''Were you?''

''No, damn it! I was not using you. I had no idea my aunt and uncle were going to give Shari and me such valuable wedding gifts. I agreed to marry you because I wanted to marry you. There was no other reason.''

''Prove it.''

She stared at him uncomprehendingly. ''What?''

''I've given this a lot of thought, Filomena,'' Trent said coolly. ''And I'm prepared to let you prove that your intentions were sincere.''

''How terribly decent of you,'' she replied scathingly. ''Just how am I supposed to do that?''

''Simple. You can either refuse the gift or put the land in trust for our own children. I don't care what you do with it as long

156 The Main Attraction

as you don't use it to finance Cromwell & Sterling's expansion plans.''

She could hardly believe her ears. Fury welled up in her again, as fresh as it had been three days ago. ''How dare you.'' Her voice was a tight whisper. ''How *dare* you. I don't have to prove a thing to you, you big, arrogant bull moose. If anyone should be trying to prove something, it's you. You're the one who's demonstrating about as much trust as a rabbit for a snake. What makes you think I would want to marry a man who had so little faith in me, let alone prove anything to him?''

''Three days ago you said you loved me.''

''That was three days ago. I'm a lot older and wiser now.''

He took a step toward her, his features harsh and rigid in the late afternoon light. ''Is that right? You find it that easy to fall out of love? Then what's the big deal about being afraid I'd announce the end of the engagement before you got a chance to clear out of town? If you didn't love me in the first place, why worry about calling off the marriage?''

Filomena found herself retreating a step as Trent came toward her. Her emotions were in a chaotic jumble. She wanted to yell, and at the same time she wanted to cry. It was too much. He had no right to do this to her. She was the innocent victim here, not him. ''I had no desire to be humiliated by another man in front of the entire population of Gallant Lake. Can't you understand that?''

''I didn't humiliate you. You're the one who was going to humiliate me by combining marriage plans with business plans. If we're going to talk about humiliation, why don't we discuss it from my angle?''

''Your angle! Shall I tell you how it looks from *my* angle? It looks to me as if you had simply made an intellectual, pragmatic, businesslike decision to get married this year because you had decided it was time you had a wife. I came along at the appropriate moment, and the next thing I know I'm engaged to you. How should I interpret that? Certainly not as the great romantic love story of the year. It looks a lot more like a convenient, businesslike arrangement to me.''

"You're the one who announced the engagement, or have you forgotten how you cheerfully informed Paxton that you were going to marry me? It seems to me I was one hell of a gentleman to back you up after you'd gotten yourself out on a very shaky limb.''

"Why you big, overgrown, insensitive Neanderthal! You told me you loved me.''

"So what? You told me you loved me.''

"I *did* love you. I would never have agreed to marry you otherwise,'' she stormed. She was still retreating in the face of his steady advance, but she had reached the end of the line. She came up against the counter that separated the kitchen from the living area and found herself unable to retreat any farther. Tears stung her eyes; rage and pain combined and burned in a white-hot flame. Her hand swept out, and her fingers closed around a napkin holder. "Stay away from me.''

"Why should I stay away from you? We're lovers.'' He moved closer.

"We're not anymore.''

"Are you going to tell me you've fallen out of love with me already? In only three days' time?''

"Don't put words in my mouth!'' She flung the napkin holder at him. He ducked the small missile. Behind him peach-colored paper napkins cascaded over the white carpet as the holder landed harmlessly.

"Tell me you've stopped loving me,'' Trent taunted, closing in on her. "Tell me you don't want me anymore. Tell me you want to end the engagement.''

"I never said any of those things. *You* said them.'' She scrabbled along the countertop and found a small woven basket full of bottles of vitamin tablets. She hurled the basket at his head. Trent impatiently knocked it aside. The bottles clattered on the carpet.

"I never said those things, either,'' Trent reminded her forcefully as he closed the gap between them. "You assumed I was going to say them so you tried to vanish. But it won't work, elf. You're not pulling any of your magic disappearing acts with me."

"Get out of here." Filomena edged along the counter, seeking another weapon. "I mean it, Trent. You have no right to barge in like this after what you said to me in Gallant Lake."

"I've got every right. I'm engaged to you." He caught her wrist just as she was about to throw a pencil holder at him. His fingers tightened on her as he crowded her up against the counter. "And what's more, I think you're still in love with me. You just need to get your priorities straight. I thought I had your full attention after that night in Portland, but there were still a few distractions left, weren't there, Filomena? You still had other things on your mind besides me. But I think deep down you do love me, and you're going to prove it to me and to yourself."

"Your ego has to be seen to be believed! Why should I bother to prove anything to you, you big buffalo?" She struggled against his hold, but it was useless. He wasn't being rough with her, but that didn't change the fact that she couldn't move. He held her with a casual, gentle strength that was overwhelming.

"Forget the rest of it, Filomena," he ordered softly. "Forget the fear of being rejected, forget the expansion plans for Cromwell & Sterling, forget the arguments about trust and just tell me the truth. Do you love me?"

"What do you care?" she wailed.

"I care," he said simply, and bent his head to capture her mouth.

Filomena struggled against the marauding kiss for a full minute, but it was useless. Her only real defense would be to go limp in his arms, but there was no chance of that. Her own emotions were burning too fiercely to allow her to react with any degree of restraint. She was too wound up, too alive with the vibrant, dangerous sensations he aroused in her. She had to react somehow, in a direct, physical way.

She couldn't fight him. The hold he had on her wouldn't permit it. Instead, all the pent-up anger and desperation transmuted into a raging desire that sent shudders through her.

"That's it, sweetheart," he breathed in deep satisfaction. "Show me how you really feel."

"You arrogant, oversized, bullheaded—"

"Hush," he advised, dragging his mouth across hers to ensure she obeyed. "Don't talk. This isn't the time. We'll talk later."

"Mmmmph." She felt his teeth nipping gently on her lower lip as he swung her up into his arms and started down the hall to the bedroom. She clung to him, aware of the fire in her veins and the hard muscled wall of his chest. She tried to think clearly, but she couldn't. Nothing mattered now that he was here and telling her he wanted her.

Trent carried her into the light turquoise and salmon-pink bedroom and dropped her into the center of the quilted bed. Before she could move he came down on top of her, crushing her into the blue-green bedding. He sprawled over her, anchoring her securely beneath him.

"Show me," he muttered against her throat. "Show me that nothing has changed between us when it comes to this."

She cried out softly, whispering his name over and over as he stripped off her shirt and trousers with sure, possessive hands. A moment later she was naked, twisting impatiently in his arms as he lifted himself away from her long enough to shrug out of his own clothes.

"You're so sweet and soft," he said wonderingly as he stroked her curving thigh. "Once I get past the thorns there's nothing but silk and velvet petals. Every time I see you walk across a room I want to touch you. I want to run my hands through your hair and feel you shiver and turn to me. I want to see you smile at me and reach for me as if there were no one and nothing else in the whole world that mattered. Do you understand?"

"I understand." She did because that was the way she felt about him, Filomena realized. She touched him gently, running her fingertips down his chest to the hard planes of his bare hip.

He was fully aroused, heavy and warm with the need that was pulsing through him. When she hesitantly moved her hand to the hard shaft of his manhood, he groaned and murmured hot, exciting words of desire in her ear.

Filomena grew bolder, cupping him gently and stroking him until he caught her hand and uttered a shaky laugh.

"That's enough for now, sweetheart. Any more and I'll explode. I want you so much. I've been going crazy during the past three days."

"Why did you wait to come after me if you…if you still wanted me?" she asked softly.

"I figured we both needed time to cool down." He grazed the tip of her breast with his thumb until the nipple hardened. Then he lowered his head and tasted the small, taut berry.

Filomena moaned and lifted one leg to curve around his thigh. She wrapped her arms around his neck and moved her hips invitingly against him. "Oh, Trent…"

"I know, sweetheart, I know. This part was never in doubt, was it?" He didn't wait for an answer. Instead he began trailing hot, damp kisses over her breasts and down her stomach. When she gasped and dug her nails into him, he groaned thickly. Then he let her feel his teeth on the soft, sensitive skin of her inner thigh. Filomena tightened her hold on him, pleading for him to complete the embrace.

"Now," she begged, "love me now, Trent."

"I will, darling. Open yourself for me. Show me how much you want me. I've missed you so."

She obeyed, parting her legs and reaching out to pull him close. He shifted his weight, centering himself over her. Then she could feel him pushing boldly against her, invading her softness with a gentle aggression that was unbelievably exciting.

"Trent."

"Say it," he muttered hoarsely as he drove himself slowly, surely into her. "Tell me you love me."

"I love you."

"Again."

"*I love you.* Oh, Trent, how could you have doubted it?"

He didn't answer that. He sank himself completely into her, pausing briefly while they both adjusted to the intimate connection. Filomena could feel the rigid sexual tension in him. When her nails curved into his hips, he groaned and began the deep, pulsing rhythm.

"Wrap yourself around me," he said into her mouth. "Put your legs around me and hold me. Show me how much you want me, elf. No tricks, no games and no disappearing acts. Show me you want me." His tongue surged into her mouth as she obeyed.

Filomena gave herself up to the enthralling embrace, lost in the spiral of desire that was consuming them both. She loved him, even if she was still furious with him. *She loved him.*

Something began to tighten within Filomena, threatening to shatter her, and then the culmination of the lovemaking swept over her with the inevitable impact of a freight train. She cried out again, whispering Trent's name over and over as the tension within her was released in a thousand glittering shards. She heard her name in a muffled shout as Trent followed her into the cascading release, and then there was nothing but silence in the room.

A long time later Filomena shifted slightly, pleasantly aware of Trent's weight along the length of her. He still lay in a careless sprawl that covered her completely. When he felt her small movement, he lifted his head from her breast and looked down at her with lazy satisfaction.

"Am I getting heavy?"

She smiled. "You aren't *getting* heavy. You were born heavy."

"I foresee a lifetime of size jokes. You've called me everything from a bull moose to a tank." He dusted a small kiss across the top of her nose. "Luckily for you I don't take offense easily."

Her smile faded. "I wouldn't say that. You were very quick

to take offense at my sister's wedding when you heard about the gift my aunt and uncle are planning to give me.''

Trent shrugged. ''That was different. More importantly, it's no longer an issue, is it?''

She saw the cool challenge in his expression and summoned up all her courage. ''No,'' Filomena agreed, ''it's not an issue. Not any longer.''

''You'll put the land in trust or tell your aunt and uncle you don't want it?''

''I'll make it much simpler than that. I won't marry you in the first place.''

''Filomena!'' Shock and outrage flared in his eyes. His fingers, which had been absently massaging her arms, suddenly sank into her flesh.

Filomena flinched at the pressure, but her eyes never wavered. ''Don't worry, Trent, I'm not going to deny either of us in a…a physical sense.''

''What the hell's that supposed to mean?'' he asked in a voice that was just one degree short of explosion.

She swallowed and forced herself to explain. ''I'm suggesting we have an affair while we find out just how serious you are about love and marriage and the trust that goes with it. You wanted me to prove my love? All right, I'm prepared to do that. My way.''

''What the devil do you think you're doing?'' he demanded tightly.

''You're not the only one who needs some proof,'' she said quietly. ''After that little scene at Shari's wedding, I need some proof, too. I'd like to be certain I'm marrying a man who knows how to give trust as well as demand it. I want a man who believes in me. I'd also like to be sure you're not marrying me just because I came along at the point in your life when you decided it would be nice to have a wife. I'd like to be sure I'm not just a solution to some mid-life crisis you're going through.''

Chapter Ten

TWO WEEKS LATER Trent lounged in a deep chair and nursed a beer while he morosely regarded his ex-fiancée from the opposite side of a small cocktail table. Around them the friendly, trendy tavern filled up with the usual Friday afterwork crowd. Trent, who had just put in nearly four hours on the freeway from Portland, listened to his companion's enthusiastic conversation and decided that nothing had proven more frustrating in his life than an affair with Filomena Cromwell.

He must have been out of his mind to let himself get maneuvered into this ridiculous situation. Looking back, he still wasn't quite certain how it had happened, but he was beginning to suspect that pride was the main problem.

Filomena's feminine pride was proving every bit as stubborn and intransigent as his own male version. He should have guessed it would, he thought moodily. The woman had had experience in using pride as a barrier against humiliation and defeat. She also had plenty of experience using it to keep men at bay.

She was bright and cheerful this evening, high on the results of her meeting with the business consultant Trent had sent her and Glenna to during the week. Cromwell & Sterling was apparently going to pursue a safer and less ambitious development plan thanks to the advice of the consultant.

"He made a lot of sense, Trent. It was obvious he'd really spent some time with our financial statement, and he spent a lot of time with Glenna and me just talking about where we really wanted to go. Then he had us sit down and make out a five-year plan. It forced us to be realistic and to think through some things we hadn't worried too much about until now. He agreed with your diagnosis that Cromwell & Sterling is at a very vulnerable stage of its development. We simply can't afford to take too many risks just now. A major disaster could wipe us out. We need some steady, sustained growth, not a flashy leap that might take us over the edge of a cliff.'' Filomena smiled at him. ''Glenna and I really appreciate your setting up that meeting with Mr. Handel. With his advice under our belts, we'll be in much better shape to approach the banks again in a few months.''

''I'm glad it worked out.'' Trent had to get the brief response in quickly before Filomena launched into another topic. Her generous thanks was unexpected. It helped lift his mood.

''I was very impressed by the way he researched the apparel trade before our meeting. He was far more knowledgeable than I expected him to be, and he seemed to know how active Seattle is in the clothing industry these days. Turns out he had consulted with another local sportswear firm a few months ago.''

''Terrific.''

She missed the sarcasm entirely, racing into a blow-by-blow description of the five-year plan she and Glenna had concocted and a detailed outline of the changes and modifications they had made in it under Handel's advice.

Trent made one or two other short responses during the next twenty minutes but decided Filomena probably wouldn't have noticed if he hadn't said a word. It had been like this for the past two weeks, ever since that afternoon in her bedroom when she'd announced she wouldn't marry a man who didn't trust her.

Now, whenever he was with her, she was bright, breezy and occasionally infuriating. Much of the time she was staying just out of reach again, baiting him, tantalizing him, slipping away from him whenever he tried to pin her down. In some ways their relationship now resembled the one they'd had during the early days in Gallant Lake, except for the fact that they were sleeping together.

Trent couldn't take a great deal of comfort from that because having an affair meant he was only seeing Filomena on the weekends and occasionally during the week. That hadn't been his intention at all. He wanted her as his wife, and she knew it. It seemed to him she was deliberately going out of her way to make him aware of what he was missing. She needn't have bothered. Every night during the week when he got into an empty bed he knew what he was missing.

He still didn't understand exactly what had gone wrong, but he was beginning to realize he should have made more allowance for Filomena's pride and her accompanying desire for revenge. She was making him pay for the demands he had made regarding that damn tract of land her aunt and uncle planned to give her.

Trent had hoped that once Handel had talked Cromwell & Sterling into slowing down their expansion plans, Filomena would realize she didn't need the land. But even if she had realized it, the knowledge hadn't done him any good. Unfortunately Filomena was now defending a principle.

So was he.

"Doesn't sound like you'll need the big bank loan," Trent managed to insert when Filomena finally wound down for a few seconds.

"No, at least not right away. Handel convinced us that our plans to open our own outlets were a few years too early."

Trent took a deep breath. "Then that makes the business of the wedding gift from your aunt and uncle a non-issue."

She gave him a sharp look. "I didn't say Cromwell & Sterling couldn't use an influx of cash. We still have growth plans, Trent, even if they're not quite as ambitious as they were before. We're going to go ahead and start a line for women who are on the other side of the average range."

An angry impatience flared in him. "You're saying you'd still like to get your hands on that land then?"

"What's wrong with being practical?"

"You're driving a wedge between us by being so damned practical."

''You're the one who turned it into a major blockbuster of an issue.''

Trent took a firm grip on his temper. He knew she was baiting him, and it irritated him to know she could get a rise out of him so easily. ''What are your plans for us?''

She looked at him over the rim of her wineglass. ''I have no immediate plans. Why do you ask?''

''Because I want to get married.'' He set the beer mug down onto the table much too loudly. Several heads turned to glance in his direction. Trent ignored them. He leaned forward and pinned Filomena with his eyes. ''What's more, you know it. You're deliberately tormenting me, trying to punish me for having the nerve to ask you not to accept your aunt's and uncle's gift.''

''I have no intention of marrying a man who doesn't trust me. This time around it's money. What if it was something else next time? What if it was another man, Trent? Hmm? What would you do if you suspected I might be seeing another man? How would you make me prove my innocence? Force me to walk across a bed of hot coals? Forget it.''

The thought of Filomena with another man sent a cold, tight sensation through his belly. Trent leaned even closer, pitching his words low across the small space that separated him from Filomena. ''If I thought you were making a fool out of me by seeing another man, hot coals would be the least of your problems. I told you once I'm good at revenge. I'm also good at holding on to what belongs to me.''

She sat back quickly in her chair, watching him carefully. Then she appeared to decide he wasn't quite as dangerous as he sounded. ''Don't threaten me, Trent,'' she said bravely.

''I'm not threatening you. I'm making a statement of fact.''

She waved that aside, obviously eager to take the argument in a new direction. ''I'll have an affair with you as long as you want to have one, but until I'm convinced you really trust me I'm not about to get married. Now what shall we do about dinner? There's a new restaurant on First Avenue near the Pike Place Market. Want to try it?''

"Don't you dare try to switch the conversation like that. We were talking about our future."

"At the moment I'm not willing to look any farther into our future than dinner."

"It's your damn pride that's doing this to us," he informed her.

"I see the problem as being your pride, not mine," she shot back. "If you hadn't gone up in flames the second you heard about that land, we wouldn't be in this mess."

"Can you blame me for thinking you might have decided to marry me because you wanted that land? Everyone assured me you didn't have any interest in marriage and then, in a matter of days, you're suddenly telling an old boyfriend you plan to marry me. You've got to admit that's a fairly quick change of heart from a confirmed lady bachelor."

"I fell in love with you!"

"I believe you."

"You didn't the night of my sister's wedding reception."

"That's not true," Trent said through set teeth. "I believed you loved me then. I just wasn't sure if that was the reason you were marrying me. I wasn't positive you *knew* you loved me."

"Now you're saying you don't think I know my own mind?"

"I wanted to be married for the right reasons, not because the property and I came together as a nice, neat, convenient package."

"So it's *your* pride that's causing the problem," she flung back, "not mine."

There were several seconds of tense silence as they faced each other across the small table. "One of us," Trent finally said with a cold, calm logic that amazed him, "is going to have to back down or we'll drive each other insane. We can't go on like this."

"Fine. I'll agree to marry you as long as you make no stipulations about the land my aunt and uncle plan to give me."

"You don't need that land. You said so yourself."

"I need some proof that you trust me, really trust me. I want to be sure you believe I'm marrying you because I love you and not because you and the land make a financially convenient package. You're very quick to demand trust from others. Your word is your bond and all that. Well, I have a right to make certain you can extend trust. I need to know you're not going to doubt my love when the going gets rough."

"It's not your love I'm doubting. It's your common sense. How can you do this to us, Filomena? You're making both of us miserable. I'm not asking that much of you when I ask you to get rid of the land. Hell, if it's cash you need, I'll give it to you."

Fury leaped in her eyes, and then unexpectedly she suddenly seemed to weary of the battle. The spark went out of her expression, and her slender body wilted slightly. The change in her was unsettling. Trent realized he wasn't accustomed to the sight of Filomena giving up in the midst of a battle. It bothered him.

"You don't even realize what you're really asking. You want me to prove my love. Do you realize how truly arrogant that is, Trent?"

He sucked in his breath and closed his eyes for a grim moment. "Put like that, it does sound arrogant, doesn't it?" When he opened his eyes she was watching him with a disarmingly hopeful expression. The bright challenge had snapped back into her eyes the instant she sensed an opening. The lady made a wily opponent. He smiled sardonically, fully aware of what was going through her head.

"Well?" she prompted gently.

He sipped his beer. "Well, what?"

"Are you going to lower your pride and drop your demands concerning that land?"

"No," he said calmly, his temper back under control. He pulled out his wallet to pay the tab, aware that Filomena was staring at him in shock. She didn't know him very well if she thought she'd won that easily.

"Why not?" she demanded, all the fire returning to her expression. "Why can't you forget that bullheaded pride of yours long enough to let us patch up this quarrel?"

"Because," he said, laying out dollar bills, "the result of this quarrel, as you call it, is too important to me. Let's go try out that new restaurant you suggested." He stood up and reached for her hand to pull her to her feet.

"Trent, wait a minute!"

"Relax, Filomena. When I first met you, I told myself I'd give you time to realize what you really wanted. The whole summer, in fact, if that's what it takes. We've still got a few weeks left. Right now I'm hungry. Let's eat."

"But, Trent, I want to talk about this."

"You didn't a minute ago." He caught her arm and steered her toward the door.

"That was different."

"Has it ever struck you, Filomena, that you have a definite streak of contrariness?" Trent asked pleasantly.

"It probably goes with the red hair," she said in forbidding tones.

"That," he stated roughly, "is not an excuse."

When the weekend drew to a close, Trent told himself he had reason to be proud. The running battle with Filomena was far from over, but at least he had managed to ensure that it was fought more or less on his terms.

She tried again and again to draw him out into a full-blown argument where she could hurl the issue of his lack of trust in his face. Trent avoided the battles largely by changing the subject. He held his own impatience and temper severely in check, hoping that Filomena would eventually run out of fuel for the fight.

She danced around him all weekend, taunting him, baiting him, challenging him, searching for a way to make him retract his demand. Trent pretended to be unaware of the various tactics, contenting himself with taking passionate revenge in bed. It was the one place she didn't try to fight him. When it came to the passionate side of their relationship, she surrendered with so much excitement and fire and sensual generosity that Trent forgot all about winning and losing. He took everything she offered, glorying in it, and gave back all he had.

Sunday afternoon, when he prepared to leave for Portland, however, it was evident that Filomena wasn't about to surrender anything outside the bedroom. Her elfin face was as determined as ever, her eyes as bright and challenging. She kissed him farewell, drawing out the embrace until she sensed his body tightening with arousal. Then she drew back slightly and looked up at him.

"Trent, please think about what you're doing. You were right when you said we can't go on like this. We have to get this matter settled, or it will tear us apart."

Aware of the ache in his lower body, Trent sighed and cradled Filomena's face in his hands. When she smiled tremulously up at him, her eyes lighting with expectant hope, he shook his head slowly. "If you want to end it, you'll have to give me your word you'll get rid of the land." When she started to protest, he silenced her with a quick, possessive kiss. "Do it, Filomena," he ordered softly.

"Why should I?" she wailed.

"Because I'm going to win this battle. I always win when the issue is important to me."

"I won't marry a man who demands that I prove my love," she said flatly. "I won't marry a man who doesn't trust me."

"And I won't marry a woman who isn't willing to prove that she wants me more than a hunk of real estate." He leaned down and kissed her again and then he walked out the door.

It wasn't easy.

Three evenings later Trent sat alone in his darkened living room and stared out at the lights of Portland. He sipped morosely at a beer and wondered if he was pushing Filomena too hard.

She was inclined to be reckless when she was backed into a corner. She was also inclined to defend a position to the last gasp. She hadn't gotten where she was in the business world by being overly cautious or timid.

When it came to men she had little reason to be trusting, even less reason to want to prove herself. The problem wasn't just her bad experience with Brady Paxton. According to Shari, it also included the fact that she had apparently run into a few fortune hunters since Cromwell & Sterling had become successful. Given her background, she probably thought she had every right to demand that a man prove himself first.

On top of everything else, she had a certain, definite taste for revenge. He'd seen ample evidence of that during those hectic weeks of trying to keep an eye on her in Gallant Lake. If he pushed her far enough, there was no telling what she might do.

Trent thought about that raw fact while he downed the remainder of the beer.

THURSDAY MORNING Filomena sat with Glenna in an espresso café near the waterfront and tried valiantly to keep her mind on business. She and Glenna were supposed to be discussing designs for a new collection of sportswear based on a fabulous print fabric Filomena had located on her last trip to Italy. Filomena had bought up a huge quantity of it and had shipped it back to the States, even though at the time she hadn't been certain what she and Glenna would do with it. Glenna had loved the material as soon as she had seen it, however, and had immediately set about creating designs that would take full advantage of the dramatic pattern.

"I think we should do skirts and blouses in the print and use emerald green and coral silk for the contrast pieces," Glenna was saying enthusiastically as she handed Filomena some sketches. "What do you think of these?"

Filomena studied the dashing renditions of a trumpet skirt and a dropped shoulder blouse. "They look wonderful, Glenna. What do you think of a vest that could coordinate with the pants and the skirts? Something dressy maybe, with a little metallic dazzle in it?"

"Umm, good idea. We're taking a chance on this particular shade of coral and green, you know. They're exotics. They could fall flat next season if everyone's going back to beiges and mauve.''

"We've made our reputation on exotics for petite women. They're just beginning to feel adventurous in our clothes. I wouldn't want to pull back now.''

Glenna, who was barely five foot two, grinned. "I agree. Okay, we'll go for it.'' She picked up her cup of caffè latte and took a sip. The amusement faded from her eyes. "Speaking of exotics...''

Filomena raised her eyebrows. "What about them?''

"I was wondering how things are going with that rather large specimen you brought back from Gallant Lake.''

"Don't ask.''

"Why not?'' Glenna's gaze was sympathetic. "I had the impression that this time around it might be for real.''

"You're an incurable romantic, Glenna.''

"And you're not? Come on, that's the whole problem, isn't it? Are you still holding out for that chunk of land your aunt and uncle want to give you as a wedding present?''

"Yes.''

"You don't care about that land, Fil, and you know it.''

"That's not the point,'' Filomena said patiently. "I have to know Trent trusts me. When he went through the roof after he heard about my aunt's and uncle's plans, I knew we had some major, unresolved difficulties in our relationship.''

"You mean he put down his foot and you drew a line and dared him to step over it.'' Glenna shook her head. "I don't know, Fil. He's got awfully big feet.''

Filomena raised her eyes to the ceiling in an expression of frustrated disgust. "You're not the only one to remark on that fact,'' she muttered, remembering her sister's comments on the subject. "Why does everyone assume that I'm the one who's going to have to back down? Why does everyone automatically leap to the conclusion that Trent will always get his way?''

"Maybe it has something to do with the fact that he could

pick you up with one hand and carry you off over his shoulder if you give him too much trouble.''

''As I've pointed out to Trent in the past, might does not make right.''

''I have the feeling he's not going to surrender, Fil.''

''It's not a question of surrender! It's a question of learning to trust. He's so damn autocratic and arrogant about his own integrity, Glenna, you wouldn't believe it. He'd probably fight duels with anyone who doubted his honor if it were still possible to do so. Trent is absolutely rigid when it comes to his own code. Everything is black and white. He doesn't allow any shades of gray.''

''He sees that land your aunt and uncle want to give you as a gray area, huh?''

Filomena nodded. ''And instead of giving me the benefit of the doubt, he wants me to get rid of it entirely. Imagine him having the nerve to ask me to make that kind of sacrifice!''

Glenna gave her a thoughtful glance. ''All right, I can understand you're not exactly thrilled with the idea of having to prove yourself to him, but there's something more involved, isn't there? You love the man. I can tell. You've never been like this with anyone else in all the time I've known you. Why won't you give in on this issue?''

Filomena drew a weary breath. ''You want the truth? I'm afraid to give in, Glenna. I'm afraid to marry a man who demands proof of my integrity. We're talking about a piece of real estate this time. What will it be next time? How many times will I have to prove myself to him? And what happens the first time I can't produce proof?''

Glenna's eyes widened with understanding. ''I think I'm beginning to see the full scope of the problem. What if...what if he thought you were cheating on him with another man or something?''

Filomena nodded bleakly. ''Exactly. Sooner or later we'd come up against a situation in which Trent would simply have to take my word. He'd have to trust me completely. I'm not sure he can do that. He's been so busy establishing his own credentials in that department that he's never had to learn to trust anyone else.''

"What a mess, Fil."

Filomena stared down into the depths of her espresso. "I know."

"But you can't go on like this indefinitely. Sooner or later something or someone's going to have to give."

"I know," Filomena said again.

"How long can you go on fighting to make him take you on trust?"

"I don't know."

WHEN THE PHONE RANG in Trent's apartment Thursday evening, he leaped for it. For some idiotic reason he was sure it had to be Filomena. It wasn't. It was Gloria Paxton, and the woman was raging through her tears.

"He's gone to her," Gloria cried hysterically. "He left this afternoon. I didn't believe it at first, but now I do. That little tramp. She's finally won. After all these years, she's finally won. She was such a mousy little thing when she was a kid. A total zero in high school. A dumpy girl with no looks, no style, no boyfriends. She used to look so out of it most of the time. Never had a date. Oh, hell, how could she turn into such a...such a homewrecker?" She broke off to sob brokenly.

Trent's hand became a vise on the phone. "Calm down, Gloria, and tell me exactly what's going on."

"I told you, Brady's left me. He's gone to her. She's lured him to Seattle so she can have her revenge on us. She doesn't even want him. She just wants to prove she can take him away from me the way I once took him away from her."

"What makes you think your husband has gone to Seattle?" Trent demanded sharply.

"He left a note," Gloria said in a strangled voice. "He said he'd made a mistake all those years ago when he married me instead of her. Said he felt stifled here in Gallant Lake. Said he wanted to change his life. The note said he was going to her because they still loved each other and...and...oh!'' Gloria's voice trailed off into another spasm of hysterical weeping.

"Gloria, get hold of yourself," Trent advised in a voice that had been known to make seasoned corporate executives back off. Gloria was unfazed by the command.

"She'll do it, you know," she told Trent in broken tones. "You saw the way she was running around Gallant Lake half naked most of the time, driving that snazzy little car and showing off to the whole town. She wants revenge. She'll seduce him just to show us all that she can and then she'll toss him out on his ear. She doesn't really want him. She can do a lot better than him, and she knows it. But she's never forgiven me or Brady for what happened all those years ago, and she's finally going to get even.''

Trent glanced impatiently at his watch. "When did your husband leave?''

"I don't know. I'm not sure. Sometime this afternoon. I got home from shopping and I found this stupid note.'' There was a ripping sound on the other end of the line as Gloria apparently tore the note into shreds. "I called you because I thought you ought to know what that little hussy is up to. She doesn't care who she hurts, does she? Or maybe she thinks she can seduce Brady and have her revenge and you'll never find out about it. At least I spiked her guns in that direction, didn't I?''

"My fiancée is not going to seduce your husband," Trent said in a savagely controlled voice. "You can stop worrying about that at any rate.''

His absolute certainty on the subject seemed to get through to Gloria. "How can you be so blasted sure of that? She wants revenge, I tell you.''

"I am sure of it because I'm sure of Filomena," Trent said coldly. "She's my fiancée, the woman I'm going to marry.''

"So what? Brady was engaged to her when he fell in love with me and started sleeping with me! Being engaged doesn't mean anything. Neither does being married, for that matter.''

Trent was getting more impatient by the minute. "You don't

understand, Gloria, and I haven't got time to explain it. Just take my word for it. Your husband won't be spending tonight or any other night with Filomena.''

Gloria was suddenly silent on the other end of the line. Trent's absolute conviction had made an impact. ''Are...are you sure of that?''

''Positive. You have my word on the subject. Goodbye, Gloria.'' He hung up the phone before she could respond. Then he picked up the receiver again and dialed Filomena's number.

When there was no answer, he dialed the airport and got lucky. There was a jet leaving for Seattle in forty minutes.

FILOMENA WAS YAWNING as she got out of the elevator and walked down the hall to her apartment. The regular monthly dinner with Glenna and a few other women business friends had been fun, but the time had flown and she was pleasantly tired.

She wondered if Trent had tried to call during the evening. She'd forgotten to tell him she was going to be out. Serve him right if he'd called and gotten no answer. She didn't want him thinking she was sitting alone every evening pining for him.

She braced herself with that thought and fished the front door key out of her small sling bag. As she did so, a large male form detached itself from a doorway and came forward.

'''Bout time you got home. You must have one hell of a social life these days, huh, Fil? Not like the old days. Does Ravinder know where you go and who you see in the evenings?''

''Brady! What in the world are you doing here?'' Filomena was so startled that she dropped the key on the carpet. Before she could grab it, Brady had it in his hand. He shoved it into the front door lock, his movements slightly uncoordinated and jerky. He had been drinking, she realized.

''I left Gloria,'' he announced grandly as he pushed open her front door and walked inside.

''What do you think you're doing? I didn't invite you in here, Brady. This is my apartment, and I want you out. Now.'' She scurried after him, leaving the door open behind her.

Brady threw himself into a chair and regarded her through

narrowed eyes. There was a dangerous glitter in that gaze. Filomena was chillingly aware of just how much larger he was than she. It was strange, she thought. She'd never thought of Brady as potentially dangerous. But tonight she was no longer so sure. Any man who towered over her as Brady did was a potential hazard.

"Have a good time tonight, Fil? You sure run around a lot these days, don't you?"

"Have you been drinking?" she asked quietly.

"Had a few at a lounge down the street while I waited for you to get home," he said with a careless shrug.

"Brady…"

"Been a long time, Fil. I made the biggest mistake of my life when I married Gloria instead of you. I've finally realized that. But mistakes can be fixed. I'm going to fix this one. I'm ditching it all, Fil. Gloria, the kids, the business. Everything. Going to start over. Going to find myself. With you."

"Not a chance," Filomena said coolly. "I've already told you I'm not interested, Brady."

"Because you wangled an engagement with that honcho from Asgard Development? Forget him, Fil. That was just a business deal, and I know it. Heard all about that land you were going to get from your aunt and uncle when you married. But deep down inside you know it's me you love. You've never gotten over me. If we get married, you can still get the land. Knowing your uncle, it'll be a choice piece of property. I'm anxious to see it."

"You've definitely had a few too many," Filomena said, reaching for the phone. "I'm going to call you a cab."

"No," Brady said decisively, "I'm not leaving. I came here to be with you, Fil. I'm going to find out how much you've learned about men during the past few years."

Chapter Eleven

"I WANT A SAMPLE of what you're giving Ravinder these days, Fil," Brady continued in slurred tones. "And I want a chance to show you what you've been missing with me."

"I haven't missed one single thing with you, Brady, and we both know it," Filomena said quietly. Her hand was on the phone.

"You want me. I know you do. *You still want me.* I left Gloria for you. You have to want me." He pounded his fist on the arm of the chair in which he was sitting, and something crumpled in his expression. The bold, aggressive male threat was gone. It was replaced by a frustrated, self-pitying anger.

"Gloria wants you, Brady. She wanted you when she was nineteen, and she wants you now. If you had any sense, you'd go back to her."

"I don't want her." The words were a childish plea.

"You wanted her at one time, Brady. You wanted her very much. Enough to sleep with her when you were engaged to me."

"She seduced me!"

Filomena shook her head. "Don't give me that. You were older than she was. You'd been through college. She was just a year out of high school, the same as me. You have to take the responsibility for any seducing that went on between the two of you. But you were never very good at taking responsibility, were you, Brady? You always wanted to take the easy path. Well, you took it and now you're stuck with it."

"It was you I loved, Fil. All along it was you I wanted."

"Love," she retorted scathingly. "You don't know the meaning of the word. You'd be better off not using it, especially around me. I know you too well, Brady."

"I've left her, Fil, don't you understand? I've left Gloria."

"That's your problem, not mine." Filomena began dialing a number she kept posted near the phone. She made her voice as forceful as possible, hoping it would penetrate his alcoholic haze. "I'm going to call you a cab. When it gets here, you're going to get into it and get out of my sight."

"No!"

"Then I will call the police."

He came up out of the chair just as she finished dialing the cab company's number. Instinctively Filomena jumped back, but her chair was in the way. Her ankle caught, and she fell to her knees just as Brady tried to take her into his arms. An instant later Brady collapsed on top of her. His weight crushed her painfully into the carpet.

Not for the first time in her life, Filomena cursed the fact that a large percentage of the population, especially the male population, was bigger than she was. She shoved with all her strength, but Brady was a deadweight on top of her.

"Get off of me," she snapped, punching him in the ribs.

"Ouch! Fil, please, just let me show you how good it could be between us now. I've got to kiss you—"

"Try it and I'll call the cops instead of a cab." Filomena stopped attempting to push him off and started trying to wriggle out from under him. It wasn't all that hard. Brady was big and heavy, but he wasn't particularly agile. Filomena used her fists again, and when he groaned and shifted his weight, she succeeded in rolling free of him.

"Damn it, Fil." Brady flopped over on his back, his arm covering his eyes in weary despair. "Why won't you give me a chance?"

Panting from exertion, Filomena ignored him and struggled to her knees. She straightened her clothes as she grabbed for the telephone. A steady hum on the line told her that the cab company dispatcher had hung up. She was about to dial again when she realized she and Brady were no longer alone in the room.

Startled, she glanced toward the door. Trent stood there, one hand braced against the jamb as he calmly took in everything from her disheveled clothing to Brady's prone figure on the carpet. Filomena froze. It couldn't get much worse than this, she thought, feeling entirely helpless. She just knelt there, staring at him and wondering why she had been such a fool to do battle with him over that piece of real estate. Perhaps if she'd given in on that, he wouldn't jump to conclusions now.

But she hadn't given in, and he was bound to think the worst now.

"Hello, Trent," she said with an aggressiveness she was far from feeling. "I'll bet you're wondering what's happening here, aren't you?"

"That's my Filomena," he responded mildly as he came through the door and strolled toward Brady. "Sassy and smart-mouthed right to the last. I'll give you credit for having the guts to defend an indefensible position. But, then, you never were short of guts." He halted beside Brady, gazing down at him as if he were examining a bug. "For everyone's information, I am not wondering what's happening here. I know exactly what's going on. I had a call from Gloria. She was kind enough to fill me in."

"That bitch." Brady took his arm away from his eyes and sat up cautiously. He glowered at Trent. "She had no right to call you."

"Paxton," Trent said as he reached down and yanked Brady to his feet by the lapels of his jacket, "you are turning into a damn nuisance."

Brady panicked and took what he saw as the logical way out. He nodded toward Filomena. "It was her fault. Blame your fancy fiancée. She lured me here. She wanted to seduce me."

Filomena stayed very still, holding her breath.

Trent slowly released his grip on Brady's lapels. "Is that

right?'' he asked, sounding amused. ''Now why would she want to do that?''

Brady stepped back, jerking his shirt into place. He glared at Trent. ''Why do you think? She wants me back. She used to be in love with me, and now she wants me back.''

Trent gave him a slow, dangerous grin. ''Paxton, you ass, if you believe that, you are a lot less intelligent than I originally thought, and believe me, I hadn't given you much credit to begin with.''

''It's true!''

Trent shook his head. ''I know the woman can be hard on a man's ego, but in this case I'm afraid you've got it coming. She doesn't want anything to do with you, Paxton.''

It was too much for Brady. ''How can you be so damn sure of that?'' he roared, totally frustrated.

''Because she's engaged to me,'' Trent said quietly. ''And Filomena would never fool around with another man behind her fiancé's back, not even for the sake of a little revenge.'' Trent turned his head and glanced at Filomena. ''Who are you trying to call?''

''A cab,'' she managed to say. ''For Brady.''

''Well? What are you waiting for? Dial.''

Filomena raised her brows at the command, but she decided this was not the time to argue about his tendency to give orders. She redialed the taxi company's number.

''Come with me, Paxton,'' Trent said as Filomena spoke to the dispatcher. ''I'll make sure you get downstairs without having any unplanned falls down an elevator shaft.''

Brady eyed Trent with open alarm. ''Now wait just a minute,'' he began forcefully.

''It's all right, Brady,'' Filomena said, glancing up from the phone. ''Trent will make sure you don't have any *planned* falls down elevator shafts, either, won't you, Trent?''

''You can trust me,'' Trent said, still smiling lethally. He gave Brady a slight shove toward the door. There didn't seem to be much weight behind the push, but the momentum carried Brady over the threshold and out into the hall. He ended up against the far wall and grabbed wildly for the duffel bag Trent tossed at him.

A moment later the door closed behind both men. Filomena hung up the phone and sat staring at her empty living room. Something was stunningly odd about the whole situation.

Trent should have been chewing nails and breathing fire. His rage should have been sufficient to shake the entire building. Instead, he seemed only mildly irritated by the whole, embarrassing scene. Furthermore, he had made it clear to Brady he knew Filomena would never cheat on him with another man.

The more she thought about it, the more she was forced to one simple conclusion. Trent might have a hangup about that stupid chunk of land, but he believed in her when it came to the important things.

Filomena heaved a deep sigh of relief and got to her feet.

When Trent opened the door a few minutes later and sauntered into the room, Filomena was waiting for him with a large, foaming mug of beer.

He dropped his jacket onto the nearest chair and took the mug from her hand. "Any other admirers hiding in the closets or under the bed?"

"No, Trent."

"Good. I think I've had about enough of Paxton, by the way. If I find him hanging around again I really might toss him down an elevator shaft."

"I'm sorry you found him here this time," Filomena said bluntly. "I didn't invite him."

He gave her a steady look. "I figured that out for myself."

"I'm...I'm glad," she said, feeling suddenly lighthearted and breathless. Her eyes were damp. "Thank you for trusting me, Trent. Not every man would have been as understanding in this sort of situation. I know how awful it must have looked."

"Do you?"

"Well, yes, I can imagine, and I realize what you must have thought when you got that call from Gloria. When I saw you standing there in the doorway, I was terrified you'd think the worst.''

"I'll admit I am getting a little tired of pulling Brady Paxton off you."

Filomena winced. "But you honestly don't believe I invited him here?''

"I know you didn't."

His certainty was disturbing. "How can you be so sure?"

"Because you wouldn't do that to me," he said simply. "You're a little wild, too independent, inclined to be reckless and you can be a severe pain in the neck at times, but you fight fair, elf.''

"Thanks. I think."

"You're welcome."

"Uh, Trent, if you didn't think I had lured Brady up here for revenge, why did you come dashing to the rescue?''

"I didn't think you'd invited Paxton, but I also didn't doubt for a minute that Gloria was right when she decided he was probably headed your way. I know it sounds old-fashioned and chauvinistic, but it occurred to me you might need rescuing. You're very small and very delicate, elf. Paxton outweighs you by about seventy or eighty pounds, and he's been stewing for weeks, wondering what he missed when he threw you back into the pond.''

"You were worried about me?''

"I was irritated as hell with you. If you hadn't been so stubborn during the past few weeks, the situation would never have arisen in the first place. You would have been safely married to me by now."

Filomena smiled. "You really do want to marry me? After all the trouble I've caused you?''

"I don't know any other way to get some peace of mind." He raised the mug to his mouth. "How about that?" he said with pleased satisfaction after the first long swallow. "It's the real thing, not a light brew.''

"I aim to please," she murmured, remembering how he had once said the same thing to her.

"The question is, how good is your aim?"

Filomena smiled tremulously. "I don't know. You tell me. And for the record, you can forget about the battle over the land my aunt and uncle want to give me. I never cared about it, anyway. It was just a principle I thought I had to defend, but I don't think I do any longer. I quit, you win. I surrender."

He regarded her for a long, thoughtful moment. "Too late. I gave up first."

Her eyes widened. "You *what*?"

"You heard me. Keep the land or sell it or grow Christmas trees on it. I don't care what you do with it."

"You don't?" she asked in disbelief.

"Nope."

"But, Trent, you can't do this to me. This is my big scene," she protested, caught between laughter and tears of relief. *He didn't care about the land.*

"I know," he said dryly. "And you're so good at causing scenes, aren't you? But this time you've been upstaged." He took another long swallow of beer and set the mug down on a nearby table. "About time somebody did it."

She hesitated another split second and then she hurled herself into his arms. "Trent, do you mean that? You really don't care about the land?"

He wrapped his arms around her and buried his face in her hair. "I knew when Gloria phoned me with her big news about Brady heading north to Seattle that I didn't care about the land. It was just the principle of the thing for me, too. Deep down I didn't care about anything except getting you tied to me legally, emotionally and permanently. I trust you, Filomena, my sweet elf. You're probably going to drive me crazy during the next sixty years, but I trust you."

"Oh, Trent, I love you so much. I was so afraid of what you'd think when you walked in here a few minutes ago and found

Brady. I could have killed him for turning up here the way he did.''

"The thought crossed my mind a couple of times on the way down to the lobby,'' Trent admitted.

"The thought of me killing Brady?''

"No, the thought of me killing him. But ultimately I decided he just wasn't worth it.''

"That's exactly the conclusion I came to shortly after I found him and Gloria in bed together,'' Filomena admitted.

"Isn't it great to start marriage off with someone with whom you have so much in common?'' Trent lifted her chin and kissed her with a thoroughness that left no room for doubt.

TWO WEEKS LATER Trent settled himself against the pillows of the wide hotel bed and glanced impatiently at the watch he had unstrapped earlier and left on the bedside table. Ten more minutes had gone by since the last time he had checked the time. Filomena still hadn't come out of the bathroom. She'd been in there over forty-five minutes.

Trent closed his eyes and willed himself to be patient. This was Filomena's wedding night. She had a right to some privacy and all the time she needed to get ready. Just because he was already experiencing a dull, sweet ache in his loins didn't mean he had the right to forge his way into the bathroom and drag his bride into bed. She would arrive in her own time.

Elf time.

Trent's fingers drummed a small tattoo on the bed beside him. He opened his eyes and took another look at the face of his watch. This was getting ridiculous. He made another bid for patience, occupying himself with memories of Filomena walking serenely down the aisle toward him a few hours earlier. It was a charming memory, one he would treasure for the rest of his life.

The small wedding had taken place that morning. Filomena's beaming family and the equally pleased staff of the lodge had been in attendance. Trent grinned briefly, recalling the relief he had detected behind the warm, loving smiles on everyone's face.

Getting Filomena safely married had taken a burden of worry off a great many shoulders. Amery and Meg Cromwell as well as Aunt Agnes and Uncle George, Shari and Jim had all come up to Trent privately during the small reception, not only to wish him good luck, but to commend him on his bravery.

"Just remember, this sale is final," Amery had said cheerfully. "No refunds and no returns."

Trent knew that more than one person in the small chapel had held his or her breath waiting to see what Filomena would wear to her own wedding. She had kept it a secret from everyone except Shari. Meg Cromwell's sigh of relief had almost been audible when her eldest daughter had come down the aisle dressed in a demure, ballet style, calf-length dress that had emphasized her slenderness and made her look like a fairy queen dressed for a secret moonlight dance. Her red hair had cascaded down her back beneath a wispy veil that had been draped from a stylish garden party hat. Trent had seen the loving laughter in her eyes as she had peeked out at him from under the brim of the hat and had thanked his lucky stars she hadn't chosen to wear scarlet red or slinky black. Elves were unpredictable.

The sound of running water in the bathroom jerked Trent out of his reminiscences. He checked his watch again. The water was shut off, but the bathroom door didn't open. Silence descended once more.

Trent waited another few minutes and then reached the end of his patience. Wedding night privacy for the bride was one thing; the extended and unexplained absence of his elf from her bridal bed required a few answers, however. He strode across the room, naked except for his briefs, and rapped on the bathroom door.

"Filomena? Honey, what's going on in there?"

"Nothing."

Trent's eyes narrowed. "Are you sure?"

"Of course I'm sure."

"Are you okay?"

"I'm fine."

Trent paused. "Are you intending to spend your entire wedding night in the bathroom?"

"No."

Another pause. When there was no further explanation, Trent asked bluntly, "What's taking so long?"

"I'm getting dressed."

"Filomena, this is your wedding night. You're supposed to be getting undressed," Trent finally said in exasperation.

"Brides get to wear peignoirs. I might never again have an excuse to wear one, so I want to get the most out of this experience."

He heard the lilting amusement in her voice and decided enough was enough. If she was going to tease him, she could do it in bed. Trent put his hand on the doorknob and twisted. She hadn't locked it.

The door popped open easily enough and revealed Filomena standing in the center of the bathroom in front of a full-length mirror. Her face was hidden beneath a cloud of soft apricot-colored silk that she was in the process of removing. On the floor around her feet were several other crumpled piles of gossamer, silky fabric. Discarded nightgowns, ranging in color from iridescent emerald green to shimmering silver, littered the bathroom like so much expensive wrapping paper.

"Trent!" At the sound of the bathroom door being opened, Filomena struggled frantically to get the apricot confection back down over her head. "What are you doing in here? I'm getting ready for bed."

Trent folded his arms and leaned against the wall. He watched the dusky rose of two pert nipples disappear beneath the apricot gown. Then the delicate fabric slipped down over her hips, hiding the most intimate part of her.

"You're not getting ready for bed," Trent decided. "You're putting on a fashion show."

Filomena smiled benignly. "I couldn't decide which one to bring with me, so I packed a whole bunch. I've been trying them all on to see which one looks best."

Trent came away from the door, reaching for his bride before she could sidestep him.

"You surprise me, elf," he said gently. "Somehow I hadn't expected to see you succumb to an attack of wedding night nerves."

"I am not nervous," she declared haughtily as his hands settled on her shoulders. She looked up at him, unaware of the hint of anxiety that was in her eyes.

Trent smiled. "Are you sure?"

"I'm sure."

"What if I told you that I'm a little nervous?"

Her eyes widened. "Are you?" She reached up to touch the side of his face, her fingers light and comforting on his skin.

"No, but I thought it might make you feel better if you thought you weren't the only one with butterflies." He laughed down at her and swooped.

"Trent, put me down," Filomena squeaked, her voice filled with laughter as he lifted her off her feet and tucked her under his arm. "I've got three other gowns to try on."

"If you think I'm going to spend my wedding night watching a fashion show, you've got a lot to learn about me, honey." He stood her on her feet beside the bed and grasped the apricot gown. With one long, firm movement he jerked it off over her head and dropped it on the rug. "That's better." His hands went to her bare waist and he pulled her against his chest. "Much better."

Filomena sighed and wrapped her arms around his neck. "I suppose I can try the gowns on some other time."

"Uh-huh." He ignored that, his mind on the clamoring desire skyrocketing through him. He felt her small breasts pillowed against him and knew an immediate, flaring response. "I can't believe I've finally got you, elf. Where have you been all my life?"

"Waiting for you," she said simply. She put her mouth against his chest, planting tiny, warm kisses on his hot skin.

Trent groaned and pushed his leg between her thighs, opening her to his touch. He could feel the rising heat in her and an exciting, feminine dampness that made the blood pound in his veins.

Filomena whispered his name, her lips moving on his skin as she clung to him. She opened her eyes and looked up at him with love and longing and an infinite promise as he lifted her and settled her onto the turned-back bed.

For a long moment their gazes locked in silent understanding and commitment.

"I love you," Trent finally said, his voice husky with need.

"I love you." She touched his shoulder with delicate nails and stirred beneath his weight. Her leg moved to twine around his muscled thigh.

"I know, my love. I know." Trent lowered his head and took her lips, secure at last in the magic that had invaded his world.

EDGE OF ETERNITY

Jasmine Cresswell

Prologue

"Give me the gun, Ned." David Powell risked another step forward and held out his hand. He hoped like hell that Ned wouldn't notice the tremble.

"Get away! I'll shoot if you come any closer!" Ned cowered behind the desk, his expression wild, his body weaving, but his grip on the .9 mm pistol obstinately firm. David was seized by a profound sense of irony. Up here, on the thirtieth floor of a Wall Street office building, drama was supposed to be about stock trading and bond issues, not about life and death.

"Killing yourself won't solve anything." David tried to sound calm, despite the fact that he felt about as competent as a novice diver confronting a great white shark. "Ned, you don't really want to do this."

"Yes, I do! I'll be better off dead. What choice have you left me?"

"As long as we're alive, Ned, we always have choices. Suicide is the only decision that leaves us with nothing." David winced at the patronizing tone of his voice. The conversation had taken on a dreadful banality, although his emotions were anything but banal. He burned inside, his stomach churning with an acid brew of guilt and fear. He'd never expected his pursuit of Ned Nichols to end up like this. Truth was, he'd never thought beyond the need to find out who was stealing the firm's money.

Great planning, he berated himself. *For this one, you win the big prize.*

Ned laughed bitterly. "You're amazing, David. Totally, amazingly stupid for a man who's supposed to be smart. Don't you realize how wonderful *nothing* sounds to me right now?"

"But only for right now—"

"Killing myself will solve everything," Ned said. "The missing money. The police. My lousy marriage. The whole damn mess."

"Think about your marriage for a moment. Think about your wife." David seized on the opening Ned had given him. "What'll happen to her when you're gone? How do you think she'll feel if you do this?"

"How will she feel?" Ned's mouth twisted into a travesty of a smile. "Hey, don't worry about my sweet lovely wife. I finally figured Amy out. And you know what? She'll do a great job of playing the grieving widow. At least until the funeral's over, and by then you can be sure she'll have some new sucker lined up to *comfort* her."

"I bet she loves you more than you realize." David heard footsteps in the corridor outside the office and wasn't sure whether to curse at the intrusion or pray for an interruption. God only knew what Ned might do if he felt cornered. David spoke quickly, hoping to cover the sounds of approaching people.

"Look, Ned, you know as well as I do that problems aren't solved by running away. Your friends and family just get left to clean up the mess. You're an intelligent person—"

Ned stroked his gun. "Yeah, smart enough to set up the scam, but not quite smart enough to get away with it. My wife won't like that."

"You almost made it," David said, then stopped abruptly. This was ridiculous. Not only had Ned Nichols done his best to steal upward of two million dollars, he'd expended considerable effort to make it look as if David was responsible for the thefts. There was something surreal about hearing himself try to reassure Ned that the scheme he'd devised for ripping off the firm's clients had been an effective one, and that he'd almost succeeded in shunting the blame onto his closest colleague.

David drew a deep breath. "Ned, you're only thirty-five. You have half a lifetime still ahead of you. Don't throw it away."

Ned shrugged, his gaze flat. "Half a lifetime isn't long enough to right this screwup."

The footsteps slowed outside the door, and sweat pooled at the small of David's back. Then the footsteps picked up again, and the person walked on past Ned's office. A reprieve, or a lost opportunity? It was impossible to tell.

David wiped his hands against the sides of his trousers and took another couple of steps toward the desk. Toward Ned and the wavering gun. This was not in the least like a Hollywood movie, he decided. Not only were his hands shaking and his stomach lurching, moisture seemed to be cascading from every pore in his body. Clearly he wasn't cut out to be a hero. In the movies, the hero never seemed to sweat, much less tremble. Bruce Willis saved Washington airport from terrorists without mussing his sweater. Harrison Ford outwitted entire galaxies without needing to change his shirt, so surely David could disarm one slightly overweight stockbroker waving a small handgun. If only he could come at Ned from an angle, he'd have a chance to grab the gun, but the desk was superexecutive size and presented a formidable barrier. Still, he had to try. David sneaked a casual sideways sashay around the desk and toward the window.

Ned noticed at once. "Stay back! I told you to stay back!" He waved the gun frenziedly, pointing it first at David and then at his own head. He cocked the hammer with an ominous click, his breath coming in frightened pants.

"There's no point in carrying on this damn-fool discussion," he gasped. "It's over. I'm not going to let you march me off to jail, and that's all there is to it. You know I'd be better off dead than shut away in prison."

"We can find you a competent lawyer," David said quickly.

"Maybe he'll be able to make a deal with the DA, come up with a plea bargain, so you won't have to do time."

"What kind of a deal were you thinking of?" Ned asked sarcastically. "A plea of temporary insanity caused by stress from trying to pay off my wife's credit-card debts?"

At this moment, a plea of temporary insanity seemed quite credible to David, but he didn't want Ned to kill himself to prove the point. He'd managed to get to the corner of the desk. How was he going to distract Ned long enough to get around it?

"You mustn't give up, Ned. Even if your lawyer can't work out a plea bargain, with the criminal-justice system the way it is these days, you're not going to spend more than a couple of years in prison—"

Ned turned white with rage. "You sanctimonious son of a bitch. Only a couple of years in prison! And what the hell am I supposed to do when I get out? How the hell am I going to find a job? And what about my wife? I did this for her, and she'll start filing for divorce the second she sees the first cop walking up the driveway."

David swallowed a comment to the effect that a wife who got her husband hundreds of thousands of dollars in debt, then applied for a divorce, wasn't much of a wife and definitely wasn't worth killing yourself for. What the heck, he thought bleakly. He wasn't in a position to be dishing out advice on how Ned should relate to his wife. His own marriage was such a travesty that he and Eve hadn't made love in six weeks, hadn't managed a friendly conversation in two months. Who was he to judge someone else's marriage, even Ned's?

He was calculating the probability of success if he leaned across the desk and simply lunged for the gun when the phone rang. With the typical ingrained reaction of a longtime stockbroker, Ned glanced toward the phone, almost as if considering picking up the receiver. For a single vital instant, his attention was distracted.

This was the only chance he'd get, and David took it. Propelled by adrenaline and guilt, he threw himself across the corner of the desk, bringing the side of his hand down on Ned's wrist in a karate-style chop hard enough to crack bone. Ned's hand jerked reflexively around the firing mechanism of the gun and a bullet exploded out of the barrel. David slumped against the desk, light-headed with relief.

"Oh my God, I've killed you! My only friend!" Ned burst into tears and collapsed into his leather swivel chair, the gun dangling limply from his injured hand.

"Hey, calm down, you didn't kill me." David removed the gun from Ned's fingers, ignoring—actually not feeling—the pain that ripped from his left elbow to his shoulder when he moved.

The door to the office burst open, revealing the distraught faces of Cyrus Frank, the managing partner, and Jean, his secretary.

"What's going on here?" Cyrus demanded. His gaze fell on Ned, now sobbing uncontrollably, and then rested horror-stricken on David's arm. "My God!" was all he managed to say.

"Don't move," Jean said. "I'll call the paramedics."

"No, don't bother," Cyrus said. "I'll drive him straight to the hospital. That'll be quicker." He visibly pulled himself together and spoke with the crisp authority that came with thirty years of success.

David tried to smile. Beneath his curmudgeonly exterior, Cyrus was a grade-A softie, but Ned needed a lawyer and a good psychiatrist, not the hustle and bustle of a hospital emergency room.

"No need to panic," he said, feeling lassitude consume him now that the major crisis was over. "No damage done. Ned's going to be okay, aren't you, Ned?"

Ned stared ahead, blank eyed, and Cyrus snorted. "He's not the one I'm worried about. It's your arm that needs attention, David, so don't argue. I'm taking you to the hospital right this minute. Come on. Jean can take care of calling the police."

"My arm?" David looked down and was astonished to see blood soaking through the sleeve of his shirt in an ever-widening stain.

Damn, he thought sluggishly. *This was a new shirt.* Several seconds later he came up with another thought.

Ned shot me.

He continued to stare at the red stain, hypnotized by the speed with which it was spreading, while Cyrus walked across the room and took the gun from him, handing it to Jean. "Take care of this, will you? Call security. Ask them to send a man up until the police get here." He slipped his arm around David's shoulder, offering his support. "Let's go, Dave, old buddy. We need to get you stitched up and pumped full of antibiotics."

David shook his head, not in denial, but to clear away the wooziness. "Call Amy," he said to Jean. "And make sure she gets here fast. Jean, whatever happens, don't leave Ned alone, not even to go to the bathroom."

"All right," she said. "I'll take care of things. Don't worry, David. I'll baby-sit Ned until the police get here. Now you go and get that gunshot wound looked at."

"Ned needs a lawyer. And we must call his wife." Had he mentioned that already? "Cyrus, we need to arrange for—"

"Shut up," Cyrus said pleasantly. "*You* don't need to arrange anything. We're leaving for the hospital. Now."

"Go on, David," Jean said, making a shooing movement. "What are you waiting for? You're dripping blood all over the office furniture."

Call Eve for me, David nearly said, but then decided against it. Eve would be getting ready to wind up the evening news broadcast, and she didn't need to have his problems added to the controlled chaos that passed for a normal working environment at New York City's most popular local TV station. He'd explain everything when he got home. Now that the facts about Ned were out in the open, he could finally tell Eve about the two million dollars in missing funds, and how he'd spent the past couple of months working his ass off to uncover the truth about the thefts. Once she knew about Ned's nefarious activities, Eve would understand why he'd spent so many hours at the office on nights and weekends, and why he'd been so vague about what he was doing.

David felt a surge of optimism, of real honest-to-God hope. Maybe this would be a chance for him and Eve to make a new start, to get some of their problems onto the table and begin to heal the hurts they'd inflicted on each other over the past few months.

Despite the throbbing pain he now felt in his arm, the prospect was almost enough to make him smile.

IT WAS A SLOW NIGHT in the emergency room, and David was only the third gunshot victim that evening. To a medical staff where even the newest trainee had already seen and dealt with a hundred bullet wounds, his injury was entirely routine. In less than an hour, his arm had been X-rayed, cleaned, stitched and bandaged.

Cyrus, reassured that his favorite junior partner was not about to expire, took off to confront Ned about his crimes, leaving David to cope with three hours of paperwork and a bored cop who seemed convinced that David was guilty of something, even if only terminal stupidity. The cop passed him to a clerk in the hospital billing department, who recorded David's economic history with extreme suspicion and excruciating thoroughness. When he was finally allowed to go, David wasn't sure whether he'd been more intimidated by the cop or his session with the billing clerk. On balance, he thought the clerk could give the cop several valuable pointers on how to maximize the fear factor during interrogation.

It was well after ten o'clock when he paid off the cabbie outside his fashionable Upper East Side apartment. He felt battered, bone weary, woozy from painkillers and distinctly sorry for himself. His mouth was dry and furry. His arm ached, his head ached, his stomach ached, and his butt ached from sitting on a hard plastic chair with rickety aluminum legs. Absurdly, even his conscience ached, as if somehow he was responsible for Ned's problems and the fact that two million dollars was missing from the firm's accounts.

He rode the elevator up to his apartment, slumped against the wall, nursing his hurt and his uneasy psyche. In a fit of misplaced bravado, he'd refused a sling. Now the muscles in his arm were screaming in protest. Cradling his left wrist, he tried to slip the key into the lock without exerting pressure on his sore muscles. He fumbled for a while and finally managed to turn the key. He closed his eyes for a split second before opening the door, shaken by the intensity of his longing to find Eve waiting inside for him, looking as she had in those magical early days when they'd fallen in love.

Resting against the corridor wall, he remembered with sudden aching clarity how she'd smiled at him on their first date. After they'd eaten lunch, they'd walked through Central Park and she'd stopped to lean against a tree. Her face had been soft and flushed, and her eyes had been warm with invitation. Unable to resist, he'd stepped close and kissed her—a light questioning kiss, filled with the promise of all he wanted them to share when they were finally alone. Now, almost three years later, he could still taste her lips, still feel the hesitant eagerness of her response. Right at this moment, he wanted to recapture the warmth and tenderness of that first kiss more than he'd ever wanted anything in his life. He shifted his weight forward against the door, pushing it open with his good shoulder, praying Eve would be there, praying she would welcome him without a barrage of questions.

She was home, but she wasn't sitting there waiting for him with gentle smiles and eyes misty with love. She was seated at her desk in the corner of the living room, files, papers and flowcharts spread out around her. Every line of her body appeared stiff with tension. She looked up as David came into the apartment, her face pale and her eyes blank. Despite the blankness— or maybe because of it—he could sense the intensity of her anger, like a physical presence in the room. He knew her guarded expression masked emotions so volatile, so fierce, she was afraid to let even a hint of them appear.

He automatically girded himself to protect his own extreme vulnerability. Tonight he simply couldn't take any more hurt. He meant to smile in apology, but he felt his forehead crease into a frown. "I'm sorry I'm late—"

"Don't bother to apologize," Eve snapped, her voice brittle. "Let me guess. You started talking with the guys at the office about Japanese rice futures or some other equally riveting subject and just forgot to call."

Her sarcasm sliced into him, cutting against the pain of his wound like the stab of a knife. For an appalling, terrifying moment, he actually felt tears burn at the back of his throat. Good God, he was a man! He couldn't cry! He turned away so that she wouldn't see the rigid, awkward way he was holding his arm, or the blood spattered on the part of his shirt not hidden by his jacket. To hell with it, he thought resentfully. He wasn't going to beg for sympathy.

"Something like that," he said, voice cooler and less emotional than an ice floe. "I'm sorry."

"That's it?" she demanded, her body ramrod straight, vibrating with the anger she wouldn't allow herself to express any other way. "That's your total explanation for why you left me alone tonight on my—" She stopped abruptly.

"That's it," David said. "There you have it. My total explanation." Misery, anger and fatigue churned inside him so rapidly that he scarcely knew where one feeling began and the other ended. The pain of his bullet wound reached inward, where it met with the pain inflicted by Eve's harshness. The two pains touched, exploding into one giant, throbbing wound.

Eve stood up. Despite the painkilling drugs and his mind-numbing tiredness, he saw that she held on to the edge of her desk, as if to stop herself from shaking. With anger, he supposed. God knows, these days their entire life seemed to be one long silence, punctuated by brief exclamation points of rage.

She was so beautiful he couldn't resist lifting his eyes to her face, searching for some hint, however small, that she still cared. He could have saved himself the trouble. Her gray-blue eyes remained blank, wiped clean of emotion. He wondered what had happened to the beguiling sparkle of laughter that had once seemed an integral part of her expression. Gone, he supposed, to the same mysterious place as their comfortable chitchat and their once-fantastic sex life.

She dropped her gaze to the stack of papers on her desk and made a notation on one of them with her pencil, almost as if he was so insignificant that she just wanted him to go away and leave her free to catch up on her administrative work.

"We clearly don't have anything pleasant left to say to each other," she said, her voice remote to the point of boredom.

"We don't seem to have anything left to say, period." *Tell me I'm wrong,* he pleaded silently.

"You're right," she said. The point of her pencil snapped, and she stared at it, rather than him. "David, this…situation has gone on long enough. I can't bear—" She stopped abruptly. "I want a divorce, and I'll do whatever it takes to get one."

He felt the words like a blow aimed right at his wounded arm. Was that how she saw their marriage? As a *situation?* His pride began to ache right along with his arm and his backside. "There's no need to sound so damned aggressive," he said. "If you want out of this marriage, then go. As you may have noticed, nobody's begging you to stay, least of all me."

Her fingers flattened for a moment against the desk. "I'm well aware of that." She turned her back and spoke over her shoulder. "We should make this as painless as possible. Are you going to move out, or shall I?"

Even though they were already in the middle of it, he couldn't quite believe they were having this conversation. Eve would never leave him. She couldn't. For God's sake, hadn't she loved him only a few short months ago? Love didn't just vanish, did it? His stomach felt hollow. His mind went blank in a fog of fatigue. "Move out?" he said. "Out of the apartment?"

Eve turned around again. She finally smiled, but there wasn't a trace of amusement in the wry twist of her lips. "Okay, David, you needn't sound so horrified. I know this is your apartment, so I'll go. My suitcase is already packed." With unmistakable bitterness, she added, "I had nothing else to do tonight but pack my belongings."

So what kind of shark was biting her flippers? David thought acridly. Why was she sounding as though this mess was his fault? While he'd been disarming a suicidal colleague and getting shot for his efforts, she'd been packing her damned bags to leave him. The injustice of her accusations left David cold with fury. The hollow in his stomach disappeared, replaced by anger, which was a lot more bearable than whatever it was he'd been feeling before.

What does it matter if she leaves? he thought. One-sided love could only take a man so far. His marriage to Eve had been unraveling for months, seriously disintegrating for at least the past eight or nine weeks. Perhaps this was as painless a way to end it as any. For a terrifying moment he understood what Ned had been feeling when he aimed the gun at his head, understood how tempting it was to fantasize about getting rid of all your problems in a single instant of excruciating, redeeming pain.

When he realized the dangerous place his thoughts were taking him, David drew a deep, steadying breath and walked toward the tiny bedroom they'd converted into his study ages ago, when he and Eve had been crazy with love. He clung to his anger, so that there'd be no room for the despair waiting to seize him.

"Fine," he said. "Move out as soon as you're ready. Tonight would be a real good time." He wondered if other men felt this roaring tidal wave of grief when their marriage ended. Wasn't there supposed to be at least a small sense of relief? "Have your lawyer call mine in the morning. Let's make this break clean and fast."

"Sounds like a great idea," Eve said. "The faster the better. Who's your lawyer?"

Good question, but of course he had no answer. Until tonight, finding a divorce attorney hadn't been high on his list of things to do. "Who's yours?" he countered.

"Jeb Goldman."

She'd obviously been planning this divorce for a while, David realized. Not only were her bags packed, but she'd even chosen her legal adviser. A friend of *his*. What the hell. He didn't care. It was time for them to split. If he was going to feel this hurt, this lost, this lonely, he'd just as soon feel it alone.

"I'll call Jeb tomorrow with a name," he said. "Unlike you, I haven't been making plans."

"Good." Eve didn't rise to the bait, didn't deny that she'd been planning for some time to get a divorce. With acid politeness she added, "Please don't get so busy making your next million dollars that you forget to disentangle yourself from our marriage. Personally, I'm ready to move on with my life without messy complications left over from past mistakes."

"I'm sure you are. Far be it from me to stand in the way of your dazzling future." What did she mean, she was ready to move on with her life? What messy complications? Did she have a lover? Was she planning to marry again as soon as their divorce was final?

He couldn't bear to ask or even to think about it. He strode into the study, slamming the door behind him. He felt a stitch pop in his arm. He pressed his fingers to the blood seeping through his gauze bandage, collapsed onto the sofa and leaned back against the cushions, eyes closed, forehead pounding.

One way and another, this had been a hell of a day.

Chapter One

Even if she hadn't been worried about the possibility of encountering her ex-husband, the town of Eternity would have made Eve Graham nervous. Picturesque tree-lined streets and distant glimpses of salt marsh, framed by winsome Greek-revival buildings, was definitely not her style.

Born and raised in Fargo, North Dakota, a graduate of rural Wooster College in Ohio, it had taken her six months to stop feeling faint every time she descended into the surreal world of the New York subway system. Now, nine years later, she was a dyed-in-the-wool New Yorker who viewed clean streets with suspicion, got headaches breathing air that wasn't polluted and developed instant insomnia unless the decibel level was earsplitting. From her perspective, Eternity flunked out on all major counts.

Jaw clenched—a permanent condition, indicative of nothing in particular—Eve drove along First Street, staring in disbelief as one imitation-antique storefront was succeeded by another. Memories and Mementos. Center Jewelers. Heritage Gowns. Windows filled with bouquets of rosebuds, displays of rings, lacy gowns and satin shoes. The merchants in this town sure had the wedding business covered. Eve felt a twinge of regret that she wasn't going to be producing her usual type of cynical hard-edged exposé, because there seemed plenty of material here just begging to be exploited.

Cynicism, however, was out as far as her report on Eternity, Massachusetts, was concerned. Eve was going to make her story cute and gushing, even if it killed her. After months spent trying to persuade Art Sonderheim that "Roving Report" occasionally needed lighter content, she wasn't about to screw up now that he'd finally agreed to go ahead and test her concept.

It was sheer bad luck that his favorite niece had decided to get married last month in the Eternity chapel and that Art—a man who normally made Attila the Hun look sentimental—had come back to New York misty-eyed over the charming wedding ceremony and the quaintness of the town. Eve and the rest of the "Roving Report" crew had been ordered up to Eternity on two weeks' notice, before glorious New England fall turned into dreary frigid winter. According to Art, if they filmed the story right, it would be utterly captivating.

The fact that Art actually used the word "captivating" had Eve sweating even before she left Manhattan. Her boss's instructions usually tended to be loaded with four-letter expletives, not fancy adjectives. His niece's wedding in the Eternity chapel seemed to have caused a definite crack in the granite organ he called a heart.

In some ways, her boss's spasm of sentiment was the least of Eve's worries. Her number-one major-league problem right now was the fact that David's family had deep roots in the town of Eternity, and she knew—her parents had made sure she knew— that after two years of chasing up and down the coast of Central America, David had recently returned to live in the area.

Given freedom of choice, she would rather film on an anthill in the desert or on an ice floe in the Antarctic, than in the Powell-family chapel. The prospect of encountering her ex-husband face-to-face sent shivers rampaging up and down her spine. And those betraying shivers made her furious. David's current where-abouts were no concern of hers. Despite the fact that her family was forever trying to pass on details about his activities, Eve wasn't willing to listen. She didn't care why he'd thrown away his profitable career as a stockbroker to pursue the risky profession of deep-sea diver. She didn't care why his career on the New York Stock Exchange, which had consumed a hundred percent of his attention during the final months of their marriage, was suddenly of no importance the day after their divorce was final. Presumably he'd become a workaholic because he found their marriage boring. Once the marriage ended, so did his need to obsess about his career.

Eve refused to waste her time worrying about past motives and lost opportunities. After two years of living alone, she liked to believe she'd put her relationship with David into proper perspective. She and her therapist agreed that her ex-husband no longer had the power to wound her, so why was she getting chills and goose bumps at the prospect of seeing him again?

A white-painted sign, decorated with a pair of wedding bells, pointed the way to the Eternity chapel. Eve raised disbelieving eyebrows, then shrugged. What the heck. She had a job to do, which didn't include mockery of the town ambience. Whatever her personal feelings about the institution of marriage, her program on the local wedding industry was going to be sweet enough to send every diabetic in America into immediate insulin overload. Or was it underload? Eve's grasp of the functioning of the human body was somewhere between minimal and nonexistent.

Back in high school, when she discovered she was required to dissect a fetal pig in order to pass biology, she'd switched at once to astronomy. Consequently she was much better at naming stars and planets than she was at identifying the functions of body parts.

Early in their marriage, she'd told David the story of her short-lived biology class, and he'd found it delightful. He'd immediately taken her to bed and given her an erotic lesson in anatomy, earning an A-plus for speed and skill in finding the erogenous zones of an adult human female.

Unfortunately his glow of romantic approval hadn't lasted very long. By the time their marriage ended, he considered the fact that she'd wimped out of biology lab as just one more infuriating example of her refusal to confront life's harsh realities. During the final hideous weeks of their foray into married bliss, he'd insisted that her view of the world was dangerously blink-ered and sentimental. With the sarcasm that seemed to drip from her tongue in those days, she'd countered with the acid comment that a desire to have a baby wasn't normally considered proof of terminal naiveté, but she could certainly see how he might consider himself unequal to the task of becoming a father. Blank eyed, stony in his silence, David hadn't cared enough about her taunt to lose his temper.

She often wondered if he'd ever watched her television show since his return to the States. If so, he must realize how much she'd changed from the shy fresh-faced newsreader he'd known. As executive producer of her own syndicated news program, she was no longer a woman who recoiled from the squalor of life's underbelly. "Roving Report" was famous—infamous?—for its hard-nosed investigations. Eve insisted that her crew examine every dirt pile and every maggot in close-up and glowing color. What's more, she was always right there on the front line, di-recting the mike and the camera lens to make sure she got the best possible view of the writhing mess pulsating beneath life's smooth surface. Nowadays, if asked to dissect a pig, she'd sim-ply have asked where she should stand and which knife would look best on camera. Two years after their divorce, Eve knew she had finally become the ambitious, thick-skinned woman Da-vid had always wanted as a wife. She admitted that there was a certain satisfaction in knowing he could no longer have her.

Stopping at the town's only traffic light, she raised an eyebrow when she glanced left and saw the statue in Soldier's Green that honored a veteran of the Revolutionary War. No rushing to keep up with the quirks of modern fashion in this town, she thought in silent amusement. Eternity was apparently well named. Not only did it believe in happily-ever-after, it clearly took a long-term view of history.

She glanced at her watch, fingers drumming on the steering wheel as the light changed and she drove through the intersec-tion. Five o'clock. Her plane had been late landing at Logan, and the traffic out of Boston had been typically horrendous, delaying her still further. She disliked being late for her meeting with Constance Powell. Although she was resigned to the fact that punctuality was almost impossible for people who lived and worked in Manhattan, she suspected that the folks in Eternity adhered to a more old-fashioned standard, and Eve retained just enough of her North Dakota upbringing to know that you didn't keep elderly ladies waiting.

Her temples were thrumming. She reached into her leather briefcase and rummaged around until her fingers closed over the zippered silk purse that contained her pills. Expertly, with one hand still on the steering wheel, she shook out a couple of aspirin and tossed them into her mouth. She swallowed with no difficulty, having learned months ago how to take them without water. The tablets slid down, and her stomach sent up an instant burn of protest.

Her gaze still fixed on the road, she scanned for signs pointing to Lafayette Street while she searched for her antacids. The roll was already half gone, but she stuck a tablet into her mouth and crunched quickly. The smarting sensation in the pit of her stomach eased slightly, but not enough, so she ate another antacid, then zipped up the pill case and shoved it back into her briefcase just as she arrived at the turnoff that led to the Powell estate.

Eve massaged her stomach. Tonight she really would have to remember to eat dinner. Grilled fish, maybe, and a baked potato. Perhaps she should drink a glass of milk before bed or something. Too much was going on in her life to risk a major health problem. With her career poised right on the brink of its next major step forward, she couldn't afford an ulcer.

The Powell mansion was much bigger than she'd expected, a huge gabled mansion built to accommodate the grandiose dreams and oversize family of a successful Victorian merchant. She drove up the long driveway and rounded a corner to the main entrance.

The porticoed front door was framed by two old maples, their scarlet leaves so vivid against the gray October sky that for a split second Eve's breath caught in her throat at the sheer beauty of their blazing branches. She turned away almost at once, reaching into the rental car for her briefcase and walking briskly to the door without looking at the trees. For some reason, their brilliant fall leaves brought a pricking sensation to her eyes. She swallowed hard. Nowadays, unless she was discussing camera angles with one of the crew, she couldn't afford to waste valuable time and emotion admiring a view, however pretty.

The doorbell was answered by an elderly woman wearing wool slacks and a lavender lace-knit sweater set. "Hello," Eve said, smiling and holding out her press card. "I'm Eve Graham from 'Roving Report.' Are you Miss Powell?"

"Yes, I'm Miss Powell, but if you're from the television station, I'm not the person you want. I'm Violet, the *youngest* Powell sister." She patted her neat gray curls in a gesture that was almost flirtatious.

"How do you do, Miss Powell. It's nice to meet you," Eve said.

Violet cocked her head. "You can call me Violet. There are so many Powell sisters, people get confused. First names make it easier to keep us all sorted out."

"Thank you, Violet." Eve stepped into the vestibule, which was paneled in exquisite antique maple. "Is your sister expecting me?"

Violet ignored the question. "You were married to David," she said, not moving out of the vestibule. "It's amazing that we never met you while you were his wife."

"Well, we were living in Manhattan, and David was very busy at the time. I met his mother, of course...."

Violet squinted over the top of her gold-wired glasses, her expression definitely skeptical. But all she said was, "Nice boy, David. Won a scholarship to Yale, you know, before he was eighteen. Brilliant mind, but the poor lad's too handsome for his own good. World's worst communicator."

"Do you think so?" Eve's smile never wavered. There was nothing like on-camera experience for teaching you how to smile no matter what. "However, I'm sure you know that David and

I have been divorced for more than two years now, and I'm accustomed to thinking of myself as single.''

"Pity. You should have been married in the chapel. Never fails, you know. If you're married there, you stay married. We call it our family miracle."

If she'd stayed married to David, it wouldn't have been a miracle, it would have been a living hell. But Eve didn't want to offend the old lady, so she smiled. Maybe she was good at smiling, but words were momentarily beyond her.

Violet didn't seem to have any problem filling the silence. "I was never married, you know. My fiancé was killed in World War II. At Iwo Jima. After that, well, nobody quite matched up to Dick."

"I'm so sorry," Eve said with genuine sympathy.

Violet turned away. "He was very brave...but it was a long time ago, more than fifty years." She finally gestured for Eve to follow her down the long hallway. "My sister Constance is waiting for you in the sitting room. We lit the fire in there and it feels very cozy. This time of year, the change in the weather bothers my sister a lot." Violet lowered her voice confidingly. "Her arthritis is acting up, although she won't admit it, of course."

"Oh, dear. I hope I haven't arrived at an inconvenient time."

"We've been waiting for you," Violet said. "Constance has been quite excited."

Eve wasn't sure what that meant. She drew a deep breath, determined to be polite, and not only because the Powell sisters were likely to be important to the success of her project. Life in the concrete canyons of New York City had changed her a lot, but not enough to obliterate the bone-deep lessons of respect for others that she had learned from her parents.

"Perhaps there's no need for me to disturb your sister. If I could just get the key to the lighthouse, I can be on my way."

"Is that where you're going to stay? In the lighthouse? Connie never told me that." Violet stopped and stared at her visitor, her mouth shaping an astonished circle.

"Why, yes, I believe that's where I'm going. Your sister said there's a guest room in the lighthouse and the Powell family archives are stored there, together with a great deal of material about the building of the chapel. It seemed a logical place to start work on the research for my program."

"Yes, I suppose it is."

The old lady sounded so doubtful Eve began to feel worried. "My plans are flexible, you know. I can easily find a room in the local inn if that would be better for you."

Violet straightened. "No, no. No need for that. It's not a problem at all, not if Connie arranged it." Violet gave Eve another swift, sideways glance, then turned and scurried light footedly down the remainder of the hall. "I'm only sixty-five, you see, but Connie's ten years older, and when you get to her age, you have to expect these problems."

Violet might be "only" sixty-five, and the youngest Powell sister, but the threads of her conversation weren't easy to follow. Was Connie's problem her arthritis? Or the fact that she'd invited Eve to spend the next week in the lighthouse? Eve devoutly hoped she wasn't going to arrive at her destination and find nineteenth-century plumbing and a resident ghost haunting the only bedroom. Nowadays Eve's definition of roughing it meant staying in a hotel with room service that stopped at midnight and no valet parking.

Violet paused on the threshold of a pleasant, comfortably shabby sitting room and waved her arm. "Ms. Eve Graham is here," she announced, with a decided emphasis on the *Ms.* "David's wife. From the television program. You know, from 'Roving Report.'"

David's wife. Eve clenched her jaw. It was precisely the sort of linkage she'd been expecting—and dreading. Odd how the simple act of putting a burned-out relationship into words could revive the hurt of old wounds.

Not letting her annoyance show, she stepped into the sitting room. Four interested faces, one male and three female, looked up from their teacups. A frail, white-haired woman, dressed in beige wool challis, rose with painful slowness from her seat by the fire and extended her hand. "Welcome to Eternity, Miss Graham. I'm Constance Powell."

"It's nice to meet you in person." Eve shook the offered hand, careful not to pump too vigorously. Her grandmother suffered from arthritis, and she knew how a friendly squeeze could cause agonizing pain.

"This is my sister June." Constance nodded to a wing chair next to the fire where an apple-cheeked woman sat drinking tea and eating a muffin. "And over there on the sofa you see my other sister Patience, together with a good friend of ours, Louis Bertrand."

Patience, a handsome woman with beautiful white hair piled high and thick on her head, sat next to a dapper gentleman with a neat mustache and a definitely roguish twinkle in his eye. Eve noticed at once that Patience's cheeks were flushed, and she sensed a tension vibrating between her and Louis Bertrand. None of the other sisters seemed even remotely aware of any undercurrents, perhaps because they were all so used to each other's company that they no longer paid each other any real attention.

Louis Bertrand acknowledged the introduction by rising to his feet and bowing with an elegant flourish that reminded Eve of Maurice Chevalier about to burst into song. He took her hand and carried it to his lips, somehow managing to murmur a deft compliment over her fingertips without appearing ridiculous.

Patience Powell, on the other hand, seemed totally discomposed by the simple fact of Eve's arrival. She started to get up, dropped her napkin, rattled her teaspoon in her saucer and sat down again without speaking, her hands fluttering as if she wasn't sure where to put them. Louis Bertrand immediately returned to his seat next to her, and Eve saw him give Patience's elbow a tiny, comforting squeeze.

What in the world was going on? Eve wondered. For some unknown reason, watching the elderly couple, she felt an odd little warming of her heart. If she needed background color for her segment, she'd certainly know where to come for it. Louis

Bertrand and the Powell sisters looked like extras sent from Central Casting for the express purpose of adding visual interest to her set.

Constance lifted the teapot with a grace that belied the gnarled knuckles of her arthritic hands. "The tea is fresh, Ms. Graham—"

"Eve, please."

Constance smiled. "Very well, Eve. Please do sit down with us for a moment and enjoy a cup."

With all that she had to do over the next forty-eight hours before her crew arrived on Monday, Eve knew she didn't have time to waste drinking tea. On the other hand, the Powell sisters owned the famous chapel that was at the heart of the Eternity legend, so she might as well sit down and absorb some insider views on the local wedding industry.

"Thank you," she said, sitting on a chair near the serving cart and taking the cup of steaming tea.

"It's nice to have you here," Constance said.

June nodded her agreement. "We're looking forward to your TV program. When will it be shown?"

"We're planning some time around Thanksgiving," Eve said, glancing toward each sister with brisk professional courtesy. It was important to get influential locals on her side, and these matriarchs were the closest Eternity came to a ruling dynasty.

"It's very good of you all to make me so welcome. As the executive producer of 'Roving Report,' I want to assure you that we have no intention of trying to destroy the town legend. As I explained to Miss Constance, our research shows that the Christmas season is second only to early summer as a time for weddings, and we plan to produce a heartwarming holiday piece, dedicated to December brides and their families."

"I saw your program last year on Reggie Perry," Violet said, gazing at a cookie she was holding as if she couldn't quite remember why she'd picked it up. "I went to school with Reggie's father. He dipped my braids in the inkwell and ruined my ribbons. Then he pretended Charles Benham had done it."

Eve's gaze narrowed. The piece she'd done on Senator Reginald Perry had won her an Emmy, and she considered it her best exposé ever—a devastating yet seemingly flattering profile of a womanizing crook at work in the back rooms of the state capitol. The senator had approved every inch of footage, never realizing the destructive, cumulative effect of the material. Eve wondered why Violet had chosen this moment to mention that show. Another symptom of a grasshopper mind? Or a shrewd warning not to try the same trick here in Eternity?

"What did you think of the program?" she asked.

Violet crumbled her cookie onto an embroidered linen napkin. "The trouble with Reggie was that nobody ever disciplined him properly. His father spoiled him, and his mother was frightened of him."

"I'm not sure you've answered my question," Eve said.

Violet looked vague again, and Constance broke in with the assurance of a woman who had spent sixty years interpreting for her sister. "What we mean, Ms. Graham, is that your program amounted to a televised assassination of our state senator. In our opinion, based on years of close acquaintance, he deserved everything that came about as a result of your show. The townspeople of Eternity, however, have done absolutely nothing to deserve the sort of muckraking exposé that is your stock-in-trade. We've taken a great leap of faith by inviting you here and offering you our cooperation. We hope you can be trusted to treat the legend of the chapel and the institution of marriage with the respect they both deserve."

Eve blanched. She was more than willing to concede that her on-camera style was hard-hitting, but muckraking seemed several steps farther down the investigative scale. "Let me assure you again I've no intention of producing a hostile story," she said.

"Even though you don't believe in the legend," Violet said.

"I'm a journalist," Eve snapped. "I don't have to believe every silly fairy tale I hear in order to report on it kindly."

"Does that mean you believe the legend about our chapel is silly?" Constance inquired with deceptive mildness.

"No," Eve lied, regretting her momentary spurt of temper. If the Powell sisters wanted to believe that getting married in their chapel guaranteed a lifetime of married bliss, who was she to tell them they were crazy? Constance Powell had shown her nothing but courtesy over the past few hectic days; the least Eve could do in return was guard her acid tongue.

"I'm sure it's a very meaningful legend to the people who choose to marry there," she said.

Constance looked at her with disconcerting astuteness. "In this day and age marriage needs all the help it can get, even from misplaced faith in old legends, wouldn't you agree, Ms. Graham?"

"Certainly. But, please, you must call me Eve." She had no intention of getting involved in a discussion of the sorry state of modern marriage. Quite apart from the fiasco of her marriage to David, she was so far from being an expert on relationships that she'd just broken off her engagement to Gordon, the assistant producer for "Roving Report," and a man who was almost as kind as he was good-looking. Her friends all thought she was nuts to turn him down and Eve almost agreed with them. Gordon still hoped that their relationship could be rescued, but she was secretly resigned to the fact that some flaw in her character made her incapable of sustaining intimacy.

She flashed the sisters one of her best and brightest smiles, and wondered how long it would be before she could escape to the lighthouse, where she could indulge in the comforts of solitude and her roll of antacids.

Constance returned the smile with one of her own. "Well, then, Eve, could you tell us a bit more about how you're planning to portray our town and the story of our wedding chapel?"

"Of course. The nature of this program is such that it needs to be a cooperative effort. I'm going to be relying on everyone in this room for help as I put the project together, so I would like you to think of yourselves as my temporary partners, with all of us united in the cause of showcasing the very best of Eternity and its legend. This is a small town, not all that far from Boston, and yet the townspeople have managed to retain a unique identity, instead of becoming just another bedroom suburb. There's a lot of material here that could be made interesting to a lot of different audience segments, not just prospective brides.''

"Audience segments?'' June murmured, stirring her tea. "Does that mean people?''

Eve counted silently to ten, but this time she managed not to snap. "Television producers have to think about the demographics of the audience,'' she said. "That doesn't mean we forget our viewers are human beings.''

Louis Bertrand spoke for the first time. "My dear young lady, we understand completely. As far as I'm concerned, you can count on me as one of your most active supporters.'' With only slight assistance from his cane, he got up from the sofa and executed another fancy flourish. This one, Eve decided, owed more to Fred Astaire than Maurice Chevalier.

"Thank you, Mr. Bertrand.''

"Please, I insist, you must call me Louis.'' He gave an airy flap of his hand. "You may already know I'm a veteran of several well-received appearances on stage, screen and radio. I would be happy to participate in your project in any capacity you think might benefit from a little extra savoir faire. You can't beat input from a talented local, you know.''

Wonderful, Eve thought with a mental groan. This was all she needed. For all his corny ways, Louis Bertrand seemed rather an appealing character with a wealth of stories to impart. In other circumstances, she would have welcomed his interest. But this was Eternity, and she wanted to get in and out of the town as quickly as possible. Before she encountered David—

Eve snapped off that thought before it had time to take hold. She smiled at Louis Bertrand, trying to squash his hopes as kindly as she could. He really did seem a nice old gentleman.

"I appreciate your offer, Mr. Bertrand, but my plan is to focus the program around a couple planning to get married in the chapel.''

"But, of course, I understand—''

This time she cut him off ruthlessly. Two years as an executive television producer did tend to leave a person somewhat short in the patience department. ''What I really need from all of you are the names of a couple who are planning to get married about two or three weeks from now. I can follow them as they make their last-minute arrangements and interview them about why they're choosing to have the ceremony in the Eternity chapel.''

"Perfect," Louis said, not looking a bit put out. ''I know the perfect couple.''

"You do?" June said, sounding surprised.

"Who?" Violet asked. ''Is it someone from town? My goodness, it isn't one of the Van Bassen girls, is it?''

Louis beamed and placed his hand on his heart. ''Indeed it is not," he said. ''At least as far as I know neither of them is about to commit herself to the perilous path of marriage. The couple I'm talking about is—''

"No, Louis!" Patience interrupted. She tugged at his sleeve, looking horrified. ''Good heavens, Louis, whatever are you thinking of? I can't imagine anything more ridiculous.''

June turned to her sister with a hint of irritation. ''Patience, whatever in the world is the matter with you? You've been squirming around like a cat with fleas all afternoon. Let Louis finish what he's trying to say. I want to know who's getting married.''

Patience subsided into blushing silence and Violet frowned. ''Are you feeling all right, Patty? You've been acting strangely this entire week.''

"I'm sorry," Patience said in a small voice. ''I've been acting strange because I feel so strange.'' Her blush darkened and she stared at her shoes. ''You see, I know who Louis is talking about. It's me. You see, I'm...um...I'm getting married.''

"To me!" Louis exclaimed, with a jubilant thump of his cane.

"Your sister has agreed to become my bride, and I'm the happiest man in the entire state of Massachusetts!"

His words were greeted with a stunned silence. Constance, June and Violet appeared to have turned to stone. After ten seconds of absolute immobility, they all moved at once, turning to stare at each other in mute, openmouthed shock. Finally, just when Eve was beginning to wonder if she should offer some congratulations to break the embarrassing silence, they all got up and rushed over to hug their sister, exclaiming with delight and chattering like a gaggle of high school students surrounding the homecoming queen.

Louis stood slightly to the side, watching the sisters with much the same air of benevolent possession as a rooster viewing his harem. He did his best to look suitably humble when the sisters finally turned around to shake his hand, but he failed miserably. He looked, in fact, as proud as a young boy who's just picked up his date in a brand-new sports car, and Eve noticed that whenever his gaze rested on Patience, his eyes glowed with an affection so deep and tender she felt her heart lurch. Louis and Patience must both be in their late sixties, or perhaps even broaching their early seventies, so presumably they wouldn't be around to celebrate their golden wedding anniversary. Nevertheless, Eve had a sudden conviction that however many or few years Louis and Patience might share, their marriage would be rich with happiness and genuine companionship.

"When are you planning to get married?" she heard herself asking during a brief pause in the rattle of questions and exclamations.

"At Thanksgiving, so that all the family will be home," Patience said, her color still high, but her eyes sparkling with a shy pleasure that made Eve realize what a pretty girl she must have been. "So you see, quite apart from the fact that you would never want to film a pair of old fogies like Louis and me, you and your camera crew are going to be gone from Eternity weeks before our wedding takes place."

"But we could come back and film the ceremony at the last

minute,'' Eve said, thinking rapidly. ''If the rest of the program was edited and ready to run, it wouldn't be too difficult to integrate footage of your wedding into the final segment.''

Louis smiled at his fiancée. ''What do you say, my dear? We've waited twenty years to do this, and I would like the whole world to share in our celebration. Shall we take the plunge with millions of television viewers looking on?''

Patience appeared flustered again. ''Heavens, Louis, it doesn't bear thinking about. Won't everyone think we're ridiculous, getting married at our age?''

''Are you suggesting they'd prefer us to live in sin?'' Louis inquired, the twinkle in his eye a bit more pronounced.

''Louis!'' Patience sounded outraged, but Eve saw that her hand crept along the sofa cushions and linked surreptitiously with her fiancé's.

For the first time since Art had pushed the Eternity project onto her, Eve felt a surge of creative excitement. She suddenly saw the possibilities of the program, saw how she could pull together interesting facts about the state of marriage in America today and interweave the bare bones of the statistics with filmed biographies of Patience and Louis. She wouldn't gloss over the appalling national divorce statistics or the misery of failure for the families involved, but she'd point out that there were millions of happy marriages, even in the last decade of the twentieth century, and millions of children who'd grown up feeling nurtured and protected by their parents' love. For visual interest, she could intersperse clips from various weddings held in the Eternity chapel over the next couple of weekends, and the climax of the program could be a two- or three-minute selection of pictorial highlights from the wedding of Patience Powell and Louis Bertrand. It would be a damn good program, she was sure of it, and provide just the sort of leavening ''Roving Report'' needed to lighten its image.

Eve knew better than to push her point when everyone was still slightly off-balance from hearing news of an engagement that was obviously unexpected, despite the fact that Louis Bertrand seemed to be an old and intimate friend of the family. She would come back on Monday, after she'd done some research, and chat privately with Patience. Louis, camera hog that he appeared to be, was not going to need any persuasion.

"If I could have the key to the lighthouse, I'll be on my way," she said in a low voice to Constance while the remaining three sisters were engaged in a discussion of who was going to call which cousin with news of the amazing betrothal. The discussion between June and Violet was becoming heated, and she grinned, a genuine smile this time, not one of her professional specials. "I have a feeling you may be needed here to referee. Age doesn't seem to be any barrier to disagreement about which relatives to invite to the wedding."

Constance smiled ruefully. "I think you may be right. Cousin Harold has caused more arguments in the Powell family than any two other relatives combined. He married three times, that's the trouble."

"In this day and age, that's not so dreadful," Eve said, hoping to be reassuring.

"Unfortunately Cousin Harold neglected to divorce wife number one before adding wives number two and three," Constance said. She gave a final wry glance toward the sofa and walked, not quite steadily, to the sideboard. "Here you are, Eve," she said, picking up a heavy old-fashioned key. "I think this is what you need." Her gaze seemed to slide sideways for a moment. "I hope everything works out for you while you're here with us in Eternity."

"I'm sure it will." Eve spoke with more sincerity than she'd have believed possible only twenty minutes earlier. "I appreciate your allowing me to stay in the lighthouse. It sounds like a fun place."

June caught the tail end of their conversation, and her head shot up. She stared at her sister. "She's staying in the lighthouse? Do you think that's wi—?"

"Yes," Constance said in a voice that brooked no discussion. "She's leaving now. I'll see you to the door, Eve. No, June, there's no need for you to come with us. I can manage perfectly well on my own.''

Constance, despite her arthritis, seemed to be a very determined lady once she made up her mind. Eve was barely allowed to say her goodbyes and repeat her congratulations before she was ushered politely but firmly to the front door.

''I shall expect to see you sometime quite soon. You have my phone number, so just call to set a time. Perhaps Sunday evening, so that we can set a firm time to discuss further the possibility of filming my sister's wedding?'' Constance leaned against the doorframe, clearly tired by the speed at which she had escorted Eve down the hall. ''It's good to meet you at last,'' she said as Eve went down the steps to the drive.

''Thank you,'' Eve said, opening the door of her car. ''It's good to be here.'' To her considerable surprise, she realized she wasn't lying. With the Powell sisters and Louis Bertrand to anchor her piece, Eternity and its wedding chapel would make a great show.

If the lighthouse had clean sheets and hot water, she thought, the week was going to turn out just fine.

Chapter Two

David zipped up his oldest and most comfortable pair of jeans and thrust his feet into a pair of moccasins he'd bought last year when he was diving off the coast of Central America. Leaving a towel slung around his neck so he could swat the occasional drop of water from his hair, he scuffed into his tiny low-ceilinged living area and hung up his wet suit on the special rack near the kitchen. Then he spread his diving gear over the scarred Formica-topped table he kept especially for that purpose.

It was chilly inside the cottage, but he didn't bother lighting a fire or turning up the central heating. His worry, mixed with a healthy dose of anger, was doing a great job of keeping him warm. This had been an exciting and productive week for him and Matt, but he didn't feel like celebrating.

Grabbing the swing arm of the desk lamp mounted on the old table, he focused a high-intensity beam first on his air tanks, and then on the seals and hoses of the regulator. His scuba equipment was new, good quality and well maintained. He harbored no illusions about the risks involved in excavating a wreck lodged under a deep-sea cliff, and he inspected his gear with meticulous care each time he made a dive. Every single piece of his equipment should have been damn near accident proof, but twice during the past week David and his partner, Matt Packard, had come close—way too close—to running out of air way beneath the surface of the Atlantic.

The first incident had occurred on Monday. He and Matt had been searching one of the massive beds of eel grass near the wreck of the *Free Enterprise* when he realized that his air supply was about to cut out. Surprised, because he'd already changed tanks twice and it hadn't felt as if he'd been submerged nearly long enough to be short of air a third time, he checked his wrist computer. Sure enough, his sense of time had been right on; he'd only been at the wreck site for eighty-four minutes and his computer informéd him that his current tank was good for almost another eight minutes of air.

Unfortunately David's lungs didn't agree with his computer. He sucked air from the reserve supply in his buoyancy jacket and cleared his regulator, but no air flow resumed. He checked the pressure gauge on his air tanks; it still showed they were a quarter full. Computer and pressure gages were in complete agreement that everything was fine. So why the hell couldn't he breathe?

Whatever his instruments might show, something obviously wasn't working right and he needed to replace his tanks immediately. He signaled Matt to let him know he was having problems breathing and swam over to the giant net that was suspended from the dive boat and contained their supplies. Matt joined him, tapping his pressure gage and indicating his surprise that he, too, was out of air.

They strapped on new tanks without making any further attempt to communicate. They'd been diving together almost daily for two years and they didn't need to discuss their options with laborious hand signals. Matt simply glanced at David, who nodded, and they began their ascent. Since the pressure gages on both their tanks had given faulty readings, they wouldn't take the chance that the remaining tanks might not be similarly short of air.

The wreck site was located at a depth of 120 feet, which meant that after eighty-five minutes underwater, they were outside the safety limits for a direct ascent to the surface. But if they surfaced at a steady pace, floating in harmony with the stream of their exhaled bubbles and exerting a minimum amount of energy to propel themselves upward, they could take minimum decompression breaks. As they paused for five minutes at ten meters, David had plenty of time to watch the haddock swim by and contemplate the various unpleasant ways in which it was possible for a deep-sea diver to die. A collapsed lung. Embolism in the brain. Toxic bubbles of nitrogen in the blood. Dinner for a hungry shark. The possibilities were many and varied, but this time he and Matt had gotten lucky.

However many times you'd dived, however many times you'd encountered life-threatening situations on the ocean bottom, lack of air still created a visceral gut-level fear. The urge to kick loose and swim like hell for the surface never entirely faded, but David had lots of experience in controlling his natural instincts. He and Matt had survived far more dangerous situations than this during the two years they'd worked off the coast of Central and South America. The occasion when an overgrown moray eel took a dislike to David's regulator hose and bit a chunk out of it before turning around and hooking its teeth into Matt's leg probably ranked as his number-one unfavorite memory. But that was closely followed by the time rival treasure hunters tried to harpoon him—and would have succeeded if Matt hadn't come charging to the rescue.

This time there were no man-biting eels to contend with, no fresh blood to attract marauding sharks and no rivals with harpoons. The air supply in their tanks held out, and David and Matt took the last ten meters slowly, watched by nothing more dangerous than a few cod. Nevertheless, it felt great to break the surface and draw in gulps of reviving, fresh-tasting air. There was nothing like breathing through a regulator hose to make you appreciate the pleasures of sucking in the real stuff.

Caleb, who owned the specially adapted fishing boat they used as their dive boat, had greeted their premature return with a grunt. "You're back early. What's up? No mermaids down there to keep you entertained today?"

"We had a problem with our air tanks," David said. "Couldn't breathe. We need to check them out before we go down again."

Caleb had responded with another grunt, but his raised eyebrows were eloquent. Like most fishermen, he had a healthy respect for the whims of the ocean and much preferred to remain safely on top of it. Not deigning to comment on their idiocy, he returned to the shelter of the wheelhouse, where he'd provided himself with a comfortable chair and a pile of motorcycle magazines. Caleb might captain a rental boat to earn a living, but his heart belonged to his Harley.

David and Matt took the tanks and pressure gages apart, then checked all the rest of their gear for good measure.

"What's the problem?" Caleb asked, leaning against the railing and viewing the dials, gages, tubes and bits of plastic scattered over the deck.

"I don't know," Matt said. "As far as we can tell, the pressure gages on two of these tanks are defective. The pins jammed. So when we thought we'd totally filled those tanks, we hadn't. Which means we were getting readings showing we still had plenty of air left, when in fact we didn't."

Caleb squinted toward David. "You mean you were down there playin' with the lobsters and you found out all of a sudden you got no air?"

"Something like that," David said.

Caleb shook his head and went back to looking at pictures of motorcycle engines. His silence spoke volumes.

Matt and David exchanged amused glances. "Are you ready to go down again?" Matt asked. "I spotted an interesting-looking chest just seconds before my air cut out."

"Sure." With the imminent threat of winter storms, they didn't have time to sit around and worry about what-might-have-been. The pressure gages could easily be replaced, and no real harm had been done. Within minutes, they had switched to backup gear and returned to the wreck site.

It was on this dive that he and Matt had made their most exciting find since locating the wreck two weeks earlier: a small leather-and-steel chest that held 543 English gold sovereigns, all of them dated before 1860. The documents at Lloyds suggesting the captain of the *Free Enterprise* had been paid off for his cargo strictly in gold looked as if they might be true.

David and Matt hurried back to shore and went out to celebrate their triumph with German beers and fresh crabs trucked in from Chesapeake Bay. In the flush of their success, neither of them had given the failed pressure gages more than a passing thought.

Until today.

Once again, he and Matt had been using sonar to scan the acres of seaweed that surrounded the final resting place of the *Free Enterprise*. Their find this time had been the ship's anchor, encrusted with calcified barnacles and submerged beneath a virtual forest of eel grass. They were cutting away at the seaweed when they discovered a half-dozen sets of handcuffs caught up in the giant links of the anchor chain.

Manacles, David realized, appalled by the size and weight of the cuffs. My God, did they really punish sailors by locking them into these monstrous instruments of torture?

Matt directed the beam of his light directly at the anchor chain and signaled for David to come closer. He saw at once what Matt was indicating. Corrosion made it difficult to be absolutely certain, but it looked as if the manacles weren't just tangled in the anchor chain; they had been deliberately locked to it. What for? David wondered, angling his light at the lock for a better view. The *Free Enterprise* had sunk with the loss of a dozen lives and all trace of its valuable cargo, although the captain and the entire complement of officers had survived. With the ship in danger of going down, why had someone on board taken the time to fasten six heavy sets of manacles to an anchor that was presumably being cut loose from the ship in a desperate effort to stop the vessel from sinking? It made no sense.

To add to the puzzle, David knew that the *Free Enterprise* had gone down within sight of Eternity Harbor and that the survivors had been rescued after displays of great bravery by the townsfolk of Eternity. According to a report in the *Courier*, the local newspaper, the weather on December 9, 1862, had been appalling, with gale-force winds and high seas. Nevertheless, at least in the opinion of the locals, the captain's failure to bring the ship into harbor until too late in the day had been a major contributing factor in the tragic loss of human life. The newspaper's dramatic story, spread over three pages, had been replete with the sort of robust invective that Victorian readers relished and contemporary society considered libelous. David had read the *Courier* report with more than a twitch of wry amusement, despite the grim subject matter. Contemporary society was pretty lily-livered, he decided. As a purveyor of moral outrage, Rush Limbaugh barely registered on the scale when compared to his nineteenth-century forebears.

David stared at the entwined manacle, trying to make sense of what he was seeing. Two questions nagged at him. Why had all the witnesses insisted that the captain could have brought the ship closer into port? And why, when a ship was sinking in a winter gale, would anyone on board waste time and energy locking handcuffs to the anchor line?

They wouldn't, David decided. Unless there had been bodies attached to the manacles. Bodies that someone on board ship wanted to be one hundred percent sure wouldn't be rescued. Bodies that would never even be sighted by the townspeople waiting in the harbor. Bodies of captives? Bodies of prisoners of war? Except this was a merchant ship, and there was no reason for the captain to have taken prisoners.

But what if the bodies thrown overboard had been slaves? Evidence of slavery would certainly be something to hide on a ship that was operating out of a northern port during the Civil War. What if the owners of the *Free Enterprise* hadn't been the loyal supporters of the Union that they seemed? The cargo manifest David had seen in the archives of Lloyds of London certainly suggested there was something very odd in the trading patterns of the ship.

He let the manacle drop and stared at Matt, seeing his own shock reflected in his friend's eyes—the shock typical of late-twentieth-century Americans when confronted with evidence of the brutality of their ancestors. David was anxious to take photographs. He signaled his intent to swim under the ledge to the wreck of the *Free Enterprise,* where he had tethered his camera to the broken stump of a mast. Matt fell in alongside his partner as they swam into the opaque darkness of the wreck.

The beam of the light at David's waist picked out the murky gleam of the fishnet a split second too late to signal a warning to Matt. The torn net, with its almost invisible nylon fibers, floated out at an angle and twined itself around Matt's flippers, clinging with the tenacity of a jungle vine.

David unsheathed his knife and started to cut his partner free, taking care not to pierce the fabric of Matt's wet suit, which would have precipitated its own chain of problems. In the northern Atlantic, at this depth, at this time of year, a damaged wet suit could be life-threatening. Because of the cold, David was wearing gloves and his fingers weren't as supple as he'd have liked. He'd barely snipped through the first couple of lines when a gush of air filled his mouth, almost choking him with its force.

Good grief, he thought, momentarily freezing. *My goddamned regulator valve has stuck!*

Every diving pro had heard horror stories about divers whose regulator valves jammed open, causing the air supply to gush out of the tanks in an uncontrolled flow. In fourteen years of amateur diving and two years as a pro, David had never even met anyone who'd undergone the experience themselves. Now he was facing it. Stuck valves weren't just a rumor. They really happened.

And he was in big trouble.

They were too deep and they'd been down too long to attempt a straight ascent back to the surface. Apart from which, he needed several more minutes to cut Matt free from the fishnet. He signaled Matt that his regulator was malfunctioning and that he was out of air. For a split second, Matt simply stared at him, eyes wide behind his mask.

Fortunately the pair of them had learned to dive together as freshmen in college, and they'd been diving as professional partners ever since David's marriage ended and he quit his job as a stockbroker. Matt didn't need any more information from David to realize the extent of their problem. He unhooked his spare regulator and leaned in close enough for David to share the air in his tank.

Working as fast as his gloved fingers would allow, David continued to cut at the net, separating the nylon strands, thread by painstaking thread. Their difficulties were compounded because Matt's legs were extended behind him and any effort to change his position risked his becoming even more entangled. To further complicate matters, Matt's knife was strapped to his leg-sheath and so was caught up in the knots of the fishing net. What might have been a three- or four-minute job if Matt could have reached his knife, took closer to six minutes with David working alone. He had a few black moments when he wondered if he was ever going to rid his partner of what seemed like an endless tangle of nylon twine.

Finally Matt had been free. They'd linked arms around his air tank and began the ascent, stopping for the necessary decompression breaks and making it to the surface with a joint air supply of less than twenty seconds remaining.

To say the least, the timing had been a damned sight too close for comfort.

David finally finished inspecting his gear. He'd found nothing suspicious, nothing that indicated future problems. He pushed the swing-arm lamp aside and stretched, massaging his forehead, aware of the pounding pressure of his headache now that he was safely home and the emergency was over. He felt tense as a guitar string, thrumming with a foreboding that wasn't entirely rational. What, exactly, was he worried about? Even if somebody wanted to sabotage his and Matt's exploration of the *Free Enterprise,* tampering with pressure gages and regulator valves was a stupid way to do it. Surely any serious saboteur would realize that such methods were much too imprecise to have any real impact beyond temporary irritation? Amateur divers might panic and get themselves into serious trouble, but a saboteur wouldn't expect seasoned divers like Matt and David to panic. So what would be the point of planning equipment failures? The most likely result of this week's accidents was that Matt and David would take more precautions and check their gear even more carefully than usual. Which, in fact, was exactly what they both were doing.

Despite the fact that there was no logical reason to suspect foul play, David couldn't conquer a nagging sense of disquiet. Why the hell did he find today's accident so threatening? He scowled at the failed butterfly valve in his regulator, but he couldn't come up with any better answer than that he didn't like coincidence, and three pieces of equipment failure within the space of five days was stretching the boundaries of happenstance a bit too far.

On the other hand, he couldn't afford to become paranoid. There was no place in the cutthroat world of underwater salvage for divers who'd lost their nerve. And the truth was that equipment malfunctioned all the time. When you were diving every day, the chances of encountering unusual problems necessarily increased. When you got right down to it, all that had happened was that two pressure gages and one butterfly valve had failed. None of the failures caused major problems, and his stuck regulator valve wouldn't have been much more than a passing inconvenience if Matt hadn't been caught in a stray piece of net at precisely the moment David's air supply blew out. And there was no way in the world that anyone could have predicted that Matt's flippers and the fishnet would connect at the same time David's regulator valve stuck.

His assessment of the situation ought to have reassured him. Instead, it increased the nagging feeling that danger lurked somewhere just outside his range of vision, waiting to swim into focus. If he'd been a cat, he was sure the fur on his back would have been standing on end in anticipation of perils hiding around the corner.

He should never have thought the word ''cat,'' David decided resignedly. Right on cue, Cat walked in from the bedroom—a room officially off-limits to felines—and stalked over to the empty fireplace, tail an upright declaration of disgust.

David looked at the poker-stiff tail and scowled. "Cut it out," he said. "I'm not lighting the fire."

Cat stared at him in mute reproach, and David hardened his resolve. "No," he said. "I have a headache, and it's too much effort to walk outside and fetch the wood."

Cat's tail drooped. He huddled close to the empty grate, looking as desperate as Garfield deprived of a year's supply of lasagna. The temperature inside the cottage was at least sixty-five. Cat shivered, his general demeanor suggesting he would expire from cold any minute unless warmed immediately by a six-log blaze.

Muttering curses that definitely would have shocked his mother, David went out to the front porch and carried in an armful of wood, throwing a couple of big logs on top of the kindling already in the grate, and setting the others on the hearth. He couldn't imagine why he'd gone through the farce of pretending to resist Cat's blandishments. He'd lit a fire every night this week for no better reason than that the cat had conned him into it. Why should tonight be any different?

"Satisfied?" he demanded, putting a match to the corner of a twist of newspaper and staring Cat straight in the eye. "Next time you pull that tail-in-the-air trick, I'm gonna take you right back to the pound where you belong."

Cat treated that threat with the contempt it deserved. Gracious in victory, he even condescended to poke the tip of one paw about half an inch toward David. His throat rumbled with the beginnings of a purr.

David refused the offer of reconciliation. He got up, brushing his hands on his jeans, and ambled toward the kitchen. He yawned. God, he was tired! He hadn't felt this exhausted and thick-witted since the night Ned Nichols tried to kill himself. The night Eve left him.

The unexpected memory of his ex-wife brought no pain. He pushed the thought of her aside without difficulty and totally without regret. David had spent months agonizing over his failed marriage, and nowadays he was numb where Eve was concerned. With the advantage of hindsight—that great instructor—he understood what had happened between the two of them. And it sure hadn't been anything earthshaking. They'd been sexually attracted. They'd married too soon. The sexual attraction had worn off, revealing their basic incompatibility. Bingo! End of tedious story.

He opened the fridge door and stared at the shelves, images of Eve smoothly banished. What were his plans for the night? Should he broil a hamburger and enter more of their research data into the computer? Or should he break out the cereal, surf through a few TV channels and do a couch-potato routine?

The couch-potato routine sounded the most appealing. What the heck, he thought, reaching for the box of sugar-frosted flakes and a carton of milk. Since he'd surrendered to Cat's demands and started a fire, zonking out in front of a "Star Trek" rerun seemed like the very best way to spend a solitary Friday evening. Updating his excavation charts could wait.

The sound of a car driving up the road that led to the cottage stopped him in the act of carrying his bowl, spoon, box of cereal and milk carton over to the coffee table in front of the fire. Dumping his armload of goodies onto the kitchen counter, he went to the window and lifted a corner of the heavy, old-fashioned draperies to see who was coming. Other than Matt, who planned to spend the weekend hitting the nightlife in Boston, David didn't get too many visitors, partly because the cottage was situated four miles outside town on a bumpy gravel road, but mostly because he didn't encourage acquaintances to come calling. After two years working on low-budget treasure hunts off the coast of Central America, David had learned that the fewer people who knew the details of a diving project, the better.

It was dark outside, but he caught a glimpse of the car, a Mazda sports coupe, as it shot past the house, heading toward the sea. Almost immediately, he heard the screech of brakes and the sound of a car door slamming, and he realized that his un-expected visitor had ignored the parking spot of sedge and sage grass in front of the cottage and driven around to the lighthouse behind.

Good grief, he thought. Who in blazes would be dumb enough—or maybe drunk enough—to take their car after dark onto a rocky promontory with no guardrails and a six-foot drop-off into the ocean?

He hurried across to the door that connected his renovated keeper's cottage with the old nineteenth-century lighthouse. Once inside the lighthouse, he fumbled around, searching for the light switch and muttering a few more choice curses when he couldn't find it. He was still searching when he heard the scratch-ing at the rusted lock.

David froze, instantly on guard. He stopped his hunt for the light switch. Instead, he eased his way around the circular room, taking care to avoid the bumps in the plank floor and the glass-topped cases that housed Aunt Constance's prized collection of Powell family documents.

The key rattled in the lock. Who the heck could it be? Surely no experienced wrongdoer would be crazy enough to throttle their car up a gravel driveway, wrestle with a corroded door lock and still expect to make a surprise attack. It seemed unlikely, to say the least. On the other hand, this obviously wasn't a local visitor paying a friendly call. The ocean-side door into the light-house hadn't been opened since David had taken up residence in the cottage, and probably not for years before that. Everyone in Eternity knew that the only access to the lighthouse nowadays was through the cottage. And everyone in Eternity also knew that there wasn't any reason to visit the place unless you had an obsession for musty papers. Papers that recorded such fascinating details as how much the Powell family paid to have their roof repaired in 1877, or what arrangements had been made for serv-ing punch after William Powell's baptism in 1905.

David flattened himself against the rough plaster wall, wishing like hell he'd picked up the poker from the fireplace. Good Lord, if he'd been this careless during his years in Central America, he'd have been fish bait before he finished salvaging his first wreck. The familiar rural calm of Eternity created a false sense of security, but he should have known better than to let himself relax. Especially in view of what had happened during his dives this week. In this business he brought his own danger with him. Underwater salvage was a competitive affair, and his diving activities could attract the human variety of shark more swiftly than blood attracted the ocean-dwelling variety.

"Thank goodness. Finally! Stupid key."

David heard the muttered words at the same moment the door burst open, shuddering free after years of disuse. The violent bang of the door triggered every self-defense reflex in his body. Even as he launched his attack, a tiny part of his brain registered that the voice he'd heard was a woman's. An even smaller part of his brain registered that the voice had sounded hauntingly familiar. No matter. Adrenaline and instinct overrode everything else. He propelled himself at the intruder from behind, bringing her to the ground with a swift efficient hook around her legs, then straddling her and twisting her arms into a vicious full nelson before she had time to take more than a couple of steps into the darkened room.

The woman screamed once, then went utterly and rigidly still.

David recognized her perfume, the scent of her, before he recognized anything else. *Eve.*

He jumped off her limp body as if he'd been stung by a dozen Portuguese men-of-war. In fact, his body itched with the same warning sensation of poison about to enter his bloodstream.

She didn't move, not even when he released her, but he knew she was conscious with a certainty that went beyond reason. He drew a deep breath, wondering why he felt as though his heart had suddenly expanded to a point where his lungs were crushed. He labored to drag air through them as if he were fathoms deep under the sea.

"Hello, Eve." He finally managed to squeeze out the words. "Would you like to tell me what the hell you're doing in my lighthouse?"

Chapter Three

Her arms felt as if they'd been ripped from their sockets. Her knees had banged on the plank floor with a force that was more or less equivalent to a rookie pilot crash-landing his plane, and she was still shaking from the shock of being attacked. But she'd be damned if she was going to plead for sympathy or understanding from David. She'd played that game for too many months and she'd always lost. Clamping her mouth shut to prevent groans of pain, Eve pushed herself to her feet at precisely the same moment David switched on the lights.

Her stockings had holes in both knees and the jacket of her nifty little designer suit had a rip in the sleeve. The odds were good that she had dirt on the end of her nose. In other words, she looked exactly how every woman prays not to look when encountering her ex-husband for the first time after a bitter divorce.

David, naturally, looked like an advertisement for an upscale line of men's casual clothing. Whatever he'd been doing since their split up obviously agreed with him. In fact, he looked so damn tanned and lean and lithe—so damned *sexy*—she was about ready to kill him. The least she'd hoped for was that he'd have gone bald or grown a beer belly. Instead, he'd matured from thirty-three and handsome into nearly thirty-six and drop-dead gorgeous. She added failure to lose his hair and develop flab to her long list of David's marital sins.

Glaring at him, inwardly flustered because she hadn't expected to feel even the faintest tug of attraction after the painful death of their marriage, she dusted off her skirt, bared her teeth in a feral smile and said the first thing that popped into her head.

"Hello, David. Still having to wrestle your women to the floor before you can get their attention? Sometime you should try saying hi. Boringly conventional, I guess, but you'd be amazed how often it works."

He showed not the slightest reaction to her bitchiness. "What are you doing here?" he asked again, his voice so cool it sounded as if he was only mildly curious about the unexpected arrival of his ex-wife at a lighthouse in the back of nowhere.

Too many of their discussions had ended with David sounding icy and bored while Eve grew more and more tearfully distraught. She was determined not to humiliate herself by following that destructive pattern. Getting a firmer grip on her skittering emotions, she answered with an indifference she hoped matched his.

"I'm supposed to be staying here at the lighthouse for the next week while I tape a segment for 'Roving Report.'" She glanced around the cavernous room, which was empty except for two small display cases, a glass-fronted bookcase filled with leather-bound volumes and a row of metal filing cabinets. Dubiously she eyed the narrow staircase that spiraled around the bare brick and plaster walls. "Are the living quarters upstairs?"

"There's nothing upstairs except an observation tower and a dismantled warning light. The lighthouse was decommissioned right after World War II."

"I don't understand." Eve was puzzled enough that for a moment she forgot to be intimidated by David's presence and spoke naturally. "Your great-aunt Constance insisted I stay in the lighthouse. There aren't two lighthouses in Eternity, are there?"

"No," David said, his voice suddenly taking on a deeper tone. "There's just one."

Eve gave the room another doubtful inspection. "Constance surely couldn't have expected me to sleep here. I mean, there's no bed. No shower..."

"There's an attached keeper's cottage, equipped with all the modern conveniences. Or at least a 1950's version of them.'' David's voice was dry. ''Around here, people say the lighthouse when they really mean the cottage. I'm sure that's where she intended you to stay.''

''Fine.'' Eve felt a wave of relief. She was tired and sore after her fall and she didn't relish the prospect of driving back into town, nursing her bruises. ''In that case, I'll bring in my luggage and my bag of groceries.''

''You might want to reconsider that,'' David said.

''Why?''

''It so happens I'm already living in the cottage.''

''*What?*'' Eve yelled. She lowered her voice a couple of decibels and tried again. ''What do you mean, you already live in the cottage? Do your great-aunts know you're living there?''

''Of course they know.''

Eve decided her brains must have been scrambled by the fall, otherwise she wouldn't have felt so bewildered. ''Then why would they invite me to stay here for the next week?''

David's smile was entirely devoid of amusement. ''Because my aunts are elderly maiden ladies and incurable romantics. I'm sure Aunt Connie imagined that once reunited, we'd instantly fall into each other's arms and say how much we've missed each other since the divorce.''

The absurdity of that idea had the contrary effect of lightening Eve's mood. ''Well, I guess they were half-right,'' she said wryly. ''We did sort of fall into each other's arms.''

David, thank heaven, didn't misinterpret her remark. He actually flashed her a grin that reminded her a little of the old David she'd known years and years ago when they were in love. ''Yeah, I guess we did.'' He hesitated for a second, then added, ''I'm sorry about jumping you like that. The locals never use the back door and I expected a marauding beach bum at the very least.''

''Heaven help the beach bums.'' Eve rubbed her arms, which were beginning to throb.

''I'm sorry,'' David said again. He stretched out his hand and took half a step toward her before retreating. "It's not an adequate excuse, but if you remember, I tend to overreact once my adrenaline starts flowing."

The only occasions Eve could remember David overreacting were in the early months of their marriage, when he'd considered everything about her adorable and sexy. In those long-ago days if she flipped the tab on a can of soda he would say she looked so beautiful he needed to make love to her. If she lifted the weight of her hair off the back of her neck when she was cooking, he'd declare she was ravishing. The pot would be left to burn on the stove while he showed her just what he meant. She felt her cheeks grow hot at the memories, but she wasn't about to share them with David, so she stared at her feet and said nothing.

He waited politely. When she didn't say anything, he spoke again. "Do you think you need medical attention? I can call the doctor, or I could find you some Band-Aids and antiseptic in my first-aid supplies."

"No, thanks. I just need a hot bath, some dinner and a good night's sleep." Eve walked toward the door, feeling sad. It was obviously better that they be polite to each other, but their descent into careful courtesy highlighted the void between them, which once had been filled with love and the beginnings of a rich, warm affection.

"Could you point me in the direction of the local inn?" she asked, anxious to get away from reminders of their failure. *Her* failure. In the end, she'd been the one who'd cracked under the intolerable pressure of weighted silences, career conflicts and David's unexplained absences. *She* was the one who'd demanded a divorce. On her thirtieth birthday. Which David, of course, had forgotten to come home for.

She managed a tiny smile. "Fortunately this town isn't big enough for me to get badly lost. I even have a map in the car."

She sensed David's hesitation, although he wasn't looking in her direction.

"What's the matter?" she asked.

"It might not be quite as easy as you think," he said. "You'd better come into the cottage. Take five minutes to freshen up. Have a glass of something and some aspirin. I'll call the inn to make sure they have a room available before you leave. You don't want to drive for nothing."

Eve's stomach performed a quick nervous flip. "Surely you don't think the inn will be fully booked?"

"Eternity is a wedding town," David said. "That means every weekend literally dozens of people arrive to watch their nearest and dearest tie the knot in the chapel. Midweek isn't so bad, but the Haven Inn runs close to capacity every weekend, even at this time of year, which is sort of off-season for weddings."

"Then I guess you're right. It would be smart to call first, but I'm sure they'll have space for me." Eve didn't want to consider the alternative. "My camera crew had no problems making reservations for next week," she said, trying to reassure herself.

"That's for next week and they called ahead. Today's Friday, the start of the weekend. We'd better check."

Eve wasn't going to let him see that the prospect of walking with him into his home made her panic almost to the point of paralysis. She couldn't understand why this chance meeting was having such a strong physical impact on her. After all, her parents insisted on keeping in touch with David, and she'd known he was living somewhere near Eternity. Long before she left her office in Manhattan, she'd come to terms with the likelihood of running into him. Why else had she consumed a roll of antacids between taking off from La Guardia and arriving here?

True, she'd spent much of the past week cursing Art Sonderheim for sending her into her ex-husband's territory, but—between curses—she'd indulged in a few daydreams about a reconciliation. A civilized reconciliation that would enable her to get on with her life, and maybe even take the plunge and make a meaningful commitment to Gordon. She'd planned agreeable scenarios where she invited David to a candlelit dinner and they managed a friendly courteous burial of the ugly skeleton of their marriage.

Of course, in her daydreams, they'd always met in a restaurant, surrounded by other people, and Eve had always looked stunning in her most fetching black evening suit. David, by contrast, had looked paunchy and regretful for all he'd lost. Sadly, the reality of their encounter tonight hadn't come close to her fantasy. Still, the basic fact was that she'd anticipated a meeting with her ex-husband—why else had she driven along the town's main street with her eyes darting from side to side like a lizard?—and there was no reason to go into a mental tailspin just because she wasn't wearing an elegant suit and David wasn't potbellied.

"I'd better get my overnight bag if I'm coming in," she said, doing a credible job of sounding bright and cheerful although she couldn't manage to meet David's eyes. "I could probably use a change of outfit before I run into any townsfolk."

"I'll fetch your luggage," David said.

"That's all right. There's no need—"

His mouth tightened with impatience. "For goodness' sake, Eve, let me show you some normal courtesy. The floor's hard, and I used my full weight against you. I'm feeling guilty as hell. For once in your life, can't you just admit that you're feeling bruised and sore without acting as if you've lost a major battle in some undeclared war with me?"

She stared at him as if he were speaking a foreign language of which she understood no more than the occasional word. Her offer to bring in her own luggage had been automatic, a meaningless civility. Why in the world was he glaring as if she'd attacked his manhood, for heaven's sake?

"Feel free to play porter," she said, aware she sounded ungracious, but too dumbfounded to moderate her tone of voice. "I need the small gray overnighter, as well as the garment bag, if it's not too much trouble."

What battle? she wanted to ask him. What undeclared war? She didn't ask, of course. Since they were no longer married, there wasn't any point in probing minor mysteries, minor failures of communication. God knows, she had taken long enough to form scar tissue over the emotional wounds of their marriage. She didn't need to start slicing the scars open now, when she was finally in charge of her life again.

Their divorce hadn't brought the immediate surcease of pain she'd hoped for, and she'd gone into therapy for several months. Under the sympathetic but firm direction of her therapist, she'd eventually managed to put her relationship with David into proper perspective. The sex had been terrific, but they'd had nothing to back up the physical attraction. Eventually David's driving ambition and her own ambivalence about their hectic yuppie life-style had messed up the sex to the point that they'd been left with nothing. Great sex, followed by failed sex, followed by aching emptiness. A sad all-too-common requiem for a modern marriage.

David came back into the lighthouse carrying her luggage. He gestured to indicate she precede him into the cottage. Despite the fact that they were in New England and the cottage was at least a hundred years old, Eve hadn't expected to be greeted by such a homey, snug sort of room. The low-beamed ceiling created a sense of intimacy, enhanced by the forest green draperies, drawn to shut out the darkness. Thick flower-patterned rugs covered most of the maple-wood floor, which was stained an unfashionable but cozy rust color. A beige sofa, piled high with needlepoint cushions, sat solidly in the center of the room, and the fireplace was flanked by two shabby wing chairs, slipcovered in a chintz fabric that might once have matched the bright flowers of the carpet but was now faded into dusky shades of faded rose and moss green. A roaring fire blazed in the old-fashioned brick fireplace, and a black cat with four neat white paws was washing itself on the rag rug in front of it.

"You have a cat!" Eve exclaimed. During their marriage, David's adamant opposition to the idea of acquiring a pet had merely been a forerunner to his even more adamant opposition to the idea of having children.

"No, I don't," David said stiffly.

Eve blinked, but the cat didn't disappear. It yawned, subjecting her to an intense amber-eyed scrutiny. Then, not finding her worthy of further acknowledgment, it stretched itself out full-length on the rug, blissfully exposing its underbelly to the blaze.

"The cat seems to think you have a cat," Eve suggested, bending down and stroking its stomach. It purred with exaggerated joy, lifting a foreleg so that she would have more fur to stroke.

David shrugged. "He's a stray. Turned up on my doorstep and wouldn't go away. I'm planning to take him to the pound as soon as I can find the time."

The cat certainly didn't behave as if he lived in hourly expectation of being evicted to the gas chambers. In fact, he had the snooty air of an animal that knows he's lord of all he surveys. What's more, the rag rug looked out of place in the living room, as if it had been brought in from somewhere else and placed there solely for the cat's convenience. Eve shot a covert glance at David, who was flipping through a phone book, ostentatiously ignoring both her and the cat. Eve smothered a grin and decided not to press the issue.

"Is there a bathroom on this floor?" she said, straightening from her stomach-rubbing duties. "I could certainly use a mirror and some hot water."

"Through the kitchen, first door on your right. It's small but adequate. I'll call the inn while you wash up."

"Thanks. I appreciate your making the call for me." It seemed they were back to scrupulous courtesy. Eve sighed. She was too tired for this brutal politeness, and her stomach was burning again. Astonishingly, despite the burn, she realized she was hungry. It had been weeks since she could remember experiencing genuine hunger as opposed to a resigned feeling she probably ought to eat. She thought of her bag of groceries sitting uselessly in the trunk of her car and stifled another sigh. It must be the sea air giving her an appetite, she decided. The pleasantly bracing tang of salt marsh had been in her nostrils ever since she'd arrived in Eternity.

The bathroom was not only small but also lit by a single dim bulb, badly positioned. However, the inadequate lighting was probably a blessing, all things considered. What Eve could see of herself in the tiny mirror over the pedestal sink didn't encourage a desire for floodlights. Her nifty designer suit appeared seriously ruined. As for her fear of having dirt on the end of her nose, she'd underestimated the problem. She didn't have one spot, she had three: one on each cheek and a long streak of dirt all the way across her forehead. As for her hair, which she'd had the studio hairdresser fix in a sophisticated coil before she'd left New York, the style could now best be described as four protruding hairpins and a straggle of untidy blond fuzz.

She combed her hair and tied it back with a thong she used when she was working out; not glamorous, but tidy. She washed the dirt off her face, then repaired the damage to her makeup as best she could. Finally she changed into wool slacks and a plain cashmere sweater and emerged from the bathroom hoping she looked smart enough to impress David with how well she'd weathered their separation. This was probably the last time they would ever be together, and she wanted to leave him with a more appealing image than torn clothes, disheveled hair and a dirty face.

She realized now that her idea—her fantasy—of a quiet friendly dinner had been ridiculous. If she and David were capable of eating friendly dinners together, they wouldn't have ended up in the divorce court. Her friends kept telling her she needed to open up and express her deepest emotions, or she'd find herself becoming a shriveled stick of a woman, incapable of handling intimacy. Heck, she *already* couldn't handle intimacy, she thought ruefully. Why else would she have screwed up her marriage to David and backed away from Gordon the moment he pressed her for a real commitment?

When she returned to the living room, David was standing in front of the fire waiting for her. One look at his face was enough to warn her that the news from the inn wasn't good. "No luck?" she asked.

He shook his head. "The inn's fully booked all weekend."

Her stomach was not only burning, it was taking a nosedive straight to her feet. "What about a motel?" she said. "Isn't there a motel? Or a guesthouse?"

"The two bed-and-breakfast places are full. So is the motel at the highway exit. There are rooms available at the Colonial Inn in Ipswich, which is a very pleasant place to stay, but it's twenty miles from here."

"Then I guess I'd better start driving." She hadn't meant to sound so darn sorry for herself, but she was bone weary, and at this precise moment a twenty-mile drive to Ipswich sounded like a journey across the Siberian tundra by open dogsled.

She was halfway to the door before David spoke. "You could stay here," he said.

She swung around. "Here?" she said. "With you?"

"There's a spare bedroom," he replied tightly. "I was offering sleeping space, not stud services."

She hadn't meant to sound like a Victorian maiden who feared being ravished. Lord knows, David hadn't made love to her for weeks before the divorce; she had no fear he was going to pounce on her tonight.

"It never occurred to me you were offering anything more than a place to sleep," she said. "I'm just surprised you're willing to have me intrude on your privacy."

"It's no big deal. Besides, it's getting late and it's the least I owe you after Aunt Connie messed up your arrangements like this. I'd call her and tell her exactly what I think of her schemes, except I want to cool off a bit first. My mother taught me I wasn't allowed to yell at little old ladies."

He sounded as if having her stay the night was about as pleasant as opening his home and hearth to a rabid rodent. Eve, who until that moment had had every intention of leaving for Ipswich, perversely decided to stay put. "Frankly, I'm exhausted," she said, "not to mention hungry. If you don't mind, I'm going to take you up on your offer, at least for tonight."

David's face might have been carved out of marble. "I'll be delighted to have you."

"Try to say that without looking as if someone is pushing needles under your fingernails," Eve snapped.

He visibly cut off an angry retort and turned to throw another log onto the fire. "Do you need anything else from your car?" he asked, his voice scratchy with the effort of control.

She cheered up a bit at the discovery he wasn't quite as unruffled as she'd thought. "I have some groceries in the trunk. Basic supplies. Stuff for dinner, that kind of thing."

He straightened, brushing his hands against the seat of his jeans. She looked away. She was about a decade too old to drool over a man's thigh muscles.

"If you'll give me your keys," he said, "I'll fetch the groceries and drive your car around to the front of the cottage. It's not a good idea to leave it with one wheel dangling over a cliff."

She took the keys out of her pocket and handed them over, taking care not to touch his fingers. In the interest of harmony, she ignored his reference to how she'd parked the car. "Could you tell me where the spare bedroom is?" she said. "I'll take my suitcase upstairs and unpack."

"The room on the left," he said. "The door's open, I expect. You'll see an old-fashioned brass bed with a blue spread. The door on the right leads to my bedroom, and the room straight ahead at the top of the stairs is the bathroom, if you want to take a shower. You'll find clean towels under the sink."

The spare bedroom was small, but comfortable, with a full-size bed and plenty of drawer space. The bathroom was white tiled and strictly functional. But by the time she'd taken a long hot shower and hung up her clothes in the cramped closet, Eve's mood had improved dramatically. A CD was playing flute music as she came downstairs, soft and sweetly sad. Handel or Hayden, she couldn't tell which. David had taught her to appreciate classical music, but she was still pretty much of an amateur listener who liked simple pieces of the sort you could hum along to. When they were first married, David had found her humming cute. By the end of their marriage, he wouldn't even put a CD on when she was in the apartment for fear she would desecrate his listening pleasure by breaking into song.

Perhaps the CD playing now was a gesture of reconciliation on his part. Or maybe he'd forgotten how much her musical ignorance irritated him. Whatever his motive, Eve resolved to avoid the temptation to sing along with the flutist. With a little care, she and David would get through the evening without any more embarrassing tension. They owed each other the dignity of behaving like mature adults.

She found him busy in the kitchen, cooking. "I thought you might be hungry," he said. He'd obviously been making resolutions similar to hers. His voice sounded almost normal and he nearly managed to meet her gaze without scowling.

"I'm starving!" she said, wincing at her own false heartiness.

"Good. I cooked the fish I found in your grocery bag and made a salad. Genuine Roquefort dressing, your favorite." He stopped abruptly, clearly not having intended to indulge in reminiscences. Forcing a smile, he waved a foil-wrapped package in her direction. "I even got some garlic bread out of the freezer. I'll heat it if you're ready."

"Great. Terrific. I'm more than ready." Her mouth was fixed into the sort of smile she gave on television when a major disaster was occurring off camera and the audience wasn't supposed to notice.

David broke an awkward little pause. "Well, ten minutes to heat this, and then we can eat." He put the bread into the oven and opened the fridge, pulling out a bottle of beer. "Want one?" he asked.

She hadn't drunk beer since the day her marriage ended, partly because beer was too high in calories, but chiefly because special-reserve California chardonnay and imported white burgundy were the beverages of choice for her crowd. But since David had already dipped the fillets of sole in batter and fried them, this didn't seem to be the moment to worry about a few extra calories.

"Thanks," she said. "A beer would be great."

"Sit by the fire," he suggested, twisting off the cap and handing her the chilled bottle. "We'll have to eat in the kitchen. You may have noticed there isn't a dining room."

"The kitchen's fine by me." If they bent any further backward to be accommodating, Eve thought wryly, they'd both fall flat on their rear ends. As she wandered back to the fire she passed a desk holding a computer and saw his diving gear. "Are you diving again?" she asked. "Isn't it a bit late in the year to dive in this part of the country?"

"We're right on the edge of storm season, but it's been a mild fall. There hasn't been a single frost so far this month, and no winds worth bothering about."

"Hasn't there? I've been traveling so much I haven't really noticed the weather. Although my flights have been surprisingly on time."

"Are you enjoying the travel?" he asked with such careful neutrality that she immediately remembered how often they'd argued about the demands of her hectic travel schedule. In fact, one of his prime reasons for not wanting a pet had been the fact that she traveled so much. Not an unjustifiable reason, now that she came to think of it.

"Work's been interesting lately," she said, then quickly changed the subject. "So where are you diving? You didn't say."

She noticed a tiny pause before he answered. "Matt and I have been fooling around along the coast. Here and there. Neither of us has done all that much cold-water diving and it's an interesting experience. More plant life, more fish, but a lot less colorful."

"Matt is here in Eternity?" Eve asked. "Is he living here at the cottage, too?"

"No, at the motel. But he's in Boston at the moment." David chuckled. "He's showing his latest girlfriend the nightlife."

She smiled back. "Some things never change. Have you met the new woman?"

"Not yet. Although she passed the thirty-day test a couple of weeks ago."

"Wow! And this time Matt's sure it's the real thing, right?"

"Right." They exchanged grins. Matt's women changed so frequently she and David had devised a rule for him: Don't introduce your latest love of a lifetime to us until you've been dating her for at least thirty days.

Eve looked away, tipping the bottle and taking a swallow of icy beer. With an ex-husband, it seemed it was sometimes hard to avoid falling into the trap of reminiscing. "I'd like to see Matt again," she said. "He's a good guy."

As soon as she spoke the words, she wondered if they were true. Did she really want to see Matt again? She'd liked him a lot and enjoyed his happy-go-lucky company, but her memories of him were inextricably tied up with her marriage, which meant they were all laced with regret.

She and David had married on the spur-of-the-moment, with Matt and his woman-of-the-week as their only witnesses. What had his girlfriend been called? Lynn? Linda? Laura? How depressing that she couldn't remember, that she'd been so self-absorbed on her wedding day that Matt and his companion had been little more than a blurred backdrop to her feelings for David.

She remembered sharing a bottle of champagne with Matt and Lynn/Linda/Laura, then she and David had flown off to Bermuda for a heady weekend honeymoon, three days crammed with laughter, sun and sex. Neither of them had bothered to call their families until their marriage was a couple of weeks old. They were so wrapped up in each other that even their parents and brothers and sisters had seemed to fade into unreality.

Looking back, Eve couldn't understand how she and David could have ignored the feelings of so many people who loved them. It was as if they'd floated through the early days of their relationship in a permanent state of intoxication, drunk on lust. She could still remember the nerve-tingling excitement that swept her the first moment she'd seen David. She could still *feel* the anguish of the final weeks of their marriage when nerve-tingling attraction had turned into vicious heart-tearing pain.

"Bread's hot. Dinner's ready," David said.

Eve carried her beer into the kitchen, followed by the cat, who was obviously so well fed that food had to be served on the table before he deigned to show any interest. David slipped him a saucer of tidbits and tried to pretend he hadn't.

"Everything looks great," Eve said sincerely. Fried fish and garlic bread dripping in butter hadn't been exactly what she planned to eat tonight, but her stomach reacted to the prospect of so much hazardous cholesterol with a rumble of pleased anticipation.

"Thanks." David pulled out her chair and sat on the opposite side of the small wooden table. He offered her the bowl of salad. "So what exactly are you doing here in Eternity? You said you were filming a segment for 'Roving Report,' but I can't imagine what about."

"I'm doing a story on the successful wedding cooperative that the town's developed," she said. "And of course I want to include the legend of the Eternity chapel."

He pulled a face at her choice of subject matter, but at least he didn't leap to the conclusion that she was planning to trick the townspeople and produce a scathing exposé. "Sounds like a pretty tame story," he said. "Is it likely to interest your viewing audience? They're used to meatier reports from you. As far as I know, there isn't even much disagreement among the co-op members. They're all working in perfect harmony."

She felt a little spark of pleasure that he'd obviously watched her program. "Meaty" was the word she'd have used herself to describe her work. "I think there's plenty to interest my audience in the story," she said, warming to the project as she outlined it for him. "There are several fascinating stories to develop here. For starters, unlike most small towns close to a big city, Eternity hasn't become just a bedroom community. It's managed to pull all its merchants together into a successful cooperative that both insures the town's prosperity and helps to preserve its unique identity. In the present economic climate, that's a story in itself. An amazing story, in fact.''

"True, but how are you going to handle the ridiculous legend my family's built up around their chapel?'' David asked. "If you expose it for the myth it is, you'll ruin the town whether you intend to or not.''

"Why do you assume the legend's ridiculous?''

He put down his fork, gazing at her in genuine surprise. "Because it is. Because half a brain—a quarter of a brain—tells you that getting married in the Eternity chapel can't possibly guarantee a marriage that lasts a lifetime.''

"No, but perhaps couples planning to marry there think things through a little more carefully than people who just rush off to the nearest town hall or marriage mill. That way, they're less likely to make a terrible mistake.''

"Are you talking about us?'' David asked.

"No, of course not,'' she said quickly. Too quickly. "I'm just trying to explain the statistics that form the backbone of the Eternity legend. My initial research shows that they're truly amazing, totally off the chart in comparison to national averages. People who marry in the Eternity chapel just don't seem to get divorced.''

He shrugged. "So what are you going to do? Film some naive young couple getting set to tie the knot? And end the program with them riding off into the sunset in a cloud of white lace and promises?''

"Not quite.'' She smiled, remembering Louis Bertrand and Patience Powell. The picture of them surreptitiously holding hands on the sofa brought a warm glow to a corner of her heart. "Give me credit for more originality than that. I'm planning to film a very special wedding.''

David broke off a chunk of bread. "Whose?'' he asked. "A local couple?''

She nodded and her smile widened. "I'd give you three guesses, but there's no point because I know you'd lose.''

"Okay. Tell me.''

"Your great-aunt Patience is going to marry Louis Bertrand—"

David dropped his fork. "What!"

"—and they've agreed to let me film the preparations and the actual ceremony, as well."

"You've got to be kidding!" David was silenced by shock and then he chuckled. "So the old rogue talked her into it at last." He leaned back in his chair, obviously delighted. "I wonder if Louis has promised to reform, or if Patience has decided to kick over the traces and live dangerously after seventy years of Yankee decorum?"

"I suspect it's a bit of both. I met them just now when I went to pick up the key from your aunt, and Louis was obviously on his best behavior. On the other hand, I saw a definite sparkle in your aunt's eyes." Eve took another bite of fish and realized she'd eaten the entire piece and her stomach hadn't emitted even a twinge of protest. "Dinner's really good, by the way. You always cooked better than I did."

"Glad you like it." A silence fell. David closed both hands around his beer. A log burned through in a shower of sparks and he cleared his throat. "What happened to us, Eve? We were so happy, and then we were so damned miserable. What the hell happened?"

He spoke quietly, a hint of pain in his voice. Eve found she couldn't look away from his hands, clenched around the neck of the beer bottle. This was it, she thought. The chance she'd been looking for to lay the ghosts of her marriage to rest. "We married for the wrong reasons," she said finally.

"For sex," he said. She didn't disagree, and he scooped bread crumbs into a pile beside his plate. "Is that really all there was between us, Eve?"

"I don't know," she said slowly, wanting to give him the courtesy of an honest answer. "We were both workaholics, and when our careers got in the way, the whole structure of our marriage crumbled because we had nothing solid to build on." Strangely enough, the heady sensation of joy she'd felt when she'd first met David had seemed solid, real, capable of withstanding anything. Obviously that had been a dangerous illusion.

Silence fell again, stretching out between them. "Well, at least the sex was fantastic," David said.

He spoke lightly, and Eve understood he was trying to ease the tension that suddenly lay thick around the dinner table. Unfortunately his tactic didn't work. The sex *had* been fantastic. Mind-blowingly fantastic. Her gaze locked with his and she saw heat darken the tan along his cheekbones. She knew what he was remembering, because she was remembering much the same thing. She closed her eyes, but that simply brought the image of their entwined naked bodies into sharper perspective. She quickly opened her eyes again. David hadn't moved, but there was a sheen of sweat on his forehead.

Her stomach felt hollow, her mouth dry. This was crazy! She reached for her beer, but her movements were jerky and she fumbled, sending the bottle flying. She and David both grabbed for the same paper napkin. Their fingers touched. They both dropped the napkin and jumped up from their chairs as if the seats were on fire.

"I'll get a paper towel," Eve said, rounding the table.

David moved at precisely the same moment. They bumped into each other and sprang apart as violently as if they'd poked each other with electric prods. Eve didn't know whether to laugh or to cry, so she stood paralyzed, afraid to move in case she touched David again.

He gave a disgusted grunt and reached for her hands, taking hold of both of them at once. "This is insane," he said, trying to smile, although his breathing wasn't quite steady. "We're behaving like certified morons. We can hold each other's hands without igniting, for God's sake."

Speak for yourself, Eve thought dazedly. If she wasn't igniting, she was coming pretty darn close. With great care, she slid her hands out of his clasp and pushed them into the pockets of her pants, where he couldn't see them shaking. She drew a deep breath and tried for a casual smile. She failed.

"I'll get the paper towels," she repeated. "Why don't you finish the rest of your dinner?"

"Fine." David was on the point of sitting down again when the doorbell rang. Eve realized that the fact neither of them had heard the sound of a car approaching was a measure of how caught up they'd been in their own ludicrous drama. She also realized that the flute music had stopped. Well, at least she'd managed to survive the entire CD without bursting into song. At this point, she should be grateful for small mercies.

David opened the door. "Matt!" he exclaimed. "What's up? I thought you were going to check out the Boston nightlife with your new girlfriend."

Matt didn't come in, but Eve could hear him plainly through the open door. "Amy got called away just as we were leaving. One of her co-workers is involved in some messy family situation. So I went back to the motel. Dave, someone broke into my room. The lock was busted, and the charts are gone."

David swore with creative fluency. "What about the site drawings? Photos?"

"Gone. All of them. We have your copies of course, but someone's on to us, Dave, and now they have everything they need to clean out the site once they find the wreck."

"Hell," David said. As an afterthought he added, "You'd better come in."

Chapter Four

Matt's news was troublesome to say the least, but David's overwhelming sensation was relief. Relief that Matt had arrived before David made any more of a horse's ass out of himself than he already had. Relief that Matt had arrived before Eve realized her ex-husband was suffering from major brain dysfunction, brought on by an acute attack of lust. Why did he feel an overwhelming urge to take his ex-wife to bed when he didn't even like her? When he knew she'd cut him off at the knees the first chance she got? He'd watched Eve in action often enough to be free of illusions; she was lethal when she chose to wield the knife.

"Come in," he said again to Matt, holding the door wide. He tried to find some casual way to mention Eve's presence but couldn't, so he didn't say anything. The old pattern of his marriage reasserting itself with a vengeance, he thought sardonically. Don't know what to say, so say nothing and look like a jerk.

Matt breezed into the cottage in his standard dressed-to-seduce outfit of black jeans, black oversize sweater and Obsession men's cologne. From the skintight fit of his jeans, it looked as if he'd solved the dilemma of whether to wear briefs or boxers by wearing neither.

Matt did an exaggerated double take when he saw Eve. "My God, Evie, is that really you? You're looking wonderful, babe. Simply spectacular. Love that hairstyle, babe. The casual look suits you." He swept her into a hug that David thought went on far too long. Eve, however, gave every indication of enjoying it.

She finally pulled away and laughed up at Matt, her eyes sparkling with some of their old teasing fire. "Hey, Matt, good to see you. You're looking terrific, too, and don't call me 'babe' or I'll report you to the thought police."

"Whatever you say, babe." He grinned at her, then thumped David on the back. "A great buddy you turned out to be. How come you didn't breathe a word about Evie spending the weekend with you?"

David felt stiffer than a steel brace in contrast to Matt's easygoing camaraderie. "Eve's here on business. Her visit was unexpected...."

Matt slanted a hot look in Eve's direction, then smirked at David. "Hope I didn't interrupt anything exciting. If I'd known what was going down between you two, I'd have waited until tomorrow morning to come calling."

"Nothing is going on between me and Eve," David said tightly. "I told you, she's here on business."

"Sure, a real credible story." Matt waggled his eyebrows in the direction of the kitchen, where the remains of their cozy dinner for two were plainly visible.

David was finally smart enough to shut up. He'd forgotten that his friend's attitude toward women lurked somewhere between a hypocritical fifties' condescension and a predatory eighties' conviction that sex was the only reason men and women got together. Eve, despite her feminist views, never seemed offended by Matt's chauvinism and tonight was no exception. She merely rolled her eyes, told Matt his mind would be like a sewer except it was too empty and offered him a beer.

David couldn't understand her indifference. He knew that if he'd given her a leer like Matt's she'd have frozen him with a glance. Hell, she'd have stormed out of the cottage, lashing him with some slogan about his lack of respect for the dignity of womanhood. But Matt acted like a slimeball and she offered him a beer. Go figure, David thought grumpily. He'd never understand her.

"Come and sit by the fire," Eve said to Matt, handing him a

frosty bottle of Coors. "Tell us what happened. What do the cops say about the break-in?"

Matt shrugged. "Nothing much. Nobody was hurt and nothing was stolen that's likely to turn up in a pawnshop or a drug deal. Even in a placid backwater like Eternity, the police don't have time to waste on that sort of penny-ante stuff. If the thieves hadn't smashed the door when they were forcing the lock, I wouldn't have bothered to report the break-in, but Joe insisted. He needs an official report, or his insurance won't cover the cost of repairs."

"Where are you going to sleep tonight?" David asked. "I know the motel's full. You're welcome to stay here if you'd like."

"Thanks, but Joe's offered me the spare room in his apartment, and we've already moved some of my things over there."

"Who's Joe?" Eve asked.

"The motel manager. I have an efficiency suite at the motel, two rooms and a bath. That way David and I don't have to spend all night together, as well as all day. It's worked out pretty well so far."

"At least nobody got hurt tonight," Eve said. "Thank goodness you didn't arrive back at the motel while the burglar was still working your place over."

"Yeah, I guess." Matt sounded unconvinced. "Except it would have been great if I could have gotten a glimpse of the guy." Almost to himself he muttered, "Dammit, I thought we'd kept a low enough profile to avoid this." He took a swig of beer and turned back to David. "Whoever broke in didn't pick my place at random, you can count on that. He singled me out, and he was looking for something specific."

David grunted, not disagreeing. "How can you be sure?" he asked, more for confirmation of his own opinion than anything else.

Matt counted off on his fingers. "First off, this guy was no ordinary thief. He didn't touch my stereo equipment or the TV or a bunch of other stuff that would have fetched easy cash from the local fence. Second, the charts were in plain view, right on the table, so they weren't grabbed by mistake, along with something more valuable. Third, any thief who knew enough to take the excavation charts would also know they're useless without another chart to pinpoint surface locations, and this guy obviously went looking for the necessary backup materials. He damn near tore the place apart searching for the rest of what he needed.''

''Do you mean that literally?'' David asked. ''Did he slash the mattress, rip your clothes? What about your diving equipment?''

''Caleb took it to the dive shop for the weekend, thank God. And no, nothing was literally torn. It looked like the thief worked in a big hurry. He emptied drawers, stripped the bed, tossed my clothes out of the closet, but he didn't actually destroy very much. Guess I should count my blessings.''

''Damn!'' David threw another log onto the fire and watched it catch in a hot red flare. He knew Eve was listening to their exchange with avid interest, but there seemed no point in warning Matt to watch what he said. In the first place, irrational as it might have seemed in view of her profession and their screwed-up relationship, he trusted her not to repeat what she heard. In the second place, it seemed that his and Matt's cover had already been blown.

''Damn!'' he repeated. ''I worked so hard to spread the story that we're here on extended vacation, doing a little fishing.''

Matt snorted. ''That may wash with the locals, but we both know it wouldn't deceive a professional salvage operator for five minutes. If word is out in the trade that we've been up here in Eternity since June, the pros are going to assume we've found a hot site.''

''It's my hometown,'' David said without much conviction. ''I planted a couple of rumors to the effect that I was having a premature midlife crisis....''

''Yeah, well, I guess somebody wondered if I was having a midlife crisis, too. And once the pros start asking why we're having our nervous breakdowns together, any diver with residual brain function is going to leap straight to the right answer. That we're fit as fiddles and we've found a promising wreck somewhere close to the town of Eternity.''

"So why do you think the burglar risked letting us know he's on to us?" David asked. "Seems to me this was a high-risk operation. Whoever broke into your room has put us on guard and gained very little advantage for himself.''

"I know," Matt agreed. "There's only one thing I can come up with that makes any sense. Somehow, he heard about the sovereigns we've already found. Maybe he thought we'd already cleaned out the wreck.''

David's head jerked up. "He must know we wouldn't be stupid enough to keep thousands of gold coins in a motel room. That's dumber than expecting us to keep a map with a giant X marking the spot where he can find the treasure.''

Matt raised his shoulders in a shrug. "He must have anticipated finding *something* in my rooms he could dispose of for big bucks. Otherwise you're right. He wouldn't have risked tipping us off to the fact we're being watched.''

David let out a sigh. He picked up Cat and smoothed the fur along his spine, soothed by the hoarse rumble of Cat's purring. "Only three people knew we'd found those sovereigns," he said, voice clipped. "You, me—and Caleb.''

Matt winced as he chugged the last of his beer. "Dammit, Dave, it doesn't make any sense for Caleb to sell us out.''

"Like hell it makes sense, and you know it.''

Matt shook his head. "No, dammit—''

"You like Caleb—we both like Caleb—and you want me to reassure you, tell you you're crazy to suspect him even for a moment. But I can't tell you that." David scowled unseeingly at Cat. "This wreck is in much better shape than we had any right to expect. If it turns out to be carrying everything we anticipate, we're talking huge sums of money. Megabucks. Enough money to tempt almost anyone.''

"Almost anyone, but not Caleb." Matt rolled his empty beer

bottle between his hands. "It's not just that I've worked with Caleb before and he's always been as honest as the day is long. The fact is he doesn't care about shipwrecks and buried gold and megabucks in profit. Darn it, Dave, you know as well as I do that Caleb wouldn't care if we'd found the lost treasures of Atlantis and El Dorado combined—not unless it turned out that Atlantis had an underwater version of a Harley."

"He sure gives that impression," David said. "But think of the terrific bike he could buy with those golden sovereigns we already brought up from the *Free Enterprise*."

"We've promised him a share of the treasure when it's raised. Why risk a big payoff a few weeks from now—a legitimate payoff—for the sake of a few illegal golden coins today?"

"Because those *few* stolen coins represent several thousand of today's dollars, and I've seen the need for money do terrible things to people." David was seized by a bleak memory of Ned Nichols, waving a gun, sweaty with fear and despair. "Maybe Caleb has an urgent need for cash, right now, without delay. We don't know much about his personal life."

"What's to know? He's in love with his bike...."

"And maybe his ex-wife is tired of the competition."

Eve bit her lip, forcing herself to stay silent. Trust David to assume that if Caleb had gone off the rails, his ex-wife must be responsible.

"I don't think Caleb's ever been married," Matt said.

"But we don't know for sure," David pointed out. "On Monday, I'm going to make a few discreet inquiries into his financial situation. He could have a string of ex-wives and be supporting ten kids through college for all we know."

"Okay." Matt was clearly reluctant to suspect a friend. On the other hand, he knew they couldn't afford to ignore the risk that their operation was being betrayed from within. "Jeez, I hate this aspect of the business, suspecting everyone who doesn't come with an FBI certificate of purity."

David smiled grimly. "Those are the first guys I'd suspect."

"You ex-stockbrokers have real nasty minds." Matt yawned.

"Let me know if you need any help with your research into Caleb's background."

"Thanks," David said. "Unfortunately, as you just pointed out, during my stockbrokering days I acquired lots of experience in running character checks and digging up financial dirt. I can probably find out most of what I need by computer."

The references to his old life brought back many memories, most of them painful. He glanced at Eve, who was smart enough to be sitting still as a mouse and more silent than a sleeping snake. Tough luck for her that he could never forget her presence even for a minute. He leaned forward in his chair and stared into her incredibly gorgeous sapphire blue eyes. He willed himself to concentrate on the matter at hand, which was a fortune waiting to be excavated from the wreck of the *Free Enterprise* and Caleb's possible betrayal. The way her eyes used to become a dark smoky blue when they made love was entirely irrelevant to their present situation.

"Eve," he said softly, "your nasty little thoughts are written all over your face."

"I can't imagine what you—"

"Yes, you can. You can imagine perfectly what I mean. I'm talking about the fact that you're an investigative reporter with a reputation for being far too nosy, and Matt and I are a couple of unfriendly guys who like to dive without any interested observers watching the flow of our air bubbles. We especially don't like observers from the media."

Eve was much too clever to continue pretending a lack of interest. "Since I'm an investigative reporter, maybe you should consider letting me help investigate what's going on here. Seems to me, you and Matt are running into some potentially serious trouble."

"Thank you, but Matt and I are accustomed to trouble, and we can manage our investigations without any help from a television journalist."

Her cheeks flushed an enchanting sexy pink. "You needn't

sound so damned condescending. I have ten years of experience in ferreting out information people would rather conceal—"

"You're not listening to me, Eve." David knew how viciously competitive deep-sea treasure hunting could be, and he was sweating at the prospect of Eve's getting caught up in the danger. He and Matt were operating legally, as agents for Lloyds of London, but there were plenty of hunters who considered rules and laws about deep-sea treasure as just so many irrelevant print-outs in a boring government handbook.

He cupped Eve's face in his hands and forced her to look at him. "If you whisper so much as a single word of what has been discussed here tonight, even to your own mother, I will person-ally take you down to the wreck site and leave you to find your way back up to the surface. Alone. In the dark."

He was lying, of course, but it was disconcerting to see that Eve seemed to believe him. She blanched. She'd parachuted from planes, gone hang gliding, climbed mountains that would have challenged a goat and even explored underground caverns, but for some reason, despite hours of instruction, she was still terrified by the idea of donning flippers and a face mask, then strapping a tank of air to her back so that she could swim un-derwater.

"I understand that you need to keep your dive site confiden-tial," she said stiffly.

"Not just the site," David said. "Everything about it. The name of the ship. What we're looking for. What we've found so far."

"As you know quite well, I have no idea what the pair of you are looking for or what you've found. Except that this is obvi-ously a high-stakes deal."

David felt Matt staring at the two of them with amused inter-est. Obviously the tension between himself and Eve had finally become sharp enough to pierce even Matt's alligator-thick hide.

Matt stretched and gave them a cheerful smile. "I guess this reunion between you two is kind of a recent thing. Some of the kinks still waiting to be worked out, huh?"

"It's not exactly a reunion," David said. "Leave it, Matt."
Now that was a ringing clarification of the situation, he told
himself. He sneaked a glance at Eve. She was very busy unraveling a thread from the cuff of her three-hundred-dollar sweater.
He was a bit surprised she didn't leap in and announce that,
except for a chapter of accidents, she wouldn't be staying at the
cottage and probably wouldn't be anywhere within a hundred-
mile radius of her despised ex-husband. For some reason, she
remained silent.

"Sure, sure," Matt said, still grinning with infuriating smug-
ness. "Hey, you know me. The soul of tact in matters of the
heart."

Eve perked up at that. "Right," she said. "Matt Packard and
Godzilla—the two people I turn to when I feel the need for real
sensitivity."

Chuckling, Matt got to his feet. "It's good to have you back,
Eve, for however long. Now I'm going to head for home before
you decide to hand me a cloth and point me in the direction of
the dinner dishes." He waggled his fingers suggestively. "These
hands are reserved for more important tasks than washing
plates."

"Such as?" Eve asked sweetly. "Holding your overinflated
male ego?"

Matt laughed and gave her a swift kiss on the cheek. "Be
kind to David," he said softly. "Remember the poor guy is a
marshmallow underneath that tough veneer he tries to adopt."

David was speechless. He considered various interesting forms
of torture as he watched Matt scratch Cat's head and make for
the door, humming a chirpy tune under his breath. He recovered
his voice just as Matt was waving a casual goodbye. "If you're
free sometime tomorrow afternoon, I'll stop by the motel and
we'll decide on what increased security precautions we need to
take before our next dive."

He spoke sternly, but Matt grinned, totally unrepentant.
"Come on Sunday around seven in the evening," he said. "Amy

and I have a busy day planned for tomorrow to make up for all we missed tonight.''

"Fine. I'll see you Sunday." David shut the door behind his friend, torn between outrage and resignation. He wasn't envious of Matt's dating plans, not exactly. He never had any difficulty finding female companionship whenever he wanted it, so he was surprised by a sudden feeling of emptiness when he contemplated the long hours of the weekend stretching ahead of him. The thought crept into his mind that it would be great to spend the day with Eve, showing her some of the small-town delights Eternity had to offer. Then in the evening, they could share a quiet dinner. He would open a bottle of their favorite chablis and grill a couple of steaks, and they could picnic in front of the fire.

He quickly corrected the disconcerting trend of his thoughts. He didn't want to spend the day with Eve. Good grief, they'd divorced because they couldn't be together for more than a few minutes without ripping each other's emotions to shreds. Why would he lay himself open to that sort of hurt again? He simply felt restless tonight, in the mood for some female companionship. His mouth twisted in a wry smile. Not to put too fine a point on it, he felt horny as hell. Having an ex-wife sleeping under the same roof seemed to be wreaking havoc with his libido.

Eve was already clearing the remains of their dinner from the table when he walked into the kitchen. "You cooked. I'll clean up," she said when he went to help.

"Sounds like a fair deal." He was determined to keep their conversation polite, friendly and as impersonal as possible. "Would you like coffee?"

"Thanks. That would be nice. We could drink it in front of the fire." She glanced wistfully toward the living room. "I hadn't realized how much I miss having a fireplace in my new apartment."

"Where are you living now?" he asked, scooping fresh coffee into the filter.

She frowned. "Eighty-second and Third. The address is deluxe, the security system is great, and my apartment has all the personality of a packing crate. The only decent room is the bedroom."

"Satin sheets? Mirror on the ceiling?"

She laughed, not seeming to hear the edge to his question. "No, I bought enough bookshelves to line three walls floor to ceiling. The books almost make it look like a room with character." Her hair was coming loose and she refastened the clip that held it in place, pushing a couple of straggling curls off her forehead. Her breasts strained against her sweater, soft and full, unbearably tempting. David glared at the cat and ordered him out of the kitchen. Cat stared back at him with the contempt he deserved and stalked to the front door, scratching to be let out.

David suddenly laughed. What the hell, even Cat knew he was being ridiculous. He crumpled the paper napkins they'd used during dinner and tossed them into the trash. "What are your plans for tomorrow?" he asked. "Anything I can help with? Do you need directions? Chauffeuring?"

She flushed. "Well, I don't want to inconvenience you..."

"You won't. The most pressing task on my Saturday agenda is a trip to the supermarket to buy milk for the cat."

She smiled faintly. "For the cat you're planning to take to the pound. What's his name, by the way?"

"Cat."

A corner of her mouth quirked upward. "How...original," she said.

He stared at her mouth. "Yeah. I have a richly creative mind."

She looked at him then, not with the teasing warmth she'd shown Matt, but at least without the cold hostility that had marked the end of their marriage. "If you really aren't too busy, I'd appreciate a guided tour of the town. My crew arrives first thing on Monday, and I'd like to have the basic structure for the program worked out by then. That way, they'll know what they need to tape and I'll have an idea how best to frame my interviews.''

"You've got a deal," David said, still not quite sure how in the world he'd *volunteered* to spend Saturday with the woman who'd broken his heart.

IF ANYONE HAD TOLD HER before she left Manhattan that she'd spend Friday night sleeping in the same house as David and that she'd spend the next day touring the town with him in his Jeep, Eve would have said that the person was delusional. And yet, here she was. Even more astonishing, she was having a good time.

True, she'd woken up at dawn, oppressed by the unnatural quiet of her surroundings. And admittedly there'd been a certain strain as she and David faced each other over orange juice and the morning paper. Still, the Eternity *Courier* made her smile with its solemn recap of the week's ''news,'' which included such events as a high school football game against the town of Ipswich and a heated vote on the size of the town council's contribution to this year's Christmas decorations. Five thousand dollars could arouse more passion in Eternity than a million dollars in New York City.

David, fortunately, seemed to be taking great care to keep their relationship—if that was the word—on exactly the sort of friendly but slightly impersonal basis Eve wanted. In the bright light of a sunny October morning, she began to hope that after this week she might have a realistic chance of laying to rest the lingering ghosts of her marriage and getting on with the rest of her life. She'd been dreading Gordon's arrival on Monday. Now she almost looked forward to it. Maybe she'd take one look at him and realize she was ready to name a date for their wedding. After all, she thought wryly, wasn't Eternity supposed to be the town of happily-ever-afters?

They visited the famous wedding chapel, then several businesses in town, with David playing tour guide and Eve taking copious notes as to who would make for the most colorful interviews. They stopped in at the travel agency run by Jacqui

Bertrand Powell, a pretty woman who was married to David's younger brother, Brent. Even that potentially sticky interview went off quite well, with the conversation focusing on the great news that Jacqui's uncle, Louis Bertrand, was marrying Patience Powell, rather than on the fact that Eve had once been married to David. With considerable tact, Jacqui made no reference to the embarrassing truth that during the entire two years of their marriage, Eve had never actually paid a visit to David's hometown and had only met David's brother when Brent had gone to New York on a brief visit for a fire fighters' training session.

"We've got time for one more quick stop before lunch," David said as they left Jacqui's. "How about a visit to the *Courier* office? You'll probably want to meet Katharine Falconer before you start filming your story. She'll be a good source for you."

Eve was well prepared with background information on the town's major figures. "Katharine Falconer's the owner of the paper, isn't she?"

"Yes, and the editor in chief, too. Her family's had connections to the area for years, but they only bought the paper about forty years ago." He stopped and turned to her. "Why are you smiling?"

"The fact that you used the words 'only' and 'forty years ago' in the same sentence. When you work in television, last week is ancient history."

He looked blank for a moment, then chuckled. "I hadn't realized that I've reverted to thinking like a native. When folks around here talk about the war, they mean the American Revolution. 'Newcomer' means anyone who arrived since the depression."

"So tell me more about this upstart Falconer family," Eve said.

"Upstart? Bite your tongue. Mrs. F. may be a newcomer to the *Courier,* but she likes to remind everyone that her ancestors on both sides of the family came over to the colonies on the *Mayflower.*"

"Once they got here, did they do anything useful?"

"Procreate." David grinned. "She also had an ancestor who was into shipping and competed with my great-great-grandfather in the nineteenth century, so her links to the town stretch back quite a way." He hesitated for a moment and Eve had the impression that he cut off some reminiscence. "Anyway, Katharine's never entirely reconciled herself to being a big fish in the tiny pond of Eternity. The *Courier*'s okay, but she feels a paper like the Boston *Globe* would be more suited to the size and scope of her talents."

"It sounds as if she's a modest woman," Eve said.

"Mmm. Modest rather like Miss Piggy."

Eve laughed. "In that case, I'll bet I can wheedle unlimited access to the *Courier* archives in exchange for the promise of an on-camera appearance for Mrs. Falconer. Thanks for the tip."

"You're welcome. Although you don't have to wheedle access to the archives. They're computerized and accessible to anyone with a computer modem."

"That's great. And surprising."

David smiled. "The twentieth century has reached even this backwater." He parked the car outside yet another building with colonial-style columns and old-world bay windows. "This is it. The *Courier*."

Eve followed him into a small reception area decorated with striped burgundy wallpaper and set off by dark green carpets. An extremely good-looking redhead was seated at a large desk behind a bank of telephones, sorting through a pile of glossy black-and-white photos. She looked up.

"Yes? Can I help you?" She sounded polite but bored. Then her mouth puckered into an excited circle. "Oh, my! I recognize you! You're Eve Graham, aren't you? From that TV program, 'A Current Affair.' I'm Amy Lewin." In a gesture Eve had seen a hundred times before in similar circumstances, the receptionist moistened her lips and smoothed her hair, adjusting her face into a smile, almost as if she expected a cameraman to spring from behind the draperies and start filming.

Eve held out her hand. "Actually, you're only half-right. I'm

Eve Graham, but my program's called 'Roving Report.' It's nice to meet you, Amy. This is a...friend of mine, David Powell. Perhaps you already know each other?''

Eve had spent most of the morning watching the women of Eternity either simper or preen when they talked to David, so she wasn't surprised when Amy glanced quickly at him, then flushed and stared down at her fingernails. David held out his hand and, after a second's hesitation, Amy stood up and shook it. Why the hesitation? Eve wondered.

"Hi, David," Amy said, sounding breathless. "It's a pleasure to meet you. I've heard so much about you."

David gave a groan. "Never come back to live in your hometown," he told Eve in a mock warning. "Who's been talking about me?" he asked Amy with a smile. "My great-aunts? My mother? Whatever they said, it's all lies."

Amy gave a husky little laugh that was surprisingly sexy. "None of the above have been talking to me," she said. "I'm a friend of Matt's."

David feigned horror. "Even worse. Really, I'm a great guy. Honest, trustworthy. Chamber of Commerce seal of approval available on request. Please, Amy, don't believe a word he's told you."

She looked at him consideringly. "He says you're smart and honest and the best friend he could ever have." The phone buzzed, and she sat down to answer the call. "Good morning. *Courier.*"

Eve actually felt sorry for David. She had rarely seen his attempt at charm so ruthlessly trampled on. This must be Matt's latest girlfriend, she reflected, the woman he'd planned to take to Boston last night, before their date got canceled at the last minute. She was very attractive, Eve decided, but much less outgoing and bouncy than the type of woman she'd seen Matt date in the past.

Amy's skin had the magnificent creamy tinge that sometimes accompanied red hair, but a fan of tiny lines at the corner of her eyes indicated she was well into her thirties and several years older than the bimbos Matt usually preferred. Perhaps, after thirty-seven years of playing the field, Matt was seriously thinking of settling down. Even the mightiest warriors fall in the end, Eve thought, hiding a smile.

Amy looked worried when she put down the phone. "I'm sorry to keep you waiting," she said, "but I have to track down Binnie Forsyth. She's our staff reporter," she added for Eve's benefit.

"What's the scoop?" David asked, smiling.

Amy didn't answer his smile. "Someone's dead," she said. She swallowed nervously. "The police think he's been murdered."

"Here? In Eternity?" David sounded more incredulous than horrified.

Amy recovered her poise. She nodded, her fingers busy dialing. "Some kids found the body down on the beach this morning. It was a man. He'd been shot."

A chill rippled over the surface of Eve's skin, leaving goose bumps in its wake. In New York, violent death might be regretted, but it sometimes seemed unavoidable, an integral part of the city landscape. Up here, in the rural peace of Eternity, it was harder to accept the intrusion of deadly violence.

David and Eve exchanged glances. They could hear the phone ringing, and finally the reporter's answering machine clicked in. Amy recorded a message.

"Binnie, you need to get over here right away. A man's been found dead on the beach. Murdered." Amy referred to her notes. "He runs a charter boat but hasn't lived here long, just the past five months. Apparently he moved up from Boston and rented a room from Marge Macdonald. His name's Caleb. Caleb Crewe. Call in as soon as you get this message."

Chapter Five

Caleb's body, shrouded in black vinyl, was being loaded into a morgue van when David and Eve arrived at the beach. Officials from various law-enforcement agencies swarmed around the bloody stretch of sand where he'd been found, like flies buzzing over rotten food. Detective Pete Pieracini stood next to his squad car, shoulders hunched, trying, with little success, to look as if he knew exactly what to do next. Shoplifting and the occasional break-in were the most violent crimes he was accustomed to investigating, and he was mad as fire that some big-city jerkoff had committed a murder on his turf.

The standard yellow tape that marked the crime scene snapped and billowed in the wind. Their shoes seeping sand, David and Eve skirted the plastic barricade and made their way across the beach toward the detective.

"Hi, Dave," the detective said. "I guess I don't need to ask what brings you out here."

"We heard some bad news about a friend of mine, Caleb Crewe." David shot a glance toward the cluster of forensic experts working on the beach. "Unfortunately it looks like the news was true."

"Yeah, he's dead, more's the pity. Shot a couple of hours before dawn this morning from what they reckon." Pete was sweating, despite the fact that a stiff breeze was blowing in off the ocean. "Didn't realize you and Caleb were acquainted, Dave. He's not from these parts." The detective made nonresidence sound like an indictable offense. "How well did you know him?"

"We weren't close personal friends," David said. "But we'd spent a fair amount of time together. I was out in his boat just yesterday. I guess there's no doubt the victim really was Caleb?"

"No doubt at all," Pete said. "We found his driver's license right next to the body, complete with photo. Age forty, six feet, 180 pounds. And his landlady already confirmed the ID."

"He'd taken a couple of rooms over in Marge Macdonald's place, hadn't he?" David asked.

"Yeah. Jeez, this has been a lousy morning. Caleb's face wasn't messed up too bad, but his guts was all spilling out—" Pete remembered he was talking to an acquaintance of the deceased and stopped abruptly. "Marge got sick to her stomach when she saw him. Couldn't stop crying, and the pathologist ended up giving her a shot. Said it's the first time he's injected somebody who's alive in fifteen years. Jeez!" He mopped his forehead with a grubby handkerchief. "I tell you, it's been like a three-ring circus down here today, and I'm not trained to play ringmaster."

"I guess we're lucky murder's such a rare occurrence in this town."

"We sure are. Wouldn't want to be a cop if I had to do this too often. Don't know how the city guys stand it." Pete stared lugubriously at the police photographer, who was stretched out on his stomach trying to get a final picture of the blood-drenched sand. "I've been with the police department in Eternity for twenty-two years, and this is only our third murder. As far as I'm concerned, that's three too many. I can't believe this happened here."

Eve had been trying to remain quiet and inconspicuous, but she couldn't let that one pass. "Murder can happen anywhere," she said. "People are still people even in a picture-postcard town like Eternity. And some of them are rotten people who do rotten things. Including commit murder."

"I know that." Pete looked at her. "Have we met somewhere, miss? I seem to recognize you."

"This is Eve Graham," David said. "She's a re—"

"A friend of David's from New York City." Eve brought her foot down sharply on David's toes at the same time as she extended her hand to Pete Pieracini. The detective would surely clam up if he realized she was from "Roving Report." "Good to meet you, Detective."

He shook hands warily. "Likewise. Don't get me wrong, Eve. I've got nothing against New York and I realize Eternity isn't paradise. I know we've got our share of all the usual problems. Folks still get drunk, they still have fights with their relatives, and our teens are every bit as pigheaded and pea brained as the kids anyplace else. The difference between us and the big cities is our gossip network. The grapevine out here tends to work real well, and that's great protection for everyone." He cracked a smile. "I guess it's as annoying as all get-out if you want to have an affair with your neighbor, but on the plus side, at least we usually hear about threatening situations before they get totally out of hand."

"I guess Caleb wasn't tied into the network," Eve said. "People didn't know him, so they didn't gossip about him."

"I guess not, although folks in this town usually like to find out the background on strangers. He must've made a real effort to keep himself to himself." Pete stared morosely at the ocean. "This murder will turn out to be drug related, you can count on it. Every damn thing's drug related these days. Jeez, I hope those Boston gangs aren't getting ready to move into our town. They'd destroy everything we've worked for."

Eve felt a surge of impatience. With superhuman effort she bit back a comment to the effect that Pete needed to stop mourning the intrusion of the real world into his idyllic life and get on with the business of finding out who murdered Caleb Crewe. She stuffed her hands into the pockets of her pants and stared determinedly at a boat scudding across the horizon. She reminded herself that she wasn't in Manhattan and that she needed to leave her big-city aggression behind. Despite the reminder, she still felt an almost overwhelming desire to give Pete a swift kick in the pants. She reached for her roll of antacids, popped one into her mouth and crunched down on it. Hard.

"You're sure Caleb was murdered?" David asked. "His death couldn't have been an accident?"

The detective shook his head. "Has to be murder. He was shot in the back with something mighty powerful and fell right where we found him. Probably killed with a .357 Magnum, according to the doc. The murderer fired off two rounds, and the second bullet exploded Caleb's heart."

David winced. "Was he robbed?"

"Don't know. His wallet didn't have any money in it, just his driver's license and a couple of credit cards. But if the killer took Caleb's money, why leave his credit cards?"

"Because the killer was high on drugs?" David suggested.

"Could be," Pete agreed. "But even a thief who's high surely wouldn't be strolling along the beach at two in the morning just hoping he'd bump into someone he could rob."

"Sure sounds unlikely. Two o'clock is when Caleb was killed?"

"The coroner hasn't given a time yet, but that's probably pretty darn close, give or take an hour. The way I see it, Caleb arranged to meet someone and they got into an argument. Then—*bam!*" Pete snapped his fingers.

David frowned. "Who the blazes would Caleb arrange to meet on the beach at two in the morning?"

"You tell me," Pete said. "I never met the guy. Who do *you* think he might want to see without anyone knowing about the meeting?"

"Beats me," David said with perfect truth. "As far as I know, most nights Caleb went to bed early and got up at dawn to tinker with his motorcycle. His heart definitely belonged to his Harley."

"If he was a biker, he must have had biking cronies, right?" The detective looked more cheerful as he pictured some chain-

and-leather biker as the murderer. Pete was clearly having trouble dealing with the possibility that a citizen of Eternity had fallen far enough outside the law to kill a man.

"I'm sure he had biking buddies, but I never met any of them." David shook his head. "Sorry, Pete. I wish I could help, but Caleb just wasn't the sort of guy who confided details of his life to his friends. We shared a couple of beers on a Friday night, but basically he was one of your real uptight Yankees."

"Maybe it was a drug deal that went wrong," Eve suggested, tired of waiting for the detective to come up with such an obvious suggestion. "That seems like a logical motive, given where Caleb was found. Somebody could be running drugs by boat and landing them on the Eternity beach at night. Caleb could have been organizing the distribution network in the town. Or maybe some of his biking cronies acted as a courier service to ferry the drugs into Boston. Hell's Angels have been implicated in several major drug busts recently. I did...I mean I saw a TV program on it."

David's protest that Caleb wasn't a member of Hell's Angels was drowned out by the detective, who gave a ferocious howl of outrage. "If Caleb Crewe was dealing drugs on my turf, then as far as I'm concerned, the bastard got what was coming to him. Where the hell was he planning to sell them? At the high school so's he could screw up the lives of decent kids? Jeez, I'd like to pull the trigger myself on some of these guys."

Belatedly he realized that his comments were hardly in line with departmental policy on communicating with the public, and he snapped his mouth closed. Even more belatedly he seemed to realize that he'd given out a lot more information than he'd received.

All formal efficiency, Pete pulled out a notebook and flipped to a clean page. "Okay, Dave, you said you were out with the deceased yesterday on his boat." Pete's ballpoint hovered over the page. "What were you doing? Funny time of year to go for a pleasure cruise, isn't it? Seas were choppy yesterday."

David hesitated a moment. "Caleb took out me and a friend,

Matt Packard. Matt and I were roommates in college and he's
visiting Eternity for a while."

Pete might be inexperienced as a homicide investigator, but
he had the veteran detective's memory for names. "Matt Packard?" he said. "Wait, he's the guy who reported a break-in over
at the motel last night."

"Right. His place was really messed up." David leaned
against the squad car, looking the picture of innocence. "You
don't think there could possibly be a connection between somebody breaking into Matt's hotel room and Caleb getting murdered, do you?"

"I don't know, but it's a coincidence, and I sure don't like
coincidences," Pete said. "Matt Packard was acquainted with
Caleb Crewe and he was robbed the same night Caleb was murdered. Nobody else in town was robbed and nobody else was
murdered. Seems to me that's a situation worth checking out."

"Maybe you have a point. As far as I know, Matt's in Boston
right now and won't be back until Sunday night. But I'm sure
he'll be happy to cooperate with you as soon as he returns."

"You don't happen to know where he's staying in Boston?"
Pete asked.

"Sorry, I don't. He went with a woman friend." Eve noticed
that David made no mention of the fact that Matt had an apartment in Boston or that his "woman friend" was Amy, the receptionist at the *Courier* offices. She decided not to fill in the
gaps until she found out why David was so reluctant to discuss
his salvage operations.

Pete turned back to his notebook. "Well, then, let's get on
with this account of the last time you saw the deceased. You and
Matt Packard hired Caleb's boat and went off—where?"

"Out in the bay," David said vaguely. "Around the estuary.
Like I told you, Matt's on vacation, so we decided to do a little
underwater sportfishing, kind of get the weekend off to a good
start, you know?"

"Was it chance that you hired Caleb's boat? Or did you
choose him on purpose?"

"We'd already made arrangements with him," David said. "We hired Caleb because we'd gone out on his boat many times before and we'd learned to trust his expertise. He's been working this coast for years. He knows—knew—all the best fishing spots in the area. He knew the navigation charts for this area like you know your way around the streets of Eternity."

"Damn cold to get in the water at this time of year, isn't it?" Pete muttered. "Jeez, you must have damn near frozen your..." He glanced at Eve and fell silent.

"We wore wet suits," David explained. "They're pretty efficient heat insulators." He hurried on, and Eve realized he was trying to avoid further questions by providing an excess of irrelevant information. "Once you get down a few feet you can find some interesting fish. Matt and I use spear guns we designed ourselves. It's a very challenging sport because the water distorts your vision and you have to learn how to make allowances for the light refraction when you aim your gun. Which is a harpoon, of course, not really a gun at all. And there's plenty of opportunity for the fish to escape even when you've speared them, which is bad for you and worse for them, so you have to chase them and try to complete the kill. Lots of times, you go home empty-handed."

"How'd you do on Friday?" Pete asked.

"Okay." David gave a disarming grin. "We're not about to put the local fishing industry out of business."

"To each his own, I guess. Me, I prefer to stand around in hip boots and wait for the trout to swim by laughing at me."

The detective obviously didn't know enough about deep-sea diving to realize that Massachusetts in October was an extremely unlikely place for anyone to go underwater sportfishing, both because of the cold and because of the almost total absence of game fish after years of heavy commercial fishing. Eve wondered why David was deliberately withholding information from the detective. He must have a pretty compelling reason to keep the purpose of his diving secret if even a homicide investigation wasn't enough to make him admit the truth about his underwater activities.

She listened with only half an ear as Pete ran David through a list of questions relating to Caleb, trying to uncover a likely motive for his murder. Eve had never met Caleb, so she had no personal reason to mourn his death, and her work as a television journalist inevitably brought her into frequent contact with human suffering. Nevertheless, she was aware of a bleak feeling of regret as she watched the police photographer finish his task and load his gear into a white-paneled truck.

The forensic crew had worked fast because the tide was coming in, and the evidence of Caleb's murder would soon be washed away by the waves. In a couple of hours, maybe less, Caleb's blood, the churned-up sand and the footprints of the investigators would all disappear, the beach made smooth and new again by the cleansing surge of the ocean. Eve felt strangely sad. A place of death, she thought, deserved a longer memorial than the interval between two tides.

She watched as a woman, one of the forensic crew, trudged up the beach and held out a clear plastic bag containing something small and gold-colored, about the size of a quarter, but oval, instead of round.

"Here, Pete, thought you might want to get a look at this. We found it buried under a thin layer of sand about six inches from the victim's right hand."

"What is it?" Pete asked, squinting through the plastic. "A piece of jewelry?"

"I'm not sure. Looks like a coin."

The detective turned the bag over. "Victoria Regina," he read. "Eighteen sixty-two."

"Victoria," the woman repeated. "She was that nineteenth-century English queen who reigned for years and years, wasn't she? The one who draped all her piano legs in velvet because they were too vulgar to be left naked."

"She's the one," Pete said. "This must be a British coin, then. Course, we've no way of knowing if it has anything to do with the deceased. Could be sheer coincidence we found it near the body." He squinted, holding the bag up to the sun. "Do you think it's real gold?"

"It's shiny and heavy enough," the woman said. "Brass would've gone green years ago. If it really dates from 1862, that is."

"It's probably a sovereign," David said. Eve could see that he was barely restraining his desire to snatch the bag and examine the coin, but nobody else seemed to notice his burgeoning tension. He drew a long, uneven breath, struggling not to sound too eager when he spoke again. "Could I have a closer look, do you think?"

"Don't touch it, even through the plastic," Pete warned. "Hold the bag by the corners so you don't smudge any prints. You know something about old coins, then?"

"Just a bit. It's kind of a hobby of mine." David held up the bag, twisting against the light to give himself the best possible view. "Yes, it's a British sovereign all right. That's the name given to a 22-karat-gold coin minted by the British government right through the nineteenth century and up into the twentieth." He cracked a faint smile. "We ought to get down to the beach, Pete, and start digging. Maybe there's a cache of buried pirate's gold down there."

"Don't waste your time," the forensic investigator said. "We checked the beach out real good. There's nothing else on that stretch of sand but seaweed and crabs."

Pete eyed the tiny oval of gold with new respect. "How much is it worth? Enough to kill someone for?"

David shrugged. "Maybe, given that kids will kill each other over a pair of sneakers or a leather jacket. But it wouldn't be rational to commit murder for the sake of a single sovereign. Its face value was a pound," he explained. "Which in 1862, when this particular coin was minted, equaled about eight dollars, or two weeks' wages for an average working man in England. It's worth a lot more than that now, of course, but not enough to make you rich. Depending on the price of gold and the condition of the coin, a sovereign might fetch eighty bucks, maybe a hundred or so if it's a special date of issue.''

The investigator looked disappointed. "You'd need a trunk of the things before you'd be rich.''

"I'm afraid so,'' David agreed.

Pete frowned. "If this sovereign belonged to Caleb Crewe, why the heck did he take it down to the beach?'' he asked nobody in particular. "What was the point? Surely he wouldn't be dragging around bags of gold to pay off a drug dealer?''

The forensic investigator shrugged, taking back the sovereign. "Don't ask me. I'm just the dumb hick who wraps the clues up in plastic. You're the detective.''

Pete's answering smile was totally without mirth. "Yeah, I can hardly wait to bring my wealth of experience to solving this case.'' He shook his head. "Maybe it was his lucky piece or something.''

"If so, it didn't bring him much luck,'' David said grimly.

"Ain't that the truth,'' Pete said with sincere feeling. "Ain't that the truth.''

NEWS OF THE MURDER had obviously leaked out all over the town's highly efficient grapevine. Binnie, the reporter from the *Courier,* arrived at the scene of the crime fresh from an interview with the high school homecoming queen. Binnie was young and eager, a graduate of Wellesley who longed to prove herself, preferably by uncovering scandal and corruption in high places. The fact that Eternity was ruthlessly democratic and had no high places to speak of didn't dampen her enthusiasm in the slightest.

She was probably the only person in town delighted to have a murder take place so close to home, and—too excited to remember that a reporter who falls foul of officialdom doesn't collect much insider information—parked her car on a stretch of sage grass at the edge of the beach, slammed the door and ran to confront Detective Pieracini.

"So what's the inside scoop? Any suspects so far? Any motive for the murder?''

If she hadn't made the mistake of whipping out her tape recorder, Pete probably would have answered all her questions without a murmur of protest. Accustomed as he was to cooperation with the local paper, he had none of the big-city cop's instinctive distrust of journalists. But the sudden appearance of Binnie's tape recorder under his nose reminded him that this was no ordinary occasion.

"The department will be making a statement at four-thirty this afternoon," he said. "Now if you don't mind, miss, you'd better move on. We got nothing to say at this time."

Binnie was not so easily defeated in pursuit of her "big chance," and she succeeded in slipping down to the water's edge when Pete was distracted by the arrival of a carload of gawking teenagers. Pete, however, was more than equal to the challenge. He might not have much experience with murders, but he was a dab hand at controlling recalcitrant crowds and pushy citizens.

"Get back up here," he bellowed at Binnie. "And you kids keep off the beach or I'll lock you all up for trespassing. There's no reason for you to be crawling all over the sand. You pay your taxes to have the police do that."

"Come on, Pete," said Binnie, "give me a break."

"You'll get a break," he said. "Four-thirty this afternoon at the police station."

"Let's get out of here," David murmured, under cover of the confusion. He took Eve's hand and headed for the Jeep. Recognizing his need for the warmth of human contact, she didn't attempt to remove her hand from his grasp. She'd filmed dozens of homicide scenes and reported on a hundred deaths equally as violent as Caleb's, but her sense of loss never diminished. If it ever did, she knew that would be the point at which she gave up journalism for good. David must be experiencing her feelings of loss in a far more intense form, since he'd known Caleb and was less accustomed to dealing with the aftermath of murder.

David drove along the coast to a small restaurant in a neighboring town. "We missed lunch," he said. "Are you hungry? They do a great clam chowder in this place."

"Sounds wonderful," she said, surprised to find that she was hungry, despite the large dinner she'd eaten the night before and the unpleasantness of the past couple of hours.

"I'm sorry I dragged you out of Eternity," David said as they settled into a sunny table by the inevitable bay window. The waitress indicated the box of crayons in the center of the table and told them they were welcome to draw on the heavy white paper tablecloth if they wished.

"I know you want to meet some more people in the town so that you can work on the structure of your program for 'Roving Report,' " David said. "But the problem is, if we stopped anywhere in Eternity this afternoon, we'd be mobbed by people wanting to talk about Caleb's murder, and I don't think I'm up to that right now."

"I certainly understand, and we don't have to talk about him if you'd rather not."

"I want to talk about him with *you*," David said. "I just don't want to spend the afternoon inventing clever half-truths, which is what I'd have to do with most of the people in town."

The waitress arrived and David gave her their order for two large bowls of clam chowder and a miniloaf of French bread. Eve selected a blue crayon and began to doodle a series of threatening-looking waves cresting on a barren shore. When she realized what she was doing, she put the crayon down.

David leaned back in his chair, his face pale and weary beneath his tan. "This is one hell of a mess," he said.

"You were doing some pretty fancy footwork to avoid answering the detective's questions," Eve said. "Why didn't you tell him what you really suspect Caleb was doing down at the beach?"

David poked at the ice in his glass of water. "Because I don't know what Caleb was doing down at the beach," he said.

"But you've got a pretty good idea," Eve said.

David's eyes met hers, then slid away to focus on the ocean. "Yeah, I've got a pretty good idea," he said. "I think the son of a bitch was planning to sell us out to a bunch of rival treasure hunters."

Chapter Six

"Treasure hunters?" Eve's breath caught in her throat. "What in the world have you and Matt discovered that's so valuable Caleb risked getting killed for it?"

"Nothing—yet." David looked as if he regretted his momentary burst of frankness. "Besides, Caleb obviously didn't go down to the beach expecting to get murdered. Maybe he didn't realize he was in danger." David picked up the menu and studied it, despite the fact that they'd already placed their orders. "They make the world's best Boston cream pie in this place if you're interested."

Eve had spent the final six months of her marriage dealing with David's unwillingness to confide in her when he had problems. In those days she'd worried herself sick about his failure to communicate, convinced it reflected her inadequacy as a wife. She was no longer willing to waste her energies in such an unproductive exercise. Seized by a twinge of impatience, she leaned across the table, forcing him to meet her eyes.

"Look, David, you can brood in gloomy silence while we eat our soup, or you can decide to talk to me. The choice is yours. Feel free to use me as a sounding board if you think that might help straighten out your thoughts. My job has given me a fair bit of experience as an investigator, and I believe I could make a useful contribution, but I'm not willing to plead for you to confide in me. I'm sick to death of playing the role of brainless bride, begging to be allowed to share in her husband's grown-up worries—'' Eve realized her voice was rising to a shrill complaint and she stopped abruptly.

David looked up from the menu, his eyes blank with shock. "What the blazes are you talking about, Eve? That outburst had nothing to do with Caleb's murder, that's for sure."

"You're right." She drew a calming breath. "I was talking about our failed marriage, I guess." She gave a rueful grimace. "I'm sorry my remarks came out sounding so aggressive. I didn't realize I was still that angry with myself over the way I behaved—over the way I let you behave during our marriage. Anyway, that's in the past and you're right, it's got nothing to do with Caleb's murder—''

"What do you mean, the way you let me behave?" David sounded halfway between annoyed and genuinely puzzled.

"I guess that was another bad choice of words," she said. "I meant that we fell into the habit of role-playing early in our marriage, and I played the role you assigned me without protest. That would have been bad enough, but then I spent the whole time being secretly mad at you for giving me a role I didn't like."

"What role do you think I gave you?" David asked. "Good grief, Eve, I felt way too uncertain of myself to be dishing out role assignments to you or anyone else. I could barely take care of being a husband without trying to prescribe how you should be a wife."

"Maybe that was part of the problem," Eve said. "We were both so overwhelmed that we fell back on stereotypes. Don't beat up on yourself about what happened. I was every bit as guilty as you."

"We were overwhelmed," David agreed. "But why? We weren't kids fresh out of high school, or even young college graduates still wet behind the ears. We'd established demanding careers, we'd had other relationships before we got married. In fact, I'd say we were a pretty sophisticated couple."

"I'm not sure that being sophisticated is a recipe for success in marriage," Eve said wryly.

"What do you advocate?" David sounded brusque. "Naiveté? Ignorance? Teenage marriages?"

"None of the above, of course. Maybe a lot more self-aware-ness than you and I had, plus a willingness to confront problems head-on, instead of burying them under layers of silent anxiety. The truth is, we were so physically attracted to each other that we never took the time to develop a mechanism for dealing with the rough spots that come in any marriage."

"We didn't seem to have any problems the first year."

"That's because we used sex to solve everything," Eve said with brutal frankness. "When we disagreed about anything, from the color of the sofa cushions to where we should spend the holidays, we'd go to bed and make love. The trouble was, how-ever great the sex, we still needed to decide where we were going to spend the holidays and what color cushions we wanted. And we ended up staying home or not buying furniture or not doing whatever. The reality is that you can't spend an entire lifetime avoiding decisions that may hurt your partner's feelings."

"I guess you're right," David said after a moment's silence. "In retrospect I can see you have a point. By the time we'd been married for a year, we each had this mental list of subjects that were too dangerous to talk about."

"We sure did," Eve said with feeling. "The backlog got to be so huge that to start a real discussion—about anything—was like deciding to take a stroll across a field of unexploded land mines."

"So naturally, every time one of us got brave enough to start an honest discussion, sure enough, one of the mines exploded." David shook his head, his expression disgusted. "When you look back, we were really pretty pathetic, weren't we?"

Eve was astonished to hear herself chuckle. "Yes, but call us typically stressed yuppies. It sounds kinder than pathetic."

"Okay, how did we manage to feel so stressed about some-thing as everyday as being married?" David asked. "Your par-ents have a great marriage, so did mine. What was our hang-up?"

"With the advantage of hindsight, I've decided our parents were a major part of the problem," Eve said.

"They were hundreds of miles away and never interfered—"

"Not intentionally," she agreed. "But we grew up in homes with very traditional values, and somewhere deep inside we expected our marriage to follow our parents' patterns. You were too much a man of the nineties to consider *asking* me to give up my career, but I'm sure you thought that if I really loved you, I'd simply *volunteer* to stay home and have your babies."

"I was never quite that moronic," he protested.

"Are you sure?" she asked. "I was. Don't misunderstand, David. I'm not trying to point the finger of blame at you, far from it. That was my whole point when I started this conversation. I *accepted* the role you assigned me without a word of protest. In my heart of hearts, I agreed with your definition of how a wife was supposed to behave. So I was more than ready to blame myself for everything that went wrong between us. I felt uneasy about the amount of time I spent at work and downright guilty about having so much professional ambition. So when you started to spend nights and weekends at the office, part of me was mad as hell, but the other part of me accepted your absence as the punishment I deserved. After all, if I couldn't be home for you, waiting with a delicious meal, the bed made and your shirts ironed, didn't I really deserve to have you stay later and later at the office?"

David gave a bleak smile. "Do you want to know why I was staying so late at the office?"

He was going to tell her he'd been having an affair. Eve's hand clenched so tightly around the crayon she'd been holding that it snapped. She didn't want to hear about his ultimate betrayal of their marriage vows, but she'd gained enough self-knowledge since the divorce to realize that it would be better to hear the truth from David than to torment herself with images of adultery that would be all the more vivid for having no roots in acknowledged fact.

"Yes," she said harshly. "I'd like to understand what was going on in your life."

David stared at the black slashing lines he'd drawn on his place mat as if he didn't quite know how they'd gotten there. "Why is it so easy to tell you this now when it seemed so difficult back when we were married? The truth is, the extra hours I spent at the office had nothing whatever to do with the problems in our marriage. Not directly."

"Then what...?"

He smiled grimly. "I was searching for a small fortune in missing company funds. I put in so many hours of overtime because I was working my butt off scanning every damn computer transaction and company record trying to find out who'd stolen more than two million dollars from the stock portfolios I managed for my clients."

"What!" Eve was so startled she nearly knocked over her glass of water. "Good grief! How come nobody ever told me about this?"

"Nobody knew. Being suspected of fraud wasn't a career achievement I wanted to spread around." David's eyes gleamed with rueful self-mockery. "Fortunately my boss had faith in me and covered the missing funds while I conducted my investigation. But I spent the last two months of our marriage with the constant threat of an indictment hanging over my head."

"And you never told me." Eve wasn't sure whether to laugh or cry. "All those days and nights, with this terrible threat looming on the horizon, and you never said a single solitary word to me. Your wife."

"In retrospect it sounds crazy, but your career was taking off to new heights of success, and I was just too damn proud to tell you how much trouble I was in."

"But what happened? Who really stole the money? Obviously you eventually discovered the truth." Eve's eyes widened with apprehension. "Or did you? That wasn't why you quit your job right after the divorce was finalized, was it? I mean you weren't fired for stealing or anything?"

"Thank God, no. Right around the time we split up, I managed to find out what had been going on. After weeks of dreary analyses, I was able to show that one of my partners had not only stolen the money, but had deliberately set out to pin the blame on me."

"David, I'm so sorry. I wish I'd known." Eve was torn between regret that she hadn't been allowed to provide him with comfort and a familiar ache of frustration because he'd shut her so completely out of his life. The questions bubbled up, thick and fast. "Who tried to frame you? I still can't understand why you never told me any of this! What was his motive? And why pick on you to frame?"

"The thefts were carried out by a guy called Ned Nichols. He needed money to pay off his wife's credit-card debts and picked me because the areas in which we traded happened to complement each other."

"His wife had run up two million dollars' worth of credit-card bills?"

"Only a hundred thousand or so plus interest. But I guess Ned figured, while he was at it, some extra spending money would be nice." David cracked a smile that contained no humor at all. "He apologized to me with great sincerity when we met in the courthouse right before his trial. He wanted to assure me that his selection of me as his victim was nothing personal. He really liked me a lot, but I'd been the easiest person to frame, and he'd needed the money so his wife wouldn't leave him."

"Obviously his was a friendship to treasure."

David shrugged. "In his own way I think he really did consider me a friend. But he was crazy in love with his wife and their relationship was so mixed up I think he kind of got torn loose from his moral moorings."

"For heaven's sake, David, stop being so damn noble. The guy behaved like a jerk. A total lowlife. Admit it."

David looked away. "I'd like to, but I can't. Maybe it would be easier for me to put the incident in perspective if Ned were still alive. But he's not. He died in prison."

"Oh, no! Did he die of natural causes?" *Please say yes,* she added silently.

"Unfortunately not." David had drawn a smoking gun on the tablecloth, and he scribbled over it. "He committed suicide about six months into his sentence."

"Oh, jeez. I'm sorry."

"Yeah."

Eve instinctively reached out to put her hand over his. "David, it's a sad way for his life to end, but you know better than to blame yourself for what happened, don't you?"

"Of course," he said. "At least in my rational moments, when I'm wide-awake and busy. Sometimes my conscience isn't quite so cooperative last thing at night when I'm trying to get to sleep."

Eve had thought her emotions were pretty much under control. She found out now they weren't. Suddenly all the old hurt and frustration boiled over. "My God, David, I can't believe you were going through all this garbage and I never knew. How could you have been under such stress and never breathe a word to me about what was going on?"

"We were divorced by the time Ned died."

"But I was your wife when he was trying to frame you! Dammit, didn't I deserve to share in something so important?"

David's mood suddenly lightened and his shoulders lifted in an ironic shrug. "Of course you did. But how come you were offered a job at CBS—a huge career leap—that you turned down without ever mentioning it to me?"

"B-because it…it involved a move to the West Coast and I knew I could never take it," Eve said. "How did you hear about that?" Before he could answer, she found herself laughing, albeit a touch wistfully. "All right, point taken. Heavens, David, for two supposedly smart people, we were a pair of idiots, weren't we?"

"Sure. But probably no more idiotic than half the other married couples in America."

"Maybe in a hundred years or so they'll develop androids so

that people can have a trial marriage with a programed dummy before they move on to the real thing.''

"Sounds dangerous," David said. "I bet most people would end up preferring the dummy. Hell, any smart person would.''

Eve was laughing when the waitress arrived carrying two huge bowls of steaming chowder, a basket of fresh-smelling bread and a dish of butter nestled in ice.

"Enjoy your meals," she said. "Can I get you anything else?''

"No, thanks, this is great." David gave her an absentminded smile and the waitress simpered. Eve sighed. David's sexual magnetism still worked with a hundred percent efficiency on all females. Including her. She realized that she'd drawn a circle of red hearts around her glass of water and quickly scribbled them out, hoping David hadn't noticed. She didn't want him to read deep significance into a meaningless doodle.

"Are you going to tell me what's going on with you and Matt?" she said when they'd both eaten some soup, which was as delicious as David had promised, thick with chunky vegetables and juicy clams. "What are the pair of you trying to find?''

"Eve, I'll agree to tell you what we're looking for if you'll agree to keep everything I say confidential. Deep-sea salvage is a cutthroat business. You saw what happened to Caleb, so you know that when I say cutthroat, I mean it almost literally.''

Eve suppressed a shiver. "You have my word," she said. "Although we shouldn't leap to the conclusion that Caleb was murdered because of his connections to your diving operation. As the detective would be quick to point out, Caleb could have been into drug dealing or a dozen other crimes for all you know.''

"He certainly wasn't a drug user," David said.

"Unfortunately that might not stop him dealing drugs to people who, unlike him, aren't smart enough to say no.''

"You're right." David frowned. "Well, I guess we'll soon find out if he sold me and Matt up the river.''

"How?''

"A team of rival divers'll turn up at the wreck site."

Eve gulped. "What'll that mean?"

David was silent for several seconds. "Danger," he said finally.

Eve's imagination kicked into overdrive as she visualized what that laconic single-word answer might mean. "Did Caleb know enough about what you and Matt are doing to cause you real problems?" she asked, trying to sound cool.

"Enough to cause serious trouble? Sure. Remember the break-in at Matt's motel? We couldn't understand who would want the underwater grid charts when they didn't show where we were diving, only what we'd found when we were down there. Well, if Caleb was behind the break-in, everything makes sense."

Eve understood at once. "Because he knew precisely where you were diving," she said. "He's the guy who took you there every day, so those disembodied grid charts make perfect sense to him, even though they'd be meaningless to almost anyone else."

"Exactly. So if he stole the charts, he had all the information a dive team would need to find the wreck we've been working on and to assess where they should concentrate their search for treasure."

"Locating the wreck is the time-consuming part of the underwater salvage business, isn't it?"

"Usually, although with sonar and underwater robots you can often cut down the search time quite a bit. Of course, using robots also increases the costs exponentially, so Matt and I decided to do our own searching on this project, rather than subcontracting out. We had precise information about where the ship had gone down, and we used a pretty advanced computer program to analyze where the currents might have carried it, but it still took us seven weeks to locate the wreck."

Eve grimaced. "Everything you've said makes it sound almost certain that Caleb stole those charts from Matt's motel room. Nobody else would be able to put them to such good use."

"I guess we'll have a better idea about that if we meet a rival team swimming around the wreck next time we go down."

Eve's soup had lost its flavor. She pushed the bowl aside. "Wh-what will happen when you and the rival team meet up with each other?"

"Nothing as dreadful as you're obviously thinking," David said. "Based on past experience with other treasure hunters, I'm guessing they'll try to negotiate a payoff for leaving me and Matt to work the wreck in peace."

His explanation would have sounded a lot more convincing if she hadn't seen Caleb's body being loaded into the coroner's van a couple of hours earlier. "We're back to my original question," she said. "What in the world have you and Matt discovered in a wreck off the coast of Eternity that's causing all this interest?"

David hesitated for no more than a second. "Gold," he said.

"Hah! I thought so." Eve gave a triumphant smile. "How much gold?"

"As far as our best estimates lead us to expect, about 150,000 gold sovereigns, each of them worth around eighty dollars or slightly more."

"Wow! That's a lot of sovereigns and a lot of dollars." Eve made a rapid mental calculation. "At eighty bucks a piece, that makes twelve million dollars. *Twelve million dollars!*" She shook her head and picked up a crayon to write down the sum. "I must have added a zero. That can't be right."

"Yes, it can," David said quietly. "Twelve million dollars in golden sovereigns is exactly what we're hoping to find locked in treasure chests somewhere in or around the wreck of the *Free Enterprise.*"

"Twelve million dollars!" Eve found the idea of salvaging that many sovereigns more terrifying than exciting. "The money won't be yours, will it? Doesn't underwater treasure belong to the federal government?"

"It depends," David said. "In the normal course of events, the federal government imposes a hefty tax on anything found in its territorial waters. And if the wreck is valuable enough, sometimes the state and the federal governments fight court battles about who has taxing and ownership rights. But in this case, all the governmental authorities are out of luck, whether they're state, federal or city.''

"Pete will be annoyed that Eternity isn't going to get a cut."

David grinned. "He'll have to take his lumps, I guess. The *Free Enterprise* was insured by Lloyds of London. It sank in a gale about half a mile outside Eternity Harbor on the night of December 9, 1862, and Lloyds paid off on the claim to the tune of more than a quarter of a million dollars.''

"That was a small fortune in those days, wasn't it?"

"It sure was. But the point is, the courts have decided in other similar cases that if Lloyds paid off the claim when a ship sank, then Lloyds owns the wreck if the ship is ever located and successfully salvaged. Which means that the cargo is also theirs, even if the wreck is found in United States territorial waters.''

"That seems fair," Eve said.

"Mmm. And that's why Matt and I have been keeping such meticulous records of precisely where we've explored and the exact location of everything we've discovered. The grid charts that were stolen show every inch of the wreck and its environs, because we need to have the backup data to prove in a court of law that the sovereigns we bring up were part of the cargo of the *Free Enterprise*.''

"And therefore the property of Lloyds and not of the American government.''

"Right. Of course, I have duplicates of all the site charts, so from that point of view, the theft of Matt's copies makes no difference.''

Eve was so interested in what David was saying that for a moment she forgot that bringing the sovereigns to the surface looked like a task fraught with life-threatening risks. "Let me get this straight," she said. "Technically speaking, you and Matt are working on behalf of Lloyds of London, right?''

David shook his head. "Not really. Matt and I are what you

might call independent contractors, working on a contingency-fee basis. We've told Lloyds what we're doing, and they've given us official permission to act as their agents, so our diving activities are completely legal. But Lloyds isn't paying our expenses, so if Matt and I don't find anything of value, we're out of luck, and out of a lot of money, too. On the other hand, if we locate the sovereigns, Lloyd's has agreed to pay us twenty percent of their total value as a finder's fee.''

Eve choked into her soup. ''That's more than two million dollars for you and Matt,'' she said.

David grinned. ''Actually almost two and a half. Has a nice ring to it, don't you think?'' His amusement faded. ''Of course, if Caleb sold us out to a group of treasure hunters who are working outside the law, their profits would be even higher. Provided they don't flood the market with too many sovereigns at one time, they'd be able to keep all twelve million dollars.''

''Wouldn't it be difficult to sell that many antique coins without the authorities getting suspicious?''

''It depends how cleverly they passed them into the marketplace. But even if they decided to melt some of the sovereigns down and ignore the antiquity or collectors' value, the coins are made of 22-karat gold, and gold fetches almost four hundred dollars an ounce.'' David's voice was grim. ''That still works out to several million dollars. More than enough money to tempt a lot of people into behaving very badly.''

''Possibly including Caleb Crewe,'' Eve said, feeling sad.

''Yes, unfortunately. Damn, I really liked the guy.'' David stared moodily into his empty soup bowl.

''Tell me more about the *Free Enterprise,*'' Eve said, wanting to get David's thoughts away from Caleb's possible treachery. ''Since it sank right here in your hometown territory, I guess the story of its fabulous cargo must be the stuff of legend, right?''

''Wrong, actually. In fact, the accounts written at the time the ship went down all indicated that the cargo was mostly what was called in those days 'English finished goods.' Things like Royal Doulton china and Axminster carpets, destined for the Boston luxury market and bought with money made by the sale of American timber in the British markets."

"So where did the gold come from?"

"That's still a mystery," David said. "But I suspect it was a payoff for the illegal cargo that the ship was running."

"You mean the *Free Enterprise* was a pirate ship?" Eve's eyes widened. "I thought piracy on the high seas ended long before the 1860s."

"It did, but during the Civil War, both the North and the South treated each other's merchant ships as fair game for seizing. Or sinking. The *Free Enterprise* was registered as a Union ship, which meant that it couldn't legally trade in Southern goods."

Eve was fascinated. "And you think that's what it was doing? Running the Northern blockade to trade with the South?"

"It seems very likely. By sheer chance, I was helping Aunt Connie sort through some Powell family papers this spring and came across a letter written by my ancestor, Bronwyn Powell. She made a couple of references to the fact that she suspected James Falconer, who owned the *Free Enterprise,* of being a secret Confederate sympathizer. My curiosity was piqued, and I got a friend in London to do some research in the Lloyd archives. He came back with the news that the *Enterprise*'s cargo, as it appeared on the Lloyds manifest, was very different from the cargo that folks in Boston and Eternity thought the ship was carrying. According to the documents my friend discovered, the ship was carrying weapons—and four trunks filled with gold sovereigns."

"It's amazing what musty old records can reveal, isn't it?" Eve said. "Is that why she sank? Because the Union navy discovered what her crew was up to and scuttled her?"

David shook his head. "No, she genuinely foundered during a gale. As far as I know, nobody around here had any idea what Falconer was up to."

"I'm almost glad she sank. Presumably, if she'd succeeded in running the blockade, not only would the Confederate cause have been advanced, but the ship's owner would have made a heap of money out of being a traitor.''

"A fortune," David agreed somberly. "The British were desperate for Southern cotton and indigo. The Confederacy was desperate for guns and ammunition. Any ship that managed to make the run in both directions without being intercepted stood to rake in a hefty profit. I'm pretty sure that's why James Falconer took the risk. Money seems to have been a strong motivator where he was concerned.''

"James *Falconer?*'' Eve was suddenly struck by the name. "That wouldn't by any chance be one of Mrs. Falconer's blue-blooded ancestors?''

"A blue-blooded and probably blackhearted ancestor," David said. "You haven't heard the worst of it. I think James Falconer was not only running the Northern blockade in order to bring guns to the Confederacy, I suspect he was also using slaves to act as crew on his ships.''

Eve recoiled. "Oh, no! What makes you think that?''

"Evidence from the wreck. When Matt and I were diving last week, we found the anchor from the *Enterprise.* Locked to the anchor chain were manacles, and nearby, tangled up in the eel grass, we actually found a couple of human shin bones.''

"Are the bones significant?" Eve asked. "I mean, several sailors drowned in the wreck, so finding the odd bone or two isn't unexpected, is it?''

"Maybe not, but underwater currents would probably tow any bodies out to sea unless those manacles were used to attach human beings to the anchor chain.''

Eve gulped. "My God! It's grotesque! You think he killed the slaves, then attached their bodies to the anchor chain…?''

"I'm not so sure he killed them first," David said grimly. "Here's my theory about what happened. When the ship started to sink, it was in sight of Eternity Harbor. The reports in the *Courier* make it clear that Ebenezer Pinnock, the captain, refused all offers to have local sailors come on board and help him navigate through the entrance to the harbor. Captain Pinnock claimed that his engines were damaged beyond repair and that he couldn't move the *Enterprise* because the sails were also inoperable. I think the truth is he was terrified that rescuers would see he had slaves on board and realize that his ship had been trading with the Confederacy. So rather than risk having the folks in Eternity find out what he'd been doing, he chained the slaves to the anchor and drowned them.''

Eve shuddered. "Oh, my God, how horrible! It's…it's so depraved."

"I guess the captain got the punishment he deserved. When he finally decided that he'd covered his tracks sufficiently to risk coming into harbor, it was too late. His engines really had failed, just as he claimed, and by this time, his mainmast had snapped in the gale. He couldn't save the ship, so he went down with it."

Eve felt not even a smidgen of pity for Ebenezer Pinnock. "I'd have preferred him to be found out in his treachery by the townsfolk. They'd have meted out a better punishment than death by drowning." With a murmur of thanks, she accepted a refill of her coffee cup from the waitress. "What about the rest of the crew?" she asked David. "Did any of them survive?"

"Several of them. Officially six sailors drowned, including Captain Pinnock, but of course nobody knew about the slaves. The rest of the crew was saved by the heroic efforts of the Eternity fishermen who took out their boats to rescue them."

Eve sipped her coffee. "Only one thing surprises me," she said. "People have always loved to gossip and hint at dark secrets, so I'm surprised rumors about the slaves never leaked out."

"James Falconer was a man who knew how to cover his rear end. He was in town the night of the gale, and he saw the *Enterprise* go down. According to the *Courier,* he hurried the surviving crew members off to Boston by first light the next day, insisting that they would suffer too much if they had to face the scene of the tragedy. The wily old fox was probably rushing them out of Eternity before they could tell anyone what the ship had been carrying and where it had been trading.''

''When you've brought up the gold, I'd love to do a program about the ship,'' Eve said. ''It would be wonderful if we could piece together James Falconer's story and tie it in to underwater scenes from the wreck. Not to mention the gold. Sunken treasure always goes over wonderfully with the viewing audience.''

''You'd have some technical problems getting good pictures,'' David said. ''The water down there is pretty murky.''

''I'll hire you as technical adviser to the shoot,'' she said.

''It's a deal.''

They looked at each other, dismayed at where their discussion had led them. Eve quickly changed the subject. ''Was that sovereign the investigator found on the beach the first proof you've had that the *Free Enterprise* really was carrying trunk loads of gold—'' She broke off, looking up with a slight smile. ''Matt, hi! How'd you manage to track us down?''

''This is one of David's favorite bolt holes,'' Matt said, barely managing a quick, distracted smile. His face was pale and drawn taut with grief. Tension kept his body twitching, as if little jolts of electricity were being shot randomly through his muscles. ''This sucks big time,'' he said to David. ''Amy told me what happened. Caleb...'' Matt's voice cracked, and he stared out of the window. Eve had the impression he was afraid to blink in case he started to cry.

''We tried to call you,'' David said. ''Joe at the motel thought you'd already left for Boston, but we knew that couldn't be true, because Amy was still at the *Courier* office.''

''Yeah, our great time in Boston was postponed again.'' Matt's voice was flat. ''Amy had to work this morning. The other girl called in sick.'' He rubbed his forehead, pinching the bridge of his nose in an effort to relieve the pressure. ''Jeez, Dave, for ten years I thought I'd really known Caleb, but now I'm wondering if I ever knew him at all. It's a rotten feeling.''

''The pits,'' David agreed harshly.

''What was he up to?'' Matt shook his head in bewilderment.

"What the hell was he doing down on the beach at some ungodly hour this morning?"

"There seem to be three possible options," David replied, his voice bleak. "I guess you'd call them the not-so-good, the bad and the absolute worst."

Matt hooked a chair with his toe and pulled it up to the table. "Let's start with the worst scenario first," he said.

"All right," David agreed. "Here it is. Caleb had made contact with a team of rogue treasure hunters, and before he died he'd already passed on to them the location of our dive site. He also made them a present of the grid charts he stole from your motel room last night."

Matt's cheeks turned sickly gray. "If he's done that, we're in deep sh—deep trouble."

"We sure are."

All smiles, the waitress approached their table. "Dessert, anyone? Sir, could I bring you a menu?"

Matt waved her away without even turning around to look. "Dammit, Dave, Caleb would never sell us out. He *couldn't* sell us out. He was a friend, not just some guy renting out his boat."

David didn't reply. His silence stretched out, painful in its implications. After several tense seconds, Matt sighed. "All right, I'm not going to argue with you. Let's approach this from another angle. If Caleb sold us out, why the hell did he get murdered? What was the point?"

This time David didn't hesitate. "To silence him," he said. "The only rational explanation for Caleb's murder is that there was a falling-out among thieves. Something must have gone terribly wrong with last night's deal or Caleb wouldn't have been killed."

"Why not?" Eve asked. "He presumably wasn't selling you out to a bunch of Sunday school teachers with high moral standards. Maybe this rogue team of treasure hunters planned all along to murder him as soon as they had the charts and knew the location of the wreck. That makes him one less person to pay off."

"It's unlikely," Matt said, shaking his head. "The last thing a rival team would want is to alert us to the fact that they're interested in our dive site. Ideally they'd just want to get in, loot the treasure and get out again before anyone knows they've located the wreck. Their interest would be in keeping Caleb alive and us innocently unaware we've been screwed."

David pushed his coffee cup aimlessly around the border of his place mat. "The police forensic team found a gold sovereign on the beach right by Caleb's hand. Did you hear that?"

"No!" Matt frowned. "Where the hell did he get it?" Reluctant understanding dawned in his eyes. "You think he stole it? From us?"

"I don't know where he got it," David said. "The date on the sovereign was 1862."

Eve couldn't see why the date was so significant, but Matt's breath drew in on a sharp hiss. "Good Lord! That's two years later than any coin we've found so far!"

"Yes. I guess he's found another source."

Neither David nor Matt said anything more, and Eve couldn't bear the silence. "So where did Caleb get the sovereign?" she asked. "If the date means he couldn't have stolen it from you, what's the big deal?"

"Maybe nothing," Matt said.

"Maybe everything," David said, sounding weary. "It could mean that Caleb and his gang have already plundered the wreck. If they found the gold, it would explain how Caleb came to be in possession of a sovereign dated 1862."

"But I thought you said Caleb didn't dive?" Eve said.

"Yes, that's what we thought," David replied grimly. "Maybe he couldn't. Or maybe we've been fooled coming and going."

"He can't have located the gold!" Matt exclaimed. "Why would anyone break into my motel room and steal the excavation charts if they've already found the treasure?"

David shook his head. "Not to mention leaving Caleb's body

in the middle of a beach where it was bound to be discovered. Why the hell did they do that?''

Eve's head shot up as she realized David had touched on an important point. "You're right," she said. "Why *did* they leave Caleb's body on the beach? There's a good chance whoever killed him arrived by boat. So why didn't they take the evidence of their crime out to sea when they left? They could have zoomed a few miles out into the ocean, tied the body in a weighted sack and tossed it overboard. Chances are Caleb wouldn't have been found for weeks.''

Matt leaned back in his chair, looking slightly less stricken now that his mind was focusing on the puzzle presented by Caleb's murder, rather than the savage reality of his friend's death. "The murderer might have been scared off by someone before he could dispose of Caleb's body, I suppose.''

"At that hour?" David said. "In that spot? And if some up-standing citizen scared off the killers, why hasn't he or she come forward?''

"Maybe they're embarrassed?" Matt suggested. "If the witness was somebody conducting an illicit love affair or a teenager who'd sneaked out of the house, he might not want to speak up.''

"It's possible," David said. "God knows, people have kept quiet about murder for the most appallingly trivial reasons.''

Matt took a crust of bread from the basket and munched on it absently. "Leaving aside the fact that I still can't believe Caleb agreed to sell us out, how could a straightforward deal go so badly wrong that murder was the only way out for the treasure hunters? Heck, we're talking a real simple trade here. Caleb provides grid maps and navigation charts. The rival team pays him. End of deal, end of story.''

"Maybe they couldn't agree on the price?" David shook his head, rejecting his own explanation. "But Caleb wasn't a fool, far from it. He'd never go to meet someone alone on a beach in the dead of night without having negotiated a price for what he was selling. Not to mention some solid guarantees to protect his own ass.''

"How do you know?'' Eve said quietly. ''Both of you are basing your judgment about how Caleb would behave on your relationship with him as a friend and partner. But that's the whole point, isn't it? If Caleb got killed when he went down to the beach to sell you out, then it seems to me you have to face up to the other side of the same reality.''

"What's that?'' David asked.

"That you didn't know very much about the real Caleb Crewe. And that you'd better get to know more about him pretty damn quick if you want to save your multimillion-dollar hoard of gold coins.''

Chapter Seven

After a lot of debate back and forth, David and Matt reluctantly agreed that they had an obligation to let the authorities know about the possible links between Caleb's death and their attempts to salvage the cargo of the *Free Enterprise*. Using Matt's car, they drove straight from the restaurant to the police station to make a report. Eve took David's Jeep and drove back into town to continue setting up interviews for the arrival of the "Roving Report" crew on Monday morning.

She worked hard, taking copious notes, soaking up the feel of the town and its citizens. At twilight, she stopped to watch a young bride and groom emerge from the chapel and pose for photographs to a chorus of enthusiastic cheers from family and friends. Usually her reaction to such a scene was a sardonic groan at the disillusionment lying ahead for the newlyweds. Today, for the first time since her divorce, she found herself offering a heartfelt wish that the couple might enjoy many years of shared happiness. Perhaps that was the secret of the chapel's success, she mused. Its legend allowed people to hope in an age clouded with cynicism.

By the time she let herself into the cottage it was dark and a light rain had begun to fall. She was aware of an odd sense of homecoming as she flicked the switch and the cozy crowded living room flooded with light. The cat jumped off the back of the sofa and stretched lazily, his mouth expanding into a cavernous pink yawn.

"Hello, Cat," she said, making her way into the kitchen and

dumping her purse on the corner of the counter as she walked by. "I guess your master isn't home yet."

Cat didn't deign to reply to the obvious. Eve scratched his ear. "I'm going to cook dinner for your owner. Something special to take his mind off what happened to Caleb."

Cat's eyes fixed on her with an expression of profound feline scorn. She smiled ruefully, then shrugged. "Okay, you're right. I'm a lousy cook, and David isn't going to forget about Caleb anytime soon, but it's worth a try, isn't it? Besides, this cottage makes me feel…domesticated, I guess. In a place like this, cooking a hearty dinner actually seems like fun."

Apparently "dinner" was a magic word to the cat. He stalked into the kitchen, whiskers twitching. Rubbing against her legs, he whisked back and forth several times until her wool slacks were coated with hair. A purr started to rumble in his throat. Eve stroked his back, muttering complaints about the cat hair decorating her slacks, but secretly enjoying the sensation of being greeted by a friendly living creature.

"David's overfeeding you," she said, giving him a final pat and swooshing him away. "Go take a run around the house—you're way too fat." She closed the blinds on the kitchen window, shutting out the darkness and the drizzle, which was beginning to turn into a steady downpour of cold rain.

Cat reacted to the uncalled-for comment on his girth by walking straight to his bowl and looking pitiful when he discovered it was empty.

Eve laughed. "Okay, I get the message. You're starving and I'm a monster. Sorry, but you'll have to wait for your dinner until David gets home. I don't know what he feeds you. In the meantime, let's decide what we're going to cook tonight."

She pulled open the freezer door and stared at an unpromising collection of prepackaged meals and plastic containers that seemed to be filled with ancient foodstuffs liberally coated with ice crystals. In the end, she selected a package of ground beef that looked as if it might, with luck, have been bought within the past week or two and set it in the microwave to defrost. The pantry yielded rice, a can of tomatoes and a container of chili powder. The fridge was stocked with surprisingly fresh cheese, a couple of shiny green peppers and a wizened onion. Eve decided that gourmet meals had been made of less.

"Chili," she announced to the cat. "My best recipe, and about the only meal David has the ingredients for. Obviously it's fate that I got home first tonight. What we have here is a perfect meeting of talent and opportunity."

Cat stared at her. Or rather, if truth were told, at the package of ground beef she'd just taken out of the microwave. His whiskers vibrated with longing. Eve hardened her heart and found a skillet, setting the meat to brown over a low heat.

"I had an interesting meeting with Bronwyn Powell this afternoon. She's David's sister, you know, and a justice of the peace. She performs a lot of the weddings in the Eternity chapel, including the one today. She tried hard to be nice although I'm sure she doesn't approve of me. She was polite, but she thinks I must be mentally deficient to have divorced her marvelous brother."

Cat gave his empty bowl a yearning lick.

Eve sighed. "Face it, Cat, as a conversationalist you lack a certain something, but as a moocher you're first-rate." She couldn't find any tins or bags of cat food, so she put a spoonful of half-cooked ground beef into his bowl and mixed it with chunks of stale bread. Cat devoured the offering as if he hadn't seen sustenance in days.

"Beats the yucky stuff that comes in tins, huh?" Humming as she arranged the ingredients for her chili on the counter, Eve reached for the chopping board. Her mood was surprisingly upbeat in view of Caleb's murder and the possible threat to David's safety. Bronwyn's quiet courtesy had helped to remind her that the world had plenty of good people along with the few bad ones. She had also learned from Bronwyn that David's mother was out of town for ten days, which meant that Eve didn't need to wrestle with the idea of whether or not to visit her former mother-in-law—a major relief. Divorce certainly threw up some interesting social dilemmas, she reflected wryly.

Cat had given up waiting for more food. Ears pricked, he marched out of the kitchen and jumped onto the battered table where David kept his scuba equipment. Eve watched his progress from the corner of her eye, ready to scold him if he tried to get back onto the counter to steal food.

Some incongruity—maybe a rippling movement of David's wet suit caused by the thump of Cat's tail—suddenly attracted her attention. Her humming stopped in midbreath and she swung around, really looking at the dark corner for the first time since she'd entered the cottage.

"Oh my God!" Eve dropped the paring knife with a clatter. Her training as a diver was minimal, but she didn't need much familiarity with scuba equipment to recognize that David's gear had been viciously damaged. His wet suit had been slashed in half a dozen places, leaving insulating rubber and plastic hanging in forlorn shreds. His regulator hoses had been cut into strips, and his face mask looked as if it had been smashed with a hammer. The fingers on his gloves had been snipped and his flippers hacked into small pieces. In fact, every single item had been spoiled in one way or another.

Rinsing her hands and grabbing a towel, Eve walked over to the table. The ruination looked even worse on closer inspection, a savage display of angry destruction. Nothing could be salvaged, she was certain. David would have to outfit himself from scratch before he could dive again.

She felt anger on David's behalf before she felt fear. She was poking gingerly through the shards of splintered metal and glass when she was struck by the realization that if all this equipment had been destroyed, someone must have invaded the cottage to do the destroying.

And that someone might still be here.

The warm glow of light in the kitchen no longer seemed cozy. Instead, it seemed a threatening spotlight, illuminating her in its glare. Instinctively she stepped backward, huddling against the table as she peered into the nooks and crannies of the kitchen and living room.

The ground floor of the cottage was small enough to check out in a couple of sweeping glances, but it was irregularly shaped, with lots of jutting walls and niches. The fact that the place appeared empty of intruders wasn't as reassuring as it might have been in her boxlike New York apartment.

Eve swallowed hard, fighting back an attack of panic as she crept along the narrow hallway to the main-floor bathroom. She knew it was stupid to tiptoe when she'd been banging pots and pans around for fifteen minutes, announcing her arrival to anyone who wasn't deaf. Still, the need to crouch, to be quiet, was intuitive. Heart pounding, she flung open the bathroom door and sighed with relief when she was greeted by silent emptiness.

Of course there was no one here, she told herself. There was no logical reason to suppose the person who destroyed the scuba gear was still in the cottage. Why would he hang around once his dirty deed was done? If he'd been anywhere nearby when she arrived home, he'd have gone after her the moment she came through the door.

A soft thud from overhead instantly banished her attempt at calm. She grabbed the poker and raced up the stairs, trying to achieve a compromise between speed and quiet. Outside David's bedroom door she paused, straining to hear the slightest sound.

There were no more thumps, but she heard the faint rustle of moving cloth and her palms grew slippery around the poker. Was somebody hiding behind the curtains? Crawling under the bed?

Belatedly it occurred to her that even if the intruder still lurked in David's bedroom, she would be crazy to burst in and challenge him. Much as she wanted to confront the person who'd vandalized David's diving gear, a poker was no match for a gun, and the intruder would almost certainly carry a gun.

She ran downstairs again and dialed the police with shaking fingers, her back turned to the wall and her gaze fixed on the stairs. She wondered why she was feeling so shocked, so violated. Caleb's death should have warned her not to trust appearances, however beguiling. She'd allowed Eternity to wrap her in its small-town embrace and lull her into a false sense of security. She wouldn't make that mistake again.

She heard the sound of a car approaching on the gravel road just as she finished dialing. She lifted the blinds and saw Matt's car, the hood ornament gleaming in the spill of light from the porch. Ignoring the response of the police operator, she let the receiver drop back into its cradle as David got out of the car, waving a quick goodbye to his friend. Eve pulled open the front door in time to see Matt swing the BMW around and race off, scattering gravel.

"David, I'm so glad you're home!" She hadn't realized how badly she wanted to see him until he was actually there on the doorstep. "I guess Matt decided not to come in?" She tried to smile, tried to sound in control, and failed miserably.

"He and Amy are finally getting together for their heavy date. Matt was just about panting. The police kept us far longer than we expected." David stepped into the cottage, shaking off a shower of raindrops. He pushed the front door closed with his foot, reaching for her all in the same motion. "What is it?" he asked. "Eve, honey, what's the matter?"

Honey. Strange how natural, how right, that sounded. "Your diving gear," she said, fighting a crazy impulse to burst into tears. "Oh, David, it's totally destroyed! Someone got into the cottage and vandalized it. And I'm afraid the intruder might still be here. I heard someone—something—moving around upstairs in your bedroom!"

He muttered a curse, and then another, more forceful. "Stay here," he ordered, brushing her cheek in a quick, reassuring caress. He took the stairs two at a time, using his foot to push open the door to his bedroom and immediately springing back to flatten himself against the corridor wall.

Eve held her breath. For two or three seconds there was complete silence, then Cat strolled out of the bedroom and rubbed David's legs briefly before continuing on downstairs and sitting on 'his' rug in front of the fire.

"I guess Cat was the intruder you heard," David said. Cautiously he entered his bedroom, disappearing from Eve's view. A minute or two later, he reappeared. "Everything seems okay," he said as he came downstairs. "Although I'm pretty sure I closed the door to my room when I left this morning, specifically to keep Cat out."

"You did, I remember. So whoever vandalized your diving equipment must have gone into your room, too, and then left the door open when he came out."

"Nothing seems to have been stolen or even disturbed. I checked the closet and my chest of drawers." David put his arm around her shoulders and walked her to the table where his ruined equipment lay scattered. He viewed it in silence for several long moments, then turned her in his arms and held her close. "They did a pretty thorough job of destruction, didn't they? Thank God whoever did this wasn't still here when you got back."

She shivered. "It looks...vicious," she said. "Almost demented. The way he ground up the glass from your face mask..."

"As long as you're all right, that's all that really matters." His arms tightened around her. "Thank God you weren't hurt."

"But you've lost all your equipment, hundreds of dollars' worth! Thousands!"

He cupped her face in his hands, smoothing out her frown with his forefingers. "Honey, don't look so stricken. It's only plastic and aluminum, with a few fancy bells and whistles tacked on. Fortunately we can buy plenty more of that. All we need is money."

"A lot of money," she pointed out.

"Last I heard, the dive shop takes credit cards." He pressed his finger against her nose, willing her to smile. "I have one of those fancy gold cards with a hologram in the corner. It's about time I gave it a workout."

His good humor calmed her fears, but for some reason, she found her throat clogging up and the tears she'd locked inside welling up in her eyes and spilling down her cheeks. She felt herself go hot and then cold with embarrassment, but still the tears wouldn't stop. She wiped her eyes on the sleeve of her sweater. More tears appeared.

"Eve, sweetheart, don't cry." David used his thumbs to staunch her tears. He looked uneasy. Tears had always reduced him to a state of flurried incoherence, and Eve had tried never to cry when he was anywhere near. They'd freely shared laughter and passion. The darker emotions they'd kept to themselves.

But this time the more she tried to stop, the harder she cried. "Eve," he said, sounding desperate. "Eve, honey, tell me what's the matter."

"It was my birthday," she sobbed. "It was my birthday, dammit!" The tears gushed out, a positive Niagara of grief.

David appeared puzzled, as well he might. "Today?" he asked. "But your birthday is in May."

She swallowed over a hiccuping sob. "Not today. The night you didn't come home for dinner. The night I asked you for a divorce...."

"I know, honey." He looked stricken. "Eve, I'm sorry. I realized later that it was a special occa—"

She interrupted, choking out the accusation that had haunted her for two years. "It was my thirtieth birthday, and you didn't even bother to call!"

Eve realized there were a lot of excuses he could make for not having called, chief among them the fact that he'd been trying to save himself from the threat of a criminal indictment. But he made no excuses. He just stared down at her, not saying a word, his blue eyes shadowed with regret. She sensed the hesitation in him, the reserve, and knew there was something he was holding back.

Dammit, he was doing it again! Eve's tears stopped as suddenly as they'd started and her cheeks began to burn, but not entirely with anger. To her dismay, the potent combination of fear and frustration she felt began to change. The simple fact of David's nearness left her hot and shivery with physical desire.

Torn between excitement and despair, she acknowledged that it had always been like this between them. Any intense emotion, happy or sad, eventually seemed to transform itself into a white-hot flame of sexual need.

David felt the change in her the moment it occurred and recognized the cause. Why not? He'd had years of practice in responding to her sexuality, years of practice in fanning the flame of her desire. His fingers trailed down her cheeks and brushed across her mouth, which—inevitably—had started to tremble.

"I guess it would complicate things if I kissed you," he said huskily.

"It would complicate things," she said. "A lot."

His head bent a little lower and his voice thickened. "Sex is never the answer to anything."

"Never," she agreed. "Absolutely never."

"We sure found that out during our marriage."

"We proved it conclusively," she said, but she didn't move away. Her hands crept up and linked behind his head. David closed his eyes. Her hips started to rock toward him, but she caught herself in midsway, freezing into stillness, terrified of where they were headed.

David sighed restlessly, pulling her against him. "I've missed you, Eve." His mouth was no more than a millimeter from hers. "God, I've missed you."

She had just enough sense left not to respond to that remark, but he closed the infinitesimal gap between them, anyway. He touched his mouth to hers and her lips parted in instant hungry response.

He tasted of the cold and the rain and a hundred nights when they'd shared the wonders of a sexual passion that seemed to have no limits, no beginning and no end. Eve felt a wave of longing start in her toes and surge through her entire body. Shuddering in his arms, she pulled up his damp sweater and pressed her mouth to his skin, drinking deep of the taste and texture of him. The thud of his heart slowed and melded with hers. In the space of a kiss, their bodies had readapted to a single unified rhythm.

When she realized they were lying on the sofa, she couldn't remember how they'd gotten there. Worse, she didn't really care. David was muttering frenzied love words, covering her neck and shoulders with feverish kisses. She preferred not to reflect on the fact that declarations of love didn't mean much when spoken in the throes of unslaked passion.

"Yes," she whispered. "Yes, David, please make love to me."

"I want you."

"I want you, too. So much." She melted deeper into his embrace, molten with longing, soft and sleek with need.

His hands shook as they pushed her slacks over her hips and fumbled when they reached for the clasp of her bra. His mouth closed over one of her nipples just as she found the buckle of his belt and unzipped his jeans. He was rock hard. She was already shivering on the brink of climax.

They pushed aside the last remnants of their clothes, scattering underwear over the floor and sofa as she pulled him on top of her. He slid into her, and she wrapped her legs around him, waiting for the deep strokes that would carry her to the culmination hovering so tantalizingly on the horizon.

He brushed her hair out of her eyes, his gaze fierce as he looked down at her. "My God, Eve, it's been torment without you. Without this."

"I know. I've missed you, too."

David's voice was hoarse. "It feels like a million years since we made love."

Eve didn't—couldn't—answer. She was suddenly seized by an edgy, restless sense of danger, as if some sixth sense warned her of emotional hazards lurking frighteningly close. Only a few moments ago they'd both agreed that sex was never the answer to problems in a relationship. So why was she setting herself up to reopen all the old unresolved issues? The painful unhealed wounds?

Perversely, the half-realized threat of danger did nothing to cool her physical needs. On the contrary, it seemed to add the final spark that set the conflagration burning out of control. Instead of escaping while she still could, she countered the sense of danger by grasping David's head between her hands, pulling his lips to hers and thrusting her tongue into his mouth. He shuddered, convulsing in response.

Yes, she thought on a sigh of silent exultation. Now, at last, she felt whole. In David's arms she would finally ease the gnawing hunger that had been building inexorably ever since she'd landed on the floor of the lighthouse and found herself trapped beneath him. Trapped beneath the powerful, muscled body that for some reason seemed to have a unique capacity to drive her wild.

She arched her hips, inviting him more deeply into her. His face contorted into a spasm of pleasure as he accepted her invitation and thrust hard, claiming possession.

In the arid years since their divorce she'd forgotten that sexual desire could be fierce enough to leave her barely breathing, suspended between agony and bliss. She'd forgotten that the need to mate could be as compelling and as elemental as the longing for water after days wandering lost in the desert. Forgotten that when David held her the universe stopped in its tracks. Forgotten that when he cupped her breasts and kissed her throat she felt stars explode and her soul shatter. Dear God, she'd been so careful never to let herself remember! But now the past was uniting with the present in a dazzling star burst of pleasure. David was tormenting her with exquisite reminders, forcing her to remember the forbidden past, enticing her to walk with him into an unknown future.

The tremble of ultimate release started deep inside her as David plunged, prolonging the exquisite moments. She soared with him into the secret universe only he could find. A place of magic and dark velvet softness. A place of light and rainbows and shimmering joy.

For a few endless, blissful moments, Eve knew that in David's arms she had found perfect happiness. For an instant carved in time she realized she would never find this much happiness with any other man.

Then reality returned. She sat up and opened her eyes.

A FEW SECONDS before she said anything David knew Eve was going to deny the reality of what had happened between them. The little pants of her breath hadn't quite stopped, and her body still quivered with the aftershocks of her pleasure, but her hands suddenly pushed against his shoulders, forcing him away. Her eyes flew open and she stared at him with something close to despair. Then she turned her head away, hiding her face in the sofa cushions.

Although he knew she didn't want him to touch her, he couldn't resist letting his hand trail down her spine, relishing the way she quivered at even this light caress. Her skin was perfect: smooth, still golden with the remnants of a summer tan. Incredibly, despite the intensity of their sexual encounter, he already felt aroused again.

She shivered, her breath quickening, even though she refused to look at him. David knew precisely the odd combination of physical response and mental rejection she experienced as his fingers stroked her back. Knew, because his own feelings were just as ambivalent and just as strong.

"David, please let me get up." Her voice was muffled since she chose to speak to the sofa rather than to him.

He dropped his hand and moved away, but only to the end of the sofa, sitting by her feet. He wondered what the hell they were supposed to do now. The sex they'd just shared had been spectacular, perhaps the most wonderful of his entire life, but where did that leave them? Whatever naive delusions he'd harbored when they first met, he'd wised up enough by now to realize that great sex didn't make a great marriage. He and Eve had enjoyed mind-blowing sex for more than a year after they got married, but that hadn't stopped them heading for the divorce court with the emotional wounds they'd inflicted on each other still fresh and painful. Since David wasn't a masochist, presumably the incredible sex he'd just enjoyed with Eve wasn't cause to rush out and apply for an immediate renewal of their marriage license. But wasn't it cause for *something?*

What kind of man was so out of touch with his needs that he didn't know how he felt or what he wanted? How could he possibly *not* know what he felt about this person—the woman he'd married and divorced? The idea of being confused about his feelings at this stage in the game was patently ridiculous. But his heart was hammering and his stomach churning. And the honest-to-God truth was that he didn't know why.

He watched as Eve scrabbled among the sofa cushions, obviously searching for something. He fished her bra from between two pillows and held it out, gaze carefully blank. Much as he loathed not being in control of his feelings, he loathed revealing his uncertainty even more. "Is this what you're looking for?" he asked.

"Thanks." She snatched the bra and put it on, hunching away from him as she cupped her breasts and fastened the front hook. He found the simple everyday action unbearably erotic. Hell, he thought, a smidgen of humor returning, that wasn't surprising. He found everything Eve did unbearably erotic.

He waited until they'd both scrambled into their clothes before he said anything else, hoping Eve would feel less vulnerable and less defensive when she was dressed. Then he took her hands, holding fast when she tried to tug them away. Growing up in a big affectionate family, he'd always assumed that important relationships took care of themselves. In his child's view of the world, mothers and fathers and brothers and sisters all loved each other simply because they were family. And this view was never challenged, because in his family, it had been true.

Only when his marriage was already well down the road to failure had he realized he might sometimes need to put complex feelings into words, however hard that might be. And only after his divorce had he understood another, subtler truth: the harder it was to find the right words, the more likely the words were needed.

"Eve," he said softly, "thank you for what we just shared. Making love to you, well, there's been nothing else like it in my life, ever. It was...wonderful."

"You're welcome." Her pulse fluttered beneath his fingertips. She ran her hand over her face, hiding a blush more of frustration than embarrassment. David found it comforting to realize that, despite her poise and fluency on camera, she couldn't always find the words she needed, either.

"I didn't mean that the way it sounded." She drew a shaky breath. "David, the sex...the lovemaking...was wonderful, but I still think it was a mistake. I mean, there's no...context for what we did."

"I know." During their marriage he'd always felt compelled to sound decisive, knowledgeable, in control. Masculine. Now he saw his bluster for what it had been: the arrogant posturing of a man afraid to reveal his uncertainties. He turned her hand palm up and carried it to his face, pressing it against his cheek. "I know one thing, though. When two people can give each other so much pleasure every time they make love, there must *be* a context."

She drew her hand away, not roughly, but almost sadly. "Maybe not, David. Maybe the only context is that we make great sexual partners." She stood up, looking down at him with troubled eyes. "We're forgetting how badly we hurt each other when we were together. The lovemaking was great. But the pain and the horrible silences in our marriage were real, too. After...after what just happened between us, it's too easy to forget the silence and the hurts."

"Neither of us seems to be finding them easy to forget. In fact I'd say we've both done a great job of remembering. We're scared to death to get close to each other again in case we inflict more wounds."

Eve gave a tiny smile. "Let's face it, David, we have reason to be scared." She gave a tiny gasp. "I don't think I could survive another two months like the last two of our marriage."

"Maybe we've both learned something about the importance of communicating," he suggested.

"Have we?" Eve seemed on the brink of walking away, then she shrugged and turned to face him. "All right, David, let's communicate. I still want to work in television and you'd like me to stay home. I still want to have a baby, and I think I can manage that without sacrificing my career."

"And what's going to happen to the baby when you go back to work?" David snapped. "Who's going to take care of this child of ours when you're away on assignment, filming drug lords and crack addicts and deposed dictators whose armed thugs are likely to rough you up if they don't like your questions?"

"I think you just proved my point," Eve said, her smile fading, leaving only the sadness behind. "The gaps between us, our disagreements about what we want out of marriage, are too wide to be bridged. You want a homemaker, David, and I want something…much more complicated."

He was very much afraid she was right, although part of him—his libido?—wanted to insist she was wrong. He ran his hands through his hair, hot and scratchy with frustration. "Dammit, Eve—"

She touched a finger to his lips. "Let's not talk about it right now."

"But that's what we always did. Decided not to talk."

"No." She shook her head. "When we were married, we didn't *decide* not to talk. We fell into resentful silences."

"And this is different?" he asked, raising an eyebrow.

"Sure it is." She risked a faint smile. "At least now we've openly acknowledged the sort of problem we're facing, and we've agreed that taking the problem to bed and burying it in sex won't work."

"It may not have worked," he muttered. "But the burial process sure was a lot of fun."

"Only for a while. Look, David, we need to spend some time thinking about solutions that might work for us. Maybe we can come up with something. Maybe we can't. But yelling at each other isn't going to help, and making love again is only going to confuse the issues.'' She drew a deep breath. ''We simply mustn't make love—have sex—again, David. We can't. It's too confusing.''

The way he felt right now, confusing the issues with sex sounded like a terrific idea, probably the best idea he'd had in months. He managed to smile. ''If we can't find a way to be married to each other, maybe we could agree to spend one month a year on a desert island making love.'' He wasn't sure if he was being facetious.

She laughed. ''Now that's a really tempting proposition. You're a truly magnificent lover, David.''

Her whole face lit up when she smiled. Looking at her, David knew that a month of lovemaking would never satisfy him. After a month in bed with Eve, he would simply be left craving more of the same. Which brought him right back to where this wretched conversation had started. He scowled, stumbling through his thoughts, trying to decide how he could persuade her to accept his point of view when he wasn't sure what his point of view was.

Eve gave him a quick, light kiss on the cheek. He resisted the nearly overwhelming impulse to grab her. ''We'll talk again,'' she said softly. ''But not now, David.'' Her breath caught in a little hiccup that was almost a sob. ''Not now, David, please.''

''Okay.'' He accepted her desire to change the subject, albeit reluctantly. He might be mixed up, but he was smart enough to know he wasn't capable of handling a renewed attack of her tears. ''Did I see signs of dinner in the kitchen?'' he asked. ''What were you planning to make?''

''Chili,'' she said with evident relief. ''Chili and rice. It'll take about an hour, though. I'd barely gotten started.''

''I'll help. I can chop and grate with the best of 'em.''

''Great. That should speed things up. I'm hungry again, even though we ate lunch late.'' Eve sounded unnaturally bright and her smile was obviously forced. David wasn't sure whether he wanted to rail at her for refusing to face the reality of what they both felt, or whether he wanted to kiss her for being so adorably stubborn. Or was that simply two different facets of the same want? He ordered himself to stop asking dumb questions and applied himself to chopping green peppers with grim determination.

"Tell me what happened at the police station," Eve said as they settled into the rhythm of slicing and dicing.

"The police were interested in what Matt and I had to say, to put it mildly."

"Did they tell you what's happening with their investigation?"

"Not much. They've contacted Caleb's sister and she's going to make the funeral arrangements. Joyce—that's the sister— maintains her brother despised drugs and would never deal in them."

"That doesn't surprise you."

"No, I agree with her. Other than that, we didn't learn much. Pete Pieracini was obviously feeling guilty about his loose tongue down on the beach today. To compensate, he very nearly turned himself into a walking, talking edition of the police guide on how not to blab to citizens. He insisted that the investigation was on track and the Boston police were digging up useful background information on Caleb Crewe."

"I'd love to know the detective's definition of useful."

David grinned. "That's easy. Anything that links the motive for Caleb's murder to big-city Boston criminals."

She added onion and chopped peppers to the garlic browning in a pan. "You'll have to tell him about the destruction of your diving gear."

"Yes, I'll make another report tomorrow morning." He grimaced. "The police station's beginning to feel like my second home."

Eve stirred a can of tomatoes into the ground beef and lowered the flame beneath the pan. "Why would anyone want to destroy your equipment, David? And how did they get into the cottage? They must have had a key because the lock wasn't smashed."

"Half the town of Eternity probably has a key to this place," David said. "My aunts dish 'em out to any friend, relative or passing acquaintance who needs a place to stay."

"Maybe we should change the lock," she suggested.

"I'll call a locksmith in the morning. That won't keep out anyone who's determined to get in, but there's no point making things easy for intruders."

"Maybe he could check the bolts on the windows at the same time," Eve said. "Although we're probably closing the barn door after the horse has bolted."

"Not if it keeps you safe," David said, surprised and embarrassed when he heard his voice turn husky with emotion. He was overwhelmed by the sudden need to hold her, a need that was only partly sexual. Unable to resist, he put his arms around her waist, nestling his face against the smooth skin of her neck. She felt warm and womanly and unexpectedly fragile. He pulled her closer, the urge to protect instantly transforming into an urge more explicitly sexual. "God, Eve, you're so beautiful."

She trembled and the wooden spoon she was holding slipped from her fingers. "Don't," she whispered. "We agreed...no more...not tonight...."

"Then walk away from me," he said, dropping his arms to his sides.

He felt the shudder of her indrawn breath. She took a single step, then stopped. He didn't dare move in case she took another one. The silence in the kitchen stretched out, a hollow dome, vibrating with conflicting emotions. When he couldn't stand the tension any longer, he reached around her and turned off the stove. Then he held out his hand and led her without speaking toward the stairs. This time he wanted to make love to her in his bed, with soft pillows and warm covers and all the time in the world to show her what he was feeling.

She gave a little sigh, half acceptance, half regret, and let her head fall against him as they climbed the stairs. Outside his room she hesitated again, and he stepped across the threshold, silently inviting her in. She followed him into the room, but he could see his own turmoil reflected in her troubled expression. Eve was too honest not to acknowledge the desire she felt, but he knew she hadn't come to terms with the disparity between her sexuality and what her common sense told her.

He risked breaking the spell by speaking. "Eve, this isn't just about sex."

She met his gaze. "Maybe that's why I'm so scared."

He smiled wryly. "Me, too." He didn't want to look away from her, so he reached behind him to turn back the covers on the bed. Still with his gaze locked on hers, he tossed back the comforter and the top sheet. But as he stepped forward to take her into his arms, her face froze in an expression of total horror.

"Eve?" He tried to hold her, but she pushed him violently away. "Eve, honey, what is it?"

She gagged, literally unable to speak. Then she pointed to the bed, closing her eyes.

He swung around to look, not sure what he expected. A rat stared back at him, dead eyes hideously vacant, its gullet spilling out of its slit throat, intestines exposed by the surgically sliced belly. The fat black body was already frozen into stiffness, and its pink tail formed a curved question mark of naked flesh against the beige sheets.

Hastily he threw the top sheet back over the grisly sight. Arm around Eve's waist, he hurried her from the room. "Wait for me downstairs," he said. "I'll take care of cleaning it up."

"I'm all right." She spoke through stiff lips. "It was the shock, that's all." She cleared her throat. "Would you...would you check the bed in my room?"

"Sure." He went into the guest room and pulled back the covers. A rat, a mirror image of the one in his bed, stared at him with sightless eyes. David stared back, momentarily transfixed. Then he realized he was wiping his hands against the seat of his jeans, as if trying to rid himself of contamination. Tight-lipped, he returned to Eve's side.

One look at his face told her what he'd found. "There was another rat." Her words were a flat statement, not a question.

"Yes. I'll take care of it. We'll need clean sheets. Clean everything, in fact."

She hardly seemed to hear him. Her blue eyes appeared enormous against the pallor of her face. "David, what's this all about? Who could have done this to you?"

He felt a twitch of gallows humor. "Well, not Caleb Crewe."

"My God, David, this isn't a joking matter. This is a serious hate crime. You must tell the police right away. A person would have to be mentally unbalanced to slit the throats and bellies of two huge rats and put them in your beds. And crazy people are dangerous." She wrapped her arms around her waist, shivering. "My God, they were enormous! I've never seen a rat that big before."

Knowing Eve, he doubted if she'd seen many rats, period. For himself, finding the dead rats in his beds had filled him with feelings of rage and a determination to find out who was responsible. Watching Eve, the rage dissipated and David was overcome by a renewed wave of tenderness.

"Come on, let's go downstairs," he said, taking her hand and holding it for a moment against his cheek. "You're ice cold, honey. Why don't you build us a fire, which will please Cat no end, and I'll call the police."

She drew a deep, hard breath. "Lord knows, I'm always happy to be of service to the cat," she muttered.

He admired her courage all the more because he knew how squeamish she was. If the rats had bothered him, he knew they must have devastated her. He gave her hand a comforting squeeze.

"I'm glad you're here, Eve," he said, surprising himself by the simple truth of his words. "I'm really glad you're here."

Chapter Eight

Detective Pieracini, commenting darkly that Eternity seemed to be in the midst of a crime wave ever since Eve had arrived in town, conducted a thorough inspection of the cottage and asked numerous questions, none of them leading anywhere as far as Eve could see. He arranged to have the table where David stowed his gear dusted for fingerprints, and concluded his visit by warning them both to take the incident seriously.

"As of now, it's my opinion the murder of Caleb Crewe will turn out to be connected to your attempt to salvage valuable cargo from the *Free Enterprise*," he informed them earnestly. "Mr. Crewe seems to have been associated with some very nasty folks, and you'd better be prepared for the worst. I'm going to call the Coast Guard and request that they patrol the area around your dive site, David. We want to know if anyone turns up there over the weekend."

David started to protest that he wasn't anxious to draw attention to the site, but the policeman cut him off. "Look, you may want to keep the exact location of the wreck a secret, but that's crazy in view of what's happened. From what you and your friend Matt Packard told me, if Caleb Crewe handed over those charts to some crowd of underwater criminals, sooner or later they're going to turn up and cause trouble. Probably sooner rather than later. So if you take my advice, you and Matt will be very cautious before you do your next dive. I don't know much about scuba equipment and such, but I bet there's a lot of opportunities for the pair of you to get into a whole heap of trouble when you're swimming around a wreck hundreds of feet underwater.''

On this ominous note he departed. Eve was exhausted, but the prospect of going to bed was unappealing, to say the least. Pete had taken charge of the rats, whether to dispose of them or send them for postmortem examination, she preferred not to inquire. To her chagrin, she was discovering that it was one thing to film the seamy side of life and quite another to live through it. Her recently acquired veneer of cool sophistication was, it seemed, just that. Deep down inside, she was still the same wimpy Eve Graham who'd ducked biology class and never went to a movie unless she was sure it had a happy ending.

She helped David remake the beds with clean linen, swallowing a twinge of nausea at the smears of blood on the sheets. Unfortunately the clean linen did nothing to obliterate her mental pictures of the dead rat, hairless tail curled obscenely among the covers. If she'd been alone, she wouldn't have bothered with dinner, but David said he was hungry, so they set up a card table in front of the fire and she served up the rice and chilli, willing to push food around her plate and pretend to eat rather than admit to a churning stomach and shaky nerves.

Surprisingly, instead of giving her indigestion, the spicy, piping-hot food seemed to help her relax. The normal everyday pleasure of eating a good meal in front of a warm fire somehow muted the repulsiveness of what they'd discovered upstairs in the bedrooms. At first she responded only mechanically to David's attempts at conversation. By the time they were sipping cups of after-dinner coffee, she realized she was truly engrossed in explaining how she and a two-man crew from "Roving Report" had managed to film a Central American dictator at the very moment an insurgent army stormed his summer palace in the mountains.

During their marriage, Eve would never have admitted to the dangers she'd encountered in capturing such an incident on film. Ironically, despite her prevarications, David would have read behind her silence and been coldly furious at the risks she'd taken.

Tonight, perhaps because she was no longer his wife, he seemed more able to accept the hazards of her profession. He simply asked interested questions about how she'd persuaded the dictator to grant her an exclusive interview and expressed his admiration for the brilliance of the program that resulted. "You deserved your Emmy," he said.

"Thank you." She smiled, flushed with pleasure. Tucking her legs under her, she settled further in the big shabby armchair. "Now it's your turn. Tell me what you've been doing these past two years. Why did you leave your job with Cyrus Frank? You always seemed to enjoy being a stockbroker."

"I did enjoy it up to a point, but our divorce, and the showdown with Ned Nichols, gave me a real need to step back and reevaluate my priorities. Matt had just spent six months working in the Galapagos Islands on a marine-research project, and he was determined never to go back to being a lawyer. He convinced me I should spend some time with him diving in the Gulf of Mexico. I asked Cyrus for a three-month leave of absence, and he agreed. Three months was all it took. By the time my leave of absence was up, I was hooked."

"On the diving?" Eve asked. "Or on the lure of finding underwater treasure?"

"Both," he said.

"It's an odd combination, stockbroker and deep-sea diver."

He smiled. "Do you think so? I've decided that the two professions have a lot in common. They're both jobs where you need to have a cool head and steady nerves. You have to be willing to do lots of meticulous research and careful comparative analyses, but in the end, you also have to be willing to play your hunches. That's how you get the big payoff in the end. Like here in Eternity with the *Enterprise.*"

"Sure," Eve said. "A two-and-a-half-million-dollar payoff in this case. Always provided the Calebs of the world don't murder you first."

"We don't know yet what Caleb was up to or why he was murdered," David pointed out. "And if you've read a newspaper recently, you may have noticed that hunting for underwater treasure isn't the only way to get yourself killed these days." He hurried on before she could dispute his point. "Anyway, after three great months in the Gulf of Mexico, Matt and I decided to formally quit our 'real' jobs and team up as full-time divers. We did some intensive research into wreck sites, moved south and started working off the coast of Guiana."

"With anyone else, I'd try to look intelligent," Eve said. "With you, I'll come clean. I haven't the faintest idea where Guiana is."

"It's a strip of coastal land between Venezuela and Brazil. The British, French and Dutch all had colonies there at one time or another. Matt and I uncovered a promising lead and went to Holland to follow up with research. We found rock-solid evidence that a group of insurgent peasants had sabotaged a Dutch colonial tax ship and that it sank only about twenty miles from the harbor, which made the salvage prospects much easier."

"Sounds exciting. Did it work out? Did you find a treasure trove of tax money and turn into instant millionaires?"

"I wish." He smiled ruefully. "We didn't find a thing. Not even a trace of the hull, much less a ship laden with treasure. Which doesn't mean it isn't down there somewhere, just that we didn't manage to look in the right place. Matt and I spent six months and far more money than we could afford, and came out with a big fat nothing. But, hey, it was great fun and we learned a lot."

David's face was alight with enthusiasm, and Eve felt a surge of affection as she looked at him. He'd been a workaholic overachiever all his life, going from high school to college to graduate school and then plunging straight into the competitive world of the New York financial markets, virtually without pausing for a break. Along the way, he'd acquired a scholastic record replete with *A*s, a scholarship to Yale and the 1978 number-one ranking in Massachusetts for long-distance swimming. Eve had a suspicion that his search for lost treasure ships made up to him in some ways for the fun he'd missed during a lifetime spent pushing himself to the limits. Living up to his own and his family's expectations had left no room for enjoying life.

Even she had been guilty of piling on the pressure, she realized. During their marriage, there had been constant competition between the two of them for professional success. Funny how a mere two-year separation could change perspectives and priorities. Looking back, she couldn't imagine why climbing the career ladder had seemed so consumingly important.

If she'd made these self-discoveries while they were still married, they might have been worth discussing. Now there seemed no point in raking over problems divorce had made irrelevant. "Where did you go after Guiana?" she asked, genuinely interested in hearing how David had filled the months since their divorce.

"Matt and I headed into the Caribbean. We worked for a couple of commercial exploration companies for a while, because we were too poor to work for ourselves. Then one of those scruffy characters that hover around the fringes of the diving world approached us in a bar and sold us an 'ancient letter' that described a fierce battle fought in 1832 between a Brazilian tax ship and three pirate ships near Belem." His eyes gleamed with repressed laughter. "There was a chart attached showing exactly where two of the ships supposedly sank. Loaded with treasure, of course."

"And you bought that load of nonsense?" she exclaimed. "Good grief, I can't believe you and Matt fell for such a corny scam!"

"We only paid fifty bucks, and I don't think either of us was entirely sober at the time." He grinned, showing a total lack of shame. "Besides, it just goes to show that virtue and sobriety don't always bring their own rewards."

"Don't tell me," she groaned. "The letter turned out to be genuine, right?"

"It sure did, and the chart showing where the ships sank was amazingly accurate. We'd only been diving a couple of weeks when we located the Brazilian frigate and one of the pirate ships within a half mile of each other. The pirate ship even had a ball still in the cannon ready to be fired.''

"What about the treasure?'' Eve could feel her eyes growing wide. There was something about tales of Caribbean pirates and sunken galleons that made a child out of even the most hardened reporter.

"Unfortunately the gold was long gone,'' David said. "We found remnants of a dozen rotted wooden chests and about three gold doubloons, but that's all. The ocean currents are strong there, and the coins were scattered so widely that we hadn't a hope in hell of finding them.''

Eve sighed. "I'm disillusioned. I have this Disney World picture of swimming down to a sunken galleon, sails still fully rigged, and discovering a treasure chest, lid open and piled high with gold. And a rope of pearls hanging over the side, of course, gleaming with a soft pink luster.''

David laughed. "It's a great fantasy. Usually what the salt doesn't corrode the sea worms eat or barnacles calcify.''

"So the end of this exciting tale is that you struck out again, despite the great 'ancient letter' and your old sea chart. There's a moral to this story, David.''

"Not exactly. We were incredibly lucky. We didn't find any gold, but the hull of the frigate was partially buried in silt, which helped to preserve it, and eventually we located a small metal object jammed between two collapsed ribs. The object turned out to be a golden casket, considerably worse for wear. But inside the casket, wrapped in layers of oiled cloth, was a jeweled tiara we believe can only have been intended as a gift for a princess in the Portuguese royal family.''

"Because it was so fancy?''

"It was *very* fancy. At the center of the tiara were three four-karat diamonds, each surrounded by ruby flowers and clusters of emerald leaves. The circlet was fashioned from a hundred more diamonds and a few sapphires just to break the monotony.''

"Ivana Trump, eat your heart out,'' Eve said. "What did you do with it?''

"We sold it at fabulous profit to a Korean art collector who has a passion for Portuguese history. We made enough on the deal to cover the costs of the entire Brazilian expedition and to finance our operation here in Eternity."

"You seem to have had a great time these past couple of years," Eve said, realizing she sounded rather wistful.

"It's been interesting, that's for sure," David said, "Although there've been moments when I've wondered about that Chinese curse. You know, the one that says, *May you live in interesting times.*"

A subtle, frightening curse. His words brought Eve back abruptly to the problems of the present. It was approaching midnight, and she would soon have to go upstairs to bed. To curl up in a bed last occupied by a dead rat. Interesting times, indeed. She swallowed hard, trying to ignore the unpleasant mental image. "I've really enjoyed hearing about your exploits," she said, "but it's getting late. What time do you have to be up tomorrow?"

"Not too early, since it's Sunday. I'd like to get started on checking into Caleb's background, but I'm not sure what I can do over the weekend, beyond talking to Marge Macdonald."

"She's his landlady, isn't she? Won't the police already have questioned her?"

"I'm sure they have. But my questions might be a bit different from Pete Pieracini's." David shrugged. "It can't hurt to ask the questions, even if she doesn't tell me anything new."

"No, I guess not." Eve cleared her throat. "I'd like to go with you, if I could. This rat thing makes whatever's going on somewhat personal as far as I'm concerned."

"I'd like your company," he said. "Your expertise as an interviewer should help a lot in putting Marge at ease."

"Great, that's settled then." Eve jumped up from her chair. "Well, if it's all right with you, I'm off to bed. Okay if I use the bathroom first?"

David wasn't deceived by her bright smile. He got up, pulling her into his arms. "Sleep in my bed," he said softly. "That's the best way I know to banish the pictures of those rats we're both trying so damned hard not to see.''

For a moment she allowed herself to luxuriate in the thought of spending the night wrapped in David's arms and waking in the morning to the enticing caress of his lovemaking. Then she sighed and pushed away from him. ''Thanks for the offer,'' she said huskily. ''But a few things in this world are even more frightening than dead rats.''

David looked at her, his eyes dark, his expression guarded. ''What scares us so damn badly, Eve? What are we running from?''

She knew the answer to that one. ''Pain,'' she said. ''Pain that nearly destroyed both of us.''

David didn't respond with words, but his hands dropped to his sides and he stepped away from her. It was all the answer she needed. It meant that, in his heart of hearts, he agreed with her. The fierce tug of attraction between the two of them was a problem to be overcome, not the basis for a renewed relationship. Slowly, sadly, Eve turned and walked upstairs.

MARGE MACDONALD appeared to be in her late thirties. She had beautiful thick brown hair, the yellowed complexion of a committed smoker and thighs that were half a size too large for her pants. Despite the fact that her face looked as if it was accustomed to laughter, she greeted David and Eve with a reserve that bordered on hostility.

''We really appreciate your taking the time to talk to us this morning,'' David said.

For once his charm had no visible effect. Marge's gaze slid over him, dull and indifferent. ''Come on in,'' she said, ''but I don't know what you want from me. Like I told the detective, Caleb kept himself to himself and never caused no trouble, not to me nor to nobody else.''

''He was very good at his job, too,'' David said, standing back to let Eve and Marge precede him into the chilly parlor that was clearly never used except on formal occasions. They sat down in high-backed chairs with prickly tweed cushions. Marge lit a cigarette and dragged on it nervously.

"What do you want to know?" she asked. Her tone of voice suggested she might or might not be willing to provide them with answers.

"Caleb and I had been diving together for several months," David said. "We got on well together, but I wouldn't say I really knew him as a person. He worked hard and he seemed to spend most of his free time fixing up his Harley." He gave a small smile. "I guess a man can't get into much trouble doing that."

Marge's expression softened. "Yeah, he loved his bike. Every Saturday morning, seemed like he had some new gadget to fool around with."

The glow in the landlady's eyes alerted Eve to the idea that Caleb had possibly played a larger role in Marge's life than temporary lodger. "You're going to miss him," she said quietly.

"Yeah." Marge had all the vaunted New England capacity for understatement. She crossed her hands and stared silently down at her lap.

With years of experience as an interviewer, Eve realized that they would never get any information from Marge unless they could somehow forge a bond of sympathy. And she guessed the best way to arouse the landlady's sympathy was to make her aware of the danger David and Matt faced in the wake of Caleb's death. The catch was to find a way to do that without accusing Caleb of having committed a crime.

"Marge," she said, leaning forward in her chair, "David and I wouldn't have bothered you this morning, but the truth is we're frightened. Or at least, I'm frightened, and I believe David darn well ought to be. We think Caleb's murder is part of something bigger."

"Yeah," Marge's voice was bitter. "The sergeant keeps yammering on about that. Drugs, he said. Caleb would never deal drugs, and that's a hundred percent sure. His ex-wife was hooked on speed, diet pills, caffeine, codeine, the works. Couldn't go through the day without chugging down handfuls of pills. Took so many amphetamines she walked through a window thinking it was the door. Broke her arm, but luckily for her it mended pretty good. Then she went right back to popping the pills. That's why Caleb divorced her—years ago now. He despised drug dealers. He says—said—it was some scuzzy bartender, anxious to make a bit on the side, who'd gotten his wife hooked on the speed. Caleb called drug dealers hollow people, with no souls.''

Eve and David exchanged a quick glance. So Caleb had been married, after all, albeit a long time ago. "I agree with you," Eve said to Marge. "I don't think Caleb's murder had anything to do with drugs. I'm sure his death was connected to the shipwreck David and his partner are trying to salvage. The three of them were working to recover some valuable cargo from a ship that went down off the coast here more than a hundred years ago. Did you know that?''

A faint spark of curiosity lightened the misery in Marge's expression. "Caleb never said nothin' about salvaging a wreck.''

"He understood it was important not to talk about what we were doing," David said. "This is a competitive business, and we prefer to avoid any gossip. Let me tell you what's been happening over the past couple of days." He went on to explain about the stolen charts, his ruined diving gear and the rats in his beds. Marge listened without any reaction until he got to the part about the dead rats.

"My God!" she said, coughing on a lungful of smoke. "My God, that's sick!''

"Not as sick as murder," Eve said. "Marge, help us out. Those rats make me wonder if whoever killed Caleb has a personal grudge against Matt and David, as well.''

"Why do you think that?" Marge asked.

"I can't believe an ordinary intruder would waste time putting dead rats in David's beds. He might tear the place apart looking for something to steal, but he wouldn't have any reason to waste time turning back beds and then carefully remaking them so that the puffs of the comforter concealed the shape of the rats' bodies.''

Marge reached for another cigarette. ''I can see what you're saying, I guess, but I don't see as how I can help any. How does me talking about Caleb help to find the person who's harassing you?''

''You can help a lot,'' she said. ''You may be able to show us the link between what happened to Caleb and what happened to Matt and David.''

''Suppose there isn't no link?''

''Then no harm has been done to anyone, certainly not to Caleb. If the police have the wrong idea about Caleb, you need to set the record straight, or everyone is going to go chasing off in the wrong direction. I bet Caleb let down his guard with you, told you more about himself than he did other people.''

''We were...good friends.''

''Then help us find out who killed him,'' Eve pleaded. ''Did he seem worried about anything recently? Was he having financial problems? Menacing phone calls?''

Marge hesitated for a moment. Then she got up and walked over to the window, lifting a lace curtain and staring out toward the sea. ''He didn't have no money problems,'' she said. ''And it wasn't his ex-wife, neither. She and Caleb hadn't spoken in years, that I'm sure of.''

''How can you be sure?'' David asked.

She let the curtain drop back into place. ''Well, there wasn't no reason for them to be in touch, was there? Caleb went into the navy right out of high school. Came out three years later and married his high school sweetheart. No kids, and they divorced a couple of years later. That was because of the pills she popped, like I told you. She cleaned up her act, married some guy from Missouri and they got kids of their own now. Neither one of them was carrying around any grudges and the divorce was finalized more than ten years ago.''

''It certainly doesn't sound as if she plays any part in Caleb's life these days," Eve agreed. "Do you happen to know her name?"

"Shelly. But I don't know Shelly what. Like I keep telling you, Caleb and I never talked about her. Wasn't nothin' to talk about."

"How about friends?" David asked. "Did he make many friends since he arrived in Eternity? Apart from you, of course."

"He used to hang out over at the Kowalsky's garage now and again, talking bikes with the guys. But he liked to go into Boston if he had the night off. We'd go dancing. Had a real good time. Caleb was a great dancer, although you'd never have expected it, him being so quiet and all." Marge covered her eyes and turned away from them to stare blindly at the peaceful view through the windows. "We'd talked about getting married, you know. We got on real well together."

"I'm so sorry," Eve said. "I really am."

"Yeah, well, guess there's no use in crying over spilled milk. He's dead." Marge found a tissue and blew her nose. Her gaze slid sideways. "You really think someone out there might hold a grudge against you folks? A big enough grudge to kill you?"

"Yes," Eve said with complete honesty. "After last night, I really think that's possible. After all, Caleb was murdered, wasn't he?"

"Wait here," Marge said. She disappeared from the parlor and came back carrying a metal cash box with sharp edges and a flimsy lock, the kind that could be picked up in any discount store. "This was Caleb's," she said. "It's got some of his personal papers in it."

David looked surprised. "Didn't Detective Pieracini want to take it away with him?"

Marge flushed. "I never told him about it. Well, the way he was carrying on, seemed like he'd decided Caleb *deserved* to be murdered. I thought, nuts to you, Pieracini. Why the hell should I help make your life any easier? You know what I mean?"

"Would you allow us to look through the box?" Eve asked quickly, before David could suggest something appallingly ethical like turning the box over to the police. "Just in case there's something in there that David might be able to recognize as being important."

"Sure, that's why I brought it down. You go ahead."

Eve opened the box. It contained the sort of things she would have expected: A record of monthly fees paid on Caleb's condo in Boston; a bank statement that showed a balance of two thousand dollars in his current checking account—healthy, but not excessive; a wad of receipted bills; tax records; the maintenance logbook for his Harley; and a loose-leaf notebook.

"You take the notebook," David said. "I'll check his bank statements and see if I can spot any significant transactions."

Marge was looking more uncomfortable by the minute, so Eve leafed as quickly as she could through the notebook, in case Marge changed her mind and snatched it back.

Caleb had apparently used the notebook as a combination memo pad and address book. She flipped through reminders to visit the dentist, buy his sister a birthday present and a notation that someone called Jed was getting married at Thanksgiving. In the alphabetized address section, she found an entry for a Shelly Hunsicker, in St. Louis, Missouri. His ex-wife? She wrote down the address and phone number without comment, trying to be as inconspicuous as possible so as not to alarm Marge Macdonald.

The only other names she recognized were David's and Matt's. In the very back of the book, just as she was closing it, she saw the almost illegible indentations of a few words and numbers, scrawled at an angle. Caleb had probably written down a note to himself on another page, then torn out the page, leaving behind the impression of his writing.

She took the notebook over to the window, lifted the curtain and squinted at the words with the help of the extra light. The first word looked like a name, and definitely began with an *A,* but the rest of the entry was too faint to read. She rummaged in her purse and found a lead pencil.

"What are you up to?" David asked, coming to stand beside her.

She ran her pencil very gently over the impression. "Trying to read this note Caleb wrote," she said. After a few seconds she handed him the page. The scrawled message now appeared in clear white against the pale gray of the pencil:

Amy. 8:30/Sat. (617) 555-6484

David looked at Eve and said, "The Boston area code is 617."

"Amy," Eve said. "Amy Lewin? And why would Caleb have been meeting her?"

Marge's voice spoke from behind them. "Caleb never had no calls from a woman named Amy, not while he was staying here. Only woman who called him regular was his sister. Joyce."

Eve wished Marge wasn't quite so quick to jump on every imagined insult to Caleb's memory. "Then this number's probably not important," she said. "Amy will likely turn out to be his dental hygienist or something." She committed the message to memory and held the notebook out to Marge. "Thanks very much for letting us see Caleb's personal papers. You might want to let the police take a look, as well. After all, they're the experts, and you want to do all you can to help them find Caleb's murderer, don't you?"

"I guess." Marge's mouth wobbled and she dashed her knuckles across her eyes. "Problem is, the police keep acting like Caleb's committed a crime. They seem to forget he's the person who got himself killed. He's the *victim* in all of this, not the guilty party."

"You're right, but you have to understand the police perspective." Eve risked a light comforting touch on Marge's arm. "They're trying to come up with a motive and they're bound to ask themselves what Caleb was doing on the beach at such a late hour. You told them you've no idea—"

An almost imperceptible jerk on Marge's part caused her to stop in midsentence. "Marge?" she questioned softly. "Do you know why Caleb went down to the beach so late at night?"

"Not exactly." Marge drew a shaky breath. "Something was bothering him that night. Been bothering him all week, in fact.

He didn't get home until almost nine, and I was annoyed, because we'd planned to go out to dinner. Anyways, it was too late for a big meal, so we decided to go get a hamburger over at the bar. That's when we heard there'd been a break-in at the motel. Caleb wasn't all that interested until I asked Hugh—that's the bartender—if it was a wedding guest who'd been robbed. The economy of this town being what it is, we don't need no motel break-ins, right?''

"Right," Eve said, steering her gently back on track. "But did the bartender know who'd been robbed?''

Marge actually smiled. "In this town? In the bar? You gotta be kidding. Hugh, he knows all the gossip. The government should give him a pair of binoculars and get rid of their spy satellites. Hugh would keep 'em up-to-date on the news and save billions of dollars into the bargain.''

David spoke with careful patience. "How did Caleb react when he heard that it was Matt's motel room that had been broken into?''

"He was upset," Marge said. "Didn't show it much, but I could tell. He made an excuse to leave the bar and we went home. He couldn't settle down to nothin'. When I went upstairs to bed, right around midnight, he said he'd come later. He had to go out because he had a job to take care of.''

"Did he tell you what kind of job?" Eve asked.

"Not exactly. I kinda got the impression he was going to take out the boat.'' Marge seemed surprised by her own words, as if she hadn't realized what she'd been thinking until she said it. She frowned. "I was miffed, let me tell you. Didn't really speak none after that. Just said goodbye and started walking up the stairs. Caleb, he muttered something about how he wished he never got himself involved with her.''

She fell silent again. "With her?" Eve prompted.

"Yeah. I wouldn't mention none of this, because it's of no account, except you seem so interested in that Amy woman.''

"We're very grateful for any information you can give us, Marge, we really are.''

She took her pack of cigarettes out, then shoved it back in her pocket. "Yeah, well, anyways, when I asked him what he meant, he said I had no cause to be jealous. He'd sooner live with a barracuda than this woman who was causing him problems. Then he said something about how she'd found herself bigger and better fish to fry than him."

"But he never mentioned her name," David said.

"No." Marge seemed to look inward for a moment. "That turned out to be the last time we ever spoke. When I thought about it afterward, seemed to me like he'd taken a lot of trouble not to say her name."

Marge seemed to regret admitting so much about a man whose reputation she was determined to defend. She took the papers and stuffed them back into the box. "Well, I've got nothing else to tell you, so if you don't mind, I need to get over to my sister's house in Ipswich. I'm going to spend a few days with her."

She was clearly not prepared to reveal anything more, however innocuous, and pressure would only make her hostile. "We appreciate the time you've given us," David said. "Thanks for talking to us."

Eve spoke softly as they walked to the door. "Marge, will you think about what we've told you, about how David and his partner may be in danger, and if you remember anything more that might help to explain what Caleb was doing down on the beach, would you call us?"

Marge didn't reply, but at least she didn't refuse outright. "Here's my card," Eve said, scribbling the phone number for the cottage next to her name. "And this is where I'll be staying for the next few days." She smiled encouragingly. "Keep us in mind, okay?"

David added more thanks and tried not to show his impatience as they got into the car. He hadn't said a word to Eve about seeing the name Amy in Caleb's notebook, but she knew he was worrying about the same thing she was.

As soon as they were out of sight of Marge's place, David stepped on the accelerator and sped to the nearest public phone, which happened to be in the local gas station. They got out together. "The number was 555-6484, right?" he said, reaching into his pockets for change. "Darn, can you give me some more quarters?"

Eve held out a fistful of change. "Help yourself."

David dialed. "It's ringing," he said. "So at least it's an active number."

Eve heard a young female voice answer the phone. "Good afternoon, this is the Fish Dish, Boston's finest seafood restaurant. How may I help you?"

David's face fell. "Damn!" he muttered, hand over the mouthpiece. "Hi," he said, lifting his hand. "I'm looking for a friend of mine whose name is Amy. I, er, believe she works there. Is this her shift by any chance?"

"I don't think we have anyone called Amy working for us, but I'm new around here. Hold on a minute, please."

Several tense seconds ticked by. An older woman's voice came onto the line. "May I help you?"

"I'm looking for Amy—she's a friend of mine," David said. "I believe she works in your restaurant."

"What's her last name?"

"I don't know." David's mouth tightened. "I mean I think her name might be Lewin. Amy Lewin."

"I'm sorry, I can't help you." The woman hadn't sounded friendly from the start, and now her voice became noticeably cooler.

"Tell them she just got married," Eve whispered. "Suggest she might have a different last name."

Matt rolled his eyes, but he complied. "What I meant to say is, Amy just got married. I'm an old school friend of hers, you see, but she got married recently and I can't remember her new husband's name."

"We have no one by the name of Amy Lewin working at this restaurant." The woman sounded hostile.

"I'm sure she isn't using the name Lewin anymore," David

persisted. "I just need to know if you have any employee at all called Amy."

"We have no one called Amy working for us." The woman hung up with a definite bang.

David held out the phone so that Eve could hear the buzz of empty static. He grimaced ruefully. "Well, I sure managed to extract lots of useful information with that call," he said as they walked back to the car.

"Maybe there was nothing to extract. Ms. Fish Dish could have been telling the simple truth. They have nobody called Amy working at their restaurant."

"Or she might have been cautious. Unfortunately in an age of lunatics, weirdos and stalkers, you can't blame her for not handing out personnel information to every Tom, Dick and Harry who happens to call."

"All right," Eve said. "Let's assume Amy doesn't work there. Why did Caleb have the number written down? There was a date and time, too. Do you think they planned to meet there?"

"Could be." David shrugged. "Or maybe Amy called Caleb when she was eating a meal at the Fish Dish and asked him to call her back because she ran out of quarters. In fact, that's the most likely explanation. He scrawls the number in the back of his notebook and then tears out the page when he's finished the call because he knows he won't need the number anymore."

"You're probably right." Eve sighed. "Anyway, I guess we shouldn't get hung up on finding her. We have no reason to suspect she's connected to Caleb's murder. Half the world's population is female. Even if he was planning to meet a woman the night he died, it probably wasn't Amy. And we have no reason to suspect that this Amy is the woman Matt's dating."

"I guess this is what detective work is all about," David said wryly as they got into the car. "Hours spent tracking down leads that fizzle away or turn out to be totally irrelevant."

"On the bright side," Eve said, "I found an entry in Caleb's address book for a woman called Shelly Hunsicker, who just might be the former Mrs. Caleb Crewe."

"Great. Maybe she'll turn out to be bursting with juicy information. Maybe she's gone back on drugs and shot him in a fit of heroin-induced paranoia."

"I have her phone number and plenty of quarters. Do you want to call?"

"Let's go home first," David said, driving out of the parking area. "We can phone in comfort from the cottage."

"Sure." Eve buckled her seat belt. "Is it worth swinging by the motel to see if Matt got back from his date? You need to fill him in on what's happened since last night."

"He won't be back yet," David said, overtaking a Cadillac filled with a cluster of fuchsia-clad bridesmaids. "We spent so long with the police yesterday afternoon that he and Amy decided..." His voice died away.

In the sudden silence Eve could hear the rush of blood thrumming in her ears. She looked at David. He looked back. He slammed on the brakes and pulled the Jeep over to the side of the road.

"Dammit, it's no use pretending we aren't worried," Eve said tersely. "We both think it could be Matt's Amy whose name was in Caleb's book, don't we?"

"Possibly." David's voice sounded tight.

"What do you know about her?" Eve asked. "Other than the fact that Matt's crazy about her?"

"Nothing much, except that he's been dating her for almost three months. She's divorced, midthirties, good-looking. I met her for the first time yesterday morning." He pulled a face. "But you know that. You were with me."

"Isn't a bit odd that Matt hasn't introduced you to her yet?"

David frowned. "Yes, although we've been working such long hours there hasn't been much time for socializing, except on weekends. And they like to spend the weekends in Boston at his apartment."

"Is that where she's from? Boston?"

"I'm not sure. She isn't a local, that's for sure, or I'd have known her in high school. From something Matt said, I have an idea she arrived in town about the same time he did.''

Eve thought back to the previous day when the news of Caleb's death had been called into the *Courier* office. "If Amy knew Caleb, she's a terrific actress. She gave the distinct impression she'd never met him. Remember how she looked down at her notes to remind herself of his name?''

"No," David said. "No, I don't remember, but I trust your memory because you're trained to observe that sort of thing." He drew a deep breath. "We need to be careful. We don't want to weave some sort of wild conspiracy theory just because Caleb and Matt both know a woman called Amy. Even if they both know the same woman called Amy, it doesn't necessarily add up to anything suspicious."

"But it might," Eve murmured. "If she and Caleb were working in cahoots, think how useful it would be if Amy seduced Matt. She'd be able to feed Caleb all sorts of insider information."

"Matt's much too smart to shoot off his mouth to every woman he happens to sleep with," David snapped.

"What about a woman he's fallen in love with?" Eve shot back. "You know how vulnerable people are right after they've made love. Each time she might get just a snippet or two of information out of Matt. But if she puts all those little snippets together, she and Caleb could accumulate everything they need to know in order to locate the treasure."

David drew to a halt at the town's only traffic light. "Are you suggesting Amy is the person who stole the charts from Matt's room?"

"It's a possibility worth considering, don't you think? Who would know better when it was safe to break in?"

"Why would she need to break in?" David demanded. "She probably has her own key."

"Maybe. But three months isn't that long for a guy, especially Matt, to give a woman a key to his place."

David clenched his jaw. "I think we're building an Everestsize mountain on the basis of a few words scrawled in Caleb's notebook," he said finally. "We have no reason to assume Matt's girlfriend and Caleb's Amy are one and the same. We have even less reason to assume she's some conniving Mata Hari, sucking secrets from Matt and spewing them out to Caleb."

"True, but isn't it worth at least asking her a few questions?" Eve said.

"We have no authority to interrogate her."

"Who said anything about interrogation? We can leave a message at the motel inviting her and Matt to dinner."

David turned onto the gravel road that led to the lighthouse. "And then what?" he said.

Eve shrugged. "Then we'll ask her how well she knew Caleb Crewe."

"And if even half of what you've suggested is true, do you expect her to answer truthfully?" David didn't bother to hide his skepticism.

Eve smiled somewhat sadly. "Of course not," she said. "But I've had years of experience in detecting when people are lying. Invite Matt and Amy to dinner, and I guarantee before the evening's over, I'll be able to tell you precisely how well she knew Caleb Crewe."

Chapter Nine

In response to Eve's invitation, Matt and Amy arrived at the cottage shortly after seven. Matt breezed in, his normal exuberance somewhat muted, carrying a giant pizza box and a six-pack of Diet Coke. Amy followed behind, her quiet personality overshadowed.

"Hello, gorgeous." Matt gave Eve a halfhearted peck on the cheek. "Here's the pizza you ordered. Double cheese, extra onion and no salami, as per instructions. It might need a couple of minutes in the microwave, but the Cokes are ice-cold. Am I a great guest or what?"

"You're a great guest," Eve said, taking the pizza and the six-pack so he could remove his jacket. She smiled at Amy, who was hanging back, seeming a little shy. "Hi, Amy," she said. "Come on in and get warm. I'm glad you and Matt got back from Boston in time to stop by tonight."

"We were glad to come." Amy hung her down vest neatly on one of the pegs by the door. She went into the living room and held out her hands to the fire. "This is lovely," she said. "It's chilly out tonight and there's nothing more comforting than a real fire, is there?"

"Nothing," Eve agreed, thinking how stunning Amy looked. At work on Saturday, her hair had been twisted into a businesslike coil at the nape of her neck, concealing its extraordinary color and thickness. Tonight she'd left it loose, and it tumbled around her shoulders in a riot of shining chestnut curls. The forest green sweater she wore with her jeans was a clever choice;

it not only highlighted the creamy glow of her complexion, but also flattered her figure by emphasizing the generous curves of her breasts and the slender column of her throat. Despite the lush sensuality of her appearance, however, Eve got no sense that the woman was deliberately flaunting her physical attractions.

Amy might be unaware of the effect she created, but Matt was staring at her with an expression of naked longing, and Eve felt her stomach knot with apprehension. If by some horrible chance it turned out that Amy had been conspiring with Caleb Crewe to strip the *Free Enterprise* of its treasure, then Matt was going to be devastated. How dreadful it would be if the first woman he'd ever seriously loved turned out to have betrayed him.

Pressing her warmed hands to her cheeks and smiling contentedly, Amy sat down in one of the armchairs by the fire. Matt watched every movement, every tiny gesture, as if hungry for the sight of her. Amy seemed unaware of his scrutiny, which Eve found astonishing. How could she not feel the waves of Matt's sexual need beating against her?

The desire was so strong, at least on Matt's side, that Eve felt like a voyeur. "Would either of you like a beer?" she asked, anxious to break the tension. "Or maybe a glass of wine?"

"No, thank you." Amy smiled politely. "I don't drink very much alcohol. I'll wait and have a Coke with my slice of pizza."

Matt blinked, and with a visible effort brought his attention back to Eve. "I'll wait, too," he said. "Where's Dave? What's going on with you two, anyway? He sounded real uptight on the phone."

"He's upstairs," Eve said, "talking to Caleb's sister. She's just arrived in town and she's very upset."

"Caleb's sister is here?" Matt sounded appalled.

"Not actually in the house. She's staying at the inn. Apparently the innkeeper gave her David's number and she called a couple of minutes before you arrived."

"Boy, am I glad David's the one handling that phone call!" Matt's expression tightened with anxiety. "I can't imagine what I'd say to her."

"You'd tell her that you're very sorry Caleb is dead," Amy said quietly. "It's always best to keep condolences simple, and it's important to tell the truth, even when someone's died. Maybe especially when someone's died."

"You're right, honey." Matt sat down on the sofa, leaning across to take Amy's hand and looking at her as if she'd imparted some great nugget of wisdom.

Boy, did he have it bad, Eve thought, torn between amusement and alarm.

"Matt is really upset about Caleb's murder," Amy explained to Eve.

He smiled sheepishly. "Translation—I've been a royal pain in the ass for the entire weekend. We came back early from Boston because I was feeling so down."

"It's tough," Eve agreed. "How are you coping, Amy? Did you know Caleb well?"

She looked mildly surprised at the question. "I didn't know him at all."

"I'm sorry," Eve said. "I must have misunderstood. I thought Detective Pieracini said something about finding your name in Caleb's diary." Well, she thought, that was only a slight stretching of the truth.

"How odd." Amy sounded genuinely puzzled. "I can't imagine why Caleb would have my name written anywhere, unless it was connected with my work. I take all the orders for the classified-ads section at the *Courier*. Maybe he placed an ad, although I don't remember ever speaking to him." She frowned. "I'll check my records as soon as I get back to work. It's kind of creepy knowing your name is in a murdered man's diary."

If she was faking, Eve thought for the second time, then she had to be the world's best actress. "I'm sure it's not important," she said. "Don't worry about it, Amy."

"That's easier said than done until we find out who killed Caleb," Matt said. "I can't get him out of my mind. You know what it's like when you get a picture stuck in your head and nothing will budge it?"

"I sure do," Eve said. "And Amy must be tired of hearing about the murder already. I'm sure the staff at the *Courier* are working nonstop on the story."

"They've never had so much news in one weekend—" Amy broke off. "Oh, here's David."

"How did it go with Caleb's sister?" Eve asked softly.

He grimaced wearily. "About like you'd expect, maybe a bit worse. She's arranging the funeral for next Thursday in Boston." With visible effort, he shook off his dejection and walked into the living room, followed by Cat. He clapped Matt on the back. "Hey, buddy, you look about as chewed up as I feel." He held out his hand to Amy. "Hello, Amy, nice to see you again."

"Hello, David, how are you doing?"

If Eve hadn't been watching Amy so closely, she would never have noticed the slight tightening of Amy's lips or the split-second hesitation before she returned David's handshake. Why? Eve wondered. She'd noticed the same infinitesimal reluctance to take his hand when they'd first met at the *Courier* offices. Had Matt said something that caused Amy to view David with a distaste too strong to conceal? What in the world could that have been? Or was Eve giving too much significance to what might be no more than Amy's natural shyness?

"So what's up, Dave?" Matt said, getting to his feet to put another log on the fire. Cat eyed the action with approval and took up his favorite position on the hearth rug. "Why the urgent phone call? We're delighted to share a pizza with you guys, of course, but you sounded like you wanted more than casual dinner companions when you called."

"I need to fill you in on what's happened over the past twenty-four hours," David said.

"Nothing bad, I hope," Amy said politely.

"Not good," David said. "Sometime on Saturday, a vandal broke into the cottage and destroyed my diving gear."

"Your gear? All of it?" Matt's voice was blank with shock.

"All of it. Every single piece, from wet suit to mask and every other damn thing you can think of. It's going to be a couple of days before I can replace most of it.''

"Oh, no!" Amy exclaimed. "That's dreadful!"

Matt and Amy exchanged horrified glances, then he muttered something obscene under his breath. Eve was still watching Amy closely, but she couldn't detect even the faintest sign that her surprise was faked. She'd interviewed too many beautiful women guilty of hideous crimes to allow herself to equate Amy's good looks and sweet smile with a guarantee of innocence. But Amy was betraying none of the telltale signs of guilt or uneasiness that Eve had trained herself to look for.

Obviously shaken, Matt got up again and paced around the sofa. "Was anything stolen?" he asked. Then he pulled up short, struck by a prospect of fresh disaster. "The charts! My God, they didn't take your copies of the charts, too, did they? How about the computer? Was that vandalized?"

"No, the hardware wasn't smashed and I keep the software locked in the safe."

Matt grimaced. "That's not much of a safety precaution, is it? Your safe's a rinky-dink kind of an affair to a professional thief."

"I'm not sure this job was done by a pro. In fact, whoever did this didn't steal anything at all as far as I can tell."

Matt thrust his hands through his hair and then into his pockets. "This whole situation is weird. Really weird. If nothing was stolen, what did they—he—expect to achieve?"

David shrugged. "Heaven knows. Maybe a delay in our diving schedule? A chance to plunder our wreck before we can get down there again?"

Matt shook his head. "If they're professional divers, they couldn't be that stupid. It may take you a while to replace your gear with exactly what you *want*. But they must know you can get everything you *need* at virtually any dive shop in Boston."

"You're absolutely correct, and I'm fresh out of ideas as to what this might be about," David said.

"Okay with you guys if I change my mind and have a beer?"

Matt went to the fridge and pulled out two bottles. "Want one, Dave? Eve?"

"Sure," David said.

Eve shook her head. "No, thanks." She was already having trouble zipping up her slacks. Another couple of days of beer, fried fish and pizza, and she'd split a seam.

Matt came back, carrying the beers in one hand and two cans of Diet Coke in the other. "So the vandals didn't steal anything," he said to David. "They just destroyed your gear, right? Was their method the same as at my place? Did they smash the locks to get in? Muss up all your clothes?"

"No," David said. "He—or she—didn't touch my clothes and seems to have gotten in with a key—"

"What?" Matt spluttered into his beer. "With a key? But who could have...? Surely a *woman* wouldn't have done this?"

"Why not?" Eve said, looking at Amy. "Hacking up a wet suit requires a very sharp knife, not brute strength. A woman could have done this as easily as a man."

Amy laughed. "Take care, Eve. You're trampling on some of Matt's favorite prejudices. He's such a total chauvinist he can barely visualize women as doctors or lawyers, let alone criminals."

"That's not true," Matt protested. Amy simply raised an eyebrow, and he grinned somewhat sheepishly. "Well, okay, maybe there's a grain of truth in what you're saying. But anyhow, male, female or whatever, how in the world did they get a key to the cottage?"

"With no difficulty at all," David said wryly. "My great-aunts hand out keys to this place like Halloween treats. Any thief who wanted to gain entry could steal a key from a dozen different places."

"Always providing he's from Eternity and knows where to look," Matt said.

"Yeah," David concurred. "I guess we can conclude that the person who vandalized this place was a local."

Matt gave a brief bark of laughter. "I'll bet Pete Pieracini wasn't a happy camper when he came to that conclusion."

"He sure wasn't," David said. "These are tough times for poor old Pete and his vision of Eternity, the fairy-tale town with no crime."

"Don't forget to tell them about the rats," Eve said, getting to her feet. "I'll heat up the pizza while you fill them in on that horrible story. I'd like to get the gross stuff over with before we eat."

"Rats!" Amy sat up, showing more animation than she had all evening. She glanced around nervously. "Do you have a problem with rats out here? I'd have thought the cat would scare them away."

"These weren't live rats." Succinctly David explained about the rats in the bed.

Amy made little murmurs of distress as he told the story, and Matt was struck speechless. "My God," he said when he regained his voice. "David, what's going on here? What the hell is going on?"

"I don't know," David replied. "Last night, Eve and I both jumped to the conclusion that the same person—or people—who killed Caleb must have destroyed my diving gear and put the rats into my beds for good measure. But the more I think about it, the more ridiculous it sounds."

"Why?" Amy asked, still looking perturbed. "Surely there must be a connection. I mean, all these incidents are happening one right after the other—bang, bang, bang."

"Even so, I'm not sure there has to be a link," David said. "We keep saying Eternity isn't the sort of town where two sets of criminals could be at work at the same time. But why not? Eternity is just a regular town with a quaint legend about its wedding chapel. It isn't a sanctuary from all the problems of the real world."

"That's true," Matt said slowly. "Besides, if you think about it, Dave, we're dealing with two very different sorts of crime.

Murder is big-time stuff. But what's happened to you and me isn't all that bad, not really.''

"I disagree,'' Eve said. "The rats were pretty bad.''

"Yeah, but I guess if it wasn't for Caleb's murder, we wouldn't be feeling so damned uptight about everything. The rats bothered you so much because you instinctively considered them a personal threat. Caleb is dead. These rats are dead. Next time, *you* might be dead.''

Eve looked at him with respect. "You know, I never expressed it to myself that clearly, but you're quite right. That's precisely the connection I was making, although I didn't realize it before.'' She brought the reheated pizza in from the kitchen and set it on the coffee table, along with a stack of paper plates and napkins. "Help yourselves, folks.''

Matt flipped the top on a can of Coke and handed it to Amy. "We need to remember that, despite all the Jacques Cousteau mystique and Mel Fisher panache, underwater salvage operations are a business. Some people conduct their diving business more ethically than others, same as in any other line of work. But if you're going to make money at this job, you can't afford to take unnecessary risks. That holds true whether you're planning to make your money on a legal salvage job or an illegal salvage job.''

"What's your point?'' Amy asked, returning a string of melted mozzarella to the top of her pizza.

"My point is I can see why a rival treasure hunter might end up killing Caleb Crewe, but I can't see why he'd put those rats in David's beds. He would be running a totally unnecessary risk. And why? What could he possibly hope to gain?''

"Don't ask me,'' Amy said, shivering. "I'm hopeless at understanding the criminal mind.''

"I don't believe there's an entity we can call the criminal mind,'' Eve said. "One of the things I've learned as a reporter is that the right combination of circumstances can push regular everyday people into committing the most incredible and unlikely acts. Sometimes they're acts of enormous courage, like when a mother fights to save her children from an impending disaster. Other times they're hideous acts that grow out of the darkness of failed and twisted relationships. More often than you'd expect, the heroes and the villains I've interviewed were regular everyday people until something threw their lives out of kilter.''

"I guess you're right," Amy said. "Still, speaking personally, I can't imagine committing a serious crime. Not because I'm so virtuous," she added quickly, "but I'm scared witless by authority figures. Give me a parking ticket and I'm convinced I'll be clapped into federal prison if I don't pay up on the spot."

Matt grinned. "Never do that, honey, or they'll arrest you for trying to bribe a cop."

Amy looked stricken. "Can they do that?" She laughed at herself before anyone could answer. "Okay, I'm being totally ridiculous. You don't have to tell me."

Cat, probably attracted by the sliver of uneaten pizza resting on the paper plate balancing on the arm of the chair, jumped onto Amy's lap and began kneading her stomach, eyes fixed on the prize. Amy wrapped the pizza in her napkin and placed it firmly out of reach. "It's not good for you," she said, scratching him behind the ears.

Cat, recognizing the undeniable voice of authority, gave up yearning after the unattainable and curled up on Amy's lap, squirming ecstatically as Amy ran her long supple fingers over his fur. "You're a beautiful animal," she said. "What are you called?"

"His name is Cat," David said. He shot Eve a defiant look. "He's a stray. I'm going to take him back to the pound as soon as I get a few spare moments."

Amy gave a little gurgle of laughter. "You're certainly not going to take him back to the pound," she said.

"Of course he won't," Eve agreed. "David's all fierce bluster wrapped around a marshmallow heart. Cat just about owns this cottage, and he knows it."

Amy chuckled again. "Sorry, Eve, *he* doesn't know anything.

David's cat is a female, and my best guess is that she'll be delivering her kittens about three weeks from now.''

"What!" David's howl of outrage might have been appropriate if someone had just told him that his Jeep was totaled and his house had burned to the ground. Eve wasn't sure whether to laugh at his panic or be embarrassed that she'd spent hours stroking a pregnant cat without noticing it was female.

"And to think I've been accusing the poor lady of being fat," she said. "Oh, Lord, we'd better take her to the vet for a checkup, and then we'll have to find homes for a bunch of kittens."

"We?" Matt asked, chugging the last of his beer. "Does that mean you and David are getting back together? Congratulations."

"Oh, no, heavens no," Eve said, flustered by her slip of the tongue.

"Not a chance," David said, a split second later.

He needn't sound so damn certain, Eve thought, irrationally hurt. The truth was that events had forced her and David into such an intimate routine over the past couple of days that the nightmare ending to their marriage sometimes fell out of focus, bringing images of happier times into view. But obviously David wasn't allowing his common sense to be blurred by romantic daydreams of recapturing past happiness.

Amy broke the embarrassed silence that had fallen over the group. "This cottage is built right onto the back of the lighthouse, isn't it?"

Everyone accepted the change of subject with relief. "Yes," David said. "There's a connecting door in the hallway near the kitchen. If you haven't visited the lighthouse, you should come back during the day and do the tour. As you'd expect, there's a magnificent view from the observation turret."

"I'd like that. I know your great-aunts sometimes take tourists around in summer." Amy gave Cat a final stroke and returned her gently to the hearth rug. "Actually I mentioned the lighthouse because I was wondering if either of you had thought to check it out since the break-in.''

David and Eve exchanged glances. ''We didn't give it a thought,'' David said. ''Chiefly because there's nothing in there except Powell family records and dismantled equipment.''

''I didn't realize that,'' Amy said, sounding almost apologetic for having brought the matter up.

''I'm glad you said something,'' David said. ''Now that you've mentioned it, I guess I should take a quick look around to make sure whoever vandalized my diving gear didn't decide to take a whack at the family records. Aunt Constance will be devastated if somebody's spoiled all those grocery lists and medical bills from the nineteenth century.''

''Are you going to check now?'' Eve asked.

''Why not?'' David took a flashlight from the kitchen drawer and led the way to the connecting door into the lighthouse. He found the light switch, and the chilly cavernous room sprung into view.

Until the light came on, Eve didn't realize she'd been holding her breath. She exhaled, her gaze traveling slowly over the glass display cases, the trunks and the walls of metal shelves stacked with cardboard boxes, specially designed to hold archival materials. Not a rat, alive or dead, in sight. Thank God.

''Everything seems normal,'' Matt said, glancing quickly along the shelves.

David opened a filing cabinet. ''Nothing but dust here,'' he said, sounding as relieved as Eve felt.

Amy had wandered over to the display cases in the center of the room. Eve realized she was staring at one of them in almost hypnotized silence. Her stomach immediately churned in sick anticipation.

''What is it?'' she asked, coming close to Amy but deliberately not looking inside the case. She'd seen more than enough rodent entrails for one weekend.

Amy gave a little jump, quickly turning around and positioning herself so that Eve couldn't see the cabinet. "Nothing," she said. "Honestly, nothing at all."

The lie was patent. "Amy, I'd like to see what's in the cabinet."

Amy pulled a face. "I don't think you do, Eve," she said wryly, but she gave up protesting and moved aside.

Eve looked into the cabinet. For a split second, she didn't recognize what had bothered Amy so much. Then she saw the photographs. There were two of them, set neatly in the top two corners. One was of her, the other of David. Or at least the heads belonged to her and David. Their smiling faces had been carefully superimposed on pictures of two naked, hideously battered bodies.

Eve blinked, then swallowed hard. "Matt, David, get over here." Her mouth had gone so dry she was amazed she could speak.

"What's up?" The men came quickly, their voices dying almost instantly into silence.

"Oh my God!" Matt said. His voice broke on the words. "How did they get in here?"

"I think they're laser prints made on a copying machine," David said. "Which means almost anyone could have produced these at one of those self-serve print shops."

"Anyone with a sick mind," Matt said.

"The lock on the display case has been smashed." David lifted the glass lid and was about to take out the pictures when Amy stopped him. "Don't," she said. "There may be fingerprints."

"I'm going to call the police," Matt said. "Those photos are obscene. There's no other word for them." He and Amy walked hand in hand back into the cottage.

Eve realized she'd started to shake and couldn't stop. "Let's get out of here," David said, putting an arm around her shoulders. "You okay?" he asked quietly as they walked back into the cottage.

"Terrific. Peachy keen." Her pretense of composure collapsed, too brittle to be sustained. She turned her face and buried it in his sweater. "No," she said. "I'm not okay. Those photos make me feel sick to my stomach."

"That's two of us, then," he said. His arms tightened around her and he held her close, rocking gently. After a minute or two, she felt his fingers stroking her hair, but he didn't speak, just held her, giving her comfort by the silent strength of his presence. Her nausea slowly faded.

She should have known such tranquil harmony wouldn't last. Not between the two of them. David framed her face with his hands and looked down at her, his gaze intent. "Eve, I want you to go back to New York," he said. "Until we find out who's behind all this garbage, you're not going to be safe staying here in Eternity."

Eve stiffened. She pulled away from him, thinking sadly that if he understood anything about her character, surely he wouldn't dare to make such a suggestion.

In the bad old days of their marriage, her hurt would have turned into instant hostility. Tonight she was determined to do better, to explain her motives for wanting to stay in Eternity, rather than attacking his motives for wanting her to leave.

"I couldn't cut and run even if I wanted to," she said. "David, you must see that. My crew's arriving first thing tomorrow morning, expecting to find me here. I have a program to produce that's already been scheduled for airing the first week in December. That means deadlines to meet and footage to tape right now."

David's mouth tightened and he half turned away. "I know your career always comes first," he said, his voice acid with sarcasm. "However, if you could bring yourself to give just a smidgen of consideration to the fact that a psychotic murderer seems to be stalking you, I'd sure appreciate it."

"How about you?" she demanded, her good resolutions flying out the window. "Are *you* moving out of town? Or is this yet another example of your desire to send the little woman to safety while brave macho David toughs it out with the bad guys?"

"Don't be so damned ridicu—" He stopped himself in mid-word, banging his fist into his palm. Then he shoved both hands into his pockets and scowled at her, eyes dark with the struggle to speak calmly. He sucked in a lungful of air. "I'm sorry," he said. "You're right. I was applying a double standard. If I can stay because I need to get on with my diving operation, you can stay because of your TV program."

She was so stunned by the admission that she couldn't think of a word to say. David's gaze became quizzical. "Speechless, Eve? Gosh, I never thought I'd see the day. I guess I should try being humble more often."

"It suits you," she said. She smiled, then reached up and touched him lightly on the cheek. "Don't get too reasonable, or I might start to like you."

"An interesting twist on our relationship," he said. "Are you sure it would be so bad if we liked each other?"

She thought of the two painful years she'd spent getting over him. "It would be…frightening," she said. As soon as the admission was made she regretted it. She turned abruptly and walked to the kitchen, where Matt and Amy seemed to be in the midst of a low-voiced argument of their own. They swung apart, and Matt greeted her with barely concealed relief.

"Did you reach Detective Pieracini?" she asked.

Matt nodded. "He's on his way."

Amy shot a glance at Matt that seemed almost defiant. "And a lot of use he'll be," she said. "Unless whoever did this signed his name on the back of the pictures, the police won't have the faintest clue about what's going on."

Eve wished she could disagree. Unfortunately she thought Amy had the situation summed up just right.

Chapter Ten

The detective, Matt and Amy finally left. David helped Eve gather up the congealed remnants of their meal. "I think Pete's planning to request a transfer to someplace less crime filled," he said, stashing paper plates and napkins into the garbage. "Like L.A. Or maybe the South Bronx."

Eve managed a small smile. "We should stop making fun of him. The poor guy has probably had almost no sleep for the past forty-eight hours, and he's doing everything he can. All anyone could do. Sherlock Holmes wouldn't have much luck in making sense out of this situation, either."

"Maybe there is no sensible explanation," David said. "Maybe we're trying to see cause and effect when there's no logical sequence to discover."

"What's happened doesn't feel random or senseless," she said. "It feels deliberate and…vicious."

He scowled. "Yes, I agree. Unfortunately."

She could see David struggling not to lapse into bad habits, such as ordering her back to the safety of New York City, and she resisted an unexpected impulse to walk over and hug him. She decided to change the subject. "What did you make of Amy tonight?"

"I'm not sure, and that worries me. I couldn't quite get a handle on her."

Eve nodded in agreement. "She worries me, David. I've conducted interviews with CIA agents who are more forthcoming than she was. I don't even know if she's attracted to Matt."

"Neither do I," David admitted. "Although it's plain enough he's crazy about her."

"About the only thing I could say about her with any degree of certainty is that she doesn't like you."

"And that doesn't make a lick of sense," David said. "As you know, I met her for the first time a couple of days ago. We've never exchanged a single word of private conversation."

Eve shrugged. "Well, I guess we're not going to solve the mystery tonight, so we may as well go to bed."

The word "bed" resonated in the sudden quiet. She'd been so busy resisting her feelings of affection that she'd walked right into another, much more dangerous trap.

David pounced on the opening her subconscious had given him. He straightened and turned to confront her, unleashing the sexual power she now realized he'd been straining to control. He was a tall man, and he'd always been strong, but the years of diving had honed his body to a muscular strength that was, quite literally, breathtaking. He didn't touch her, didn't even move close, but she couldn't look away. "Eve, sleep with me tonight."

She heard the note of harshness in his voice and realized that it was caused not by the arrogance of demand, but by the fear of rejection. David's sexual charisma had always been overwhelming, but never predatory. Even in the darkest moments of their marriage, he'd never used the power of his sexuality to subdue her, only to respond to her own desires.

She touched her hand to his cheek, not sure what she was going to say, but the feel of his stubbled cheek was so achingly familiar that she instinctively leaned toward him, brushing his mouth in a soft kiss.

Slowly, his eyes on hers, he combed his fingers through her hair. "I've never felt this way about another woman, Eve. You know that, don't you?"

She knew it and was scared as hell. Nervousness caused her to babble. "Maybe that's why we shouldn't do this. God knows, I'm not ready to handle... We've had a rough few days.... My shrink says never to make important decisions at a time of crisis...."

"She sounds like a smart woman," he said. "Last time we reacted to a crisis, we got divorced."

"Was that a mistake?" She stumbled over the question. "And anyway, how do you know my shrink's a she?"

He smiled. "I took a wild guess. And yes, I think we gave up too quickly on our marriage." He lowered his head and pressed his mouth against the sensitive skin of her throat. She closed her eyes on a low moan. Their bodies flowed together, melding from shoulder to knee. "Eve, let's go to bed."

"David...don't..." Her nails dug into his back.

He found the clip of her bra and rubbed his thumbs gently across her nipples. "Don't what?" he asked.

She gave a shuddering sigh. "Don't stop," she said.

BY MONDAY MORNING, Eve was so exhausted by the emotional roller coaster she'd been on that the prospect of starting work seemed almost like a minivacation. She had arranged to meet Gordon and the rest of the crew fifteen minutes after they checked into the motel. She arrived promptly at ten and discovered that the town grapevine had worked its usual infallible magic. Everyone in the motel, including her crew, knew not only about the murder, but also that she was staying with her ex-husband in the lighthouse cottage, where two dead rats and two obscene photographs had just been found.

After listening with what she considered superhuman patience to the film crew's chorus of tactless questions, Eve's temper finally frayed. "The next person who asks me how those damned photos got into Constance Powell's display case is fired, got it?"

The crew snickered, monumentally unimpressed by her threats. "Testy this morning, aren't we?" the cameraman said, grinning. "Anyway, you can't fire us. We've got a union."

"Watch me," she said grimly. "The way I feel this morning, the pleasure of firing one of you guys would make a strike seem worthwhile. Now get this gear over to the Powells' house. We have a tight schedule. Let's stick to it.'' The crew, no more worried than before, departed for their van.

"You sound like you've had a rough weekend,'' Gordon said, tucking her hand into the crook of his arm. "I told you before you left New York that you needed me to come up here with you. You know you don't do well in the boonies.''

"I'm not sure how your being here would have prevented Caleb Crewe from getting murdered,'' she retorted as they got into her rental car. "Or even how you'd have stopped some lunatic dumping a pair of dead rats in David's cottage.''

He made soothing noises. "Mike's right, you *are* testy this morning. But I can understand why. Poor you. You must be feeling devastated by all that's happened. And having to spend so much time with your ex, too. That must be like salt rubbed in the wound.''

With a little shock of surprise, Eve realized she wasn't feeling in the least devastated. Actually she felt great, despite her fatigue and her inability to understand the way David had behaved last night. In fact, she was secretly delighted that Gordon had been safely stashed in New York over the weekend. Which probably said something wretched about her character since he was the kindest man imaginable and she ought to be grateful for every minute spent in his company.

"I'm fine,'' she said, giving him a smile. "But let's concentrate on work now, please. If I never hear the words 'murder' or 'rat' again it'll be too soon.''

She should have known better than to expect the Powell sisters to have put the excitement of the weekend murder behind them. They all clustered around, demanding the latest information. Finally Eve managed to persuade them to sit down, so that the crew could start adjusting microphones and setting up lighting.

Eve never liked Gordon better than when she worked with him, and this morning his enthusiasm was particularly infectious. As the associate producer on "Roving Report,'' he was responsible for the technical aspects of filming a story, and he had a magic touch for setting up cameras and microphones in just the right places to capture unexpected facial expressions and details of the setting that would have escaped less-talented eyes. Eve prided herself on her acute powers of observation, but she had no doubt that when she viewed Gordon's film of the Powell sisters and their cozy sitting room, she would see both the room and the people in an entirely new light.

He also had a skill that amounted almost to genius for persuading people to forget they were being filmed. Today he had the added advantage of the sisters' being already agog with the double excitements of the murder and Patience's wedding. He guessed that the more meticulously he explained the technical aspects of placing his cameras and sound equipment, the quicker they would lose interest and revert to chatting informally among themselves. Sure enough, after a tedious forty minutes of watching the crew exchange jargon and adjust yards of electronic cable, while Gordon droned explanations replete with technicalities, the sisters lost interest in the crew and their alien equipment. After offering the technicians cookies, tea and fresh-brewed coffee, the sisters temporarily abandoned their efforts to explain the events of the weekend and started a discussion of wedding arrangements, carrying on the sort of lively intimate conversation that couldn't be staged, even by the most talented reporter.

Sitting as unobtrusively as possible in a darkened corner of the room, Eve shot an inquiring glance at Gordon. He nodded, answering her unspoken question. She sat back and relaxed, knowing that the equipment was all fully operational and that Gordon was capturing the scene on tape.

In view of the fact that Patience would be marrying at Thanksgiving, the sisters had decided to decorate Eternity's famous wedding chapel with bronze and yellow chrysanthemums and branches of pine. "So that it will smell wonderful," June said, beaming. "It will feel as if we've captured the holiday spirit and brought it right to your wedding. Oh, Patty, this is such fun! Why didn't any of us do this before?"

"I can't think why none of us ever got married!" Violet exclaimed.

"In my case it's easy to explain," Constance said mildly. "It's because I was never asked by a man who seemed even half as interesting as my own company."

The sisters laughed. "There is that," June said. "The supply of entertaining men never seems to meet the demand." She seemed not at all cast down by this realization and quickly returned to the decorative arrangements for her sister's wedding. "Well, Patty, if the flowers for the chapel are going to be in fall colors, what color are you going to wear? You'd look lovely in a deep rose, but does that clash with yellow?" She smoothed her skirt as if she were mentally visualizing the wedding gown she would choose if she was the bride.

"I'm going to wear my beige suit," Patience said.

"Your beige suit?" Violet's mouth formed an astonished circle. "But you bought that last year!"

"That's irrelevant." Patience knotted her hands in her lap. "It's excellent quality and I've only worn it once."

June and Violet exchanged appalled glances. "Yes, you wore it to Judge Fritzheim's funeral!" June exclaimed. "Patty, you can't wear the same suit to your wedding that you last wore to a funeral!"

"Why not?" Patience's mouth thinned into a stubborn line. "What about that saying? You know, something old, something new, something borrowed, and so on?"

"But your wedding dress isn't supposed to be the something old!" Violet protested.

"I don't see why not. People wear antique gowns all the time, don't they? Heritage Gowns is one of the town's most successful stores."

"That's different." June's forehead wrinkled in distress. "Heavens, Patience, you run an antique store! You of all people ought to know the difference between last year's suit and an heirloom gown! It's as if you were comparing yesterday's empty soup can to a nineteenth-century jam jar!"

"If it makes you happier, I'll buy a new silk blouse," Patience said, sounding defensive. "I should be able to find one in a nice cream color, perhaps with a touch of lace at the throat."

"Last winter's beige wool suit and a new blouse. The perfect outfit," Violet muttered. "At least, it's perfect if you want to apply for a job as the town librarian."

Patience flushed. "Good heavens, Vi, I'll be seventy years old next birthday! What do you expect me to wear? White satin and a veil?"

"I expect you to wear something that suggests you're pleased to be getting married!" Violet retorted. "A velvet dress maybe. Something in burgundy would be subdued and yet…festive!"

June cheered up. "That's a lovely idea, Vi. Burgundy velvet would be charming. Or how about hunter green, like the pine branches? Dark green can be such a rich color—"

"I'm wearing my suit," Patience repeated doggedly. "Let's face it, I'm a piece of mutton, and it's no good pretending I'm a joint of tender lamb. Louis will have to take me as he finds me. Old and tough."

Constance, who'd been silent so far, spoke up at that. "Well, dear, it may be true that mutton can't pretend to be lamb, but who's to say you shouldn't put a frill on the roast even if it is mutton? Particularly since it seems to me that Louis Bertrand is definitely the sort of gentleman who enjoys frills." Her eyes twinkled. "On his ladies, that is, if not on his roasts."

"Then perhaps he should have asked Carlotta Ormsby or Dodie Gibson to marry him, instead of me!" Patience snapped. The coffee cup she was holding rattled as she returned it to the saucer. Her sisters stared in silent astonishment as she reached for an exquisite lace hanky tucked into her sleeve and pressed it to her nose. Tears welled up in her eyes.

June and Violet exchanged horrified glances. "Patience, dearest, we certainly didn't mean to upset you," June said.

"Of course your suit will be fine. Very…elegant. Louis will love it." Violet almost managed to sound sincere.

Patience wiped her eyes and gave her sister a wry smile. "Vi, you're a hopeless liar.'' She put the hanky away and squared her shoulders. "Heavens, I'm sorry to have been so grouchy.''

Constance smiled. "My dear, you're not—''

"No, I was being ridiculous, and you're all quite right. Last year's suit is a dreadful excuse for a wedding dress, but it felt...safe. Familiar.'' She shrugged deprecatingly. "My goodness, it seems getting married at my age is just as nerve-racking as it would be if I were forty years younger!''

"I'm sure it's worse,'' Constance said, reaching over the arm of her chair and giving her sister's hand an affectionate squeeze. "You're old enough and wise enough to know what an important step you're taking. How intimidating that must be!''

"It *is* intimidating.'' Patience cleared her throat. "The truth is I feel all jittery inside. When Louis and I are together, everything seems wonderful. As soon as we're apart, I start wondering why on earth he wants to marry a cranky old spinster like me.''

"You're not cranky,'' June protested. Her eyes twinkled. "At least, not most of the time.''

"Besides, brides are supposed to feel nervous and on edge,'' Violet said with all the authority of a maiden lady who hadn't dated in at least a generation. She took her sister's coffee cup and carried it to the sideboard. "Never mind, Patty. If you want to wear your beige suit, you can.'' She smiled mischievously. "And I shall wear burgundy velvet. I've seen the perfect dress in Emma Webster's shop.''

On this note, the conversation changed from what the sisters would wear for the ceremony to what would be served at the reception afterward. Complete harmony was soon reestablished as they ran through a list of favorite dishes and recipes, many of which they planned to cook themselves and freeze in advance of the wedding. After about twenty minutes, Eve realized that although nobody was taking notes or giving orders, the sisters had arrived at a clear understanding of what needed to be done for the reception, who was going to be responsible for what, and the precise role the catering service was going to play in the affair. Not bad for a quick lesson in how to establish positive family dynamics, she thought, smiling absently at Gordon.

"From my point of view, we have enough," Eve said to him. "Everything okay technically?"

"Perfect," he said, signaling to let the cameraman and the sound technician know they could stop recording. "Give us fifteen minutes to pack up the gear and we'll be out of here."

The sisters stopped in mid-discussion of whether to have ice cream for dessert, as well as wedding cake. "But what about the interview?" Patience asked. "When is that going to start?"

Eve smiled. "You already gave us a wonderful interview. I couldn't possibly have asked for anything better."

The sisters stared at her, torn between doubt and dismay. "But we were talking about such trivial things," June said. "Aren't we all going to sound silly when you broadcast that on television?"

"Not at all," Eve said. "You're going to sound like a group of people caught up in making wedding arrangements for a much-loved member of the family."

Constance looked perturbed. "I trust it won't end up boring your viewers. Not to mention embarrassing us."

"In the first place, none of you did or said anything to be embarrassed about," Eve said. "But apart from that, I've already promised you that this program isn't intended to humiliate anyone. Please trust me on that. My edit will be entirely tactful."

Patience was only half reassured. "But why did you need to film all that ridiculous gibble-gabble about what I'm going to wear?"

"It was anything but ridiculous," Eve said with complete sincerity. "If this program is going to be worth watching, I need to give our viewers some insight into the dynamics of modern marriage. I hope to show that decisions about relationships are never easy, at any stage of our lives. From a personal point of view, listening to your discussion this morning, I realized for the first time that bridal couples share a lot of the same anxieties and pleasures, regardless of their backgrounds or their personal situations. I'm sure viewers will be as fascinated as I was to realize that age doesn't necessarily take away all the tensions surrounding the arrangements for a wedding ceremony.''

"But all that fuss over what an old woman is going to wear," Patience murmured. "By the time you become a senior citizen, you're supposed to have more important things to worry about other than clothes!"

"What could be more important than the dress you choose for your wedding day?" Eve leaned forward, smiling warmly. "Everyone already realizes that a young bride gives a lot of thought to the dress she wears. It'll be intriguing for our viewers to see that being mature doesn't necessarily make the decision any easier. In fact, you've whetted my appetite." She grinned. "No pressure of course, but I'm really looking forward to seeing what you eventually decide on."

"In my next life I'm going to be a man!" Patience exclaimed. Eve laughed aloud. "Any special reason why?"

"A dozen at least, jealousy chief among them. Louis is just breezing through the arrangements for this wedding. He's already told me that whatever I decide will be fine. Fine, my foot! He's only being so darned accommodating so he can escape from all the difficult decisions!"

"At least he'll have to choose his own wedding outfit," Eve said.

"Hah, big deal! He'll wear a dark suit and one of his trademark vests with his grandfather's big gold watch tucked into the pocket. Then he'll put a dark red carnation in his buttonhole and everyone will say how distinguished he looks. Now tell me life is fair!"

"It isn't," Eve said, sharing a rueful laugh with the sisters. "I'd register an official protest with the authorities, but I don't quite know how to contact the appropriate party."

While she and Patience had been chatting, the technicians had carried most of the gear out to the van. Gordon came up to her as they stacked the final load. "We'd better hurry, Eve, if we're going to grab a sandwich before our next interview."

"Please do stay and eat with us," Constance offered. "I believe June has prepared a delicious chicken casserole, and there's plenty to share."

"It'll be ready in twenty minutes," June said.

Gordon spoke before Eve had a chance, giving the sisters one of his most charming smiles. "Thanks, you're very kind, all of you. I wish we could stay, but Eve and I really need to have a working lunch. We've lots of technical filming details to discuss, that sort of thing." He put his hand beneath Eve's elbow, drawing her to his side in an unmistakably possessive gesture. "Are you ready to leave, honey?"

Eve sighed, the harmony she'd felt earlier in the morning and her admiration of Gordon's professional skills dissipating in a flash. Five months ago, when Gordon decided he was in love with her, she'd made the mistake of not rejecting his advances flat-out. He was a nice guy, she respected him as a colleague, and at the time, she'd felt oppressed by the solitariness of her life. For the past few months she'd tried to work up a spark of enthusiasm for the idea of Gordon as a husband, and she'd dated him on those nights when the emptiness of her apartment seemed even worse than the alternative—sharing dinner with a kind, talented, good-looking man who bored her.

A month ago, Gordon had stopped suggesting that they marry "sometime" and proposed that they get married before Christmas. Confronted with an ultimatum and a deadline, Eve had panicked. She was thirty-two years old and she longed to have a child. Gordon would be a kind father and a faithful husband, so she wasn't entirely sure why she was hesitating. She'd promised him an answer by Thanksgiving.

Unable to beat herself into saying yes, she couldn't quite bring herself to deliver an unequivocal no. For the past several weeks, she'd berated herself for her being too much of a workaholic and too emotionally shallow to make a commitment. Now she realized she'd been neither shallow nor work obsessed. She'd simply been smart. Smart enough to realize instinctively that marrying Gordon because her biological clock was ticking and she found him agreeable were lousy reasons for getting married.

Gordon, however, wasn't willing to have his ultimatum rejected, and so far nothing she'd said had convinced him she wasn't a candidate for a second trip into the marital combat zone. His refusal of Constance's invitation to lunch and the possessive way he put his arm around her waist were just two of the many ways he tried to assert a claim that didn't really exist. Eve was annoyed, but in all honesty she had to admit that her own past ambivalence justified some of his behavior.

Not wanting to start a scene in front of the sisters, particularly since they were David's great-aunts and presumably more than capable of reporting back to him, Eve made no protest. She didn't want any garbled maiden-aunt version of a fight with Gordon to reach David's ears. So she added her warm thanks to Gordon's and followed him out to his car. They were going to have a working lunch all right, she decided. She was going to lay it on the line for him: he needed to keep his feelings out of the workplace and his hands off her person, or it was going to become increasingly difficult for them to work together.

The town had mostly emptied of its weekend contingent of wedding guests, and they were able to find a quiet table at the Bridge Street Café. Eve ordered a chicken-breast sandwich, surprised to discover she was hungry again. Gordon's possessive behavior was the sort of thing that usually reduced her appetite to zero and drove her to crunch an entire roll of antacids. Today she felt mildly irritated, but that was all. Obviously murder and mayhem agreed with her, she thought wryly. Or maybe she felt more in harmony with herself because events over the weekend had forced her to step back from the pressures of her career and get some perspective on her life. Murder and mayhem did tend to shed a different light on personal problems.

Gordon added his order to hers, then leaned across the table, gazing deep into Eve's eyes. He was extremely good-looking, she thought abstractedly, with the sort of amiable expression and ready smile that went perfectly with his easygoing disposition.

At moments like this, she wondered if she was crazy not to leap at the chance to marry him.

"You're mad at me, aren't you?" he asked, gaze tender.

"No, not mad. Irritated would be a better word."

"Why?" he said, looking crestfallen. "Eve, honey, how have I managed to upset you? Tell me, and I'll try to put things right."

"You refused Constance Powell's invitation to lunch without consulting me." She took a sip of ice tea. "I don't like it when you speak for me, particularly in a work situation. You shouldn't just assume my wishes are the same as yours. For all you know, there might be important background information that I need to get from the Powell sisters in an informal off-the-record setting. Like lunch."

He looked contrite. "You're right. I shouldn't have refused their invitation until I'd checked with you, but we work so well together I always feel we have a sort of telepathic communication where the program is concerned. I think of us as a team. A couple—"

"We're not a couple," she said flatly. "And professionally you're right, we're a great team, but the fact is, I'm the boss."

He stroked his thumb over her knuckles. "I know you are," he said, "and I have no problem with that because I respect your work enormously. I couldn't work for someone I didn't respect."

She sighed, ashamed of her crabbiness. "The feeling's mutual, Gordon. I was thinking only this morning how much I admire your work. I'm really looking forward to seeing the film you shot today at the Powells'. I think it's going to be spectacular."

He flushed with pleasure. "Thanks, Eve." He clasped her hands. "Honey, I know in your heart of hearts you realize we're going to get married sooner or later, so why do you insist on putting off the inevitable?"

"Gordon, please—"

He hurried on, not letting her interrupt him. "Why don't we get married right here in Eternity this month? I'd say this week, but I'd like us to be married in the chapel, a real old-fashioned wedding with all the trimmings." He smiled coaxingly. "You know what the legend says—if we exchange vows in the chapel, we'll live happily ever after.''

"I think we'd need more than a legend to keep the two of us happily married." She removed her hands from Gordon's clasp, reaching automatically for her antacids. She already had the roll unwrapped before she realized what her fingers had done. She refolded the silver paper and dropped the roll back into her purse. Antacids, in the quantities she'd been eating them, couldn't possibly be good for her. And a dozen packs of double-strength pills wouldn't cure the problem of her relationship with Gordon. What that needed was a refreshing dose of honesty, something Eve had been remarkably reluctant to dispense.

She drew a shaky breath. There was something frightening about rejecting Gordon in the unequivocal terms that left no room for doubt. She procrastinated a little. "Actually I think the legend about the Eternity chapel is more subtle than most people imagine. All it promises is that people who marry there will stay together for life." She flashed him a rueful smile. "For the two of us, that would probably be a guarantee of eternal misery, rather than a promise of lifelong wedded bliss."

He chuckled, not a whit put out. "That's my Eve! Always a cynic. But you're such a cute cynic I still love you."

She decided not to dispute his claim that she was *his* Eve or ask him how a cynic could be cute. "At least you don't seem to have any illusions about me," she said. "Tell me something, Gordon. Since you realize I'm nothing at all like you, why do you want to marry me? You're so good-natured yourself you deserve somebody equally as kind and easygoing. Why in the world do you want to spend your time with someone as scratchy and ambitious as me?"

He flushed and didn't answer for a moment. Then he looked up and gazed deep into her eyes again. "Because I'm in love with you, Eve." He cleared his throat, but his voice remained raspy with emotion. "Everything about you seems wonderful, even things like your ambition and your determination, which would be unattractive in other women."

Edge of Eternity

There was a compliment buried in there somewhere, Eve thought wryly. Gordon, it seemed, was in love with her even though he didn't really like her. Whereas she liked him and found many things about his character admirable, but she was never going to fall in love with him. What's more, she'd done him a major disservice in not telling him in clear, unmistakable terms that marriage was out of the question. She pushed aside her glass and leaned forward.

"Gordon," she said gently, "I'm truly honored that a man as worthy as you has fallen in love with me, but I can't possibly marry you. Trust me, it wouldn't work, and we'd make each other bitterly unhappy."

"Why?" he demanded. "We like each other. We respect each other professionally. We have interests in common. We've talked about our beliefs and our family values, so I think we could raise a child together."

What he was saying made a lot of sense, Eve reflected, so why was she so sure a marriage between the two of them wouldn't work out? The answer came in a flash of unexpected insight. *Because my feelings for him are tepid.* She didn't desire Gordon sexually, and there was no real emotional connection between them. He left the deepest level of her heart untouched; in some fundamental way, they lacked the capacity for intimacy.

"Gordon, you're a very attractive man, but there's no...spark between us." She reached for his hand, feeling no more than a mild spurt of affection as his fingers interwove with hers. "You see? We don't connect," she said. "There's no passion, no fire between us."

His grip tightened. "You're just talking about sex," he said. "But sex isn't especially important to me because it doesn't have much to do with making a marriage work in the long-term. Sex fades all too fast, Eve. You, of all people, ought to realize that passion is nothing compared to good solid friendship."

"How do you mean? Why do I know that?"

He reddened. "Well, I was around when your marriage to David was breaking up. Remember, I'd just started at the station when things began to go wrong between the two of you. Everyone knew how in love you'd been, how attracted you were to each other, and look what happened to your marriage.'' He leaned across the table, tense with sincerity. ''I'll say it again, Eve. Sex isn't everything. In fact, I'm convinced it isn't important in a marriage as long as the partners like each other a lot.''

He was wrong, Eve thought with sudden overwhelming conviction. For her, at least, he was totally wrong. Sex might not be everything in a marriage, but without physical passion there was no glue to hold the relationship together, no gateway to lead into the unique world of marital intimacy. Marriage was made up of a thousand splintered moments that combined to create the magical whole. But surely some of the most important moments were spent together in bed when a man and a woman shut out the rest of the world and shared everything that they were—their hopes, their fears, their longings—in an outpouring of mutual desire and satisfaction.

She didn't quite know why she understood this so clearly today, when for months she hadn't been able to put her feelings into words. Perhaps, if she hadn't seen David again, she might have been able to convince herself that friendship was an okay basis for marriage. But after the incredible pleasure she and David had shared this past weekend, she knew better. Maybe she was oversexed. Maybe she had a skewed understanding of what marriage ought to mean. But the truth was she could never substitute a friendly union with Gordon for the passionate fire of her relationship with David. The end of her marriage might have been hell, but the beginning, God, the beginning! The first few months of her marriage to David was the standard against which she secretly judged what it meant to be truly happy.

The waitress arrived with their lunch before Eve had time to probe her feelings further. ''Here're your sandwiches, folks. Sorry for the delay. Enjoy!''

''Thanks.'' For once, Gordon didn't manage to produce his usual cheerful smile. ''What were you thinking, Eve?'' he asked as soon as they were alone. "You looked a million miles away just now."

"Nowhere near as far as that," she said. "I was thinking that I've treated you badly."

"No, of course you haven't—"

"I've taken advantage of you," she said, admitting the truth to herself, as well as to him. She drew a deep breath. "Gordon, I wanted to fall in love with you because I was lonely, and I knew you'd be a great father for the baby I'm longing to have...."

He smiled in relief. "You see, we are in agreement!"

"No," she said. "Gordon, I wish I could marry you, but I can't, and I should have realized it a long time ago. You're a good friend, and maybe we'd even manage to stay friends after we got married if we worked really hard. But I'm greedy. I want more than friendship from my husband."

"What do you want that I can't give you?"

She smiled sadly. "I want the moon and the stars and all the planets, too. I want to fall madly, deliriously, insanely in love with my husband."

"But you could fall in love with me," he said plaintively. "Surely you could if you tried."

She realized then what it was she'd been trying to grasp a few seconds earlier. The truth that came to her was so simple and so shocking that she didn't know whether to laugh or to cry. "I can't fall in love with you because I'm in love with David," she said. "And I'm afraid I always will be."

Chapter Eleven

Having spent a productive day in Boston shopping for replacement diving gear, David wasted the entire drive back to Eternity trying to convince himself he was heart-whole and fancy-free. He was sure that what he felt for Eve was simply a nostalgic burst of sexual attraction for a beautiful woman. Despite the incredible hours of lovemaking they'd shared last night, his deeper feelings remained untouched.

He admired Eve's work, of course. How could he not when she was so talented? But that didn't mean he missed her insightful conversation or longed for her company or yearned for the soft warm sound of her laughter. No sirree. He was past the age of believing in romantic fantasy and understood the practical basis on which marriage needed to be built. He would never again fall into the trap of marrying a woman striving for professional success and especially not the same career-obsessed woman who'd already made his life a living hell.

He was smarter now than he'd been when he fell in love with Eve. He had his life planned out. Once he and Matt finished salvaging the *Free Enterprise,* he would buy a house in the suburbs, marry a sweet home-loving woman who had no professional ambitions and settle down to raise a family. It was a great plan. So why did it have him breaking out in a cold sweat?

He knew the answer to that when he arrived in Eternity and realized that, instead of driving straight home, he was roaming the streets, searching for the "Roving Report" van and hoping for a glimpse of his ex-wife. These were not precisely the actions of a man caught up in the throes of indifference, he reflected ruefully. Was he so damn frightened of his feelings that he couldn't risk being honest even with himself?

The truth was he was half-out of his mind with worry. He was scared that Eve wouldn't consider marrying him again, scared that she wouldn't be interested in a man who was no longer dedicated to the goal of climbing high and fast up the corporate career ladder, chewing up rivals and spitting them out with a triumphant gnash of his teeth. He had good reason to be scared, he decided. Eve was the one who'd demanded a divorce, and from her point of view, nothing in the past two years had changed for the better. Other than the fact that he managed to give her a great time in bed, why would she want to start their failed marriage again?

Besides, he decided gloomily, peering through the gathering darkness in search of the van, even their lovemaking might not seem special to Eve. She was so wonderfully responsive, so warm and generous in her sexuality that half the men in America could probably give her pleasure in bed.

He immediately felt murderous jealousy toward half the men in America. When he realized he was scowling ferociously at some innocent middle-aged male who happened to be standing at the traffic lights, he finally managed to laugh at himself.

I'm behaving like a lunatic, he thought. *Takeover of brain cells by testosterone. The ultimate and unmistakable sign of a man in love.*

He spotted the van at last, parked outside Marion Kent's jewelry store. Eve came out while he watched, smiling as she said goodbye to Marion and had a few words with one of the cameramen. His heart began to pound. Lord, she was beautiful!

He pulled to a halt behind the van, then stuck his head out the window. "Hi, Eve. Hi, Marion."

Eve barely nodded. Marion gave him a friendly smile. "Hi, David. Haven't seen you in a while."

"I've been busy. How are the babies?"

"They're gorgeous, of course, but quite a handful. I think Geoff is turning prematurely gray."

"And loving every minute of it, I'll bet." For once, David regretted that he hadn't paid more attention to his mother's gossip. He vaguely remembered hearing that Marion and her husband had split up, then spent a summer hovering right on the brink of divorce. He wished he knew Marion well enough to ask what had happened, how she and Geoff had reconciled and if they were truly as happy now as they appeared. Marion seemed to have found the perfect balance in her life. She was a devoted mother, but she still managed her store and found time to create custom jewelry designs in addition to caring for her twins. Maybe life did sometimes provide second chances, he thought, turning to look at Eve. God, he hoped so.

Eve finally finished going over the following day's assignment sheet with a good-looking man in his thirties whom David recognized instantly as a rival. He resisted the urge to bristle or strut. "Any need for a chauffeur?" he asked Eve, trying to sound like a normal person and not a man suffering from a terminal case of longing. "I'm available."

A faint flush crept into her cheeks. He didn't know if it was a good or bad sign that she appeared uncomfortable with him. "Thanks, but I have the rental car back at the chapel," she said, her voice sounding a little breathless.

"Leave it there. I can drive you to your first appointment tomorrow morning," David said.

"Okay. It's a deal." Eve climbed into the Jeep without quite meeting his eyes. David turned to wave to the people on the sidewalk and realized Marion was staring at the pair of them somewhat quizzically. He wondered if his state of adolescent longing was as visible as he suspected. Suddenly aware of the comic side of the situation, he gave Marion a huge grin. "'Bye, Marion. We have to get home," he said. "We need to feed our pregnant mother."

Marion looked surprised. "Oh, how…great. I didn't realize you were pregnant, Eve."

"I'm not," Eve said sharply. "David and I are divorced, remember?" She bit her lip, then smiled in silent apology. "I guess David's talking about our...about the cat." Her eyes suddenly twinkled. "Say, would you like a kitten when ours are born?"

"Heaven forbid! We've got enough babies!" Marion laughed and waved goodbye. David rolled up the window and sped toward the lighthouse.

"*Our* cat?" he queried. "*Our* kittens?"

Eve stared at the passing traffic. "A slip of the tongue. Cat is definitely all yours."

"I'm in a generous mood. I'm willing to share."

"Thanks, but my life-style doesn't lend itself to caring for pets. You were quite right to point that out when we were married."

"It's a relief to know I did something right. In retrospect, I can only remember all the occasions when I behaved like a total horse's ass."

"We both made mistakes." She looked away from him and spoke quickly, her voice excessively bright. "I had a good day, how about you? This is a nice town, full of nice people. I can understand why Pete Pieracini is so protective of his turf."

"I had a frustrating day, I guess. The face mask I want is out of stock in every dive shop in Boston, and the weather forecasters are predicting the imminent arrival of two major storms, which will screw up what's left of our diving schedule."

"Oh, dear, that sounds bad," she said.

"Yeah. But it gets worse."

"How?"

"I can't stop thinking about you, Eve. You're there, dammit, wherever I go, whatever I do."

She became preoccupied with buttoning her jacket. "Having me on your mind is worse than the imminent arrival of two winter storms?"

He looked away when he made the admission. "Yes, it's worse, because I don't know what to do about it."

She didn't say anything. He parked the Jeep in front of the cottage and cut the engine. In the sudden quiet David heard the rustle of wind in the sage grass, the soft indrawn sigh of Eve's breath and the heavy pounding of his own heart. He wanted more than anything in the world to reach out and take her hand, but the gap between them seemed like the chasm between two sky-scrapers. If he reached out and missed, the landing could be fatal.

"Eve, we need to talk," he said.

Her smile was strained. "A whole new concept in our relationship."

"We talked a lot this weekend," he reminded her. "It's been…good."

"We spent a lot of time in bed, too." She drew a quick, shallow breath. "It seems old habits are hard to break."

"What happened last night wasn't just about sex or hiding from our problems," he said.

"I know."

"Then what was it about, Eve?"

She'd twisted the button on her jacket so many times that it came off. She stared at it sightlessly for several seconds, then clenched her fingers around it and swung her head up, meeting David's eyes for the first time since she'd gotten into the Jeep. "I think it might have been about love," she said.

His hands shaking, David reached for her, closing the chasm and landing safely in Eve's arms. "Yeah," he said. "I kind of thought that myself."

THE PHONE RANG, rousing David from a blissful state of grogginess. He pushed Cat off his stomach—when the devil had he…she jumped up onto the bed?—and reached for the phone. "Hello."

"Mr. Powell? David? This is Marge Macdonald."

Caleb's landlady sounded distressed. He sat up, ignoring Eve's mumbles of protest. "Yes, Marge, what can I do for you?"

"I've been talking to Joyce," she said. "You know, you spoke to her, too. She told me you had a real nice talk."

"Sure," he said. "Caleb's sister. I hope she's okay."

"She's fair." Marge Macdonald fell silent for a moment. "For a while, I wasn't sure I should tell you this, but I thought about it some and I decided you need to know."

"We'd be grateful for any help you can give us."

"The other day you asked me if Caleb was worried about anything, and I said no, because I didn't want you to know—" Marge pulled herself up short and started again. "I told you Caleb had been involved with another woman," she said, the admission coming out fast and breathless. "He didn't want to be, kept telling me I was a good friend and he wanted to spend his life with me, but there was this other woman. He couldn't break free from her. It was like she had some magic hold on him, you know?"

"Yes, I can understand," David said, his grip tightening around the phone. "But you said Caleb never mentioned her name."

"That's right. Caleb never told me. Said it was better if I didn't know anything about her, that I didn't want to tangle with her. But when I was with his sister today, we started chatting. Nothing special, just remembering a picnic we went on this summer. Joyce told me how glad his family was that Caleb had found me. How he'd had this girlfriend a couple of years back that got her hooks into him and wouldn't let go. Joyce said this woman's name was Amy and she'd been a real piece of work. Caleb never had much sense about women, according to Joyce. First he got involved with his wife and her pills, and then this Amy. Like I told you, Caleb never breathed a word to me about no Amy, but Joyce knew the name real well."

Eve was now fully awake. She sat up, leaning close to him in an effort to hear the conversation. "Marge, I really appreciate your calling," David said. "Did Joyce happen to know Amy's last name or where she lives? And has she passed this information to the police?"

"She's gonna give 'em a call, although when I showed the detective Amy's name and the phone number written in the back of Caleb's notebook, he didn't seem to think it was important. I wasn't gonna say anything, then I got to thinking as how you both seemed to find that note about Amy real interesting and I remembered Eve said to call her if anything came up. I guess if he was involved with this Amy, you need to know, right?''

"We sure do." David tried again to get her focused. "We're glad you called, Marge, very glad. Especially if Caleb's sister was able to tell you where Amy lives or what her last name is."

"She doesn't know her address, but she knows her name. Joyce never met this Amy, mind, because Amy was married when she and Caleb started dating, so he didn't exactly introduce her around. Joyce says there was something real strange about their relationship right from the start. She says as how she seemed like a quiet, polite little thing on the surface, but she had Caleb so tied up in knots he didn't know which way to turn. If she'd asked for the Brooklyn Bridge, Joyce thinks Caleb would've tried to buy it for her."

"She must be some woman," David said. Hanging on to his patience, he asked for the third time. "And what was her last name?"

"Nichols," Marge said. "Her name was Amy Nichols."

Amy Nichols! The name exploded into David's consciousness, momentarily stunning him into silence. He paused so long that Marge spoke again. "Hello? David? You still there?"

"I'm still here," he said. "Marge, I think what you just told us might be very important."

"Is it going to help find out who murdered Caleb?"

"It might," David said grimly. "It very well might. Marge, I'll get back to you as soon as we know anything more. And thanks for the tip. Ask Joyce to think hard and see if she can come up with an address for Amy, will you? Some clue as to where we might find her."

Eve was already out of bed, picking up their clothes from the floor. She pulled on her sweater and tossed David his socks. "I heard what Marge said. She's found out Amy's last name. Nichols. Why are you looking as if you've been poleaxed?"

"Amy Nichols," he said. "That was the name of Ned's wife."

"Ned?" she repeated. Memories clicked into place. "Oh my God! Ned Nichols! Do you mean that Ned?"

"The very one. Good ol' Ned. The guy who robbed my clients of almost two million dollars, tried to shoot himself and then finally committed suicide in prison."

Eve stood, belt dangling from her fingers as she mentally connected the pieces. "We'd better not jump to conclusions here. It'd be an amazing coincidence if Caleb's girlfriend and Ned Nichols's wife turned out to be one and the same Amy."

"But it's certainly a compelling possibility, wouldn't you agree?"

"I sure would." Reluctantly she admitted, "Still, the world's full of amazing coincidences."

"And I guess it's not that unusual a name," David said.

"But it's not exactly John Smith or Mary Johnson, either."

David paced the bedroom, his mind buzzing on the brink of overload. "If Caleb was once head over heels in love with Amy and anxious to get her back, we have to accept that he knew she was here in town. And that she knew likewise. Which means little Amy Lewin has been lying through her teeth when she denies being acquainted with Caleb."

Eve nodded. "But that doesn't necessarily mean they were up to no good. In fact, lovers who split up usually prefer to avoid each other, and they often lie about their past."

"True. But we invited Amy and Matt to share a pizza with us last night just so you could check her out. Did you conclude she was lying? In your opinion, is she what she appears on the surface?"

"I don't know," Eve admitted. She shook her head in frustration. "I thought I'd be able to make a pretty firm judgment about her honesty once we spent some time together, but she was too...opaque. I've interviewed a lot of people since I started work at 'Roving Report,' but I can't remember ever encountering a woman who was harder to read. Even after last night, I have no *sense* of her. No idea whether or not she knew Caleb. No idea whether or not she feels anything for Matt.''

''Nor me,'' David said. ''But whatever she may or may not feel for him, I'm a hundred percent sure Matt's in love with her, and if Amy Lewin turns out to be Amy Nichols, ex-wife of Ned, ex-lover of Caleb, it's going to be traumatic for him.''

''Really traumatic,'' Eve agreed. ''We have to face the likelihood that if all these women are one and the same, then there's a good chance Amy developed her relationship with Matt strictly in order to set him up.''

David couldn't see the exact shape of it, but he felt a cloud of dread form on his mental horizon. ''Matt's already upset about what he considers Caleb's betrayal. He'll be devastated if it turns out Caleb and Amy were *both* using him.''

Eve winced. She sat down in the armchair, and Cat immediately curled into her lap. ''David, tell me exactly what you suspect Amy of doing.''

''Too many things,'' he said. ''I'm leaping to conclusions like an Olympic hurdler.''

''Take me through your leaps one by one. I think I fell by the wayside right around the first jump.''

David tried to order his chaotic thoughts. Strange how the simple fact of hearing Amy's last name could change his entire concept of what had been happening over the past few weeks. If Caleb and Amy were old acquaintances, if they'd been working together to rob the *Enterprise* of its treasure, so many puzzles became easier to explain.

''Let's go back to the beginning,'' he said. ''To Amy Nichols and her husband, Ned.''

''Is that the beginning?'' Eve asked.

''I think so, from our point of view. I never met Ned's wife, but I have a clear impression of the sort of woman she was. She didn't testify at Ned's trial, but from some of the evidence he gave, it's obvious she had the guy twisted up in an emotional morass. He testified that he stole because Amy had an almost pathological need to spend money and that somehow she made him feel he was a failure as a man if he couldn't provide it.''

"How did she spend the money?" Eve asked. "On possessions, or on high living?"

"Both, I guess. Jewels, cars, trips, you name it. Ned knew he had to provide her with a luxurious life-style or she'd leave him, and he was unable to bear that thought. In the end he understood what she'd done to him, how her manipulations had corrupted his judgment. He even understood that she didn't really love him, but he still couldn't break free.''

"That's exactly the sort of thing Caleb's sister was complaining about to Marge, isn't it?" Eve said. "On the other hand, we've seen Amy and Matt together, and I didn't detect any sign that she was obsessed with money or riches, did you?"

David shrugged. "No, but that may not mean much. Ned wasn't a stupid man and neither was Caleb. Presumably Amy's techniques for exploiting her lovers are a bit more subtle than sitting down every night and demanding champagne and diamonds. On the other hand, I agree with you that it's hard to visualize the Amy Lewin we met last night as a scheming woman, involved in a nefarious plot to get the men in her life to shower her with riches. Her character seems so...bland.''

"Bland isn't the right word," Eve said. "*Concealed* would be better. And she doesn't like you."

David was surprised. "How can you tell? I didn't feel any negative vibes.''

"I noticed that she didn't want to shake your hand, and every time you came near, she moved back so that there was no chance of the two of you accidentally touching. The desire to avoid you was about the strongest sign of emotion she gave all night.''

David thought about that for a moment. "If she's really Amy Nichols, she might well have reason to dislike me," he said. "After all, I'm the man who uncovered her husband's fraud. I was the star prosecution witness at his trial. Maybe she blames me for his suicide. And in a roundabout way she's right.''

"Of course she isn't!" Eve protested. "Besides, she'd already divorced Ned months before he killed himself. She's in no position to claim emotional distress or blame you for anything.''

David sat down on the edge of the bed. "When it comes to feelings, people aren't always logical or consistent," he said. "Amy could divorce Ned at the first sign of trouble and still be genuinely distraught over his death.'' He looked up and caught her gaze. "Consider the two of us," he said. "I hated you the night you asked me for a divorce. Hated you with a passion, because you wanted to end our marriage when I loved you so damn much.''

"Oh, David!" She put Cat off her lap and came to kneel on the floor beside him. "I was hurting," she said, her expression dark with remembered anguish. "I just wanted the pain to stop. I didn't care how I did it or how much I wounded you in the process.''

"I understand that now." He framed her face with his hands, aching with the intensity of his longing. "Marry me, Eve." The words came out of the most deeply buried layers of his subconscious, but as soon as they were spoken, he knew he meant them more than anything he'd ever expressed.

Her cheeks paled and her blue eyes clouded with panic. "I don't know," she said. "David, I'm not sure... Oh God, we made such a wretched mess of it last time!"

"Maybe we both learned something from picking up the pieces," he said. "I think I did.''

"I'm not ready...''

"We can go slowly," he said. "Let's take it one step at a time. Do you love me?" He wondered what the hell he'd do if she said no.

Color flooded her cheeks, then retreated, leaving her paler than before. "I love you," she admitted. "Only you. Always." She gave a broken little laugh and dashed the back of her hand across her eyes. "I'm just not sure I can live with you, that's the problem.''

He was so relieved that the love was still there for both of them that he wanted to grab her and dance a jig. With a great effort of will, he managed to do nothing more violent than press a quick hard kiss on her lips. He decided to back off for a while. He could live without her immediate promise to marry him. For a week or two. Maybe. But he was a determined man, and he knew there wasn't a chance in the world he was going to let her slip away from him a second time.

He smiled and hauled her up on the bed, holding her close. "I'm willing to settle for being your lover for now. But be warned, I plan to keep nagging until you agree to make an honest man out of me." He shot her a sideways glance. "Besides, Cat needs a respectable home to bring up her kittens."

She laughed, but he saw the strain behind her smile. He kissed her lightly on the nose. "Okay, now that we've got the important things taken care of, maybe we should get back to our discussion of Amy Nichols."

"All right." As he'd suspected, Eve grabbed eagerly for the change of subject. She began to tick off the points on her fingers. "Let's assume the Amy who was married to Ned Nichols is the same Amy we know here in Eternity. Amy Lewin Nichols persuades Ned to steal two million dollars for her spending pleasure. Then Ned gets arrested and she turns to Caleb Crewe for comfort." Eve stopped in midstride. "That poses a problem right away. Why would she turn to a man like Caleb?"

"Because she fell hopelessly in love?" David suggested.

Eve shook her head. "The woman you've described would never be motivated only by love."

"Then I can't begin to guess. Amy Lewin is good-looking. Very good-looking. If she craves money and high living, you'd think she'd go after some rich elderly executive willing to trade in wife number one for a younger, sexier model."

Eve thought for a moment. "The woman you've described wants power, along with her jewels and expensive vacations. With a man who's already rich Amy wouldn't be in control. She'd be the supplicant, always waiting for her husband to dish out rewards, always the subservient person in the relationship."

"You're suggesting that she needs to be in control of her

lovers?'' David said. ''That persuading them to steal for her is part of her pleasure?''

''It's a possibility, don't you think? Maybe she gets her kicks from knowing that she's twisted an honest man until he's willing to do anything to keep her, even commit a crime. You told me once that Ned was an honest man who lost his moral bearings. From what you and Matt have said, I'm guessing that Caleb was an honest, decent sort of guy until he met Amy. Maybe that's the point. Maybe she's only interested in honest, decent guys.''

David found the picture Eve was painting uncomfortable. ''You're making her sound like a black widow spider crossed with Prince Machiavelli.''

Eve grimaced. ''I interviewed a woman exactly like that once. She'd set up a drug-dealing network that covered half the college campuses in New England. She had an IQ well above the genius level, and she could have had a glittering academic career. Instead, she got her kicks from running hard-and-fast on the wrong side of the law. She liked the challenge of outsmarting the rest of the world. She took on organized crime, the college authorities and the law-enforcement agencies, and for a few years she won. It could be that Amy has the same sort of twisted lust for power. An insatiable desire to corrupt.''

David remembered Amy as he'd seen her the previous night, sitting placidly in the armchair, teasing them because Cat was a pregnant female and neither of them had realized it. He shook his head. ''It's easy to agree with what you're saying until I actually visualize Amy Lewin. Then I think we're creating a monster out of a woman who's so ordinary we'd never notice her in the normal course of events.''

''But she isn't so ordinary,'' Eve said. ''She's stunningly good-looking, and yet she doesn't act like a beautiful woman. She doesn't seem to send out any sexual vibrations at all. Why not?''

''I can't begin to guess.'' David's voice was dry. ''I guess you could say my sexual attention has been focused elsewhere these past couple of days.''

Eve blushed, but looked rather pleased at the backhanded compliment.

"I guess the question now is what we do next," she said. "Do we talk to Detective Pieracini?" She shook her head. "No, bad idea. Lousy idea. Can you imagine his reaction if we walk in and suggest he should investigate Amy Lewin on the grounds that Caleb wrote the name Amy in his notebook and you once helped prosecute the husband of a woman called Amy Nichols?"

David flinched. Expressed in such bald terms, the theory they'd constructed looked little short of ridiculous. Were they making mountains out of very small molehills? He got to his feet and took a restless turn around the bedroom. "Pete'd be right to ignore us," he said. "Right now he's taking statements, waiting for lab reports, coordinating with the Boston police and dusting half the surfaces in Eternity for fingerprints. He's not going to drop all that because we believe—no, have a vague hunch—that Amy Lewin once had an affair with Caleb."

"How about if we told him we suspect Amy Lewin may have killed Caleb?" Eve said.

The rumble of Cat's purr echoed in the sudden quiet. "That would certainly raise the stakes," David said at last. "But knowing Pete, my guess is he'd tell us we were risking a suit for slander and carry on dusting for prints."

"She's the most logical suspect for putting rats in our beds and destroying your diving gear. We'd already decided that looked like a classic act of revenge, and Amy definitely dislikes you."

"She could have put those obscene pictures in the lighthouse, too," David said. "Remember how she was the one who sent us in there?"

"And when it looked as if we might leave without finding the photos, Amy was the one who pointed out the broken display case with the pictures inside."

"This is all speculation," David said. "Pete still isn't going to listen to us."

"Maybe we should talk to Matt." Eve got up from the bed

and paced the room. "He must know more about Amy's background than we do. Besides, he needs to be told what we suspect."

"We can't approach Matt." David's friendship with Matt went back to college days, and he knew that his friend was a lot less self-confident than he appeared. Matt's mother was an alcoholic and he'd grown up emotionally abandoned by an ambitious, indifferent father and a stepmother who disliked children. Myriad unresolved hurts swirled beneath Matt's happy-go-lucky surface, and David dreaded having to approach his friend with the news that Amy might have deceived him. Matt was already depressed by the probability of Caleb's betrayal. He would be devastated to learn that the woman he loved had been conspiring with Caleb to steal treasure from the wreck of the *Free Enterprise.*

"Matt's head over heels in love for the first time in his life," he explained to Eve. "If it turns out we're wrong about Amy, he'd never forgive either of us for suspecting her. Talking too soon could literally destroy our friendship. And even if we're right, he sure as heck wouldn't cooperate with us to investigate Amy's background. We need solid proof she was conspiring with Caleb before we breathe a word of this to him."

Eve sighed. "You're right. Of course you are. But solid proof means we need something like documents, or incriminating photos...."

"Or even one of Pete Pieracini's much-loved fingerprints."

"But how are we going to get that sort of hard evidence?" Eve asked. "If the police with all their resources haven't found anything, we aren't likely to do any better."

"We might," David disagreed. "If we searched Caleb's apartment, we'd specifically look for links between him and Amy Lewin. The police aren't doing that. If they come across a snapshot of Amy and Caleb arm in arm on the deck of his boat, it won't mean a thing to them. They'll put it right back in the album."

"True." Eve gave a frustrated shrug. "But we aren't going

to get the chance to search Caleb's apartment, so we're stymied. The police aren't looking for a link between Caleb and Amy, and they won't start looking for one until we've already established that the link exists. At which point they don't need to look. A classic case of the vicious circle.''

David refused to surrender to her seeming logic. ''We're both approaching this with too much negative personal baggage,'' he said. ''We're not thinking straight. Eve, you're a talented investigative journalist. If you were working on an assignment for 'Roving Report,' you wouldn't give up this easily. Imagine you're in the midst of filming an important program and you want to get the inside scoop on Amy Lewin. How would you do it?''

Eve straightened, energized by the appeal to her professional expertise. ''I have a research team of course, and in this sort of case the initial procedure would be routine. I'd have them run a credit check on both Amy Lewin and Amy Nichols—that's easy to do and can turn up information you wouldn't believe.''

''A credit check isn't going to show that Amy Lewin was working with Caleb or that she invaded the cottage and planted dead rats in our beds, so what would you hope to turn up?''

''You'd be surprised at how often a credit check will give you evidence of what you're looking for, even if not in the way you expect. Aside from that, I guess I'd ask the team to look for proof that Amy Nichols and Amy Lewin are one and the same person. Even if they established that, it wouldn't prove Amy was involved in a conspiracy with Caleb Crewe—it wouldn't prove she was involved in anything—but it certainly ought to justify asking her some tough questions.''

''We can't access bank records or driving-license bureaus,'' David muttered. Then he jumped up, ignoring the howl of protest as Cat tumbled to the floor. ''That's it!'' he said. ''Her social security number! We can go after her employment records and show that Amy Nichols is registered under the same social security number as Amy Lewin. After that, it should be much easier to track her movements over the past couple of years and establish her connection to Caleb Crewe." He stopped in mid-stride. "Always assuming she didn't use fake ID."

"As far as we know, there's no reason for her to do that," Eve said. "After all, she and Caleb presumably planned to leave Eternity with the treasure long before anyone considered checking into her background. Or his."

"Great, then let's go." David marched to the bedroom door.

"Wait! Don't get too cheerful. I hate to rain on your parade, David, but did Amy have a job during the time she was married to Ned Nichols?"

"No, but that doesn't matter." David was seized by a surge of adrenaline so strong his hands were twitching. "I can call in a favor from my old boss, Cyrus Frank. He can give us Amy Nichols's social security number, providing he's willing to disclose it. That would provide us with at least half the information we need."

Eve looked puzzled. "Why would your former boss know Amy's social security number?"

David grinned, unable to avoid feeling a little smug. "As Ned's wife, she was part of the company health plan, and I know they kept track of plan members by means of social security numbers. That's the way most health plans work. Cyrus can access that number for me with a couple of phone calls to the personnel department. Always providing he's willing, of course."

"Then let's get started." Eve glanced at her watch. "It's almost nine o'clock. Do you know his home number?"

David took his Rolodex off the dresser. "I think I have it," he said, flipping through the cards. "Yep, here it is. Home and office." He dialed the number and gave Eve a thumbs-up when his old boss answered.

"Cy, this is David. David Powell. How are you doing?"

"All the better for hearing from you. I thought you were hunting pirate gold in the Caribbean."

"You're a few months out of date," David said. "This time

I'm going after Confederate gold off the coast of Massachusetts.''

Cyrus snorted. "Damn-fool waste of time. What provoked this
call? Are you broke? If you want your old job back, you're
hired.''

David laughed. "Cy, I'm not broke, and I'm so out of touch
with the market, your clients would sue you for incompetence if
you let me loose on their portfolios.''

"A couple of months and you'd be right back on track. You
have a magic touch with investments, David. You're wasting
your talents harpooning doubloons, or whatever the hell it is you
do. You can produce more gold on the stock exchange than
you'll ever find rotting on the ocean bottom.''

"Gold doesn't rot, but thanks for the compliment, if that's
what it was. I'll give your offer some thought.''

"Do you mean that?''

"Yes, I mean it." He glanced at Eve. "I may be moving back
to New York. But the real reason I called, Cy, was to ask a big
favor.''

"Ask away, but I'm a hard-nosed old bastard. If I want to
refuse, I will, even though I like you.''

"It's about Amy Nichols," David said. "Ned Nichols's ex-
wife.''

There was a momentary pause and when he spoke again, Cyrus Frank had sobered. "Yes," he said. "How can I help you?
That was a bad business all-around.''

"Call someone in personnel and ask them to look up Ned's
file. I need to know his wife's social security number. They
should be able to find it listed somewhere in Ned's application
for medical insurance.''

"Why do you want this information?" Cyrus asked, his tone
suddenly all business.

"I recently met a woman I think may be Amy Nichols, but
she's going under a different name," David said. "I'm trying to
confirm her identity by comparing social security records.''

"It's not illegal to use a different name, unless it's for the purpose of committing a crime."

"That's the problem. I think Amy may have killed someone."

"Killed someone! Who?"

"One of her lovers. Who may have been stealing on her behalf."

Cyrus didn't speak for a while. "Have you a shred of evidence for suspecting her of such a thing?" he demanded finally.

"Not evidence that would hold up in a court of law. That's precisely why I need her social security number. It's a long, involved story, Cyrus, but that number could be the crucial key."

There was a heavy silence. "I took you at your word the last time you asked for a favor," he said after a moment. "And I wasn't disappointed. I guess I can trust you one more time."

David's grip around the phone relaxed fractionally. "Thanks, Cyrus. I appreciate your confidence. How long do you think it might be before you can get hold of Ned's records?"

"About a minute," Cyrus said. "I don't have to contact anyone to get Ned's personnel file—it's right here in my study. When we were making the legal preparations for his trial, I duplicated the disk containing his personnel records, so that I could work on his case at home. I can check for the information you want myself. Hold on."

Neither David nor Eve spoke as they waited for Cyrus to come back on the line. "I've accessed Ned's file," he said, returning to the phone. "We have two entries for Amy Nichols in connection with the company health plan. She was born on January 12, 1962, in Ithaca, New York. And her social security number is 555-36-4420."

David let out the breath he'd been holding. "Thank you, Cy. Thank you very much. I owe you one."

"Yes, you do. Think about that job offer I just made if you want to give me a worthwhile payback." Cyrus hung up without waiting for David's reply.

"That was terrific," Eve said. "You have all the makings of a decent research assistant." Her eyes gleamed with laughter.

"Ask me nicely, honey, and I'll see if I can find you a place on my team." As soon as she'd spoken, she went bright red and turned away. David knew why. During their marriage, they'd both been so damn sensitive about their career successes that he would have reacted with icy withdrawal to Eve's teasing. What fools they'd both been, he thought ruefully.

He touched her arm. "Gosh," he said. "I'm really flattered. Between you and Cyrus, this seems to be my night for job offers."

She swung around, her face flooding with relief that he hadn't taken offense at her teasing. "You told Cyrus you might consider going back to your old job. Were you serious?"

"That depends," he said, holding her gaze. "If you and I get married again, I can't very well go off chasing treasure all over the world, can I? Especially if we have kids."

Eve shoved her hands into her pockets, looking worried. "But do you want to be a stockbroker?" she asked. "I thought you were tired of living in New York?"

"It wouldn't be my first choice," he said. "But I want to be your husband, and all the rest comes way down the list in terms of importance."

"Oh."

Eve fell silent. He wished she would run into his arms and reward his willingness to compromise with a promise to marry him. She didn't of course, but he supposed it was progress of a sort that she didn't protest yet again that marriage between the two of them was doomed to failure.

He took her hand. "It's getting late," he said, "and we've still only solved half the problem. We know Amy Nichols's social security number. Now we have to find out Amy Lewin's."

"Yes, you're right." As usual, she eagerly seized the change of subject. "How are your contacts at the *Courier?* You did so well with your old boss. Any chance you can bribe or flatter someone at the paper into accessing Amy's file?"

"No chance," he said. "Katharine Falconer runs a tight ship."

"Darn. Maybe I can get my research team on it tomorrow morning. They can sometimes work miracles."

"No need to wait." He grinned. "I'm just full of hot ideas tonight. Come on." He grabbed her hand and ran downstairs to his computer, switching it on and pulling up another chair for Eve as he waited for it to come on-line. "With luck, I may be able to access the *Courier*'s records myself."

"How?" Eve asked. "David, it can take hours—days—to find the access codes you need to break into a company's files."

"You sound as if you speak from experience," he said, moving his mouse to access his address file. "Ah, here it is." He gave a grunt of satisfaction as the listing for the *Courier*'s research center appeared on screen. He activated his modem and dialed the number.

"What are you doing?" Eve asked.

"Last year, when Eternity celebrated the two-hundred-year anniversary of its incorporation, my great-aunts made a donation to the town and paid for all the back issues of the *Courier* to be scanned and made accessible to researchers by modem. It's a great system and a great resource for local history buffs, not to mention serious historians. When Matt and I were researching the fate of the *Free Enterprise,* we scanned the data base for references to the shipwreck and accessed the articles without ever leaving the cottage. It's a tremendous time-saver."

"It sounds like a wonderful gift your family made," she said. "You mentioned it before. But what has a research data base got to do with finding Amy Lewin's personnel records?"

"Nothing in the normal course of events. Except twice I misdialed the number to access the data base and found myself staring at the paper's personnel files."

"Good grief, surely you can't remember the number you misdialed!"

"Not precisely, but I remember it was the last digit I got wrong. My fingers slipped on the key and I think I hit a seven instead of six."

The computer whirred and bleeped, then flashed a message onto the screen. REQUESTED NUMBER NOT AVAILABLE.

"Damn. I guessed wrong." David quickly keyed in another number. "Maybe I keyed one down instead of one up. Five, instead of six."

The computer bleeped again. REQUESTED NUMBER NOT AVAILABLE.

David scowled at the screen. "Dammit, I know I did this! I accessed the personnel files by mistake. What number did I dial?"

"The *Courier* could have changed the number," Eve suggested. "Maybe they found out that too many people were making the same mistake you did."

"Could be," David said. He glanced down at the computer keyboard and his gloom lifted. The pad of number keys at the right of his keyboard mimicked a touch-tone phone, with the six centered between a nine and a three. "That's what I did," he muttered. "My finger slipped down and I keyed in a three instead of the six."

He dialed the number, and after a few beeps and whirs, a heading appeared. COURIER PUBLISHING CORPORATION.

He and Eve exchanged delighted smiles. A list of menu choices appeared beneath the heading and he moved the mouse to PERSONNEL RECORDS.

The screen darkened, then lit up with a new message. ENTER APPROVED SECURITY ACCESS CODE.

"Good grief," David muttered. "This always looks a lot easier in the movies."

"Let me try," Eve said. "You'd be surprised how unimaginative people are at inventing passwords." She leaned across and tapped in a single word—Falconer. The screen flickered. The hard drive hummed and obligingly coughed up a new series of commands, including ENTER FILE NAME.

David gave a small whoop of triumph. "How the devil did you guess that Katharine Falconer uses her own name as an access code?" he asked.

"Because I've done this sort of thing before," Eve said wryly. "At least twenty percent of people use their names or birth dates as security passwords, even though all the manuals advise them not to."

David finished entering Amy's name. A new header appeared at center screen. RECORD OF EMPLOYMENT: AMY M. LEWIN. Beneath the heading were listed Amy's biographical data, tax and salary information, her three-month performance review and her application to enroll in the company health plan.

He scanned the information quickly. Amy M. Lewin was born in Ithaca, New York, in January 1962 and had been divorced since 1992. No record of her ex-husband's name. She was hired at an hourly wage of $8.50, which was raised to $9.00 after an "excellent" three-month review. Her social security number was listed as 555-36-4420.

He looked up at Eve. They smiled at each other in faintly punch-drunk approval.

"Bingo!" she exclaimed softly. "We've got her."

Chapter Twelve

Eve's euphoria faded when David began pacing the room, his expression forbidding. "What's the matter?" she asked. "For someone who's just completed a pretty nifty detective job, you don't look too pleased."

"Detection is fun when you're playing Clue," David said. "In real life, it hurts real people."

"You're worried about Matt," she said, understanding at once. "Because he's in love with Amy."

David nodded. "I have to talk to him," he said. "We've been friends for a long time, and before we take this any further, he deserves to know what we've discovered."

"Let me come with you," she said. "I know from experience that when people are confronted with news they don't like, they tend to blame the messenger. If I'm with you, he'll have two messengers to blame."

"So he can be furious with both of us, instead of just with me? Is that an improvement?" David asked. Nevertheless, he went off to call Matt looking slightly more cheerful. He came back to say that Matt had invited them to the motel.

"Let's go right now and get it over with," Eve said, not looking forward to the next couple of hours. This was the sort of situation that could very easily destroy a long-term friendship if it wasn't handled right.

"Maybe we'll get lucky," David said. "Maybe he'll be able to convince us that Amy was never involved with Caleb Crewe, then we won't have to take any of this stuff to the police."

"How could he convince us that Amy didn't know Caleb and had nothing to do with his murder?" Eve asked.

David looked bleak. "I can't imagine," he said.

THE NEW LOCK on Matt's door at the motel gleamed silver in the fluorescent lights of the parking lot.

Eve found her steps slowing after they got out of the Jeep. She'd been relieved and excited when they discovered that Amy Lewin and Amy Nichols were the same person, but she was beginning to realize that suspecting Amy of being secretly involved with Caleb Crewe didn't solve all the mysteries of the past few days.

She took David's arm, forcing him to match her pace. "We need another couple of minutes before we march into Matt's room and start flinging around accusations," she said. "So many things have happened over the past couple of days that I keep losing track of the details. But in retrospect, thinking back to the night when Matt's room was vandalized, don't you think it's odd that Caleb was dumb enough to invade Matt's room, trash the place so that it looked like a robbery and then steal nothing but the charts?"

"You mean because stealing only the charts immediately made Matt and me suspicious of him?" David asked.

"Yes. And if he was working in cahoots with Amy, why would he need to *steal* the charts? We thought before there's a good chance Amy has a key to Matt's rooms, and she must have a pretty good idea of Matt's schedule. She could slip into his suite when she knows he's away, take the charts to the instant-copy shop and return the originals all in the space of an hour. Why have Caleb run the risk of breaking into a motel room when they could get all the information they needed without you or Matt having a clue that your security was even breached?"

"Good question," David said.

"I sure hope you have a good answer."

He looked down, gaze troubled. "Only that criminals often seem to do dumb things."

"Definitely not a good answer," she said. "The more I think

about it, the more it seems that Caleb was flat-out stupid to steal *only* the charts. It was like pointing a finger of suspicion straight at himself.''

''And Caleb wasn't stupid,'' David said. ''Far from it.'' He spread his hands in a gesture of defeat. ''Eve, none of this affects the fact that we need to talk with Matt. Let's get this session with him over before we play detective again. We need to tackle one problem at a time. Right now, our problem is warning Matt what we suspect about Amy.''

''Okay.'' She hooked her arm through his as he rang the doorbell. Matt had obviously been waiting for them and answered the door within seconds, wearing his trademark black jeans and a baggy sweater. He leaned forward to kiss Eve's cheek, frosted beer can held out to the side. He gave an exaggerated sigh when he saw her arm linked with David's. ''Eve, sweetie, how come you're still hanging around with this good-for-nothing guy? Haven't you noticed yet that I'm twice as handsome and twice as smart?''

''Mmm. And twice as conceited, too.'' She smiled to take the sting from her words, wishing they didn't have to destroy his good cheer by raising doubts about the woman he loved.

''So what's up, old buddy?'' Matt punched David's arm in casual greeting, then invited them to take a seat with a wave of his beer can. He tore open a package of pretzels and set it in the center of the coffee table with a flourish. ''Okay. Your gourmet refreshments are now served. Dig in. I can offer you beer, Coke or apple juice. Take your pick.''

''Nothing, thanks.'' David jingled the change in his pockets. He looked as edgy as she felt, Eve decided.

''I'm fine, thanks,'' she said. ''Nothing for me, either.''

Matt slumped deeper into the chair, stretching out his long legs and propping his beer can on his flat stomach. He yawned. ''What's up, guys? Much as I love your company, I've had a hell of a long day, so if you don't mind, let's cut to the chase.''

Eve and David had spent the fifteen-minute drive to the motel planning exactly what to say and how best to alert Matt to the squalls looming ahead. It had seemed a lot easier in the car than it did in his sleepy, unsuspecting presence.

David shifted on the narrow sofa, almost visibly girding himself for battle. "Look, Matt, there's no way to ask this tactfully, so I guess I just have to go ahead and ask straight-out. It's about Caleb and Amy. Do you think there's any chance they could have known each other before we all arrived in Eternity?"

"Why the big buildup to such an innocuous question?" Matt asked, puzzled. "Anyway, you already know the answer. Amy never met Caleb. She'd never even heard his name until he was murdered. Good grief, you were with her when the news came in to the newspaper. You must *know* she'd never heard of him."

"Actually we wondered why she didn't recognize his name," David said. "It seemed strange that you'd never mentioned it to her. After all, we worked with him every day, and you see Amy every night. It's only natural to discuss the day's work."

"You know damn well that in our trade you learn to keep your mouth shut, even in bed," Matt said. His eyes gleamed teasingly. "Besides, we had better things to do than talk about Caleb."

"When you love someone it's hard not to discuss your daily activities," Eve ventured.

Matt didn't deny that he loved Amy. "We talked some," he said, beginning to sound exasperated by their persistence. "I tend to keep the various parts of my life separate. I didn't talk to David about Amy any more than I talked to her about Caleb."

It was certainly true that he hadn't discussed his new love with David, Eve reflected. When she and David had met Amy at the *Courier* offices, they hadn't even known for sure that she was Matt's girlfriend.

"Amy knew David and I were excavating a shipwreck," Matt continued. "But I never discussed the details of the operation with her, and so there was no reason for Caleb's name to come up in conversation. In fact, it's such an ingrained habit for me to be cautious, my subconscious probably screened his name out whenever I talked with Amy about my work." He took a swallow of beer and yawned again. "Dave, old buddy, I wish you guys would stop beating around the bush. What are you really trying to get at?"

"All right, I'll tell you why we came," David said, his voice flat. "Caleb's sister claims her brother had an unhappy love affair with a married woman called Amy Nichols and that the affair was ongoing."

Matt waited, not saying anything, and Eve realized he found the information so irrelevant that he didn't understand that David had finished his point and expected him to reply. For the first time since Amy Lewin's social security number had flashed up on the computer screen, she began to question Amy's involvement with Caleb Crewe. She didn't doubt that Amy Lewin had once been married to Ned Nichols or that Caleb Crewe had been in love with a woman called Amy Nichols. But she wondered if she and David were stretching that pair of facts into an enormous theoretical balloon that was all hot air and no substance. There were a dozen good reasons Amy Lewin might not want people to know she'd once been Mrs. Ned Nichols, none of them related to Caleb. The fact that Ned was a convicted embezzler who'd killed himself in prison, for a start. No wonder Matt was looking so blank, Eve thought.

"We believe that Caleb Crew might have been in love with Amy Lewin," she explained. "We think your Amy Lewin and Caleb's Amy Nichols might be the same woman."

Matt's blank expression was replaced by an astonished stare. "My Amy? Involved with Caleb?" His gaze flicked from David to Eve. He looked as if he wanted to laugh, but was too shocked. "Sweetie, what have you and David been smoking?"

His words were teasing, but underneath Eve could hear the throb of anger. This session was going much as she'd feared. Not surprisingly, Matt was hurt by the suggestion that a woman he loved and trusted might be two-timing him, and his anger was turning not toward Amy, but toward them.

She was glad when David cut into the mounting tension with

an abrupt question. "Do you remember a colleague of mine called Ned Nichols?"

"Of course I do. He worked with you until he went nuts and started plundering the company profits. Sure, I remember your talking about him, although I never actually met him."

"His wife's name was Amy," David said. "Amy Nichols. And we've run checks on her social security number. It's the same as Amy Lewin's."

Matt didn't say anything, but his hand clenched tighter around his beer can and all trace of laughter drained from his expression. He stared at the television, his gaze suddenly as gray and blank as the screen. "Are you sure?" he asked at last.

"There's no doubt about it," Eve said gently. "The woman living here in Eternity and working at the *Courier* is the same woman who was once married to Ned Nichols. Amy Lewin and Amy Nichols are the same woman."

Matt's face had about as much expression as a diver pulled unconscious from the ocean. "That doesn't mean she was also involved with Caleb Crewe," he said.

"No," David agreed. "But since Caleb had an affair with a married woman called Amy Nichols and, according to his sister, was still involved with a woman in Eternity called Amy, it's pushing the long arm of coincidence rather far to believe that the Amy living here in Eternity is a different woman."

"Coincidences happen all the time," Matt said stiffly.

His eyes had turned dark with pain, and Eve knew he didn't really believe his own protests. She wished with all her heart that he could have found some other woman to fall in love with. She wished that his face wasn't so revealing. She could almost see the thoughts chasing through his head. Any minute now, he would realize that if Amy had lied about her past and about knowing Caleb Crewe, she had probably lied about a lot of other things, too. Including what happened the night Caleb Crewe was murdered.

With exaggerated care, Matt set his empty beer can next to

the untouched package of pretzels. "What are you going to do about this?" he asked.

"We have to tell the police," David said. "Matt, I'm sorry, really sorry, but I guess you have to face the fact that Amy may know more than she's been telling about Caleb's murder."

"Why the hell is that?"

"Matt, if Amy knew Caleb, why did neither of them admit to knowing the other? Don't you think it's likely she was involved with him in some scheme to rob the *Enterprise* of its treasure? We need to point the police in her direction."

Matt turned away, refusing to meet David's eye. He said nothing.

"I know how devastated you must feel," Eve said.

"Do you? I doubt it."

"Matt, we'll both be thrilled if the police come back with the news that Amy had nothing to do with this," David said. "But we need some answers."

"Yeah, I guess you do." Matt sounded so weary, so depressed, that Eve wanted to take him in her arms to comfort him, but she was rebuffed by the emotional barricade he'd erected. At this point, she could tell that Matt didn't want comforting—at least not from her or David.

He got up and walked over to the bar, bending down to open the fridge. When he stood up and turned around, he was holding a gun.

Eve stared at him, horrified. "Matt, we don't need a gun, for heaven's sake."

He looked at her, eyes blank, voice cold. "You don't. I do. Unfortunately."

My God, he's going to commit suicide, Eve thought, her stomach plummeting with fear. She got up quickly. "Matt, don't! Amy's not worth it. Nobody's worth killing yourself—"

"Eve, stand still. Don't move!" David's words were harsh with the urgency of his command.

The jagged note of fear in his voice shocked her into obeying. She came to a halt about two feet away from Matt. A sick, incredulous understanding began to build deep inside her. *Matt,* she thought. *Oh my God, not Matt.*

Matt gave David a brief sad smile, but his grip on the gun had tightened, and he was pointing it straight at Eve. "This was never supposed to happen," he said. "That's why we tried so hard to keep you in the dark, so we'd never need to do this. But I can't let you go to the police, not for the next few days, anyway. Don't try to get the gun away from me, David, or I'll shoot Eve." He looked at her, mouth tightening in frustration. "Damn, I hate this! It's all Caleb's fault."

"Why is that?" David asked, sounding almost casual.

"He backed out of our deal at the last minute," Matt said. "The truth is he was jealous of me and Amy, of our wonderful relationship."

"I suppose he was still in love with her," David said.

"Everyone who knows Amy falls in love with her." Matt spoke with total conviction. "Caleb was crazy about her."

"She must be a very...special...woman," David said.

"She is." For a split second, Matt's smile was one of unalloyed happiness. "She makes a man feel strong and sure of himself."

Eve bit back the impulse to point out that inspiring her partners to commit terrible crimes was a rather strange way to make a man feel sure of himself. Not to mention the fact that her two previous lovers had both ended up dead. A high price to pay for self-confidence.

"What happened between you and Caleb?" David asked, taking a couple of steps toward Matt. "What went wrong the night he was killed?"

Matt might be mentally unbalanced by his obsession with Amy, but his reflexes were still in great shape. He saw David move toward him and reacted instantly. "Get back!" he ordered, his aim never wavering. "Don't try anything, Dave, or I swear I'll shoot Eve."

"That wouldn't be very smart," David said quietly. "People would hear the shot."

"Are you willing to gamble Eve's life on the chance that I won't shoot her?"

"No."

Matt gave another sad smile. "You're a good guy, David, but you'd go a lot further in life if you could only learn to lie a little."

"I didn't think lies were necessary among friends."

"That's where you need them the most," Matt said bitterly.

"When did we need to lie to each other?" David asked.

Only since Amy arrived on the scene, Eve thought.

Matt didn't answer the question. "You know what?" he said. "Caleb didn't like the idea of lying to you. We argued about that a lot. He said he didn't mind defrauding the government, or Lloyds of London, but you were a friend, and he wanted to cut you in on the deal."

"I'm flattered." David allowed only a hint of irony to color his voice. "I guess the gun you're waving at Eve means you don't share his high opinion of friendship and its obligations."

"You know I do," Matt said. "You're the best friend I ever had. But I'm a realist. If Caleb had known you for as long as I have, he'd have realized you're a damned straight-arrow kind of guy. You'd never agree to any sort of illegal deal."

"Why did you?" David asked.

"I need the money," Matt said. "Amy has very expensive tastes." He sounded almost proud, as if he was discussing an endearing character quirk, such as an insistence on baking her own bread or always wearing purple underwear.

Eve finally recovered her wits enough to speak. "Matt, you know you can't get away with this. What are you going to do if David and I both move at the same time? Mow us down in a hail of bullets? I don't believe you're capable of such a thing."

"Don't put your theory to the test," Matt said. "I love you, sweetie, but in comparison to Amy and twelve million dollars in gold sovereigns, you just don't stack up."

"But you don't have twelve million dollars," Eve said. "You and David haven't found the treasure yet. What's more, you need

David's help if you're going to locate it before the winter storms put you out of business."

"He doesn't need me because he's found the treasure," David said. "That's what this is all about, isn't it, Matt?"

"Of course not—"

"Matt, there's no point in lying anymore. That was the reason for the mysterious failure of the pressure gage on my air tanks and the fishing net that kept us both tangled up outside the hull of the ship." David sounded impatient with his failure to have seen something so obvious. "I kept wondering how a saboteur could have controlled those incidents, even if he gained any benefit from them. But for you, the control was easy, because you were right down there with me. You faked your shortage of air. You deliberately tangled yourself in that fishing net. And in the process you kept me away from the place in the ship where you'd found the treasure."

"I didn't know your regulator was going to jam open," Matt objected. "It was a sheer fluke that it happened at the same time I got caught in the net."

"A damn convenient fluke," David said. "Where did you find the treasure? Somewhere close to where you laid that trap of fishing nets, right?"

Matt shrugged. "I lied to protect you, David, because you're my friend. But I guess it's too late for lies if you're determined to set the police on Amy's trail. So I'll admit you're right. Yes, I've found the treasure, and yes, it's hidden behind those fishing nets. Now all Amy and I have to do is bring the chests to the surface." He gave a grin that was a parody of his familiar, jaunty smile. "Then we're outta here, folks. Rio de Janeiro here we come!"

"When did you find the gold?" David asked. "How? Why didn't I know about it?"

"That's easy. Caleb took Amy and me out every weekend when you thought we were in Boston."

"Amy dives?" Eve asked.

"She's been certified since she was a teenager," Matt said.

"We've been going down to the wreck every weekend working the aft section of the ship, and that's where we found it. Two huge trunks, filled right to the brim with gold sovereigns."

"Even working overtime, you couldn't be sure you and Amy would find the gold before I did," David said.

"Amy...we..." Matt drew a deep breath. "I had a contingency plan in case you found it first," he said crisply.

An accident on the ocean bottom? Eve thought, shivering. God knows, there would have been a dozen ingenious ways to arrange that, and no witnesses to contradict Matt's version of events.

David didn't waste time asking Matt to explain what he meant by a contingency plan. He'd obviously reached the same conclusion as Eve. "How did you plan to bring up the treasure?" he asked.

"We arranged with Caleb that we'd raise it this past Saturday night," Matt said. "He brought in the special gear, the pulleys and the buoys. He was supposed to rendezvous with us on the beach so that Amy and I could get ready for a night dive. Then Caleb got cold feet. We knew he was getting ready to sell us out to you, David—that's why I faked the robbery of those charts. I had to find a way to point suspicion at him and away from me." His voice took on an apologetic tone. "He was so damned stubborn. Amy really had no choice but to kill him."

"It was Amy who fired the fatal shot?" David asked.

"She's a very decisive woman."

"Matt, listen to me," Eve pleaded. "If Amy shot Caleb and the gold is still on the bottom of the ocean, then you haven't committed any crime. For God's sake, take a hard look at yourself! See what this woman is doing to you and walk away from her before you get into even worse trouble."

"He can't do that." The door to the bathroom opened and Amy Lewin came out. Her chestnut hair was piled in a thick, lustrous knot on top of her head, and her stunning figure showed to maximum advantage in faded jeans and a jade green turtleneck. Like Matt, she was holding a gun—in her case, a .357

Magnum—and it looked almost obscenely large and heavy in her slender hands.

Amy walked up to Matt and stood close beside him. Eve had wondered why her personality always seemed so bland, and now she knew. Amy had been hiding behind a mask so thick that it had cut off all the natural human vibrations. Now that Amy had chosen to toss her mask aside, the impact of her presence was literally breathtaking. The blatant force of Amy's sexuality affected even David. Eve saw his eyes widen and color flare briefly in his cheeks before contempt replaced his reflexive masculine response to a truly beautiful female.

Matt's reaction was far stronger. He literally shuddered, his expression changing from melancholy to helpless longing. "What do you want us to do, darling?" he asked.

"This has gone on long enough," Amy said. "We don't owe them any explanations." She jerked her head toward the door. "You take her. I'll take him." She walked up to David and pointed the gun straight at his heart. "Listen up, big boy." Her voice was raw with hatred. "We're going to walk out of here arm in arm, and you're going to look like you're loving every minute. Same with Evie over there. She's going to lean up against Matt, real close, and look like she's having fun."

"And if we don't?" David asked. "What if we scream and yell? How do you expect to get away with murdering two people in a motel parking lot?"

Amy's smile was tinged with scorn. "It's nearly midnight on a Monday, and the good people of Eternity are all tucked in bed. I expect to get away with it long enough to bring up that treasure and hightail it to Brazil."

Eve didn't believe that Matt and Amy had a chance in a million of getting away with murder in the motel parking lot. The trouble was, though, her opinion didn't count. Matt and Amy were cockeyed enough to believe they could succeed, which meant they'd shoot first and worry about escape afterward.

Eve realized that her mouth was dry with terror. She hadn't taken Matt's threats seriously, because she simply hadn't believed him capable of killing her. That had been a bad mistake. She and David should have jumped Matt when the odds were two to one in their favor. Amy looked as if she was more than capable of killing anyone who got in her way, and Matt was besotted enough to go right along with her instructions.

"Where are you taking us?" she asked as Matt grabbed her arm and pulled her toward the door.

"For a little boat ride," he said, shoving her through the door.

Behind her, she heard a scuffle. Matt spun around, dragging her with him, holding her against him, arms pinned to her side. Eve saw the flash of motion as David's elbow went smashing into Amy's ribs. Amy doubled over, coughing, but she managed to retain her hold on the gun and David sidestepped quickly as she swung her arm up, trying to aim. In a move almost too quick for the eye to follow, he got behind her and brought his arm around her throat, immobilizing her in a stranglehold. Amy clung desperately to the gun, but David was much the stronger of the two, and in a few seconds, he'd forced her fingers open and taken possession of the weapon.

Matt's voice was harsh with panic. "Let her go, or I'll shoot Eve!" To show he meant business, he braced his back against the door, sliding the gun up Eve's neck until it was pressed against her temple.

"Seems we have a standoff," David said, panting. "You shoot Eve and I'll shoot Amy. Is that what you want, old buddy?"

It was a good thing Matt was holding her so damned tightly, Eve thought. Otherwise her legs would have given way beneath her. In TV hostage dramas, crazed gunmen held weapons to the heads of innocent victims all the time. The reality wasn't even remotely like that. It wasn't even like interviewing the perp and the victim after the incident was all over. She was so scared, she was afraid she would vomit all over Matt's restraining arm, and each breath she drew caused a painful cramping in her stomach. At the same time, she was aware of a distinct sense of unreality. This was Matt Packard holding a gun to her head. The friend who'd shared more happy evenings with her and David than she could count.

"Matt, be reasonable," David said, his voice steady but implacable.

"I am being reasonable," Matt said. "Amy and I are going to take care of you two guys, then we'll bring up the gold and fly off to a new life in Brazil. Once we're there, it doesn't matter what you tell the police."

"That's not going to happen," David said. "Amy doesn't plan to leave Eve and me alive, and you know it."

"That's not true, is it, babe?" Matt sounded almost pleading.

Amy didn't reply, and David tightened his grip around her neck. "Face it, Matt, the only way you're going to get out of this room is by killing Eve. And then I'll kill Amy, and you, too. You know I'm faster with a gun than you are." He spoke almost gently. "Give it up, Matt. It's all over. Don't add Eve's murder to the list of sins on your conscience."

The gun trembled against Eve's temple. She closed her eyes, praying that Matt's finger wouldn't slip on the trigger. Then she felt his body go limp and his arm fall from around her throat. She had just enough presence of mind to pull herself out of his arms and drop to the floor.

"No! No! Don't let her go!" She heard Amy's agonized scream from far over her head. She rolled to the side, hunching against the wall as Amy, demented with rage, tore herself out of David's grip and launched herself straight at Matt.

"Give me the gun," Amy yelled, almost incoherent with frustrated fury. "Give me the damn gun!"

Matt warded her off, his gestures limp and defeated. "It's all over," he said sluggishly. "Amy, it's too late. Face reality. We've lost."

"*This* is reality." Amy brought her hand down in a sharp chopping movement on Matt's wrist. He winced, but he managed to ward her off, still clinging to the gun.

Amy wasn't willing to give up, and she clawed at his face,

literally berserk with rage as she tried to wrest the gun from his grasp.

"Amy, stop. Enough," David said. He stepped forward, intending to haul her away from Matt. Just as he moved, Eve heard the muffled explosion of Matt's gun and Amy fell forward, collapsing against Matt's chest.

"Oh my God!" Eve got to her feet, but David ran across the room and stepped in front of her.

"Amy?" Matt said, pushing her head back from his chest and staring into her eyes. "Amy! For God's sake, speak to me!"

Silence echoed off the walls.

Matt gave a howl of anguish that sounded more like an animal caught in a trap than a human being recognizing death. He swept Amy into his arms and carried her to the sofa. Still moaning, he put his fingers against her neck. Then he looked up, his eyes staring unseeingly toward David and Eve.

"She's dead," he said. "I killed her."

"It was an accident," David said. "Matt, it wasn't your fault."

Matt brushed his fingers over Amy's eyes, closing them. "I killed her," he repeated dazedly. "I killed her." He looked down at the gun he was still holding and turned it slowly toward his mouth.

"No, Matt, don't do it!" Through a haze of horror, Eve saw David hurl himself at his friend. David grabbed for the gun. There was an explosion, a flash of blue flame. Matt slumped against the back of the sofa and David fell across his chest.

"Oh, dear heaven!" Eve rushed across the room, heart pounding, stomach lurching with dread. *Please don't let David be dead,* she prayed. Just as she reached his side, David sat up, holding Matt's gun.

Eve knelt on the floor, reaching up to touch his face. "Are you all right?" she asked urgently. "Dear God, David, where did you get hit?"

"Nowhere," he said, standing up and pointing to a spot high

in the far wall where plaster was flaking around a bullet hole. Only the wall got wounded.''

"You saved Matt's life," she said. "He sure as hell didn't deserve it."

David looked down at Matt, who was staring vacantly into space, hands splayed at his sides. "I was paying back old favors," he said, unloading the bullet clips from the guns. "Let the legal system take care of him. Without his help, I'd have been food for the Caribbean fishes on at least two occasions."

"He was willing to cheat you and rob you."

David took her into his arms. "Yes, but in the end he wasn't willing to kill me. Or you."

"He came too damn close for comfort." She choked on a hastily swallowed sob. "I thought you were dead."

"I'm not that easy to get rid of." He kissed her softly on the forehead. "I love you, Eve. Don't ever leave me, please."

"I love you, too." She tightened her arms around him, overwhelmed by the need to be close, to feel the strong thump of his heart against her breasts. "Marry me, David," she said.

He cradled her head against his chest. "Sometimes," he said, "you have the most wonderful ideas."

Epilogue

The marriage of Patience Powell and Louis Bertrand was undoubtedly one of the happiest occasions ever seen in the Eternity chapel. Accompanied by his son, Paul, the groom waited at the altar, looking tall, distinguished and appropriately nervous for an anxious soon-to-be ex-bachelor. Overcome by emotion, he pulled his dashing scarlet silk handkerchief from his breast pocket and dabbed at his eyes when the bride, preceded by her three sisters, entered the little chapel.

Patience had settled the problem of who should escort her down the aisle by deciding to walk triumphantly alone. Encouraged by her sisters, she had chosen a satin dress of burnished gold in a style that carried hints of the Edwardian era in its high, antique-lace collar and deep buttoned cuffs. With her snow-white hair swept on top of her head, she looked as elegant and beautiful as every bride is supposed to look. Even the technicians from ''Roving Report,'' a crew not noted for their sentimentality, were seen exchanging sappy smiles when Bronwyn Powell declared the couple husband and wife.

The chapel had been jammed to capacity for the service, but the overflow crowd had now departed for the reception at the old family mansion, where the culinary talents of the Powell sisters and the caterers would be jointly on display at the overflowing buffet tables.

The ''Roving Report'' crew had packed up their gear, with Gordon declaring confidently that they had the perfect finale for the upcoming program on winter brides. The bright lights necessary for taping had all been switched off, leaving the chapel bathed in soft shadows and its usual glow of diffused lamplight.

The flowers and pine branches arranged so lovingly by June and Violet Powell remained on the window ledges and at the center of the simple stone altar, their scent lingering in the air and their rich colors radiant in the gleam of candles. Glancing around her, Eve thought there couldn't be a more serene and beautiful place to be married in the whole world.

Bronwyn Powell had finally finished shaking hands with guests and posing for group photographs. She returned to the chapel and stepped once again into the center of the sanctuary. She smiled at the dozen or so guests still waiting at the front of the chapel.

Opening her service book, she turned first to Eve, then to her brother David. "Are you ready?" she asked them quietly, her gaze warm with approval.

David kissed his mother, then glanced to where Eve was sitting, across the aisle with her parents. "I'm ready," he said.

Eve rose to her feet. Her mother smiled up at her, eyes misty. "Be happy, sweetheart."

Eve squeezed her mother's hand. "I will be. Thanks for coming, Mom." She bent down and kissed her father. "You, too, Dad."

Her father made the inarticulate harrumphing sound that meant he was deeply moved. She gave him another quick hug, and then walked the two or three steps to David's side.

"I thought you could never look more beautiful than you did on our first wedding day," he said, taking her hand. "I was wrong."

Her heart contracted with love. "Thank you," she said.

"We're going to make our marriage work this time," he promised her, his voice harsh with the force of his conviction.

"Yes," she said softly. "We are."

MY PHONY VALENTINE
Marie Ferrarella

Chapter One

"I WANT YOU to be me."

T.J. stared at the telephone receiver in her hand, stunned.

It wasn't until the telephone on her desk had rung three times that Theresa Jean Cochran had even become aware of it. With her mind on the statistics she'd pulled up on the screen, T.J. had groped for the receiver, managed to hit the speaker button instead and mumbled a preoccupied "hello."

"T.J."

Theresa *Joan* Cochran's voice had filled her cousin T.J.'s sunbathed seventh-floor corner office. Uncertainty had nudged at T.J. as she'd glanced at the telephone. Why was Theresa calling her on the phone? Why hadn't she just swept in without knocking, the way she normally did? It never occurred to Theresa that she had to knock. As the president of C & C Advertising, she was accustomed to going anywhere she chose within the three floors that the agency occupied in the Endicott building—short of perhaps the men's room. And entrance into the latter might have been ventured on a dare. So far, no one had wanted to see just how far the flamboyant executive would go if challenged.

Even if Theresa hadn't been the head of the company her grandfather had founded and her father had so diligently developed into a top advertising firm, she would have felt absolutely no compunction about invading her cousin's space. It was something Theresa had been doing with fair regularity ever since they had been children. By now, it was as natural to her as breathing.

T.J., named after the same paternal grandmother Theresa had

been, had reached for the receiver then. Light was flooding in through the two adjacent windows behind her, but the office had suddenly seemed chilly, as a feeling of déjà vu waltzed through her, doing double time.

She was more than familiar with the tone her cousin was using. Theresa was out for something. Like as not, it was a favor. A teeny-tiny little favor.

It was always some "teeny-tiny little favor" that would somehow snowball, embedding T.J. along with it as it built up momentum. When they were children, some of the favors had been pretty outrageous, but of late, they usually involved work, one account or another that had to be diplomatically rescued after being in the path of Hurricane Theresa. That was the name some of the older employees had pinned on her behind her back.

T.J. suspected that Theresa was aware of the nickname and took it to be a compliment.

They'd been born nine months apart, with T.J. the senior; it was Theresa who was the flashy, outgoing one. Theresa who was constantly being photographed as she was squired around by one after another of the country's most eligible bachelors. And it was T.J. who burned the midnight oil at the company. T.J. who was by far the creative force that propelled them into new contracts and new accounts and who helped cement the old ones by breathing new life into them.

Which was fine with T.J. She preferred remaining in the shadows and doing something she considered worthwhile and creative. T.J. had always enjoyed pulling her weight. Theresa enjoyed pulling off coups. They worked well together.

Because the computer was too slow for her taste, T.J. had pressed two buttons to automatically save her work. Bracing herself, she had taken a deep breath. She'd had a feeling this was going to take a while.

"To what do I owe this pleasure?" T.J. had looked at her watch. It was going on to nine o'clock. She wondered if Theresa was still home. It wouldn't be the first time Theresa was late.

She'd heard Theresa sigh dramatically. No one could sigh dramatically like Theresa. This had the makings of something big.

"T.J., I need help."

T.J. had leaned back in her chair. Yup, big. "Help as in help with a campaign, help with an ad idea or..." Her voice had trailed off, waiting for Theresa to fill in the proper ending.

Theresa had picked none of the above. And that was when she had laid the bomb at her feet and said, "I want you to be me."

T.J. now raised her brows. Bangs the color of milk chocolate threatened to mingle with dusky eyelashes. "That wasn't going to be my next guess." Not at this point in their lives, anyway.

Theresa didn't seem to hear her. It was a habit she had long honed to perfection, shutting out everything that didn't mesh with what she was thinking. "You're the perfect choice, T.J."

Not for nothing was she called Hurricane Theresa, T.J. thought. T.J., on the other hand, liked things spelled out and neatly organized.

"I think I missed a step here, Theresa. I'm a little slow before my fourth cup of coffee." Forsaking the computer entirely, she gave her undivided attention to the woman on the telephone. "Fill in the gaps for me, will you?"

There was a long pause, as if Theresa was searching for the right words. This probably had to do with conducting some meeting for her, T.J. mused. If she knew her cousin, there was a slope out there that needed skiing, or a man who needed her company at some secluded cabin hideaway. That left her to tie up ends for Theresa. Her cousin had a unique way of keeping a thriving business going while having a hell of a good time herself—elsewhere.

But Theresa was gorgeous and charming and rich, so everyone forgave her. In that respect, T.J. was no different from anyone else. And in T.J.'s case, there was also the matter of genuine affection and a sense of protectiveness that, if Theresa had thought about it, would have made her laugh in delighted amazement.

T.J. decided to prod Theresa along. "Why would I have to be you when you can be you so much better?" T.J. wanted to get to the end of the riddle before she grew too old to make sense of it.

"That's just the problem. I can't. I'm in the hospital."

T.J. bolted to attention. "In the hospital? Oh, God, Theresa, are you all right?" She began searching with her bare feet for her shoes under the desk. "What hospital are you in? I'll be right there." She drove too fast. Theresa always drove too fast. Why didn't she ever listen to her and slow—

"No, don't. I'm okay, really. But the car isn't." Theresa's voice sobered. "It's totaled. And it was such a beautiful shade of blue, too."

T.J. ran her hand over her face. If Theresa could express sorrow over the loss of a car, then she was probably all right. T.J. took in a cleansing breath and let it out slowly, calming down. She needed facts. "You were in a car accident?"

"It wasn't my fault." Theresa's voice was tinged with a note of defensiveness. "The other car ran a light."

Maybe, maybe not. What mattered now was Theresa. "But you're sure you're all right?"

"Of course I'm sure. But the doctors are being difficult." T.J. could visualize the pout on Theresa's face as she said that. She wasn't accustomed to taking orders. "They want to keep me here for observation. Of course," she continued, her voice becoming loftier, "there's this one who I wouldn't mind having examine me by candlelight...."

Theresa was fine, T.J. thought with relief. "You're digressing."

"Right as always." Assured of her audience and the response, Theresa pushed forward. "I need you to be me with Christopher MacAffee."

"Christopher MacAffee, as in MacAffee Toys?"

"Yes."

A copy of the presentation T.J. had labored over for the man was housed on the blue disk on her desk. She'd scanned her hand-drawn sketches in just last night. Christopher MacAffee was the newly appointed president of MacAffee Toys, taking the position over from his ailing father. MacAffee Toys was a hundred-and-twenty-year-old toy manufacturing company that had managed to hang on to integrity as well as healthy profits through several generations.

But knowing all this still didn't answer any of the questions that were crowding T.J.'s brain. "You're losing me again."

"Christopher MacAffee is coming down this afternoon to meet with me about finalizing the account. He has some questions about the presentation. You worked on the campaign," Theresa reminded her needlessly.

Some of her best work had gone into that campaign. "Yes?"

"You know how stuffy that man is."

Actually, T.J. thought, she had no idea how stuffy the man was or wasn't. She had dealt only with his production assistant, and then only by telephone, but she said nothing as Theresa continued.

"He is completely inflexible about his policies and he insists on only dealing with the head man—or head *woman* in this case."

Despite Theresa's sometimes capricious nature, T.J. knew that her cousin took pride in the fact that she was the head of a large, respected advertising firm. An advertising firm with a quality reputation.

A sinking feeling was beginning to take hold. T.J. felt herself being drawn in. "And you want me to go in your place. Completely. Not just represent you but *be* you?"

"You have to."

"Theresa, I don't have to do anything but raise Megan, pay taxes and die." Now there was a pretty thought, T.J. mused. But there were times when her cousin got her frustrated. And she really didn't like the idea of trying to fool the president of a large company whose account they were courting.

"T.J., I know what this is about. You don't have any confidence. Listen to me. You're solid, dependable, and if you tell him you're me, he'll believe you." As if rolling her own words over in her head, Theresa quickly added, "If you do something with your hair besides run your fingers through it and put on something decent, you could carry it off. You know you could." It wasn't the first time they had pretended to be each other, although the last time had been years ago. "We do have the same bone structure, even though mine is a little finer."

The additional comment was pure Theresa, so pure that T.J. merely shook her head at the evaluation. Theresa didn't mean anything by it. As children, they had been almost carbon copies of each other. But while Theresa had devoted herself to zealously enhancing what nature had so bountifully granted in the first place, T.J. had shrugged it off and concentrated on her studies and being her father's daughter.

That meant vanity never entered into the picture. Shawn Cochran had a selflessness that bordered on religious fervor. He had long ago detached himself from the family firm, leaving it to his younger brother to develop. Instead, Shawn had devoted himself to whatever cause needed him the most at the moment. It was T.J.'s mother who had supported the family. Responsibility and hard work had been a part of T.J.'s life for as long as she could remember. That didn't leave much time for being carefree and frivolous.

Or spending hours looking into a mirror, perfecting the perfect pout.

Theresa took care of that in spades.

Like her father before her, Theresa knew just how to hire and retain good people who in turn made her look good. She rewarded them well and expected a great deal in return. Her cousin was no exception.

Theresa's father, Philip, had seen T.J.'s creative talents early on and, in his own no-nonsense way, had decided to nurture them. Accepting no excuses from his sister-in-law or his niece, he sent T.J. to Harvard when T.J.'s parents had had barely enough money to send her to a community college.

Upon graduation, T.J. had come to work for the family firm

out of gratitude, loyalty and a need to create. She had been at it for seven years now and she loved her work as well as her cousin. But this was asking for something above and beyond the call of duty.

And T.J. had a bad feeling about it. "I'd rather you played you. After all, you're better at it."

"You're not giving yourself enough credit," Theresa insisted. "Remember high school?"

The feeling of déjà vu turned icy.

"When I took your SATs for you?"

"You saved my skin, then."

That was because they hadn't been caught. But they easily could have been. "It could have very well been both our necks," she reminded Theresa.

T.J. still hated thinking of that. It had been a stupid thing to do, risking both their futures, but Theresa had come to her in tears, completely unprepared for the test that T.J. had taken the month before. Theresa had been terrified of not doing well and bringing down her father's wrath on her head.

Moved, T.J. had gone in for Theresa. Shaking inwardly, she had managed to fool everyone and take the test. She had scored high enough for her cousin for Philip Cochran to reward Theresa with a keepsake diamond.

The diamond was the first of many she was to go on to collect.

This time, though, there was a very simple solution before them and T.J. couldn't understand why Theresa was missing it. "Look, Theresa, it's not like you're deliberately standing him up to go skiing. Why don't we just tell him the truth? That you were in an accident and are being held hostage against your will by a muscular doctor. I can't see MacAffee not being reasonable about it. We could reschedule—"

"Can't." The single word cut T.J. short. "This was the only pocket of time he had available that I could accommodate. Besides, if we reschedule, he might just decide to go with that other company that's been courting him. Whitney and Son." Theresa fairly spat out the name of their number-one competitor.

"C'mon, T.J. You could do it again. MacAffee is coming by just to give me the once-over. You're probably more his type than I am." Theresa meant it without malice, unaware of the way the appraisal hurt. "You know, serious."

Defensively, T.J. slipped on the oversize glasses she used for reading and went back to work on her computer. "Stuffy."

Theresa glossed over the wounded tone, only vaguely hearing it. There wasn't much time. "You said it, I didn't."

T.J. knew Theresa was waiting for an answer. "I'd really rather not, Theresa."

Theresa wasn't prepared for any opposition. Taking her by surprise, it left her speechless for exactly half a second. Then she rallied.

"Please?" Like a train leaving the station, Theresa's voice took on momentum as she spoke. "It'd only be for a few hours. Show him the rest of the campaign you've been working on. He really liked the preliminary drawings we sent up."

It was a royal "we" and T.J. was used to it. She had been the one who had worked on the preliminary drawings, faxing them up to MacAffee Toys' headquarters in San Jose as she went along.

T.J. felt herself weakening. Not that she really wanted to pretend to be Theresa, but in her recollection, she had never actually said no to her cousin.

"Theresa, I—"

Theresa heard what she wanted in T.J.'s tone. "Done. Well, I'm going to see if I can get that doctor to give me a sponge bath—"

Her screen saver came on, a little mouse running madly in a wheel to keep from slipping and being rattled around. T.J. knew exactly how the mouse felt. She hit a key and the tiny cartoon rodent disappeared.

"Doctors don't give sponge baths, Theresa. They have the nurses do that."

The chuckle was deep, throaty and entirely sensual. "Always

a first time. Give me a call later. I'm at Harris Memorial. Room 312. Bye.''

Like a leaf falling to the ground in the aftermath of a whirlwind, T.J. felt dizzy.

"Wait! When is he supposed to be here?" In typical Theresa fashion, Theresa was leaving her without any details, depending on the fact that she could ferret them out herself.

T.J. wasn't in the mood to ferret.

Theresa hadn't quite hung up. "Eleven o'clock. He's arriving from San Jose at LAX. American Airways. Flight 17. Emmett is going with the limo to pick him up. Might be nice if you were in it," she added.

"Be nicer if you were in it." But T.J. was talking to a dial tone. She sighed, replacing the receiver. Eleven o'clock. That didn't give her much time.

Heidi Wallace, Theresa's executive secretary, peeked into T.J.'s office less than a minute later. An understanding smile swept over the woman's finely lined face as she walked in. She laid a black garment bag over the back of the only other chair in the office.

"Swept right over you, didn't she?"

T.J. looked down at herself before glancing back at the other woman. "Do the tread marks show that much?"

Heidi laughed. A sense of humor was a prerequisite for working with Theresa Cochran.

"Wide and deep."

T.J. sighed, unconsciously eyeing the garment bag. "How did you know?"

"She called me first." Heidi was already heading for the door. "Emmett will be around to pick you up in the limo at ten-thirty." T.J.'s brows rose in surprise. "Seems she didn't think you would say no."

And why should she? I never have so far. "I suppose there's no harm in it."

Turning her swivel chair so that she faced the windows, T.J.

looked at her reflection in the glass. With a resigned sigh, she held her hair away from her neck. Maybe if she wore it up...

Heidi could see half a dozen ways it could cause harm, but she wasn't being paid to comment on that. "If you say so. But if you're going to take La Cochran's place, I'd say you need a bit of a quick makeover." She nodded toward the bag Theresa had instructed her to bring to T.J. Inside was one of her business suits, complete with matching shoes and purse.

T.J. was dressed more casually than usual, having slipped on jeans and a baggy pullover before leaving home this morning. Theresa had never cared what she wore as long as she held up her end of the load. T.J. pointedly ignored the garment bag.

"Christopher MacAffee is coming to talk business. I don't think he's going to care what I look like as long as the campaign is conducted with dignity and profit."

Heidi had her instructions. "Humor me—and her. The head of C & C Advertising shouldn't look as if she was taking in laundry on the side." Heidi picked up the garment bag and laid it across T.J.'s desk. "She keeps a change of clothing in the office in case she's, um, working all night."

Or entertaining a client, T.J. thought.

"Why don't you make use of it?" Heidi prodded.

T.J. pushed herself away from her desk and rose to her feet, eyeing the bag. "She really was sure of me, wasn't she?"

Heidi crossed her arms before her. T.J.'s easygoing disposition was a matter of record. "When have you ever given her cause for doubt?"

T.J. didn't answer. Instead, she took the garment bag and went to Theresa's suite of offices to change.

Okay, so how bad could it be?

EMMETT MITCHELL, C & C Advertising's chauffeur for the last three decades, held up a large placard with Christopher Mac-Affee's name on it. He aimed it at the sea of people disembarking from the airplane that stood tethered to the side of the building by means of a carpeted corridor.

Beside him, T.J. shifted uncomfortably in Theresa's high

heels, scanning the crowd. She had never met Christopher MacAffee, but she knew that he was a tall, stately-looking man with dark hair and a demeanor that would have easily placed him at the head of a Victorian household a hundred years ago.

Her eyes flickered briefly over the tall, dark-haired man who was just emerging from the plane in the distance. He was the kind of man Theresa would pounce on with relish, T.J. thought. Her own pulse scrambled a little as she watched him walk toward her.

Of course he was walking toward her, she thought disparagingly. Everyone on the plane was walking toward her. She was in the direct path of the disembarking passengers.

T.J. glanced at the chauffeur on her left. Emmett looked like a gnarled gnome, his skin a leather brown that seemed to complement the light beige livery he wore. "Do you see him anywhere, Emmett?"

In response, the snowy-haired man who had once driven her uncle and her grandfather before him shook his head firmly.

"Can't say I do, miss." He raised the placard higher with a touch of impatience. "But I haven't the faintest idea who I'm looking for to begin with."

"That makes two of us." She sighed. "It would have been easier on us if his father was still president. I once saw a photo of him in a magazine—a tall, thin man in his mid-sixties."

"Oh, a young guy."

T.J. struggled to hide her smile. Emmett had changed his mind about his age several times in the past fifteen years, fearing retirement would be forced on him. He pushed the number back periodically.

"Yes, like you," she agreed.

That drop-dead-gorgeous-looking man in the gray Armani suit was still coming toward her, T.J. noted out of the corner of her eye. As she turned her head, he made eye contact with her.

Her pulse jumped as Mr. Gorgeous stopped right in front of her.

The man nodded at the placard in Emmett's hands. "I believe you're looking for me."

The words *All of my life* materialized on her lips and it took effort to actually keep from saying them. Instead, she heard herself saying, "You're not Christopher MacAffee."

He smiled and T.J.'s blood warmed several degrees, turning the cold airport lobby almost balmy. "Why wouldn't I be?"

"No reason." *Smooth, T.J., smooth.*

The grin widened, showing off teeth that rivaled Theresa's precious snow-capped mountains. "I'm happy to hear that, because I am." He put out his hand to her. "Christopher Mac-Affee."

It took her a second to assimilate the information. Belatedly, T.J. put out her own hand and shook his. Christopher's grip was firm and warm. She felt something twist within her stomach and knot.

"And I'm—" *Tongue-tied.*

"Theresa Cochran," Christopher finished for her. Eyes the color of sunlight-warmed grass bathed her in their light as he smiled at her. "I'd recognize you anywhere, although I have to say you're even better looking in person than you are on the society page."

"There's a reason for that," Emmett muttered under his breath as he lowered the placard to his side.

T.J. shot him a silencing look. They had gone over the charade and the need for it during the ride to the airport. She knew exactly what Emmett thought of it. Not much, but winning the account would be a prestigious feather in their cap.

Emmett chuckled.

In an attempt to draw Christopher's attention away from what would cause her chauffeur to chuckle like that, T.J. spoke quickly, though her voice sounded a little squeaky to her ear at first. "Thank you, Mr. MacAffee. Why don't you just follow me?"

With a slight inclination of his head, Christopher linked his arm through T.J.'s. "With the utmost of pleasure. And it's Christopher, please."

"Christopher, please what?" T.J. heard herself asking. Oh, Lord, she was flirting, just like Theresa. It had to be the suit.

He laughed then, a deep throaty laugh that curled through her like hickory smoke, warm and scented. "They were right about you," he murmured as he took out his handkerchief and dabbed at the fresh perspiration on his forehead. "You really are something else."

Her heart skipped a beat, even though she knew that the compliment was meant for Theresa and whatever preconceived notions she must have conjured up in Christopher's mind.

"You don't know the half of it," she replied with what she hoped was a sexy smile.

Chapter Two

THE PALM THAT GRIPPED the hand rest on the escalator undulating its way down to the ground floor of the airport was clammy and Christopher was very aware of it. He was also acutely aware that the world around him was spinning ever so slightly if he didn't concentrate on hanging on to it with both hands.

Christopher refused to give in to the feeling that had accompanied him all during the flight and threatened to overwhelm him now. He didn't have time to be sick.

Instead, he forced himself to concentrate on the reason he was here in this overcrowded, stuffy airport. His brain felt as if there were a fog descending upon it. He was halfway through the electronic doors before he remembered. Christopher stopped abruptly. It took him a moment to focus on the woman next to him.

"What?" T.J. turned luminous blue eyes up at his face. Was it her imagination, or did he look a little pale?

"I forgot. I brought a valise with me. It should be coming onto the luggage carousel by now." Wherever that was, he thought. Disorientation mushroomed.

Reluctantly, T.J. backtracked into the airport lobby, her arm still hooked through Christopher's. She had the impression she was steadying him. "Oh, I didn't know you were staying overnight."

Damn, wasn't it just like Theresa to neglect to fill her in on the details? Just how long was she supposed to keep up this charade, anyway?

Christopher blinked to clear his vision, but his eyes still felt moist and watery. And a tremendous pounding had begun in his temples. Terrific way to conduct business.

"I'm not." Moving on leaden legs, Christopher found a place by the carousel. Luggage from two flights comingled on the conveyor belt as their owners stood around the perimeter, trying to spot individual pieces.

He'd gone to meet with his father yesterday. The old man was just getting over an intense twenty-four-hour case of the flu. He'd spent more than half the visit going on about it. Christopher was getting the uneasy feeling that perhaps advice hadn't been the only thing the older man had given him.

"I brought along some of our latest toys so that whoever is assigned to the account could get a feeling for them if and when I sign."

If and when. The man knew how to keep people on their toes. T.J. nodded. "That would be me."

He narrowed his brows. It took more effort than he would have thought. "You work on the account directly?"

That was a slip. Theresa never did, but maybe he didn't know that. *This isn't going to be easy,* she thought.

"Sometimes," T.J. amended quickly. She decided to embellish. How would he know the difference? "When the account really interests me." And working on the proposals for MacAffee Toys had really fired her imagination. "I guess I've never outgrown my love for toys." She laughed quietly. A small woman elbowed a towering hulk of a man out of the way as she claimed three pieces of garish luggage. T.J. stepped aside. "Which makes playing with Megan very easy."

All the suitcases were beginning to look alike. He wondered uneasily if his had been lost.

"Megan?"

Just the sound of the little girl's name brought a fond smile to T.J.'s lips. Her marriage had been a mistake from the moment she and Peter had left the church, but Megan had been a wonderful consolation prize. Thirty pounds of trouble, energy and sticky fingers. "My daughter."

Christopher raised his eyes from the carousel. "You have a daughter?"

She wondered if he had brought anything that would capture Megan's imagination. "Yes," she murmured absently as she scanned the spinning collection of luggage. Why hadn't he just carried it on with him?

Christopher always liked to know who he was dealing with. Nothing in the background his people had presented him with mentioned that Theresa Cochran had ever been married or given birth to a child.

"I didn't know you had a daughter."

T.J. caught the warning look Emmett flashed her. Abruptly, her words replayed themselves in her head. Damn, she had to keep her mind off the way her heels pinched and on the fact that she was supposed to be Theresa and not herself. Theresa had no children. She had never been married.

T.J.'s mouth twisted in a self-deprecating smile. And if it hadn't been for a really horrid eight months she would rather forget, neither had she. But the brief union had given her Megan and that had made all the difference in the world to her. Megan was worth enduring anything.

She ignored Emmett's knowing look and stared straight ahead at the luggage carousel, willing the valise to materialize.

"I'm sorry. I love her so much that sometimes I forget she really isn't mine." She could feel both Christopher and Emmett looking at her. Emmett, no doubt, was dying to see just how she intended to pull herself out of this. "She's my cousin's two-year-old. T.J. knows how crazy I am about her and right now, she's letting me play Mom. I have her for the weekend."

Mentally biting her lip, T.J. forced herself to calm down and take it slow. People, after all, saw what they thought they saw. And Christopher thought he was seeing Theresa. That made things a little easier for her. She just had to perpetuate that impression—and stop tripping over her own tongue.

She smiled, letting the expression drift sensually over her face and eyes the way she had seen Theresa do so many times.

"At times I really do feel as if she were my own. Megan's a terrific little girl." As an addendum, T.J. grabbed onto the first thing that occurred to her. "My cousin is away on a skiing trip."

"Skiing." How long had it been since he had allowed himself to get away for a skiing trip? He couldn't remember. "That sounds like fun."

The idea of standing on two skinny boards while sailing down a mountainside slick with snow did not come under her definition of fun.

"So they say."

Christopher looked down at T.J. quizzically. She made it sound as if she didn't care for it. "'They?'" he echoed. "Funny, I thought I read somewhere that you were an avid skier."

Dummy. You've got to stop answering as you. Theresa loved to ski. "I am," she said quickly. She let another rosy smile curve her mouth. "I was just being flippant. They tell me I do that a lot."

He looked as if he bought it, she thought. T.J could feel her heart fluttering madly. She was way out of practice. There had been a time where a simple switch would have been a challenge to her, not an obstacle course to overcome. Frazzled nerves insisted on knitting together, causing more unrest inside her.

"Do you ski?" she asked, turning the conversation away from "herself" and onto safer ground. *Damn it, Theresa, why did you have to pick today to get into an accident?*

"I used to." For a moment, an isolated scene from his past rose in his mind's eye. College. Winter break. And powdered snow so pure, it looked as if it belonged in a Currier and Ives painting. "Maybe we could get together sometime and test the powder at Vail."

This was probably the nineties equivalent of "We'll do lunch sometime," she mused.

"Maybe," T.J. agreed slyly, giving him her best Theresa imitation. She glanced back toward the carousel. A large black valise was just being belched out onto the conveyor belt. Mentally, she crossed her fingers. "Is that your suitcase?"

It took him a moment to recognize it. "Yes, that's mine." Christopher reached for it just as a sharp abdominal pain cut his breath away.

When Christopher hesitated, Emmett closed his fingers round the handle. "Nice save," the chauffeur murmured to T.J.

T.J. lowered her voice. She knew he was referring to her lapse about skiing. "Glad someone is enjoying themselves."

"Best time I've had in years," the old man said with a chuckle. Thin, sinewy arms strained beneath the livery as he hefted the suitcase off the carousel.

Emmett had all but raised the Cochran girls in the limousine and although Theresa was now his boss, he was partial to T.J. They all were. T.J. had grown up to be one of them, without any airs or pretentiousness. Theresa, pampered, spoiled, accustomed to being obeyed, always behaved—perhaps without even meaning to—as if she was a cut above the people who worked for her.

They had no choice but to forgive her, but the line that divided her from them was always there.

There was no such line with T.J., despite the fact that she and Theresa shared the same company-founding grandfather. Its absence bred the strong bond of loyalty T.J. inspired.

Christopher moved to take the valise from the old man. Chauffeur or not, it didn't seem right that the man should have to struggle with the luggage.

His strength failed him.

Christopher had told himself it was because he hadn't taken the time to eat anything this morning. Never a fussy eater, he usually enjoyed almost everything he sampled. This time around, however, he'd skipped breakfast. And the food on the plane had been completely unappetizing to him. Even the sight of it being passed out to other passengers had caused his stomach to lurch in protest.

Just as it was doing now. The cold sweat that accompanied it wasn't welcomed, either.

He was turning as gray as his suit. T.J. took Christopher's arm, suddenly envisioning him passing out at her feet. "Anything wrong?"

Christopher shook his head, which was a mistake. Dizziness descended over him, bringing with it little pointy spears that jabbed him from all sides.

T.J. braced her shoulder against Christopher just as he sagged.

He flashed what he hoped was an apologetic smile, struggling to straighten. It took effort for him to do both. "I'm not sure."

Perspiration was now popping out all along a very handsome brow. This wasn't good.

"Emmett," T.J. called to the back of the man's head.

Shifting the weight of the valise to his other hand, Emmett turned. Concern slithered over his bony face. He left the valise behind him as he hurried over. "What happened?"

Christopher felt like a fool. He also felt weak. Weaker than he could ever remember feeling in his life.

"I don't know. Suddenly I feel as if I have tissues for knees." He looked at T.J., who had propped herself under his arm. Any other time, he would have enjoyed having such a beautiful woman so close to him. Now, even the light delicate scent he detected on her hair was making him dizzy. He tried to raise another apologetic smile and had no idea if he succeeded. "Must be the company."

"Yeah, I have that effect on men." The quip was equal parts sarcastic and self-deprecating. The last time anyone had said she'd made him weak in the knees, it was because she had hit him from behind. She'd been eight at the time.

"But not this bad," she realized. Mothering instincts took

over and T.J. felt Christopher's brow. It was damp and feverish to the touch. "You're hot," she said with dismay.

"I've been told that," Christopher mumbled, or thought he did. It was an effort to keep from being swallowed up by the lightheadedness that was reaching out for him.

Nervousness faded. What she had on her hands was a situation and T.J. was never better than when she was handling problems. It was a hell of a lot easier dealing with a crisis than it was pretending to be someone else, even if it was Theresa.

"Emmett, help me get him to the limo." As the smaller man lent his support on Christopher's other side, T.J. caught the attention of a passing attendant. She commandeered him into service. "I need help with this man's valise."

Picking it up, the man followed them out to the loading zone.

Five minutes later, with the attendant's help, T.J. got Christopher into the back seat of the limousine. Pressing a tip into the man's hand, T.J. climbed in beside a rapidly worsening Christopher.

Even before the limo left the curb, T.J. got to work. She loosened Christopher's tie quickly. The shirt beneath his jacket was wringing wet and plastered to a surprisingly muscular chest.

Christopher was vaguely aware of the fluttering, light fingers working over him. He didn't like not being in control and he hated being ill, which was exactly what, to his enfeebled disgust, he was. Out of control and sick as a dog.

He tried for flippancy when all else seemed to be eluding him, escaping like mice leaving a sinking ship. He laid one hand over hers, stilling her fingers. "Why, Ms. Cochran, we hardly know each other."

She wondered if deep down, there was a Southerner mixed in with his ancestry. The man oozed charm even as he perspired. "I don't have to know you well to loosen your tie. You're sick, Mr. MacAffee."

Tell me something I don't know. "Beautiful, intelligent and clairvoyant, too, what more could a person ask for?"

How she wished Theresa was here to handle this. "A lot of things."

Emmett glanced over his shoulder. The limo was in the far lane, the one that ultimately wound up threading into the freeway. He needed a destination before then. "Where to?"

Christopher had the most beautiful dark lashes, T.J. thought, looking at the man's pale face. Lashes that any woman would have killed to have. Right now, they fluttered along a very pale cheek. Emmett cleared his throat dramatically. Caught, she flushed, her eyes shifting to the chauffeur.

"What?"

"Where do you want me to drive?" Emmett nodded toward Christopher. Slumped in his seat, Christopher looked as if he was only semiconscious. "You don't want to take him to the office like this, do you?"

"No." T.J. bit her lip. She bent over closer to Christopher. "Do you want to go to the hospital?"

There were two of her now. He tried to pick out which one was the real Theresa. He chose the one on the left. "No, this is exactly what the old man had. It'll pass in twenty-four hours." Although, right now, it felt as if he was going to pass with it.

"A virus with a wristwatch," T.J. muttered under her breath with a shake of her head. Now what? She blew out a long breath as Christopher's head drooped onto her shoulder. "Well, you're in no condition to fly home or to go to the office." She looked at Emmett. "Maybe we'd better book him into a hotel."

Emmett snorted. "Good luck with that."

"What do you mean?" He was obviously privy to something she didn't know. The last thing she was in the mood for was games.

"Haven't you heard? There's a computer convention in town. It's so big, they had to split it in half. One half's at the Anaheim Convention Center, the other's in L.A. There're computer nerds spread out all over the place and probably not a single thing left except a manger behind the inn."

She blew out a breath. "Great."

Christopher looked as if he were unconscious. There was no other choice available to her. Besides, she really didn't like the idea of just dumping him in some suite, no matter how high priced. After all, the man was sick. It wouldn't be right to leave him alone.

T.J. made up her mind. "Take him to my house, Emmett."

Emmett's tufted brows disappeared beneath the brim of his cap as he turned to look at her. "Your place?" His expression was dubious. "Are you sure?"

"I'm sure," she answered, resigned.

"No, I CAN WALK," Christopher protested when Emmett tried to brace himself on one side of him. T.J. was holding him up on the other.

The protest died as Christopher sagged between them. They both made a grab for him, barely succeeding in keeping his knees and his very sharply pressed crease from making contact with the driveway.

"Maybe tomorrow," T.J. promised. "You can walk all you want tomorrow." *In fact, I'll insist on it.*

There were no more words of protest. "You make a nice crutch."

T.J. shifted to get a better position beneath his outstretched arm. She held on to his hand for balance. "I'll include that in my résumé."

He looked at her, or tried to. He was beginning to feel mildly giddy. "Do presidents of family-owned companies need résumés?"

She thought of her father, who would have been president if only his sense of moral duty hadn't taken him into parts unknown. "Sometimes."

"I'll have to keep that in mind," Christopher mumbled. He blinked, trying to focus on the two-story house before him. He vaguely wondered if it was real, or, like the two images of Theresa in the limo, this was an illusion, too. "This isn't what I expected."

T.J. thought of Theresa's large, rambling three-story structure in Beverly Hills. It was as homey as a museum and often reminded her of one. Had Christopher seen a photo of it somewhere? T.J. seemed to vaguely recall that Theresa had opened the estate up to a film crew from a popular tabloid program a year or so ago.

"I like to live unpretentiously," she answered crisply, hoping that would put an end to his questions for now.

Whatever else Christopher was about to say in response, he didn't. Instead, the front walk seemed to come spinning up at him. When he closed his eyes to avoid the sight of the pending impact, he found himself wrapped up completely in darkness.

T.J. felt the difference immediately. She almost tumbled backward as all one hundred and eighty pounds of Christopher MacAffee turned into deadweight. "Oh my God. Emmett!"

"I have him," the older man cried with more confidence than he exhibited. His voice was strained as he struggled to keep from sinking to his knees beneath the weight. Emmett couldn't even move his head to look at T.J. "I'm asking for a raise after this."

T.J. gritted her teeth. Between the two of them, they managed to keep Christopher upright. "I'll put in a recommendation."

She pressed the doorbell urgently, hoping that Cecilia hadn't taken Megan out somewhere for the afternoon. There were house keys in her purse, but T.J. was afraid that any sudden move to initiate a search would throw them all off balance.

"C'mon, c'mon, Cecilia, open the door." T.J. leaned on the bell.

A moment later, T.J.'s housekeeper threw open the door. Bewilderment transformed into amazement, and then satisfaction, all in the blink of an eye.

The six-foot-four woman grinned at T.J. as she got out of the way. "You brought home a man."

"Don't get excited, Cecilia. We can't keep him. He's only on loan from Theresa." Was it her imagination, or was Christopher getting heavier with each step?

Dark gray eyes did a quick appraisal. The grin broadened. "I do like the cut of the lady's castoffs." Cecilia peered at Christopher more closely. It wasn't her imagination. The man *was* unconscious. "What's the matter with him?"

"He's sick." T.J. huffed out the words. Perspiration was sliding down the small of her back. "This way, Emmett." She inclined her head toward the right. "We'll put him in my room."

"I'll flip you for him," Cecilia said with a deep, throaty laugh, leading the way to T.J.'s bedroom.

Their path was suddenly blocked by an animated little girl. Her honey brown hair fluttered all around her head like a fluffy halo, giving her a cherubic look that camouflaged a mischievous streak.

With an elated cry, Megan dropped the action figures she had been playing with and hurried forward, about to throw herself into her mother's arms.

T.J. snapped to attention. "Catch the flying daughter" was a game she couldn't play today. The last thing she wanted was to expose Megan to whatever it was that had struck down Christopher.

"Cecilia, quick, take Megan to the family room. I don't want her coming in contact with Christopher."

Cecilia caught Megan by the edge of her rompers and scooped her up. Holding on to thirty pounds of wiggling child was a challenge. She bounced the little girl against her hip.

"Don't blame you." She grinned as she retreated. "If I had a man like that leaning all over me, I wouldn't want to share him, either."

T.J. was in no mood for Cecilia's sense of humor. "Because he's sick, Cecilia, because he's sick. And he's not mine. He's a client."

Cecilia paused in the hall to give Christopher a long, last appraising look. "I'd say that business seems to be looking up."

The woman was impossible. Not even her own mother, with

her prim sense of decorum and traditional roles, had been this bad. Ever since she had hired Cecilia to help care for Megan, the older woman had appointed herself T.J.'s personal match-maker. T.J. wanted no matches. All she wanted out of life was to do her work and devote her spare time to Megan. That was enough happiness, she thought, for any person.

"He certainly is a big guy." Emmett was visibly struggling as they brought Christopher across the threshold and into the bedroom.

"Just be glad my bedroom's not on the second floor." The bed had never looked so far away from the door.

"So what are you going to do with him?" Emmett puffed as they deposited Christopher's inert body onto the bed.

Waiting until her own breathing leveled out before answering, T.J. took Christopher's shoes off and placed them beside her bed.

He looked completely out of place here in her room, in her bed.

Like some fantasy come true, she couldn't help thinking. If her fantasies ran in that direction. Which they didn't. Marriage to Peter had taken care of that for her.

T.J. shrugged in answer to Emmett's question as she raked her fingers through her wayward hair. "Undress him, I guess."

"Oh, please, let me do it," Cecilia called from the next room.

Despite everything, T.J. laughed. "You get to undress the next sick man I drag in. Besides, one of us exposed to this twenty-four-hour virus of his or whatever he has is enough."

Reaching for Christopher's jacket, she stopped. The idea of even partially undressing Christopher was suddenly far too personal, virus or no virus.

T.J. looked at Emmett. "No, wait. You undress him and I'll go to the supermarket and get some orange juice and aspirin."

Megan was safely planted in front of an elaborate fort Cecilia had constructed for her earlier. That meant she had bought them about five minutes. Using it, Cecilia ventured back into the narrow hall, eyeing the man in T.J.'s bed.

"You're passing up a chance like that?" There was no way she would have let modesty dictate her actions if she had the choice.

This was getting old. "Cecilia, he's a client. Which reminds me, don't call me T.J. around him."

This had come out of left field. "Why? What should I call you?"

T.J. frowned. "Theresa." She had been T.J. ever since Theresa had been born. It had been an incredible sense of competition that had prompted Philip Cochran to mimic his brother and name his firstborn and, subsequently, only daughter after their mother.

Cecilia's small eyes became even smaller as she narrowed them. "I thought you hated being called that."

She shrugged. "I do, but he—" she nodded toward Christopher "—doesn't know I'm me."

Cecilia watched as Emmett peeled Christopher's shirt away and sucked in her breath at the sight of the almost perfect torso. "He passed out on your shoulder and he doesn't know who you are?"

T.J. didn't feel like getting into it now. "It's complicated." Cecilia obviously wasn't budging without some sort of an explanation. T.J. gave it grudgingly. "Theresa was supposed to meet with him, but she got into a car accident. She's okay," she said quickly before Cecilia could ask, "but they want to keep her in the hospital overnight for observation just in case. Christopher heads MacAffee Toys and only wants to deal with the head man, or woman in this case. Which would be Theresa."

Cecilia was trying to keep up. "Who is in the hospital."

Emmett, T.J. noted, was really struggling now. Christopher was much too large for him for manage. "Now you're getting it."

Cecilia put her hand to her forehead. "What I'm getting is a headache."

"You can have some of the aspirin when I get back."

Exhausted, the chauffeur looked toward the two women. "I need some help here."

As Cecilia went to oblige, T.J. placed her hand on the woman's arm. "I think you should avoid contact with him. Megan, remember?"

The wide lips split into a fresh grin. She gestured toward the bedroom. "Be my guest."

T.J. heard the older woman laughing to herself as she went back to the family room and Megan.

Squaring her shoulders, T.J. marched back into her bedroom.

You owe me for this, Theresa. Big-time.

Chapter Three

CHRISTOPHER MACAFFEE couldn't remember a day in his life when he wasn't in control of a situation, when he was not *expected* to be in control of a situation. His father had been a stickler for discipline and decorum. His mother hadn't been there to temper the senior MacAffee. She'd divorced his father and left his life almost before he could form a clear memory of her.

A parade of solemn-eyed nannies with a clear-cut sense of what he was expected to do had marched through his formative years, teaching him by word and by example what sort of behavior was expected of him. And he was expected to always, always, be in control. Of his emotions, of his destiny, of basically pretty much everything.

That meant, among other things, being aware of where his pants were and where he was at any given moment in his life.

Christopher was aware of neither when he finally opened his eyes again.

The unfamiliar feel of satin greeted him along parts of his body that had never had firsthand acquaintance with the material. Sliding a hand beneath the covers informed him of two things: that he didn't have his pants on and that he was wearing what felt like a dress.

That alone startled him into complete wakefulness, a condition the rest of his body protested with feeling. The room he opened his eyes to was completely unfamiliar to him. That wasn't something he was unaccustomed to. He traveled a lot.

But there were subtle, female touches here and there—soft,

filmy curtains billowing at the window, for instance, and a white eyelet comforter, which led him to believe that he wasn't in a hotel room.

The sound of childish laughter wafted from another room, like a tiny silver bell being rung in three-quarter time.

He was in someone's home.

Whose?

Christopher tried gathering his thoughts together and it was like trying to pick up peas that were being scattered from an overturned colander. The more he grasped at them, the more they rolled away from him. He tried again.

The last thing he remembered was sagging against a very soft shoulder. Cochran's. Then this was her house? He attempted to focus his mind.

Slowly, from behind a hazy curtain, fragments of a memory returned. A modest two-story house. A tremendously long walk from the door to...

Where?

Try as he might, Christopher couldn't remember where the walk ended. Probably here, which was why he didn't recall the room.

Digging palms into the mattress on either side of him, Christopher tried to sit up. A thousand disembodied hammers simultaneously began whacking away at his joints. The groan was involuntary and as much of a surprise as the sudden pain was.

Damn, he felt weak. Training had him struggling against the feeling and denying its very existence. He didn't have time for this.

The door to his room opened almost immediately in response to the groan. The woman he'd met at the airport stuck her head in.

Cochran.

Theresa, he thought, putting a first name to her. She looked concerned. Vaguely, he wondered why.

T.J. had just been about to enter her unexpected guest's room when she'd heard him groan. Her haste to open the door had almost made her drop the pitcher of orange juice she was carrying on a tray.

Recovering, she made it inside with glassware intact. T.J. peered at Christopher's face. He still looked pale, although it wasn't easy to detect at first. The man's olive complexion tended to make him look healthy. The sheen of perspiration along his hairline along with the cast of his eyes negated that.

Maybe she should have taken him to the hospital. It still wasn't too late. Emmett was killing time in the kitchen, just in case. He'd been there for the past five hours. Their guest had been sleeping that long.

T.J. eased the tray onto the nightstand. "How are you feeling?"

Like hell on a bad day, but he wasn't about to admit that. "Where are my pants?"

His voice was gruff. Maybe he wasn't as sick as she thought.

T.J. nodded toward the mirrored wardrobe. "In the closet." The expensive trousers were better off on a hanger than wrinkling beneath her comforter. "I thought you'd be more comfortable without them."

Had she undressed him? he wondered. "Only when I'm showering."

T.J. shrugged. "Suit yourself."

Taking the gray trousers out of the closet, she deposited them at the foot of the bed, then smiled at him. Actually, it was hard not to laugh out loud. He wasn't the type to wear a dark blue, flowing nightshirt with flair.

"There, you can make good your escape anytime you want, although I wouldn't suggest going just yet." Crossing to him, she touched her palm to Christopher's forehead. It only confirmed what she already knew. "You're still very warm, but then, it's only been a few hours."

There might be a sickly cast to his eyes, but they were still far too green for her comfort. T.J. looked away. Picking the pitcher up, she filled his glass up halfway.

"I brought you some orange juice." She offered the glass to him. "You need plenty of fluids to flush out your fever."

Her touch had been soft, light. It stirred something distant within him. Something that responded to the concern he saw in her eyes.

Just went to show you couldn't believe everything you read. His report on Theresa Cochran had her pegged as a social butterfly, more interested in making temperatures rise than in lowering them.

Apparently, she was capable of both.

"A few hours?" he echoed, suddenly registering what she'd said earlier.

She nodded. "Five. You've been asleep."

"I have a flight," he began weakly. What time was it, anyway?

"I already took care of that." She'd gone through his pockets to find the return ticket. "You're booked on a flight for Sunday." Two days should do it, she thought. If he got well faster, they could always reschedule again. "And I called your assistant to tell him what happened."

All he could do was nod weakly and let things happen. "Very efficient," he managed.

"We try to please. Now drink."

After a beat, he finally took the glass from her. "Is this your house?"

"Yes." T.J. looked pointedly at the glass.

He didn't care for orange juice, but because she'd gone to the trouble of getting it for him, he drank. There was something about her that told him she would press the issue if he refused. He wasn't up to carrying on a debate.

The juice stung his throat. "Why did you bring me here?"

She lifted a shoulder casually and resisted the temptation of pushing a wayward lock of hair from his forehead. There had been enough touching. "You were sick. Tossing you out by the side of the road just didn't seem right."

Flippant. Flippant usually irritated him. He found it vaguely amusing this time and didn't have the energy to question it. "Why not a hotel?"

She could have sworn he was challenging her. It made her wonder how he would have treated her if the tables had been turned.

"There's a huge computer convention in town. The only room I could have gotten you was with a church mouse. Upper berth." An easy smile curved her mouth. "Besides, leaving a sick man in a hotel room by himself didn't seem quite right, either."

He tried to evaluate her motives. The hammering in his head made it difficult.

"Bad for business," he guessed. In his experience, people didn't go out of their way for one another unless they wanted something. There was no mystery here. He represented a lucrative contract for her company.

T.J. sighed inwardly. He was a cynic. Sad that someone so young and good-looking was so turned off by the world. But that, she reminded herself, was none of her business. Her job was to convince him that she was Theresa, get him to approve the contracts, then pack him up and send him on his way, nothing else.

How would Theresa have answered him? "Yes, that, too."

Dark brows drew together and furrowed over an almost perfect nose. "Too?"

She mimicked a smile she'd seen on Theresa's face countless times. Sexy, yet aloof enough to be intriguing. She looked at his wrist before answering. "I'm a pushover for a racing pulse and yours was."

T.J. took the glass from his hand and placed it on the tray, then very deliberately smoothed out the comforter. She leaned over so that her face was just inches from his. For a moment, she felt her own pulse scrambling, then dismissed it.

"Now get some rest," she ordered sweetly, "and we'll discuss business whenever you feel up to it."

Even in his slightly confused state, he could feel the woman fairly sizzled with sex. It went along with her reputation, but seemed almost incongruous with the jaunty ponytail that bobbed to and fro atop her head. She'd somehow managed to wrap a rubber band around the voluminous mass of hair he remembered earlier. For a split second, he entertained the thought of snapping that band and watching her hair come tumbling down again.

He wasn't really well yet, Christopher thought.

It didn't keep him from trying to get up. "I feel up to it now."

The hell he did. You only had to take one look at him to know he was pushing it. She placed a firm hand against his chest and forced him back down. It wasn't hard.

"All right, when *I* feel up to it," she amended. "I don't at the moment. Why don't you take the opportunity this lull provides and get some more rest?" she proposed sunnily.

He was being patronized. Christopher knew he should argue with her, but he suddenly felt too tired. Resigned, he supposed that no vast eternal plan would be altered if he waited a few hours before beginning this meeting that fate seemed determined to postpone.

With a sigh, he slid down against the pillows.

T.J. took it as a victory. Smiling, she retreated from the bed.

Christopher had never been aware of jeans looking quite that enticing before. He felt vaguely aroused.

"Theresa," he called after her.

Theresa. She was Theresa. Widening her smile, she turned at the door. Edginess buzzed in her brain. She hoped it didn't show. "Yes?"

He had to know. Christopher picked at the dark blue nightshirt, holding it away from his chest. It was way too large to fit Theresa. It was almost too large for him. "Who does this belong to?"

T.J. grinned. She'd wondered when he'd get around to asking. "Cecilia, my housekeeper."

He was six-two. That meant she must have one hell of a housekeeper. "Oh, I thought perhaps it belonged to some former lover."

T.J. caught the tip of her tongue between her teeth. He had

tactfully refrained from commenting on Cecilia's size. She rather liked that. Maybe he wasn't so brittle after all.

"I won't tell her you said that."

"Thanks."

He was asleep before he saw her close the door behind her.

THE SOUND OF LAUGHTER called to him, rousing Christopher and drawing him to the surface.

It intruded on his formless dream, pouring over it like sparkling golden honey, until it completely blotted out what had been before, substituting, instead, an incredible urge to join in the sound. To become one with it. Without the reserve his life had instilled on him, Christopher wanted it with every fiber of his being.

It was a child's laugh.

And yet it wasn't.

With effort, Christopher pried open his eyes and discovered to his relief that the room did not shimmer and swim before him when he raised his head. More than that, it remained still as he sat up.

Pleased, Christopher smiled as he took a deep breath. The queasiness he'd experienced earlier was still there, but on a scale of one to ten it had gone from a twelve to a two.

The laughter came again, surrounding him. Giggles. Little-girl giggles. He tried to concentrate. Hadn't the Cochran woman said something about a niece spending the weekend here?

A child. Christopher frowned slightly. It wasn't that he didn't like children; he just wasn't any good with them. Not the best thing to admit, he supposed, given the fact that the family fortune was built on an impish-faced doll called Moppsie that had found its way into thousands of homes more than sixty years ago. But he'd never gotten the knack of being at ease around children, even when he had been one himself.

It hadn't improved with age.

But the sound was inviting. Curiosity got the better of him.

The room tilted only slightly and then only for a moment as he reached to the edge of the bed for his trousers. He waited to get his bearings, then swung his legs over the side of the bed and got dressed. Partially. He had no idea where his shirt was and the uneasy feeling nagged at him that if he stopped to look for it, he would exhaust his supply of energy.

So, muttering under his breath, Christopher tucked in the long, flowing tails of the nightshirt into his pants. It took a lot of tucking. Christopher glanced down. It looked as if he was smuggling a spare tire. He looked absurd. Wearing the shirt out would have made him look even more ridiculous.

Opening the door, he let the sound of the laughter guide him. There were more giggles, accompanied by a deep, throaty laugh Christopher attributed to his hostess. Either that, he amended, or the housekeeper who probably moonlighted as a basketball player.

In either case, he wanted to see for himself. The laughter was coming from down the long hallway. He didn't bother closing the door behind him. Padding on the Spanish tile with bare feet, Christopher felt he was being led like one of the mice in *The Pied Piper of Hamelin*.

Might make for a good commercial, he thought, pleased with the image he'd conjured up.

He was even more pleased with what he saw when he reached what appeared to be the family room, because it fleshed out the sketchy image.

His hostess had forsaken her ponytail. The effect was akin to standing still for a one-two punch to the gut. Mechanically, he passed his hand over his abdomen.

Theresa, her hair partially tucked behind one ear, tumbling down on the other side, was kneeling on the floor beside an animated-looking little girl who could have been a magically enhanced miniature of the woman with her.

More giggles and squeals of pleasure ricocheted about the room, which was filled with toys. Theresa was entertaining her, speaking in a high voice and pretending to be the comical, stuffed royal lion she held in her hand. The lion was carrying on a discussion with a shorter, squatter-looking penguin. The latter had a lopsided crown on its head.

She was playing with the toys he'd brought down with him, Christopher realized. The annoyance that she'd taken it upon herself to go through his things faded in the wake of the pleasure the scene generated.

If it worked on him, it would certainly work on others, he decided.

Feeling as if he were privy to something that belonged in a video put out by a greeting-card company, Christopher leaned his shoulder against the doorjamb and watched in charmed silence.

T.J.'S BACK WAS to the doorway. Christopher had slept through the night. She'd gone in several times to check on him. Since he was still asleep this morning, T.J. had taken the time to play with her daughter. Having found the toys earlier in MacAffee's suitcase while she was rummaging for something more appropriate for him to wear during his convalescence, she'd decided to put them to good use.

Megan made a great audience.

T.J. twisted her hand from side to side, making the lion appear to be hopping from one foot to the other. His sorrowful expression almost seemed to change, reflecting the words she put into his mouth.

"Boy, oh boy, I wish I had a little girl to pull my string and help me talk. Talking is hard work." She turned the lion so that he faced the penguin. "Do you know where I can find a helpful little girl, Mr. Penguin?"

"King Penguin," the latter corrected indignantly, raising his head regally. Then he attempted to scratch his head, puzzled. The penguin shook his head haplessly. Both stuffed animals turned to Megan for help. "Do you know where we can find a helpful little girl?" the penguin asked her.

Megan's eyes shone with excitement. She jerked her thumb dead center into her chest. "Me," she cried. "Me. Me. Me."

The penguin nodded his head so hard, his crown fell over one eye. When he spoke, he had a definite Bronx accent. "Yes, you, you, you. Do you know where we can find a helpful little girl?"

Megan laughed, then narrowed her golden brown brows until they formed a V over her pert little nose. She placed her hands on the penguin, but knew better than to yank him away from her mother.

"Me, me liddle gurl."

Turning them so that they faced one another again, T.J. had the lion and the penguin exchange exaggerated looks, then jump as if the weight of a revelation had been physically dropped on them.

"She *is* a little girl," the lion said the way Sir Issac Newton might have once announced the discovery of gravity. King Penguin was appropriately speechless. Megan clapped her hands with glee. In unison, the stuffed animals presented their backs to Megan. "Do me?" the lion asked.

"No, *me,*" the penguin entreated. "Pull my string first." The stuffed animal moved his royal butt adroitly and pushed the lion out of the way.

Holding her sides, Megan fell over on the floor, laughing at the show. The two stuffed animals promptly beset her on either side, cuddling, burrowing, adding to the source of her giggles.

If he could have found a way to bottle this, Christopher thought, he could make a fortune. Bottled happiness.

Megan's laughter was infectious. The more she heard it, the more T.J. laughed herself until both mother and daughter were rolling around on the floor like two children amid their toys.

"Man." Megan pointed a chubby finger abruptly toward the doorway.

T.J. looked and sucked in her breath when she saw Christopher standing there, watching them. *Yes, Bambi. Man has entered the forest.*

Christopher MacAffee looked a great deal taller when perceived from ground level on the rug. Embarrassed, T.J. quickly scrambled to her feet. She brushed her hands on the back of her jeans. They suddenly felt sweaty.

She cleared her throat, desperately wishing she had thought to close the door before entertaining Megan. "I'm sorry. Did we disturb you?"

The scene he'd happened on was so disarming, Christopher forgot that he felt awkward around anyone under four feet. Taking a step into the room, he couldn't take his eyes off the little girl. She looked like an exact copy of her aunt. Or the way he would have imagined she looked as a child.

If he were given to imagining things like that.

"If you mean did you wake me, yes. But I don't think you could call it being disturbed when the source of your merriment are two of the new toys I brought along."

"Oh, um, the suitcase." T.J. flushed like a child caught with her fingers in the cookie jar. He probably wasn't the type who would shrug off having his privacy invaded. She thought it was worth a shot. "I was really just looking to see if there was something a little bit more suitable for you to put on besides Cecilia's nightshirt." She bit her lip, then turned toward her daughter. Feeling herself on shaky ground, she decided to summon the cavalry. "Megan thinks your toys are great."

"So I see." Flanked on either side by the lion and the penguin, the little girl had a possessive arm wrapped around each. "Would you like to keep them, Megan?"

He had no idea what prompted him to give away the prototypes. It certainly wasn't like him. It just seemed like the thing to do at the time.

Megan looked up at the man who was as tall to her as some of the trees in the backyard. T.J. called the girl her little warrior. Megan was afraid of nothing. There was no hesitation in her response. Her head bobbed up and down as her eyes sparkled.

Maybe they could use the little girl in the commercial, he thought. "Then they're yours."

T.J. looked at him in surprise. A smile bloomed on her face. She hadn't had much time to be filled in on the new head of MacAffee Toys, but Heidi had given her a quick thumbnail sketch before she'd left for the airport yesterday. From what she was told, the man was efficient and all business. Never married, he had no children and had little tolerance for them.

Maybe they'd been wrong. He obviously knew how to get on the right side of a little girl.

T.J. laid a hand on his arm and brought his attention back to her. "That's very generous of you."

There was something about the look in her eyes that had him retreating. He wasn't sure from what, only that he needed to place some distance here.

The solemn expression changed his appearance entirely. It stripped him of his humanity. "They don't cost that much to produce. Besides, I presume you're going to want to keep them if we do wind up giving the account to you."

If. Well, that certainly took the shine off any thoughts she might have entertained about Mr. Christopher MacAffee and his generous nature.

"Yes," T.J. replied with just a touch of coolness, "we will." And then she saw Megan snuggle up against King Penguin. The ring of frost melted from T.J.'s heart. A good deed was a good deed, never mind about the ramifications. "Still, it's nice of you to let Megan handle the merchandise."

Christopher turned and then had to grab hold of the doorjamb to steady himself. Damn flu. "You did that before I had anything to say about it," he retorted with more gruffness than the situation warranted.

He was like a wounded bear. A cute, wounded bear in a blue nightshirt. The grin was spontaneous. "Don't you know how to accept a compliment graciously?"

"I thought I was."

Deftly she hooked her arm through his, determined to lead him back to the bed he had vacated.

"Maybe it's the fever." She touched his head. "You're cool." Now there was a surprise. Despite what Christopher had said at the airport, she figured he'd be ill for several days.

He could smell her hair. What was that? Jasmine? He would have thought someone in her position would have been wearing perfume that cost a few hundred dollars an ounce, not cologne. Still, it had a certain pleasing, arousing quality.

"Is that your medical opinion, or a social assessment?" he asked.

He was still a little shaky on his feet, she thought, and hoped that he wouldn't collapse the way he had yesterday. She glanced toward her room, then back at Megan. The little girl was busy with the stuffed animals.

"I don't know you socially." The words would have easily fit into Theresa's mouth, she congratulated herself. Theresa flirted whenever the opportunity presented itself.

He fell into the coy game effortlessly. "I'm told you know a lot of people socially."

Christopher saw a very formidable-looking woman emerging from another room. Taller than he, she made no attempt to disguise the fact that she was eyeing him. He was outnumbered.

This had to be the housekeeper, he thought. If anything, the nightshirt looked as if it might be too short for her.

Think Theresa, think Theresa. "I do," T.J. told him, "but you're not one of them. Yet." They were at her bedroom door. She coaxed him across the threshold. "Now why don't you get back to bed and I'll bring around some chicken soup? I think you're up to eating that."

He did still feel a little shaky. Suddenly the bed looked incredibly inviting. Only when he got into it did he look at the woman he thought was Theresa Cochran, thunderstruck. "You're kidding, right?"

She grinned, relieved that he hadn't passed out before she'd gotten him into bed. "I never kid when leading a man into my bedroom."

There was no sense in fighting it. "Any chance of some chicken in that chicken soup?"

"Every chance in the world," she promised with a smile, easing out of the room.

So far, she thought, *so good.*

Chapter Four

THE FRAGRANCE that seemed woven into her hair surrounded him, replacing the very air as she bent over his bed to remove the tray she had brought in earlier. It was all Christopher could do not to reach out and touch the dark strands, to see if her hair was as soft as the scent of it led him to believe it was.

He fisted his hand around the sheet instead.

"It was good. The soup," he added when she turned her eyes up to his questioningly.

And it had been. So had the company. She'd remained in the room while he was eating, talking about trivial things that somehow seemed important when coming from her lips. And somewhere along the line, as she talked and he ate, he realized that he was feeling a great deal more human than he had just a little while ago.

He looked a little tense, T.J. thought. Well, that made two of them. Who would have thought that this charade would be so wearing on her? She didn't like lying; it always tangled things up.

Just like her stomach seemed to tangle up when he looked at her like that.

"We aim to please," T.J. answered as blithely as she could. She was about to whisk the tray away, but something kept her rooted to the spot. Deep, dark, green, the man's eyes were more potent than Super Glue.

Maybe it was the virus. He couldn't blame it on the fever because that was gone. But something—he doubted it was inherent business sense, since this had nothing to do with business—told him she was sincere. That his comfort was of concern to her and that it went beyond the fact that he was a potential client.

Or maybe he was just hallucinating. He tested the waters. "I believe you mean that."

T.J. cocked her head, as if that could somehow give her a better view of the inner workings of his mind. She would have been naive to believe that the toy business wasn't as cutthroat as any other competitive business, but if she'd had her druthers, she would have wanted to believe that it wasn't. Toys were the realm of children and nothing as jaded as cynicism should ever touch it.

What sort of people was he used to dealing with? "Why wouldn't I?"

He shrugged. The ridiculous blue nightshirt swished against his shoulder blades. "Because I'm a stranger."

She leaned the tray against the bureau and smiled. "Not really. Your people have talked to my people." Tongue in cheek, she teased, "In the nineties, that makes us practically family."

"Maybe." He didn't want her to leave. Not just yet. Christopher searched for something to say, for a way to make her remain just a moment longer. "You're nothing like what I expected."

"Oh?" She took a breath, knowing she should stop right here, right now. There was no point in having him elaborate. It would be just asking for trouble. But she'd come this far, and curiosity was pushing the buttons. "And what was it that you expected?"

He thought of the *People* magazine article his assistant had handed him just before he'd boarded his plane. Meant to supplement the report he already had on her, the article had been on Theresa Cochran and it was entitled "Beauty with Brains." He was in complete agreement with the assessment, but it didn't go far enough. Nowhere in the article did it mention the traits he'd been fleetingly privy to.

Without thinking, Christopher reached for her hand. Wrapping his fingers around it, he continued. "Someone less nurturing for one. Someone who didn't know her way around a kitchen." He thought of the scene in the family room. "Or a child."

Did he realize that he was rubbing his thumb along the pulse in her wrist, or was he doing that unconsciously? Whichever it was, she wished he'd stop. She didn't like the effect it was having on her knees.

"Always Be Prepared, that's my motto." Tactfully she disentangled herself.

Another piece of the puzzle presented itself to him. He tried to fit it in. Ordinarily he liked to know things about the people who worked for him only because then there was no room for surprises. He didn't like surprises. Until now.

"You were a Boy Scout?"

"No, a Girl Scout." A dimple flickered in the corner of her mouth. "Hey, we have Girl Scouts, even in Beverly Hills." She *had* been a Girl Scout. Theresa, on the other hand, had viewed the idea of camping and selling cookies as beneath her.

It occurred to him that he still didn't know where he had been brought. "Is that where I am? Beverly Hills?"

She didn't know just how much he knew about Theresa. Her estate was in the most expensive section of Beverly Hills. Finances as well as preference had dictated that T.J. choose a far more down to earth area to settle in.

"That's where the office is, and we're close to the office."

Was it him, or was she being deliberately vague in her answer? He decided that perhaps, in this case, he was being a bit too suspicious. He was accustomed to having to read between the lines. Rarely were things as aboveboard as they were here.

Picking up the tray again, T.J. began to leave. "So, can I get you anything else?"

The answer, *"You"* whispered along his mind like a soft spring breeze, surprising him.

For a moment, he thought he'd said it aloud, but her expression hadn't changed, so it must have been just his imagination. Something he was going to have to rein in. He hadn't come here to play pattycake with a stunning woman. He'd come here to give or withhold his final seal of approval to a new advertising firm.

But Christopher had to admit, if only to himself, that sick or not, the word *merger* was taking on a whole different meaning.

He was getting better fast.

There wasn't even a television set in the room. And he was restless. More so now that she was in the room, bringing the scent of spring in with her.

"I'm getting stir-crazy," he admitted. He was used to doing things, not lying flat on his back.

She smiled. "You're getting better." It took her only a moment to make up her mind. Any longer and she might have thought better of the idea. "How about if I let you graduate to the sofa?"

"Excuse me?"

Her tongue was getting ahead of her. He really was rattling her. "You can come into the family room and watch cartoons with Megan and me." She saw that the suggestion wasn't bowling him over, but if she was going to be around him, it was safer if she had something to divert her attention away from his eyes. Megan was the likeliest choice. "I have over twenty-four hours' worth of tapes for you to choose from if the programs that are on don't please you."

What the hell? He'd never watched Saturday-morning cartoons, even as a child. His nannies hadn't approved of "mindless animation." It might be interesting at that. At least he could say he'd actually done it once.

But something wasn't quite right with the picture. "That's an awful lot of cartoon tapes to keep for someone who doesn't live with you."

The dossier he'd received on her hadn't hinted that the woman who periodically turned up at parties on both sides of the Atlantic was someone who would watch cartoons or stock them for a niece. But then, it hadn't led him to believe that she was capable of rolling around on the floor with a two-year-old, either. And he had seen that with his own eyes.

The lady was full of surprises. Pleasant ones.

She was going to have to remain on her toes. It made her feel weary. This, at least, was easy enough to explain away.

"Megan's here a lot. I send T.J. off regularly on business trips. She's very good at what she does." T.J. bit her lip, then decided that there was no harm in building herself up. What she said was, after all, all true. "She put together the campaign for MacAffee Toys."

He'd been told that, too. "I'm impressed." He knew he wouldn't have admitted that so readily if he wasn't in the process of recovering. Praise from him was hard-won and he doled out it slowly. Otherwise, whoever he was dealing with could capitalize on that and hold him at a disadvantage.

But somehow, slowly didn't seem to fit the situation here. "I'd like to meet her sometime."

Meet, as in return. The sinking feeling in the pit of her stomach was becoming a familiar sensation. "Oh, I thought this was just a one-time visit. You know, to look over the troops to see if they're battle fit."

He thought he detected nervousness in her voice and thought it rather odd. "That's the way I usually operate, but it's not something written in stone."

"I see." He wasn't supposed to return. It was what she and Theresa were counting on. So why did the thought of his returning bring such a rosy warmth with it? She had no time to analyze it or to upbraid herself for having ambivalent feelings. "Well, as I told you, T.J. is away this weekend. But I'm sure she'd be flattered by your assessment of her work if she were here."

Time to retreat before she tripped herself up. T.J. nodded at the tray in her hands. "Why don't I clear this away and see about getting things set up in the family room?"

There had already been a lot of time lost. Given a choice, he didn't want to waste any more watching cartoons. "We really should—"

She knew where he was going with this. She also knew that she had promised Megan she'd watch TV with her. T.J. loathed to break a promise. "I promise to have your briefcase in full view the entire time." She saw that Christopher's brows drew together. *Misstep.* Maybe he couldn't be teased about work. She reconnoitered. "No one's going to take any points off if you kick back, you know."

And with that, she left the room.

Well, so much for choice, Christopher thought. He didn't realize he was smiling until he saw his reflection in the wardrobe mirror.

WALKING INTO THE KITCHEN, T.J. sighed as she deposited the tray on the table. Mechanically she rinsed off the soup bowl before placing it into the dishwasher. That made it a full load, she noted.

Cecilia stood silently watching her and wasn't quite sure how to read what she saw. "Well, you certainly don't look like a woman who's got a hell of a handsome-looking man in her bed."

T.J. could feel a headache building just behind her eyes. "That's just the problem."

Cecilia laughed and shook her head. "Never heard it called that before." She jerked her thumb in the general direction of T.J.'s room. "That's the kind of 'problem' most women pray for. Have you taken a good look at that man?" She covered her chest with her hand. "Makes my heart flutter just to think about him."

Notwithstanding the fact that Cecilia's view of male-female relations could stand a bit of updating, T.J. laughed. She shut the dishwasher door firmly and set the dials. The sound of rushing water followed. "He's too short for you."

At six-four, Cecilia had gotten used to the fact that most men were. "Good things come in small packages."

T.J. wondered how their houseguest would have reacted to

being called small. And how he would react if he ever discovered that he was being duped.

"Not this time."

T.J.'s voice was definitely too pensive. Placing her hands on the younger woman's arms, Cecilia turned her around until they faced one another. "All right, give. What's wrong?"

Where did she begin? "He thinks I'm Theresa."

Cecilia's eyes narrowed. "I thought the whole idea was that he was *supposed* to think you're Theresa." And then it hit her. Clear as a tide pool in Miami. "Hey, wait a minute, you don't *want* him to think you're Theresa, do you?"

T.J. shrugged her hands away. Cecilia had a way of seeing too much. "I don't like lying."

There was more to it than that and they both knew it. Or at least one of them did, Cecilia thought. "It's all a matter of interpretation. Sometimes a little lie moves things along."

"Little?" T.J. echoed, then laughed shortly. "The man thinks I'm the president of C & C Advertising."

Cecilia didn't see what the big deal was. "And if your father hadn't dropped out of the business world and disappeared into the African jungle, you might have been."

"South American jungle," T.J. corrected. An uncustomary impatience reared its head. "And I like my position at the firm just fine." She had no desire to be at the helm of the company. P.R. was Theresa's specialty, not hers. "That's not the problem."

Cecilia was grinning at her like someone who had the answer to the question in the bonus round.

"What?"

"You like him, don't you?" There was a God, Cecilia thought with relief. At one point, she'd despaired that T.J. would waste her life in what amounted to seclusion. The way she had. Surrounded by people, but alone.

T.J. wanted to deny it. Heatedly. But the truth was, she just didn't know. "Whether I do or not doesn't matter—" She made a futile attempt to discredit Cecilia's assumption. "And he hasn't been here long enough for me to form any opinions about him. I just feel like I'm trying to walk across quicksand.''

Cecilia wrapped one long, comforting arm around T.J.'s shoulders. ''Everyone knows you don't walk across quicksand, you sprint if you can't get around it any other way.'' She dropped her hand to her side. ''Is he going to be eating dinner at the table with us?''

Where the man ate dinner didn't affect the quantity prepared. ''If he feels up to it.'' She looked at Cecilia suspiciously. ''Why?''

''No reason.''

The expression on Cecilia's face was entirely too innocent and made T.J. feel uneasy. She prayed the woman wouldn't attempt to try her hand at matchmaking. The sooner Christopher MacAffee was on a plane back to San Jose, the better she'd feel.

''If you want to look at him, he's going to be sitting in the family room as soon as I find a tape to put into the machine.'' T.J. turned to leave.

Cecilia raised her voice, calling after her. ''I could run to the video store and rent *Wild, Passionate Nights* for you.''

T.J. hoped her houseguest hadn't heard that. ''We'll probably be watching *Mr. Duck Goes to the City,* thank you.'' It was Megan's favorite.

Cecilia's mouth dropped open as she stared at T.J. incredulously. ''A cartoon? You're going to have a gorgeous, unattached man sitting beside you on the sofa and you're going to be watching cartoons?''

She wasn't going to be drawn into a debate about this. ''Yup.''

Cecilia could only shake her head. ''You don't believe in opening doors when opportunity pounds on them, do you?''

It was time to place kidding aside. ''This is not an opportunity, Cecilia. I just want to get through this charade intact. The sooner he gets well and goes back to San Jose, the sooner I'll breathe easy.''

The problem with experience, Cecilia thought with regret, was that you couldn't pass it on. No one wanted it secondhand. "I hear you, but I just can't believe you."

"You don't have to believe me, as long as I do."

The thing of it was, T.J. thought as she began to rummage through the drawers of the video cabinet in the family room, that she was beginning not to believe herself, either. Not completely, at any rate.

Since her divorce, she'd gone out a number of times socially, always with friends. Always with the thought of enjoying the evening and the company, but only in the spirit of friendship. She wasn't out for romance. Not anymore. She was much too busy these days and there were more important things in her life than the search for romance. Megan headed that list.

But there was something about Christopher MacAffee that cut through all the stories, all the excuses she had sold herself on. An excitement that bubbled up within her just at the very sight of him.

Damn, but she sounded like some teenager with a budding crush.

She was going to have to find a way to put a lid on that, she lectured herself sternly. Even if she were inclined to let things happen between them—which she wasn't—he thought she was Theresa. There was no future in getting close to a man who thought she was her cousin. You couldn't build a relationship on a lie. And she certainly couldn't tell him who she was now. If he found out the truth, he'd take his business and his indignant, bruised ego elsewhere. Nobody liked being fooled, least of all a man in a position of power.

Business was the bottom line here. She had to remember that.

T.J. sighed as she selected two tapes and pulled them out of the drawer. Talk about painting yourself into a corner.

"So what are we watching?"

She jumped, startled at the sound of his voice. The tapes went clattering to the floor. Chagrined, she picked them up quickly.

She looked like a tax dodger who had just been summoned

by the IRS. Christopher crossed to her, puzzled. "Hey, I didn't mean to sneak up on you. I thought I was supposed to be here."

She had to get hold of her nerves. Taking the first step, she smiled up at him. The family room was bathed in sunlight. It gave his complexion a healthy glow. Now that she thought about it, he did look a lot better. The man would definitely be on his way by tomorrow morning.

Why didn't that make her happy? Relieved, yes, but not happy. What was the matter with her, anyway?

"You are and you didn't," she assured him, though she doubted he bought the latter. "I was just preoccupied." The blue shirt he was wearing looked much better on him than Cecilia's nightshirt had. "I see you found your shirt."

He held out an arm, looking at the sleeve. "It's a better fit." Christopher lowered his voice, glancing toward the door to see if they were alone. "Just how tall is your housekeeper?"

"Six-four."

He readily believed it. "Sounds more like a bodyguard."

"She's my housekeeper," T.J. assured him. "Actually, Cecilia's more of a friend than anything else."

Tucking the tapes under her arm, she cleared off the oversize coffee table. She and Megan spent hours playing Candyland and putting simple puzzles together on it. Right now, the table was covered with papers, half-finished coloring books and scattered, chunky crayons.

Sitting down on the edge of the sofa, Christopher automatically began replacing the crayons into the empty crayon box he found under the table. "Where did you find her?"

"Christmas card," she answered absently. Glancing up, she saw that Christopher didn't understand. "We exchange them each year." T.J. backtracked further. "She was my gym teacher in high school. She went on to coach a girls' basketball team at UCI from there."

"Now that I believe." He tucked the lid flap into the crayon box. "How did she make the transition from coach to housekeeper?" It wasn't the kind of thing that readily came to mind.

Pleasure filled her voice as she spoke of the older woman. She had always gotten on well with Cecilia, even when their relationship had been teacher and student. "One Christmas, she wrote to fill me in. She'd given up coaching, didn't really have a place to call home." Cecilia didn't believe in owning things or letting things own her. She'd lived in a small trailer park until a developer bought the land out from under her. "I invited her to come stay with me. Then—"

T.J. almost slipped and said that it was just after she'd given birth to Megan. In her typical no-nonsense fashion, Cecilia had taken over running the household and helping her with Megan. Making life manageable. So much so that T.J. knew she'd be lost without the woman and her friendship.

"The rest is history." She held up the two tapes for his inspection. *"Mr. Duck Goes to the City."* She turned one, then the other. "Or *Crickets in My Bed.* Take your pick."

Christopher looked at her to see if she was serious. She was. She was really going to show him cartoons. Someone else might have tried to impress him with a vast collection of the latest videotapes, or rushed to cull his favor by renting something a little more provocative. He rather liked the fact that she was being herself. And that "self" was someone who was apparently guileless and sure enough of herself to *be* herself.

"Which one does Megan like?"

He won points by bringing Megan into the decision. *"Mr. Duck."* T.J. looked at the lime green cover on the tape. "She's seen it umpteen times."

He had trouble watching anything all the way through once, much less more. "And she doesn't get tired of it?"

T.J. thought he was kidding, then realized that he was serious. "You know, for someone in the toy business, you don't know very much about children. I think psychiatrists call it reinforcement. Familiar things give children a sense of security. All I know is that Megan likes to see things over and over again until she knows exactly what's coming."

She'd obviously taken the time to understand the little girl.

As he saw it, that took an inordinate amount of patience as well as love. Something else that hadn't been in the report. "Megan's very fortunate to have you for an aunt."

She wished he'd stop complimenting her. She felt like such a fraud. T.J. lifted a careless shoulder. "Yeah, well, Megan is a pretty terrific little girl. I hope to have one like her someday," she added for good measure.

The party girl making domestic noises. He found that rather appealing. It made him stop and think about his own situation. Chronologically, he was more than ready to settle down. So far, though, he hadn't found the right woman....

Christopher realized he was staring at her and looked away.

Megan came tumbling into the room, chasing a mechanical poodle and laughing. He immediately became aware that the woman beside him lit up like a Christmas tree.

"Speak of the devil." T.J. held up the tape. "Look what I have for you, Meggie."

"Missy Duck!" Megan crowed. She wrapped her hands around the videotape.

"Why don't you put it into the machine and we'll all watch it?" T.J. suggested.

Megan whirled around on one sneakered heel and made a beeline for the machine nestled beneath a wide-screen television set.

Christopher had visions of the little girl jamming the tape into the VCR. "Do you think you should let her handle that?"

T.J. grinned, watching Megan. Shaking the tape out of its cover, her daughter popped it into the slot. "She knows how to operate the VCR. At least how to hit the play button."

He leaned back on the sofa, making room for her. Jasmine again, he thought as she sat down beside him. Christopher filled his lungs with the sweet scent.

"We have something in common, then. You would have had me worried if you'd said she knows how to get rid of the flashing twelve. That would have put her one up on me."

T.J. laughed. It was the same sparkling sound he'd heard earlier, when he had gone searching for the source. And it had the same effect on him now as it had then. More so. It reeled him in, a fish caught on a silver hook. Something within his gut tightened even as a warmth flowered all through him.

T.J. turned to look at him. The laughter died on her lips as her eyes met his. The cartoon theme song droning on in the background faded. There was nothing but silence in the room. Silence, except for the frantic beating of her heart, which had somehow managed to slip all the way up to her ears.

There was nothing else to do except give in to this incredible pull. If he explored it, maybe it would go away.

"I don't think I'm infectious anymore," Christopher said softly, his fingers slipping around her cheek, cupping her neck.

Her eyes couldn't leave his. "Oh, I wouldn't say that," she whispered through lips that were barely moving.

Chapter Five

HE COULD SAY that he didn't know what came over him. That he was still a little disoriented by the virus. Any one of a number of excuses would have sufficed. But they would have all been lies.

Christopher knew exactly what came over him. She had. Theresa, with her laughter and her wit, with her warmth and her caring ways. It exuded from her without her having to say a word.

There was no recourse for him but to kiss her. It seemed his destiny, a destiny he readily embraced without wondering what the hell was going on in his mind. All he knew was that somewhere it was written that at this time, this place, Christopher MacAffee, scion of MacAffee Toys, was to kiss Theresa Cochran, president of C & C Advertising.

He would have bet his soul on it.

As soon as his lips touched hers, there was an inexplicable rush whirling through him, around him. Christopher felt he was being drawn into a vortex and there wasn't a single thing he could do about it.

And he wasn't all that sure that he wanted to.

The organizer within him, the man who was determined to make logical sense of everything, struggled to make sense out of this. Logic seemed to be out of order here. At the very least, it was taking a holiday.

This was just a kiss. Nothing more. He had to remember that. So what if he heard a rushing noise in his head and his body had suddenly ignited with a bittersweet agony he was in no position to do anything about? It was just a kiss. And if he felt unsteady, that was because of the virus, or the bug, or whatever the hell he'd come down with. It wasn't because of the kiss.

It couldn't be.

But it was.

Swallowing a groan, he deepened the kiss, determined not to be the only one bowled over here. His mouth played along hers, a concert pianist suddenly inspired to write a concerto.

T.J. didn't remember grabbing on to Christopher's arms to hang on, but she must have. Because she was. Hanging on for dear life. As if she were afraid that if she let go, she would be sucked under. Or blown away.

She was anyway.

Her fingers curled around the material of his sleeves, clutching.

This couldn't be happening. The thought desperately telegraphed itself through what was left of her mind. She refused to feel like this, as if she were hurtling down a steep mountainside atop those silly fiberglass sticks her cousin loved strapping onto her feet. But she was, hurtling fast and hard. Her breath was completely snatched away and her lungs were bursting for air.

This had to be what navigating without ski poles was like. She didn't like it.

It was far too exhilarating to be safe.

Christopher wanted to gather her into his arms, to feel her, to explore her until he knew his way around every inch of her body like a blind man touching a familiar, treasured object. He tried to remember when he'd last felt like this, and couldn't.

Because he hadn't. He'd never felt like this before. It would have scared him if he'd thought about it, but thinking had been the first thing to go.

"Mama kiss."

The childish voice, filled with glee, penetrated their consciousness simultaneously. The unexpected spontaneous combustion had made them both forget that they weren't alone.

They remembered now.

Reluctantly, Christopher drew his lips away from hers. He blinked as he held T.J. at arm's length, then looked at the small figure that was standing beside them, openly staring.

"Did she just call you Mama?" he asked, bewildered.

Oh, boy. Be cool, T.J., be cool. Think, for heaven's sake.

No easy feat when her brain felt like a scrambled egg on a hot skillet. She mustered a smile, then ran her hand along the little girl's arm affectionately.

"Maybe." T.J. looked at Christopher. "T.J. and I look a lot alike." Her explanation met with a cocked brow. "More than likely, though," she went on as her brain began to defog, "Megan was just saying that she's seen her mother kiss like this." Thank goodness Megan didn't speak in complete sentences yet.

"Not," Christopher assured her, "like this." She had a one-two punch that had sent him reeling—and wanting more. It was a good thing that the child had interrupted when she had. He needed a breather to figure out just what had happened here. And what he wanted to happen in the future. "I'm beginning to understand why you have men lined up six deep on both sides of the continent."

"Yeah, well…" It took effort to sound nonchalant, but somehow, T.J. managed. "I think they're attracted to the business as much as to me."

She'd nearly said Theresa instead of "me." It was her personal theory that at least some of the men who flocked around Theresa were only after what being connected to the Cochran name could do for them. But it was all right because Theresa knew exactly who was after what. And in as much as she was after fun and nothing more, it all worked out for her.

T.J. knew she could never lead the kind of life Theresa did. Theresa was all bright reds and splashy colors. T.J. was subtle, muted blues. She was a nester and had been right from the beginning. She'd never cared for parties that lasted into dawn, or for being seen on the right arm. She liked quiet, intimate dinners and the love of one man, not the admiration of a squadron.

Which was why her breakup had hurt so badly. When she had exchanged vows with Peter, she had meant forever. Peter, on the other hand, had obviously meant to the end of the month. That was how long it had taken him before he'd found someone else to dally with. Someone to break his vows with.

"Really?" Christopher couldn't see how any man in his right mind would have wanted her for any other reason than because she was a beautiful, sensuous woman who was capable of heating a man's blood at ten paces. "Why do you put up with it?"

She gave him Theresa's stock answer. "Because I'm not taken in by it. I'm just out to have fun." T.J. needed backup. She patted the place beside her on the sofa. "Come here, Cupcake." T.J. looked at Megan. "Come sit up here."

Christopher noted that she placed the little girl between them.

Just as well, he thought. He didn't believe in mixing business with pleasure. Which was why, he supposed, there was very little pleasure in his life lately. The last couple of years it had seemed consumed by business.

Maybe, he mused, looking at Theresa, it was time that stopped.

Megan wiggled into a comfortable position on the sofa, then flashed a killer smile at him that was very reminiscent of her aunt's. Like a queen, she pointed her finger at the screen and ordered him to watch by loudly announcing, "Missy Duck."

"Mr. Duck," he corrected automatically.

Megan nodded, her brown curls bouncing around her head like coiled springs being shaken out of a bag. "Missy Duck."

Laughing to himself, Christopher gave up the language lesson and settled back to watch.

Much to his amazement, he discovered that he liked cartoons. At least the one Theresa had selected for them to watch.

Bright blue credits soon rolled up against a blazing white background, accompanied by the song Mr. Duck always sang to himself when times got rough for him. Was the cartoon over already?

Christopher glanced at his watch in disbelief. He'd been sitting here for almost ninety minutes. Time seemed to have just flown by.

Curious, T.J. had looked over Megan's head several times to see if Christopher was actually watching. Each time she was surprised and pleased to see that he was. She didn't exactly know why she got a kick out of that, but she did.

"So, what did you think?" Pointing the remote at the VCR, she pushed the stop button. The credits abruptly disappeared, to be replaced with a black-and-white rerun of a popular late-sixties sitcom. It was about cousins who looked enough alike to be twins. T.J. quickly hit the power button and the set faded into darkness.

Christopher looked at Megan. She had sat stock-still for the entire movie, mesmerized as if she had never seen it before. But now she was all unharnessed energy. She dove toward the VCR to reclaim the tape. Obviously something her aunt had taught her, he thought.

He smiled at the question. "Kind of like a morality play with feathers."

The description tickled her. "It's never too early to instill basic decent principles in kids."

"I certainly can't argue with that."

Out of the corner of her eye, she saw Megan slip the tape back into its box. Leaving it on the floor, the little girl began to play with the castle she'd abandoned earlier. T.J. shifted in her seat, facing Christopher. She tucked one leg under her. It was time to mix in a little business.

"I like the fact that MacAffee Toys doesn't go in for flooding the market with action figures associated with blood-and-guts video games." It was gratifying, in this time when the dollar was the bottom line, to find a company with such integrity.

It had never occurred to Christopher to conduct business any other way. He was a great believer in tradition.

Christopher's mouth curved when he thought of the alternative. "I'd have several generations of ancestors spinning around in their graves if I did that."

She leaned her elbow against the sofa and propped her hand against her head, studying him. There was more to it than that.

"You don't strike me as a man who would be all that worried about nocturnal visitations from reprimanding ghosts." He was the type to do what he wanted. That he wanted to maintain a tradition brought up his personal stock with her.

The trouble was, she caught herself thinking, his stock with her was already too high.

He told her what she already instinctively knew. "No, but I believe in the credo myself."

"Good toys for good children." The motto was written across the top of each box that housed a MacAffee Toy. Her smile was soft, gentle. "A bit outdated sounding for the fast-track children of the nineties, but the sentiment is timeless."

It felt right, sitting here, talking to her like this. Even though the topic was business, it felt more intimate than that. He raised a speculative brow. "Are you trying to butter me up?"

Was that what he thought? She looked up into his eyes and decided that he was just teasing her. "No, I'm speaking the truth."

She had eyes, he thought, that a man could go wading in. Deep, fathomless, gorgeous eyes. It took him a moment to realize that she had said something, and another moment to replay it in his mind so he could respond.

"I know. That's why I've decided to go with you. Your company," he amended, lest either of them misunderstand. He was talking business. But there was a part of him that *really* wanted to go with her. Somewhere dark and romantic. And isolated.

There was something in his eyes that she found unsettling. Something that was reaching out to her on a far different level than the verbal one they were on.

She was having trouble keeping her mind on the conversation. T.J. reminded herself that business was the only thing that mattered here and the only reason she was having a conversation with Christopher in the first place.

"I'm flattered. Without even reviewing the rest of the campaign?"

He had already looked over all the preliminary drawings and proposals before flying down to meet with her. And he had no corrections to offer. It was as if they were of one mind about the direction he wanted the ad campaigns to go. But he did want to hear what Theresa had to add, if anything.

"Call it icing on the cake." If he didn't get off this sofa, he was going to reach out and kiss her again. Christopher got up. "I'd really like to get down to work right now."

She nodded, relieved that he didn't try to kiss her again. And disappointed.

"Your call." She bit her lip. "Are you sure you're feeling up to it?"

The grin he gave in response to her question had color rushing to her cheeks. Yes, he'd proven that he was certainly over whatever had laid him low. No sick man could have kissed like that.

Tactfully, he made no reference to their kiss. "After watching *Mr. Duck Goes to the City,* I think I'm ready for anything."

"Well, then," she said breezily, rising to her feet, "let's get to it, shall we?" She gestured him out of the room. Her den, where she did most of her work, was located at the rear of the house. "Cecilia," T.J. called, glancing over her shoulder to see if Megan was still occupied. She was, but that could change at any moment.

Within a minute, the housekeeper appeared, filling the hall with her presence.

She'd been pretty once, Christopher thought, studying Cecilia's profile as she walked by him. He'd go so far as to venture that she'd been a knockout. She was still a striking woman.

He thought of Lester, his father's chauffeur. Lester hadn't been the same since his wife, Edith, had died. Edith had been a tall woman, though not as tall as Cecilia. He saw resemblance between the two women and wondered if Lester would be interested in meeting Cecilia.

The thought stunned him. What the hell was coming over

him? He'd never thought of matching people up before. It had to be this house. There was a warmth here that permeated everything. And Theresa, he realized, was its source.

Cecilia let her eyes wash over Christopher approvingly before she looked at T.J. "You called?"

T.J. nodded. "Would you mind watching Megan for a while, please? Mr. MacAffee and I have a little business to go over."

Cecilia lowered her voice as she walked into the room. "Yes, I know. I saw a glimpse of negotiations when I passed by earlier."

T.J. flushed. She let the comment go. Saying anything in her defense would only lead to further embarrassment. Her eyes darted toward Christopher's face. Had he heard? He had and was apparently amused.

That made one of them.

"This way," she muttered, leading the way to the den.

IT WAS A SMALL ROOM that caught a corner of the sun when it set in the evening. Because the afternoon was dreary, T.J. had turned on the lights. There were several of Megan's drawings, Christopher noted, tacked strategically onto the bulletin board behind her desk. There was a bookcase against one wall, but the room was dominated by a desk. There wasn't much room for anything else.

She had a computer. State-of-the-art, from the looks of it. But it was dormant. She seemed to prefer drawing by hand. All the sketches she had spread across her desk for his perusal were hand drawn. He liked that. It seemed more personal that way and that was what his company had always striven for. The personal touch. It was how they had managed to survive in a world where everyone else was in the fast lane, scrambling toward the next goal. The perpetual race had created a void, a backlash. His company capitalized on the need it generated. Nostalgia had people wanting to return to the toys of their youth, of their parents' youth. And his company was there to fulfill that desire.

She'd insisted that he sit at her desk, utilizing the only chair in the room while she moved about before him, making what amounted to an impromptu presentation. And doing it brilliantly.

He was fascinated. She didn't just use her mouth when she spoke, but her entire body. Hand gestures, facial expressions, eyes that glinted and lit. She was a symphony of motion. And he found himself wanting to buy a season's ticket to the concert.

Christopher congratulated himself on finding the right person to do justice to his company. And maybe, he mused, he'd found a little more than that.

It bore further exploring.

Finished, T.J. waited and then frowned to herself. Christopher had just sat there, listening to her for over twenty minutes. She knew he was awake because his eyes were opened. But he hadn't commented or given her any input whatsoever on the work she'd placed before him. Had she managed to bore him into a coma?

Bridling her frustration, she still allowed a sigh to escape. "You're not saying anything."

She'd completely mesmerized him. "That's because you're still talking."

T.J. gathered her drawings together. They represented a great deal of late-night work, and she was proud of them. She wanted him to be proud of them, too. Very much so. Maybe she was asking too much.

"I'm done," she said quietly.

He nodded, pleased at what he'd been shown. "Then I'm impressed."

It was just too simple. She'd heard that he was a hard man to win over. Maybe she'd missed something. Maybe he was just toying with her for some perverse reason. It wouldn't be the first time. "And you're still going to sign with us?"

He wouldn't have pegged her as being insecure. Not from what he'd heard. Hurricane Theresa, they called her. Hurricanes weren't insecure. So far, not much of the report he'd received on her rang true. Except that she had great insight into what his company needed.

"More than ever."

She blew out a breath. She had done it. She'd clinched the deal. Theresa was going to be very happy about this. Her cousin had actively been after MacAffee Toys ever since Christopher's company had terminated its association with Random Ads.

"That's a relief."

Her reaction puzzled him a little. "I didn't think you'd care that much." He rose to stand beside her. She was a petite woman, he thought, with delicate bone structure that begged for a man's hand to caress worshipfully. "Acquiring new clients must be routine by now."

"It's never routine," she answered, quickly covering her slip. Theresa never seemed eager about anything, except maybe the hunk of the month, and then only at the beginning of the month.

Christopher liked her response. He found it refreshing. "Maybe that's why MacAffee Toys is going with you. You seem like you care." He looked down into her face and wondered fleetingly what it would be like if she cared for him. "You're awfully good at this. Blending work and play."

It was all she could do not to take a step back. He was standing way too close to her for comfort. She couldn't help wondering if he was referring to the kiss in the family room. For her part, she couldn't think of anything else for long and was surprised that she had even managed to make the presentation at all. Her pulse still felt like scrambled radio waves of a long-lost transmission endlessly traveling through space.

"And even finding time for your niece," he added when she didn't say anything.

He *was* talking about the kiss, she thought, suddenly nervous. What else could he be referring to? That was what "play" meant to him. Small wonder. Theresa had a reputation for going from man to man.

For a loquacious woman, she was being unusually quiet. Unable to help himself, he wove his fingers through her hair, combing it away from her face. "I don't think I've ever met anyone quite like you before."

Guilt took a giant step forward. "Maybe you're not meeting anyone like me now," she murmured under her breath.

What she said didn't make any sense. He had to have misheard her. "What?"

Damn it, she was going to have to stop feeling guilty about this. There was nothing to feel guilty about. This was business, pure and simple. It wasn't as if she was trying to reclaim the throne of Russia by posing as the long-lost Anastasia. She was just filling in for her cousin.

"Nothing." T.J. took a deep breath that sounded uncomfortably shaky to her ear. And the words were hard to push out. He had to stop touching her like that. "T.J. will be very pleased that you liked her work."

"These are T.J.'s?" He'd gotten the impression that she had personally drawn each one.

"Yes. I just make the presentations."

"And very convincingly. One would have thought they were yours."

His eyes were definitely too familiar, she thought. What made it worse was that she was enjoying it. And what made it worse than that was that he thought he was looking at Theresa.

She wished she'd never let herself be talked into this. With effort, she managed to move aside, stepping away from him. The back of her legs bumped against the desk.

"I'll let her know you liked them when she gets back." Her mouth felt dry. Turning, she began straightening papers that had already been straightened.

She almost sounded skittish. It had to be his imagination. Someone with her reputation was as far from skittish as he was from being a biker. Pleased with the way things had turned out, he felt like celebrating. With her.

"I'd like to take you out to dinner tonight."

An intimate table for two. Soft lights. Maybe music. She didn't think she could handle that. "That's not necessary."

He caught her arm as she moved past him. "No, please, I

insist.'' She opened her mouth to protest again. Christopher deftly headed her off before she could. ''To cement relations.''

She wondered which he meant and hated herself for knowing which she wanted him to mean. Those relations had already gone further than she'd ever dreamed.

T.J. tried to get him to change his mind. ''Are you sure you wouldn't just rather stay in? You know, gather your strength together to fly home tomorrow?'' It annoyed her that in her heart, she wanted him to stay. But she did. ''You were pretty sick yesterday.''

If he didn't know better, he would have said she was trying to get rid of him. But he did know better. Call it gut instinct, but he had a feeling that the woman before him wasn't the type to lie or use people. She was just being concerned. He liked that. Probably more than he should.

''It really did turn out to be just a twenty-four-hour bug. I feel great now.'' More than that, he felt as if he'd never been sick at all. ''And I won't take no for an answer.'' .

She smiled up into his face while her stomach turned to Jell-O. ''Well, then I guess I won't give it.'' *Although I know I really should.*

Chapter Six

"THIS WASN'T REALLY necessary, you know."

T.J. raised her eyes to Christopher's across the table. Dinner had been far more pleasant than she had expected. Deciding to take out all the stops and play Theresa to the hilt, she discovered that she thoroughly enjoyed the role. Maybe more than she should.

She told herself that it was just for the night and since he already believed that she was her cousin, there was no harm being done. The wine she'd had with her meal helped mute her conscience.

Christopher couldn't remember when he'd enjoyed himself so much. And in such a simple place. "I think it was."

She leaned her head on her upturned palm. The wine had taken a path straight to her head, stripping inhibitions away as it went. "Oh, you did, did you?"

"Yes." He wanted to repay her for kindness that had gone over and above the call of duty. That, and spend some time with her. He glanced around the family restaurant. It was fairly full. They'd been lucky to get a booth off to the side. "What I didn't think was that you'd be caught dead in a steak house."

Theresa wouldn't have. She wouldn't have eaten a steak unless the menu proclaimed it to be filet mignon and thirty dollars a cut. But T.J.'s tastes ran in a less complex direction. Adroitly, she covered her slip by flirting. The more she did it, the more natural flirting seemed to her. And the more she enjoyed it.

"You seem to have a lot of preconceived notions about me."

"Some." Other notions, he thought, were brand-new. And growing in volume.

She toyed with the last of her baked potato. Strangely, her appetite had all but disappeared, but she felt full. Full and light at the same time. There was a rush that came over her when she looked at him that frightened her. The only way she could savor it was by taking refuge in her role.

"Homework?" she guessed, smiling.

What would he say if he knew that he wasn't sitting across from the subject of the report she knew was sitting somewhere in his office? For one wild moment, she was tempted to tell him, just to see his reaction. But then she would have to give up the charade, not to mention suffer the consequences for it. This was much better. Safer.

And more exciting.

He spread his hands expansively. Some women would have resented the intrusion. But Theresa Cochran was more sophisticated than that. She knew it went with the territory.

"All right, you caught me. I believe in thoroughly knowing who I'm dealing with." He studied her face and knew that he'd guessed correctly. She didn't mind. "Don't you?"

"Yes and no." Her mind elsewhere, she let her eyes glide over his lips and relived the moment he'd kissed her.

He hadn't kissed *her,* she reminded herself. Christopher had kissed Theresa. She knew it was the wine that was creating the small, sharp prick of jealousy she felt, but that didn't make it any less hurtful.

"I like surprises," she elaborated, her voice deep, husky.

There was an impish gleam in her eyes. He just bet she did, he thought. It seemed her style.

"I didn't. Until now." The corners of his mouth pulled into a grin. He found her incredibly easy to talk to. Something else he hadn't expected. "You've turned out to be quite a pleasant one."

Ambivalent feelings warred within her. Theresa would have coyly laughed here, absorbing the compliment as her due. T.J.

couldn't quite bring it off. Guilt wouldn't allow it. Conscience made her want to warn him. "Maybe you're just jumping to conclusions."

Modest, too. Now there was a surprise. It just kept getting better and better. "I don't think so. I'm a fairly good judge of character."

Leaning over, Christopher topped off her wine, finishing the bottle. He debated asking for another, then decided against it. He wanted a clear head tonight. He had a feeling that it might be a long while before it was over.

A good judge of character? Not hardly, T.J. thought. She took a sip before answering. When she did, she gestured with her glass. "May I remind you that most of your judging time has been spent under covers, comatose."

"Some things you just have a gut feeling about." He placed a hand over hers on the table. There was an intimacy between them in this noisy, brightly lit steak house. He felt it far more strongly than on the occasions when he brought a companion to a posh, romantically dim restaurant. It was the woman and not the place. "Like the fact that this merger is going to be a good one. I think your firm can do a great deal for mine."

She raised her glass in a silent toast, reinforcing his words. "No doubt about that. We have a great many ideas to put into motion."

His eyes skimmed over her. She was wearing a simple black dress with the air of a princess swaddled in velvet. He had a feeling she could bring off wearing burlap. "Suddenly, so do I."

Oh, boy. T.J. took a long sip this time, fortifying herself. She could plainly read what was on his mind. Perhaps because it was on hers, too. And it shouldn't be.

Christopher drew back a little. This was far too public a place to indulge in displays of affection. He wasn't certain what had come over him. Being with Theresa appeared to loosen him up. It was something, he realized, that he could get used to.

"You don't know what a relief it is, meeting someone like

you. I can relax, without worrying that perhaps it's MacAffee Toys you find attractive—''

Her eyes widened in surprise before she remembered she was supposed to be sultry. She slanted her gaze. ''Instead of you?''

Had all the women in his life been blind up to now? He was gorgeous. If she had met him as herself instead of Theresa, he would have been the one to make her want to give romance another chance.

But she hadn't met him as herself. She'd met him as Theresa and she was stuck with that. There wasn't anything she could do to change that now.

Christopher lifted his shoulders, then let them drop carelessly. ''Well, I wasn't going to put it exactly that way.'' He felt a little foolish. ''I'm not always that good with words.''

''You're doing just fine.'' Maybe too fine, she added silently. It was getting increasingly harder to remember just where the line was drawn between role-playing and reality. Her mind kept drifting, as did her feelings. Having him extol her ''honesty'' wasn't making things any easier on her.

He slowly twirled the wine stem. The overhead light reflected in the pink liquid, making it gleam. Christopher studied it before continuing. He wasn't accustomed to baring his feelings. But somehow he thought she'd understand.

''You'd be surprised at how many women have ulterior motives when it comes to relationships. Not that I've had the time for that many in the last few years.''

There was more here than that. There had been a flicker of sadness in his eyes. Compassion made T.J. forget to feel uncomfortable. ''But the one you did find time for ended badly?'' Empathy filled her. She remembered the pain when she'd discovered the truth about Peter.

''You might say that.'' He finished his glass, then set it down beside hers. ''I fell hard.''

He was being unabashedly honest with her, more than he'd ever been with people he'd known most of his life. Funny how he felt closer to this woman he hadn't known forty-eight hours ago than he did to his friends. But there was so much under-standing in her eyes, it drew him out.

And in.

"She, on the other hand, fell for my name and my bankbook. And the family connections." Christopher looked at her. "Do you ever run into that?" She'd mentioned something about it earlier, but he thought she was just making polite conversation. He couldn't imagine anyone using her.

T.J. thought of Theresa. Of the jet-setting life she managed to conduct along with a fair amount of business. And of the men who swarmed around her cousin. In comparison, there were times she felt like the family ugly duckling, even though they were essentially cut out of the same cloth. They looked alike, but it was Theresa's zest for life, her flair that made her beautiful. There were times, just a few, when she had envied Theresa her free and easy style, her way of drawing the fun out of life and discarding the rest.

With sobering determination, T.J. reminded herself that she had Megan and a career she loved. That was enough for her.

It *was,* she insisted silently, trying to negate the power of his gaze.

With the air of a conspirator, she leaned into Christopher, lowering her voice as she resumed her role. "Do I ever run into that? All the time."

"I guess that gives us something in common." He thought that over for a moment. "Actually, we have a great deal in common." He saw by the look in her eyes that she was unconvinced. "We both helm family businesses, both are only children and both have to glean the wheat from the chaff."

And we're both unattached, he added silently.

"Except that you're all business and I'm not." *Oh, and just one more tiny little thing. I'm not who you think I am.*

He inclined his head. Maybe it was the place, or the humbling effect of waking up to find himself in a flowing nightshirt. More than likely, it was the company. The light in her eyes, the husky laugh. All of which made him want to turn over a new leaf. To finally enjoy the life he'd been so busy rushing through.

"Maybe I shouldn't be. All business, that is. I don't have to be," he corrected. "Not with the right person."

Completely sobered now, T.J. looked down at her plate, wishing there was a way to disappear. What was he going to say when he found out that he'd been pouring his heart out to a fraud? A phony? She felt for him. And for herself.

T.J. did the only thing she could—she diverted him with work. Desperate, she grabbed on to the first thought that surfaced. "You know, speaking of the right person, I've been thinking. Valentine's Day is less than two weeks away—"

"I know." He cocked his head. What was she getting at?

She lowered her eyes. This wasn't going to come out at all if she was looking at him. He had a way of making her mouth grow dry. "If we hurry, we can launch a TV campaign a couple of days before it hits—"

"A Valentine campaign for MacAffee Toys?" Humor twisted his mouth. "Toys aren't generally associated with Valentine's Day."

"No, but stuffed animals are." Mercifully, the idea began to take form in her head. As far as she knew, there were no commercials featuring stuffed animals for the day. That was strictly the domain of flowers and candy. "I was going through your catalog last night. You've got several items that would make wonderful gifts for men to give to the women in their lives."

Warming to her subject, her enthusiasm grew. "For instance, that white bear you have. The one that says, 'I wuv you' when you squeeze it." Pulling a pen out of her purse, she made a quick sketch on her napkin, turning it around for Christopher to look at. "It's perfect. We could say something like, 'Can't find the words to tell her? This Valentine's Day, send an emissary in your place.' And then we can feature the bear."

He laughed, amused, but he was taken with the idea. Her enthusiasm was infectious. Just like she was. "So that the lady in question can think she's getting a message from Elmer Fudd?"

She grinned. "Trust me, all women love stuffed animals."

Her eyes were shining. Did she like stuffed animals? It seemed almost incongruous. "I would have thought you preferred jewelry."

Theresa adored anything that sparkled and came in carats. T.J., on the other hand, had a weakness for plush.

"There's room for both. As an added touch, you could have the bear holding a diamond ring box in its paws. They could be tied around it with a bright red ribbon." Hastily she added a few more lines to the drawing. It was of a woman hugging a man, a toy bear dangling from her fingers. "So, what do you think?"

"I like it." It would open up a whole brand-new avenue for them. "Get on it."

"Consider it done." She beamed, pleased. And then remembered. Nothing had been formalized. They were getting ahead of themselves. "We have contracts to sign first."

Christopher waved the obstacle away. "A formality I'll have taken care of before the end of the week. I've already had our lawyers draw up preliminary papers."

She leaned back, looking at him. "So you were pretty sure you were going with us?"

Experience had him answering cautiously. "Not really. I wanted to check you out myself. I don't believe in dealing with companies whose CEOs don't care about the quality of the work, only the money it generates. You've completely won me over." He put his hand out to seal the bargain.

Something fluttered inside her as she slipped her hand into his. It was pleasure, mingled with satisfaction and a degree of anticipation, that overwhelmed her.

Christopher didn't break the connection immediately. Instead, he sat, holding her hand, savoring feelings that had nothing to do with the bargain their lawyers and accountants would ultimately solidify. They had to do with a man sitting across from a beautiful woman.

He raised his glass. There was only a drop left in it, but he toasted the merger anyway. "Here's to a long association."

She touched her empty glass to his. She fervently hoped it wasn't prophetic that they were toasting with empty glasses.

"Amen to that." *And may you never find out that we pulled something over on you.*

He felt the flutter in her wrist as he released her hand. "You seem nervous. Do I make you nervous?" It didn't seem possible, and yet...

Maybe a pinch of honesty would placate him. "No, *I* make me nervous."

That was enigmatic. "Why?"

The words just seemed to fall from her lips of their own accord. T.J. hadn't meant to be this open, but once she began, there was no way of gracefully turning back.

"Because I'm having all these thoughts I shouldn't be having."

His eyes held hers. The amusement in them slowly faded into something far more intense. "About?"

She had come this far, she might as well admit the rest. Or as much as she could. She couched it in terms that Theresa might have used. "Mixing business with pleasure."

He watched in fascination as her long, sooty lashes swept along the swell of her cheeks. Christopher felt something tighten in his gut. "Funny. Me, too."

It would be so easy to let things just evolve.... Easy, but not right. T.J. drew herself up. "But we can't."

Reserve? Christopher hadn't expected that. "Why not? Sometimes these things work out."

She thought of the consequences that loomed ahead if they were to become involved. "Not this time."

She was far more reticent than he would have thought. Shy even. The lady was a box just filled with surprises—each more pleasing than the last, Christopher decided.

His eyes caressed her face. He liked the light that rose in her eyes, and the tiny, nervous flutter he detected in her throat. This wasn't an act she was putting on for his benefit. This was genuine. Christopher found himself charmed all over again.

"You'll never know until you try."

Her mind scrambled for a way out. She thought of the conversation. "I don't want you to think that I'm seducing you for your business."

A couple passing their table just then looked from Christopher to T.J. and shook their heads disapprovingly as they moved on.

T.J. sank down in her seat, but laughter bubbled in her throat. "They probably think I'm propositioning you." The thought of her propositioning anyone was completely ludicrous.

And yet, he was generating these unfamiliar feelings within her. Reckless, delicious feelings.

"Instead of the other way around." He didn't want her misunderstanding. This had nothing to do with business. "And we've already sealed the deal, so anything that happens between us is after the fact."

He looked at his empty plate and the empty glass beside it. Suddenly Christopher knew exactly what he wanted for dessert. He was rarely so sure of anything outside of business. But he was sure of this.

It just felt right.

Nodding at her place setting, Christopher asked, "Ready to go?"

"Yes."

The answer, she knew, had come a little too quickly and perhaps breathlessly. But she wanted to be out of here, away from the setting of just the two of them and back home, where there was Megan and Cecilia and a shower that had cold water. She planned to stand under the shower head for a few hours.

Picking up her purse, she slid out of the booth. Christopher was beside her by the time she rose to her feet. He slipped his arm around her shoulders and guided her out. He'd already paid the bill before the food had ever arrived. There were some advantages to eating in a steak house, he mused, glad the mood could continue unbroken.

As they walked out the door, he thought he felt her shaking. It couldn't be because she was nervous. Theresa Cochran was too sophisticated for that. And yet, it wasn't cold out. On the contrary, the night was warm and sultry, adding to his mood.

Another explanation occurred to him as he directed her toward her car at the far end of the lot. "Theresa, are you feeling all right? You're not coming down with what I had, are you?"

It was her way out.

She wanted to jump at the excuse. But she was already hip deep in lies. She didn't want to add to the pile any more than she already had.

"No." Reaching the car, she turned toward him. When she raised her eyes to his, her expression was somber. "I don't think we should take this any further." She'd never hated saying anything more in her life. But it was for the best.

Had he misinterpreted the signs? No, he was better at reading people than that. Christopher searched her face for a clue. "Why?"

Theresa could have come up with something, created a dozen excuses. T.J. could only whisper the truth. "Because I want it too much."

Funny how six simple words could change his life. He'd never been a public creature, never one to display his feelings. But that didn't seem to matter right now. Unmindful of where they were, and of the fact that there were people coming and going in the lot, Christopher gathered her to him.

His arms felt as if they belonged around her. As if she belonged against him. His body needed the warmth that hers generated. Inhaling deeply, he drew the fragrance of her hair into his lungs.

"I understand."

She looked at him uncertainly. Anticipation trembled within her. What was she doing, jeopardizing everything because the touch of his hand made her heart flip-flop? After tonight, she was never going to see the man again. She didn't subscribe to the "Two ships in the night" theory.

And here she was, wanting him to touch her. To want her. To make love with her.

She had to be crazy.

"You do?" she asked.

He nodded. "You're afraid to surrender to your emotions. You always have to be in control."

Boy, was he wrong. She opened her mouth to protest, but he laid a finger against her lips.

"I know," he confided, "because I'm the same way. But it doesn't have to be about surrendering control. No one has to be in control. It can just be about two people enjoying each other."

He made it sound so simple. If only it were, she thought in despair. If only she had met him as herself, instead of as Theresa.

Guilt and desire warred with one another. Guilt won. But she had an uneasy feeling that it might not be a permanent victory.

Worse, that she didn't want it to be.

"Funny, that sounds like something I would say." Or that Theresa would say, she amended silently.

"See? We're of one mind. The more I talk to you, the more alike we turn out to be."

"Incredible, isn't it?" Her laugh sounded a bit hollow to her ear.

"*Incredible* is the word for it." And for her. His voice was soft, and the look in his eyes as he lowered his mouth to hers threatened to make her heart stop altogether.

Feelings took over. Without waiting for him to make contact, she rose on her toes and buried her hands in his hair. An eagerness she was unaccustomed to filled her as she pressed her lips to his.

And then she was completely swept away.

She never stood a chance. She didn't want one. She wanted, instead, to have this wonderful, wild, heady feeling to completely drain all thoughts, all feeling of guilt and deception away from her.

T.J. felt his hands along her back, pressing her to him, felt the leap of joy as he deepened the kiss until it anesthetized her. She felt limp even as her blood roared through her veins.

She was trembling again, he thought, mystified. Or was that

him? He didn't feel his knees. A first. Christopher had never been shaken up by a woman before. It was an experience he would have found frightening if it wasn't so thoroughly enjoyable.

He tasted the wine on her lips. Wine and desire. It was a hell of a heady combination, but he thought he could handle it. And do it justice.

Her heart pounding madly, T.J. managed to place her hands on his arms and push herself back. An ache of regret accompanied her words. "I think we'd better be getting back, don't you?"

"I'm not sure I can. I didn't drop any bread crumbs to mark my way."

Oh, please let him be talking about where she lived and not about his emotions. Because she felt it, too. She tried to ignore the thrill that created.

T.J. opened the driver's side and got in. "That's all right. I'm the one driving and I remember the way back."

Flipping the lock open on his side from the control panel, she silently added, *Maybe.*

Chapter Seven

CHRISTOPHER HAD ALWAYS exercised extreme caution in his relationships. Suspicion of motives had been second nature for him. It was the way his father had raised him. He thought it was the way things would always be.

There were no suspicions now. It was as if something had fallen away from him. A protective glass shield. A force field around his heart. He had no desire to be guarded.

The woman beside him in the car completely captivated him. She was everything he had ever wanted in a woman: smart, funny, resourceful, nurturing. A sexy Mary Poppins with a dash of Andrew Carnegie's business acumen. Hell, what more could a man want?

To build on the foundation before him, Christopher thought. That was what a man could want. It was what he wanted.

He was never slow about making up his mind. And he'd made it up this evening.

All things considered, the steak house had been an improbable place to find himself falling in love.

Improbable, but not impossible. It had to be love, he reasoned, because he'd never felt anything like this before.

He wanted to take her dancing along the banks of the River Thames. To Paris to sip wine in the shadow of the Eiffel Tower. To Tahiti to make love on the beach. He felt wild, reckless, none of which he could even vaguely remember feeling before. It had to be love. Or total insanity.

Maybe, he mused, watching her profile, it was a little bit of both.

They were almost home. If T.J. weren't driving, it would have been a struggle for her not to knot her fingers together in her lap. It wasn't something Theresa would do. Theresa would never have allowed an outward display of nerves to be witnessed. T.J. didn't think Theresa was even capable of being nervous. They were very different in that respect.

What did Theresa have to be nervous about, anyway? She led a charmed life. That was because her cousin knew that she would always be there to bail her out. T.J.'s jaw clenched as she turned onto her street.

Well, maybe she was sick of being the dependable one. Good old dependable T.J., always living in Theresa's shadow.

But tonight was different. Tonight she was Cinderella. Or Theresa, she amended. She glanced at Christopher and saw that he was looking at her. Warmth bathed her all over again. T.J.'s stomach quavered as she offered him a wide smile.

What the hell? If he thought she was Theresa, then she was going to *be* Theresa. All the way. And tomorrow, when he was on his plane, flying away from her and into forever, she would revert back to being dependable, safe, unexciting T.J.

But right now there was tonight.

She shifted in her seat, chafing, anxious. Anticipation marched through her like a well-drilled military band playing John Philip Sousa's *Stars and Stripes Forever*. The seat belt dug into her shoulder, a reminder that things were best played safe. Should she? Should she just continue being safe? Or should she, just once in her life, grab the brass ring and run with it? No one would know the difference.

They wouldn't, she thought, slanting another glance at Christopher, even know it was her.

Temptation whispered seductively in her ear. Would Christopher do the same if she let him? Would his warm breath skim along her skin when he spoke?

That was something, T.J. decided, she really wanted to find

out. A smile curved her mouth as her blood began to hum with mounting excitement. Desire was winning the battle against common sense.

Guiding the car into the driveway, she pulled up the hand brake and turned toward him.

"You're awfully quiet." He'd hardly said anything on the way home. "Was it something I said?"

He'd been content just watching her. Just watching the shadows from the towering trees that lined the neighborhood streets play over her face as streetlights shone through them.

"Everything you said."

Uh-oh. One layer of her newly applied bravado began slipping away. But the look on his face told her that everything was still all right.

"Actually, I was just thinking how funny fate is."

Yes, it was a riot, all right. Otherwise, how would they have ever wound up here, in front of her door, contemplating a step she'd never taken so rapidly before? Covering the sudden burst of nerves dancing through her, T.J. opened her door and got out.

"Oh?" She tried to keep her voice nonchalant, light. Her stomach felt as if it were knotting up.

Getting out on his side, Christopher looked at her over the roof of the navy car. "I almost didn't come down here to meet you," he admitted.

She didn't understand. It was his practice to conduct these interviews. And his father had done it before him. "But you always—"

He nodded, casually slipping his arm through hers as they came up the walk. "Yes, that's just it. I 'always,' just like my father 'always' before me. It was a pattern and perhaps a rut. Life's gotten too complicated and busy for luxuries like two people meeting and sizing one another up before contracts. Besides, we both know that contracts can be easily broken if one of us is dissatisfied, no matter how ironclad those contracts appear."

With a calendar teeming full of appointments, he'd almost

made a fatal mistake. He'd almost not come here and missed the opportunity of his life. "I toyed, if you'll forgive the expression, with the idea of perhaps implementing a new set of procedures. Trusting my investigators to give me the entire background on the people I deal with."

T.J. had taken out her key, but was just holding it, stunned. Christopher took it from her hand and unlocked the front door. Opening it, he waited until she crossed the threshold before following. When he gave the key back to her, she felt a jolt where his hand touched hers. It shocked her back to awareness.

He wouldn't have come and she wouldn't have been here with him now, not being herself. T.J. didn't know whether to laugh or to cry.

The living room was dark. Only a small lamp pooled light along the hallway. Cecilia and Megan were asleep. The house was quiet.

She was alone with him, she realized. Completely alone. The thought must have occurred to him, as well. She could read that in his eyes. They were touching her, stirring her. She found the breath backing up in her throat.

"I'm glad I decided against it. They certainly were wrong in their report on you."

She tossed her head the way she'd seen Theresa do when she was flirting. Her stomach churned nervously as she hoped she hadn't overplayed her hand. How desperately she wanted what she knew she shouldn't have.

"And why is that?" The question rang husky, uttered through cotton dry lips.

Very lightly, he combed his fingers through her hair. She wore it unadorned, free, like a dark ocean beckoning him to swim in it. He watched her eyes grow large and it pleasured him.

"What they said led me to believe that you were a rather vain, rather shallow party girl who left the running of her company to very capable subordinates." Reynolds and Wagner were guilty of slacking off and letting the tabloids do their work for them. They'd been good men up to now, but he was going to have to talk to them about this when he returned. They hadn't managed to dig below the surface.

"But I'm—"

"Not," he corrected.

She couldn't spring to Theresa's defense without risking giving herself away. She wished he wouldn't look at her like that. Wouldn't touch her like that. She couldn't think when he did. And if she couldn't think, she was going to make a fatal blunder. It was only a matter of time.

"They were obviously wrong on all counts." He stood back just a little to regard her in the dim, silvery light the moon was shepherding through the bay window. "You're not vain, although there's a great deal you could be vain about. You're certainly not shallow and you've obviously worked on the presentation yourself, not left it to any subordinates to put together."

"T.J.—" The protest never managed to even leave her lips.

Loyalty, too. The tally was mounting. He couldn't help wondering why she wouldn't take credit for her own designs. "That, I think, is a smoke screen."

She shook her head. "No, she—"

Theresa was going to insist that T.J. had done the work. He might have believed her if she hadn't made that impromptu sketch.

He placed his hands on her shoulders, stilling her. "That sketch you did for me on the napkin at the restaurant... The style matched the drawings in your den."

She licked her lips, trying again. "Our styles are a lot alike—"

She'd just proved what he had surmised. Very slowly he glided the palms of his hands along her bare arms. "See, if you were vain or shallow, you'd be preening, taking the credit instead of trying to lay it on someone else's doorstep. I'm very impressed, Theresa. With the campaign." His eyes held her fast. "With you."

Her pulse quickened again as she began to feel herself turn to liquid. She wanted this, wanted this oh-so-desperately, and yet, it was dishonest. He thought—he thought—

Christopher lowered his mouth to hers and her mind joined the rest of her liquefied state.

The hell with what he thought.

T.J. fisted her hands in his thick, dark hair and gave herself to him, body and soul. She didn't think how this might make things sticky for Theresa later. She couldn't think that far ahead. Or even clearly. If she had to put up with the discomfort of pretending to be Theresa, she was damn well going to reap the rewards, just this one time. Theresa wouldn't care that he was leaving tomorrow. Theresa would be counting on it, happy not to be involved with a commitment.

Just once, she was going to see what it was like to *really* live like Theresa.

Not that she had a choice about it. And not because of him. She knew instinctively if she said no, it would stop here, in her living room. Dark, sensual, incredibly exciting, Christopher just wasn't the type to force himself on a woman.

No, the choice she didn't have was her own. She wanted this, needed this, more than she'd needed anything in a very, very long time.

The rush felt wonderful, timeless. If his hands weren't on her, she was fairly certain that she could float.

In another moment, he thought his self-control would snap. Though he saw desire in her eyes, he wanted to be sure that this was what she wanted.

"Maybe we'd better go somewhere a little more private?" Christopher laced his hand through hers, waiting for her to demur, praying that she wouldn't. "There's this little out-of-the-way room I've been staying in that would be perfect."

It was all she could manage to nod her head. T.J. didn't even know if she smiled in response. But the rest of her was smiling. One huge grin from top to toe.

He made her feel as if she were glowing.

Christopher led her down the hallway. To her bedroom. She

didn't remember walking. T.J. heard the door close behind her and the sound reverberated in her head as she looked up into his eyes.

Waiting.

Theresa wouldn't wait, she told herself. She would act.

With hands that were surprisingly steady, she undid his tie, slowly sliding the silken material down his shirtfront.

He'd never experienced anything so sensual in his life. He'd been with enough women to know. It was all he could do not to rush this. To bring it to where this pent-up feeling within him would be released.

But he didn't.

Wouldn't.

This was going to be a night to remember, for both of them. Christopher wanted their time together to stand out in her mind. He wanted to be head and shoulders above the others who had been in her life before.

There weren't, he vowed to himself, going to be any in her life hereafter. By her own choice. And for that, he was determined that he would go slow, that each moment would be burned into her brain so that there could be no room for any other men in her mind.

He would do whatever it took for her to choose him. For he had already chosen her.

It wasn't what she had expected, this lovemaking with him. It was soft, slow, liquid. Lyrical poetry. She'd never experienced agony that was sweet before. He made her ache for him with every movement, every kiss, every touch. Every tender caress. Ache for fulfillment and yet pray that it wouldn't come too soon. Not yet. She wanted this wonderful sensation of hot, palpitating anticipation to go on just a little longer.

She had no idea she could feel this way. Drugged yet excited, eager yet hesitant. Wild. He brought things out of her that she would have never believed existed. She hardly recognized herself. T.J. forgot to playact and just reacted.

Laughter bubbled and mingled with the fire in her veins.

Their clothes strewn on the floor, their limbs tangled up with each other, they left the earthly confines of her bedroom to enter a world where there was room for only two.

And that was enough.

And when it was over, when his sleek, hard body had left hers limp and glowing, he held her against him, cradling her lovingly. As if they'd always been this way. As if he'd always been her lover.

Theresa's lover, she tried to remind herself, not hers. It didn't matter. Right now, it didn't matter. For tonight she was Theresa. Her heart was bursting with happiness and she hugged it to her.

She wanted to tell him that she had never done this before, never reacted with such intensity to a man before. Even with Peter, it had taken six months before they had made love with one another, and then only after he'd slipped an engagement ring on her finger. And that had turned out to be more promise than fulfillment.

Not this. This was something entirely new, entirely different.

But she couldn't tell him that, couldn't tell Christopher that she'd never made love with a man she hardly knew, and yet knew with all her soul. Theresa had had men in her life. He knew that. If she said anything, he'd laugh at her. Or think she was lying. Her mouth twisted. Ironic, wasn't it?

Yet she desperately wanted to tell him something. Wanted him to know how special this was for her. How wonderfully different.

The words came without preamble. "I've never done this before."

Propping himself on his elbow, he raised a quizzical brow. He could feel her hair feathering along his chest as she picked up her head to look at him.

"Made love to a client."

He didn't know if he believed her. He knew he wanted to. "Then I guess this makes me your first." He'd settle for that, he thought. For now. Bowing his head, he brushed his lips against hers.

The combustion was instantaneous. The fire roared hotter than before.

THE TELEPHONE ROUSED HER. The jangling noise intruded into her dreams, breaking them up like so many soap bubbles in a sink.

When she managed to open her eyes a crack, she saw that light was flooding the room. Morning. How had it come so quickly?

The noise persisted. The phone—she had to answer the phone.

As she groped for the receiver, T.J. realized that she wasn't alone. There was a warm body next to hers. A nude warm body.

Christopher.

Last night.

This morning.

Oh, God!

T.J. jerked into wakefulness as she simultaneously glanced over her shoulder to see if he was still asleep and rasped a "hello" into the receiver.

"T.J.?" Theresa's voice, far too exhilarated, filled her ear.

Christopher was stirring beside her. The telephone had woken him up. T.J. turned her body away from him, gathering the sheet to her as she lowered her voice.

"Yes?"

"T.J., it's Theresa." This time, she sounded puzzled. "I'm finally home. Just got in this morning. The resident doctor wanted to check me out himself." She laughed, the sound pregnant and familiar. "I'm seeing him again tonight, So, how did it go Friday?"

"Fine." The response was terse. She hoped that Theresa would take the hint and hang up.

Luck wasn't with her. All she had managed to do was rouse Theresa's curiosity. "Why are you whispering? Is something wrong?"

"I'll explain later," T.J. whispered. Theresa had certainly received enough inopportune phone calls herself to know when someone else wanted to get off. Why wasn't she taking the hint?

T.J. felt Christopher's hand on her bare shoulder and nearly groaned as his fingers lightly skimmed along her skin. She knew she squirmed as memories of their lovemaking haunted her body.

Theresa sounded as if she wanted to settle in for a chat. "No, tell me now. Did MacAffee like what you had to show him?"

The man in question cupped her breast, teasing the end with his thumb. T.J. sucked in her breath. The words were tight when she spoke. "I think so."

"Are you all right?" Theresa repeated. "You sound funny."

"I'm fine, just fine. I'll get back to you later, Th—T.J." Biting the tip of her tongue, T.J. broke off the conversation. That had been close.

"T.J.?" Theresa's voice echoed as T.J. hung up the telephone. Suddenly she found herself being turned around until she was flat on her back, gazing up into the greenest eyes God ever created.

"That was T.J.," she murmured.

He began to nibble at her neck, loving the way she twisted beneath him. Excitement pulsed through his loins in anticipation.

"So I gathered."

T.J. could feel the words along her throat. She arched, wanting to feel more. To feel him.

"She seems very conscientious, calling you on a Sunday."

T.J. swallowed before she could continue. "You don't know the half of it." She tried to muster some strength. There wasn't much to spare and what there was, she had a hunch, she was going to need soon. "So, what do you want for breakfast?"

He raised his head to look at her, his eyes teasing. "You."

Once more with feeling, she thought, happiness spreading like golden marmalade all through her. T.J. twined her arms around his neck, bringing him closer to her. "One serving, over easy, coming up."

It was the last thing either one of them said for a while.

"ABOUT TIME THE TWO OF YOU showed up for breakfast." Cecilia raised her brows, amused, in Christopher's direction. "I see you got your strength back.'' She made no effort to hide her knowing grin as she placed a plate of French toast before each of them on the table. She grinned at Christopher before turning to T.J. ''I am taking Megan to the park in case you would like to continue those undercover negotiations you were conducting.''

Certainly wasn't shy about things, was she? ''How did you know?'' he asked the woman. They hadn't made any noise. And the hour had been sufficiently late when they returned. He'd assumed the housekeeper had been asleep.

''Cecilia likes to think she knows everything. She makes good guesses.'' T.J. looked at Cecilia pointedly. ''But not this time.''

T.J. could see it in the other woman's eyes. Cecilia was thinking, *Yeah, right.* T.J. pressed on. What she'd shared with him had been exquisite, but now it was over and she had to come to terms with that.

''There aren't going to be any more negotiations,'' T.J. told her. She deliberately avoided Cecilia's eyes. ''We seemed to have settled everything to both our satisfaction.'' The housekeeper was chuckling to herself. T.J. looked at Christopher. ''What time do you want Emmett here to take you to the airport?''

''Oh, didn't I tell you?'' Christopher smiled at her. He knew perfectly well that he hadn't. It was a surprise. One he'd just come up with. He'd made the necessary arrangements while she'd been in the shower. ''I've decided to stay around for a few more days.''

T.J. dropped her fork.

Chapter Eight

T.J. QUICKLY PICKED UP her fork again. She stared at the man sitting across from her at the kitchen table. The man who had made her body sing.

The man who had to leave before he found out he had made love to the wrong woman.

T.J. had to clear her throat twice before she could speak. "Excuse me?"

He'd hoped for a slightly less violent reaction. "I've decided to remain here for a few more days."

To be here with you. He almost said it out loud, but stopped himself. It would sound absurd for him to have developed such strong feelings for her so quickly. And maybe it was. He had to find out.

"But why—?"

He thought she'd be more pleased. It disturbed him that she looked as if she was in shock. "I want to come down to the office with you. Kick off the Valentine's Day campaign."

That was only partially true. It had come out of nowhere this morning, hitting him with the impact of a detonating six-megaton bomb. Christopher wanted to be part of all the other facets of her life. He savored the rush this new feeling created. Like Christmas Day when his mother had still been part of his life. He couldn't remember details, only a feeling. If he concentrated very hard, he could remember an aura of happiness surrounding him. He'd felt contented then.

Just the way he felt now.

She was the woman for him. He could feel it. But years of caution couldn't be readily ignored or dismissed. It wasn't in his nature. He had to spend a little more time with Theresa before he said anything to her about the way he felt. Although, if she was as intuitive as he thought, words weren't going to be necessary.

And it wouldn't hurt to lay a little groundwork for himself while he was at it, either. Just because things came easily to him, Christopher wasn't so naive or so pompous as to believe that the lady would just fall into his arms. Not even after a night of incredible lovemaking. There had been other men in her life, even if casually. There probably still were now. He wanted to create a situation in which Theresa Cochran would do some voluntary house cleaning on her own.

"The office?" she repeated dumbly, still staring at him. A numbness washed over her before panic set in. Her mind began to scramble, searching for alternatives. "But I thought you had to be getting back."

The noise behind her told her Cecilia was still in the room, listening. She glanced at the woman over her shoulder, silently asking for help. The look in Cecilia's eyes told her that there wasn't going to be any coming from that quarter. Cecilia was amused by this turn of events. But then, Cecilia would have matched her up with the mailman if the man had stayed around longer than just to deliver the mail.

Feeling like the activities coordinator on the *Titanic,* T.J. turned around to look at Christopher again. He *had* to be kidding.

"I do have to get back."

T.J. almost breathed a sigh of relief, but it would have been wasted in light of what Christopher said next.

"But I called Abrams," he said, naming a vice president she'd dealt with herself when she'd called the main office, "while you were showering. Told him I was going to be detained for a few days overseeing the new advertising campaign."

How many days in "a few"? T.J. wondered, fragments of

thoughts floating through her mind like so much driftwood as panic grew.

"I think I'll be leaving now," Cecilia announced. She draped her apron over the back of a chair. "Looks like a good day for playing to me." She winked at T.J.

T.J. glared at the retreating back as Cecilia went to find Megan.

She was usually so creative when she was staring at a blank piece of paper or a pristine computer screen. Why was her mind turning to mush now, damn it, when she needed it most?

The excuse that rose to her lips was a lame one at best. "Well, we usually work best without someone looking over our shoulder."

She was acting almost shy, he thought, bemused. Why? Maybe he was just being overly sensitive. Small wonder—he'd never gone out on a limb this way before.

With the appetite of someone who was starving, he began to make short work of his French toast. "I won't get in the way," he promised.

If you only knew.

Okay, he was staying. She had to work with that. Gathering her wits together, T.J. began to mount a defensive. There were things that had to be done if they were going to get away with this. Placing her hands on the table, she began to push herself away.

"All right, let me make some calls of my own about this."

He caught her wrist before she could stand up. "But it's Sunday." Even he didn't work on Sunday. Usually.

Very carefully, she reclaimed her wrist. "Your vice president isn't the only one on call Sundays." She tried to make her voice sound casual. It wasn't easy with her heart and stomach both lodged in her throat. "Here." She pushed her untouched plate toward him. His was nearly empty. "Have mine. I don't really eat much in the morning."

Which was a lie. She always woke up hungry and enjoyed having a huge breakfast. But this morning, she wouldn't have been able to sneak a bite past her lips. Not when her insides were lurching like this.

Leaving Christopher to eat, T.J. went straight to the den. Cecilia and Megan were preparing to go out. T.J. gave her daughter a quick hug and a kiss before she left. As the front door closed, T.J. breathed a quick sigh of relief. One less worry, at least for the time being.

Two million to go. Shaking her head, she locked herself in the small room. She didn't want to be overheard.

Her hand was shaking as she tapped out the familiar numbers on the keypad. She wished she could just sit back and enjoy this instead of trying to reconnoiter and head off this latest turn of events.

Why did everything involving Theresa always have to be so complicated?

Theresa's answering machine came on after four rings. Impatiently, T.J. listened to the low, sultry voice on the other end apologize for being unable to reach the telephone. "Leave a message and I *will* get back to you."

Was it just her, or did that almost sound like an obscene promise?

"C'mon, c'mon. Pick up. Pick up, Theresa, I know you're there." Her teeth were clenched as she ordered, "Pick up the damn telephone."

Just as she was about to give up and leave a message, T.J. heard the receiver on the other end being lifted from the cradle.

"I knew there was something wrong," Theresa told her, not even bothering to say hello. "We lost the account, didn't we? He saw right through you and knew you weren't me. Oh, God, T.J. if you weren't such a mouse—"

She didn't have much time. Christopher was going to come looking for her soon. T.J. cut through the rest of Theresa's lecture, one she knew by heart. Theresa was always after her to change, to kick up her heels and follow her example.

Well, she had, and now look at the trouble they were all in.

"Theresa, you can't come into the office tomorrow."

The request took her completely by surprise. "Why?"

Feeling as if all the air had suddenly been drained out of her, T.J. sighed as she sagged against the chair. "Because Christopher is. He wants to look around, see where I—where *you* work."

"Christopher?"

T.J. drummed her fingers on the desk impatiently. Didn't Theresa ever do her homework? She was sharper than this. T.J. *knew* she was.

"MacAffee." T.J.'s clenched jaw was beginning to ache. "He's decided to stay over a few days and see how we operate."

"Why? I thought you said he was satisfied with your performance."

Theresa didn't sound nearly as distressed as T.J. thought she'd be. Definitely not as distressed as she was. Probably because her cousin figured she could handle this. Well she didn't think she could. Not this time. It was like trying to juggle with torches that had been set on fire. Sooner or later, she was going to get burned.

"He is." T.J. dragged her hand through her hair. "Maybe too much." A germ of an idea took seed. It was their only chance. "Listen, I don't have time to give you all the details now—" *Not that I ever would.* "But don't be there tomorrow. No, wait, you do have to be there tomorrow," she realized. "You have to tell everyone to pretend that I'm you. At least the head staff." T.J. began scribbling notes to herself on the pad. There was so much to remember. "Oh God, Theresa, this is turning out to be such a mess."

Theresa sounded completely unruffled. "We'll get through this. I've got a lot of faith in you."

Easy for you to say. You don't have to face him. "I really don't like lying to the man like this."

The laugh was light, amused and perhaps just the slightest bit patronizing. "Once you start, T.J., it's easy."

"If you say so. Oh, by the way." About to hang up, she remembered what would have been the most important part—if last night hadn't happened. "We've got to get started on a Valentine's Day campaign for MacAffee Toys."

"This Valentine's Day?"

Even in the midst of the storm, a flicker of satisfaction went through her. "Yes."

There was a genuine note of admiration. "Boy, you do work fast."

More than you know, cousin, more than you'll ever know. T.J. rose from the desk. She had to get back. "All right, I have to go now. I left Christopher in the kitchen and he might start to wonder what happened to me."

"The kitchen?" Theresa echoed. "What's MacAffee doing in your house?"

"A long, long story. It starts out with a virus."

"Computer?"

"Human. Bye."

T.J. hung up, then spared a satisfied look at the telephone. She'd deliberately left Theresa hanging and she had to admit it felt good just once to turn the tables on her cousin.

Maybe she had wanted this more than she'd admitted to herself, T.J. thought, unlocking the door. Otherwise, why would it feel so good?

She had no time to dwell on that. She had to come up with a plan to fall back on.

And she didn't have an idea in her head.

Nothing had occurred to her by the time she walked into the kitchen. She was just going to have to play this by ear and pray things worked out.

Man, but he was gorgeous, she thought as she approached Christopher. If Theresa had known what he looked like, she would have found a way to get to the airport, even if it meant having her hospital bed transported with her.

Christopher threaded an arm around her waist and pulled her onto his lap. "Missed you."

She tasted honey on his lips when he kissed her. Or was that just him? She could really get used to this, she mused. Too bad she was never going to get the chance.

He could smell the shampoo she'd used. Something herbal. Who would have thought herbs could be sensual? "How long does Cecilia usually take when she brings Megan to the park?"

Her hands seemed to have a mind of their own as they wound themselves around his neck. "Oh, I don't know. A couple of hours. Maybe more."

It was just what he wanted to hear. "Good, that gives us some time."

Anticipation began to nudge forward. She squelched it. He probably wasn't talking about what she was hoping he was talking about. "Time?"

"Well, I'm going to check into a hotel this afternoon." He couldn't remain here. It wasn't proper. Besides, it would give them somewhere private to go without having to worry about the housekeeper. "I imagine the conventions are over by this afternoon." He saw the surprise in her eyes. "I don't want to compromise your reputation."

Now *there* was a first, she thought. Someone actually worried about Theresa's reputation. It certainly didn't bother Theresa. Gossip just rolled off her back.

But he really wasn't talking about Theresa's reputation, T.J. thought. He was talking about hers. Never mind that he thought it was one and the same. She took it for what it was: a chivalrous act.

"Very noble of you."

"But before I leave..." He pressed a kiss to her throat and felt her sigh. "I thought that perhaps we could review some familiar ground."

T.J. melted against him, done in by the look in his eyes. She'd never seen anything so tender, so loving.

She damned Theresa and blessed her in the same breath as he kissed her again. If not for Theresa, she wouldn't have been able to sample heaven. And if not for Theresa, she wouldn't have to relinquish it again.

His mouth still sealed to hers, Christopher rose with her in his arms. He carried T.J. to her bedroom where they did indeed cover familiar ground. And make it new all over again.

PERPETUALLY TENSE, T.J. felt like a soldier picking his way through a mine field. The only time she felt at ease was when the door was shut and there was just the two of them in a room. At least then, she only had to worry about tripping herself up and not about anyone else accidentally addressing her as T.J. or making some sort of other slip.

In the few days that she'd been showing Christopher around the office, she had been a nervous wreck. Dressed in the suits Theresa had covertly sent over via her maid, T.J. did her best to play the role of the flamboyant company president.

She'd taken to the part so well that after a while, people were hard-pressed to tell her apart from the original. T.J. had overheard Heidi tell one of the secretaries in the pool that she looked more like Theresa than Theresa did.

She just acted a little differently, Heidi had gone on to say. More savvy, and, it turned out, more daring when it came to business.

By the end of the third day, T.J. finally began to relax a little. Giving orders actually came easily to her. She was on familiar ground. She'd been on both sides of the drawing board.

It was going to turn out all right, T.J. assured herself. At least, as far as business was concerned. The rest of the problem was another matter entirely. But she couldn't think about that now, not in the middle of her charade. There was just too much to do, too many torches to keep in the air at the same time. So far, she hadn't gotten burned.

And when Christopher was around her, in the privacy of his suite, she couldn't think at all. She didn't want to. All she wanted to do was feel. To store up every delicious sensation, every wondrous moment for a lifetime. Because she knew it was going to end all too soon.

The nights they spent together were as exquisite as a flawlessly cut diamond placed in a perfect setting. It wasn't just the lovemaking, which only seemed to grow more magnificent with practice. It was more.

It was the little things. Like standing on his balcony and looking up at the stars, so high above the city, so close to them that she thought she could just reach up and touch one. Like sipping champagne from the same glass, with their eyes on one another. Or like holding one another in the afterglow of lovemaking and feeling his heart beat beneath her cheek.

All little things. All precious.

She was hopelessly in love with the man and there was nothing she could do about it. Only enjoy the tiny moment in time she'd been granted.

T.J. managed to get away a few times and touched base with Megan. Gratefully, the little girl was none the worse for the separation. Because she did travel, her daughter was accustomed to not seeing her on a daily basis. T.J. knew she had to pack a lifetime into the short stay. But as the days whirled by, she was getting the very clear impression that it wasn't going to be over once he boarded the plane.

Heaven knew she didn't want it to be. But how could it continue? If he came back, he was going to have to be told the truth. And then what? What man could laugh off being deceived?

He would never trust her again.

The thought brought a pang to her heart, even as she lay curled beside him in the hotel suite bed.

Drawing her even closer to him, Christopher pressed a kiss to her forehead. These last few days had been incredible. He felt alive for perhaps the first time in his life. He was grateful to her for that, for opening his eyes to this brave new world.

She was a dynamo in the office. And even more so in bed. He was damn lucky to have found her.

The sigh that escaped her lips lingered over his chest. "A penny for your thoughts?"

There was no way she was going to volunteer that. T.J. forced herself to smile. "Only a penny?" she teased. "Is that how you managed to make your fortune? Underpaying people?"

He laughed. "The fortune, as you call it, was made long before I came into the picture. I just pulled the company a little further into the twentieth century, that's all."

She brushed aside the one wayward lock of hair that fell into his eyes, trying not to think about how much she was going to miss him. "I think you're going to have to push a little harder. We're approaching the twenty-*first,* you know."

"No hurry." It was hard deciding which flavor he enjoyed most. The one at her neck, the one behind her elbow. The one he'd discovered behind her knee. He enjoyed sampling and trying to make a choice. "I figure we'll make that transition in about another fifty years. There'll be another MacAffee at the helm by then and it won't be my concern. What I'm concerned with," he told her as he forged a slow, sensuous hot trail along her body, "is the here and now." He raised his head, his eyes on hers. "And you."

He was looking at her as if she was something precious, and she felt like such a fraud. Her body, so fresh from lovemaking, was heating again. It always would. To his touch.

"You always get so caught up in your work?"

"Never." The affirmation skimmed along her taut belly, making it tighten. "I didn't know what I was missing." The kisses were becoming more ardent, making it harder for her to form a coherent thought.

No, not harder. Impossible.

Christopher raised himself on his elbows, looking down into her face. He didn't like what he was about to say. "I'm going to have to leave tomorrow."

She knew that. Had known that. It was what she'd planned on.

The sinking sensation she felt was almost unbearable. "Tomorrow?"

He liked the echo of loneliness he heard in her voice. It matched his own.

"I have to. Everyone at the company thinks I must have lost

my mind." His mouth curved. "I've never taken time off before."

She held him then, as if having her arms around him formed a magic circle where no harm could come to either of them. And the truth stood just outside. "Never?"

He shook his head, his body curving into hers. Savoring it. "Not more than a day or two. I love my work. It reaffirms me. Maybe it even defines me. Or did," he amended with a fond smile as he gazed at her. "I hadn't realized just how nice it was to 'kick back.' Those were the words you used, weren't they?"

She wouldn't have been able to swear to anything right now. "Sounds like me."

He had an inspiration. "Come up with me," Christopher proposed suddenly. "Fly up to San Jose. I'll return the favor and show you around."

She was tempted. Tempted to continue the charade just a little longer. What would it hurt?

Everything.

With more regret than she had thought there was in the world, she shook her head. "I can't. We're launching your campaign Monday, remember?"

It hadn't been easy. The whole company had dropped everything to mount this television commercial. Buying a time slot so close to the holiday had been almost impossible. But Theresa had put in a few phone calls, pulled in a favor and a prime thirty-second opening on the most popular sitcom on the airwaves came their way. Once that was known, several others had materialized. The price tag had been hefty, but the returns, T.J. was certain, were going to be tremendous.

Her parting gift to Christopher, she thought sadly.

He frowned slightly. "You don't have to be here to do that."

"Yes, I do," she contradicted. And it was true. She did have to be here. It was her baby to oversee. "It's more complicated than you think."

"Can't you give it to T.J. to do?" he suggested. "I still haven't met her, you know." She'd promised to introduce him to her cousin, but each time he brought it up, the woman was elusively missing.

Yes, you have. I'm right here, in your arms. "She's been very busy this past week."

He shrugged, not really interested in anyone else. Only Theresa. He'd asked to meet the woman only because T.J. was related to Theresa and Theresa seemed to think so highly of her. The only person he wanted to see was right here, in his bed.

"There's time for that later." The meeting was already forgotten. There was something far more pressing on his mind. "Are you sure I can't convince you to come with me?"

She wanted to say yes. No one knew who she was at his company. But that would only be drawing a host of others into the deception. Others who might hold it against Christopher for some reason. She couldn't do that to him. "I'm sure."

He blew out a breath, disappointed. And then he smiled, shifting over her. "Well, then I guess I just have to make the most of the time I have, don't I?"

She couldn't go on this way. The burden of the lie was killing her. "Christopher, I have something to tell you."

He didn't like the look in her eyes. It had to do with them. He could sense it. He didn't want to hear her say something like this past week had been fun, but that now it was over. He didn't want it to be over. And he was going to do his damnedest to make her not want it to be over, either.

"Shhh." He pressed a kiss to first one temple, then the other. "I don't want to talk about business right now."

"This isn't about business."

The words were getting harder and harder to get out. He was kissing the hollow of her throat and tears sprang to her eyes. Tears of joy, of regret. This would be the last time, she promised herself, the last time she'd let him make love to someone she wasn't.

The last time.

She was going to make the most of it.

He thought he knew her. Knew what she was capable of. He

didn't know a thing. The woman in his bed became a whirlwind of passion. A tigress. He had always been the one to take the initiative, to lead the way. Now the reins, it seemed, had passed into her hands. He surrendered them willingly.

When she rolled over and pushed him onto his back, pleasuring him in ways he'd never even dreamed, he became weak as a kitten. It wasn't a role he would have thought he'd enjoy.

But then he'd already realized that he didn't know a damned thing.

She reduced him to a mass of wanting, of ignited passion that seemed to know no end, no resolution. Her fingers lightly glided along his body, kneading, touching, possessing, sculpting. Taking his breath away as he realized the depths to which his desire extended.

"Where," he breathed, hating the man who had taught her this even as he was grateful to him, "did you learn to do this?"

"Instinct," she whispered raggedly against his ear. "Pure instinct."

She couldn't have given him a better gift if she'd tried.

Chapter Nine

HE'D BEEN IN and out of airports all of his life, flying away to boarding school, then home for holidays. Away on business. They all blurred in his mind. Christopher couldn't really remember a single instance clearly.

This time, he knew, he would remember. He would remember the way he felt right now, standing here with Theresa saying goodbye, until the day he died—no matter what came after.

Christopher looked down into her upturned face. He could have been standing in the middle of a ''Star Trek'' convention and he wouldn't have noticed anyone else but her.

The loudspeaker squawked as the announcement came to an end. They were calling for final boarding of his flight.

He didn't want to leave.

One last time, he lost himself in her eyes, in the dimple that winked at the corner of her mouth as she smiled at him.

It was a sad smile and they shared it.

Standing near the entrance of the boarding ramp that funneled its way into the airplane, Christopher leaned his head against hers and sighed.

''You know, I caught myself wishing that I'd miss this flight. Where are those famous L.A. traffic jams they're always talking about when you need them?''

The same thing had occurred to her. And the same wish. But Emmett had had almost a clear path from the house to LAX. It was as if some unforeseen hand had moved aside all the excess vehicles, sweeping them away.

The flight attendant at the entrance cleared her throat, waiting. Urgency hummed in T.J.'s veins. This was going to be the last time she saw him like this. The last time, in all probability, that she saw him at all. It had to be.

"That was pretty much of a miracle, wasn't it? Maybe it's a sign that you should go back." *I don't want you to leave. I don't want this to end. Most of all, I don't want you to ever find out that I lied to you.*

But he would, she thought, a fathomless sadness filling her. He would. And then...

There was something in her eyes, a depth of sadness that spoke to him. She didn't want him to leave any more than he wanted to go. There should be a way around this. But for now he knew there wasn't. He couldn't forsake the businessman in him entirely, even though for the first time in his life he desperately wanted to.

Christopher framed her face with his hands. These last few days had been indescribably incredible. He felt almost as if he were being struck by lightning. Or born for the very first time. Strange sensation to relish at the age of thirty-three. He wasn't about to relinquish what he'd just found. This separation, Christopher promised himself, was just temporary.

"I only read the signs I like," he assured her with a grin.

You won't like any of this, once you know the truth. She glanced over her shoulder at the flight attendant. There was understanding in the blond woman's eyes as she gestured them forward. There was a time schedule to adhere to, love notwithstanding.

T.J. slipped her arms around his neck. One kiss, one last kiss. "If you don't hurry, you're going to miss your flight."

Would that be so bad? he wondered. There'd be another one in its place. But there were things he had to attend to. He couldn't just shrug off responsibilities because his insides felt as if they'd been drop-kicked by a mule. Or just because he found himself lost in a beautiful woman's eyes.

Ignoring the attendant's light touch on his arm, Christopher kissed T.J. Long and hard, with the passion of someone going away for a very long time, instead of the week he silently planned.

"Sir."

He broke contact and began to back away down the ramp, still looking at T.J. "I'll send one of my people down with the contracts as soon as they're signed."

To make their mutual lawyers happy, he'd signed a temporary agreement so that C & C Advertising could get the Valentine's Day commercial underway, but a ream of legal documents were waiting for his signature before the deal was final.

T.J. watched as the distance between them lengthened. The sadness within her grew in direct geometric proportions. "I'll be waiting for them."

At the last moment, just before he would have disappeared around the corner and into the plane, Christopher sprinted back up the ramp. The attendant, taken by surprise, didn't follow immediately. When she did, she was exasperated.

"Sir—"

He didn't bother to turn around. He wanted to keep looking at the woman who had brought rainbows into his world. "Just another minute."

Frazzled, the attendant looked over her shoulder at another woman who emerged from the far end of the ramp near the plane. She shrugged at her helplessly.

"But the flight—"

There wasn't time for anything more than a fleeting kiss. It wouldn't be fair to keep a whole plane waiting. Releasing her, he hurried back down.

"Valentine's Day," he called out to T.J.

She didn't understand. Was he telling her something about the TV campaign? "What?"

"I'll be back for Valentine's Day," he promised, raising his voice above the noise emerging from the end of the ramp. "Keep it open."

And with that, he disappeared into the waiting airplane and out of her life.

"Goodbye," T.J. whispered.

She stood there, immobile, even when the attendant returned to close the door. The woman flashed her a sympathetic look.

T.J. was vaguely aware of the attendant nodding at her. She stepped back, lost in a sea of emotion. Relief and misery joined hands in an awkward minuet. She was relieved Christopher was finally on the plane and the danger of exposure was temporarily over. And yet she was so miserable, she felt she could curl up and die.

Valentine's Day.

He said he'd be back on Valentine's Day. Ironic, wasn't it? She'd always wanted someone to make a fuss over her on Valentine's Day. Theresa had always been the one inundated with gifts and dates. No one had even thought to send her a card.

Not even Peter. She'd met him in late February, just after Valentine's had passed. By the time the holiday had rolled around again, they were together, but he was so complacent in their relationship, he hadn't bothered to even take note of Valentine's Day.

A sad smile curved her lips. She'd always strongly identified with Charlie Brown and the empty mailbox, knowing just how he felt.

And now, with a promise of romance lingering fresh in the air, she still couldn't look forward to the day. Because she didn't want him returning. Didn't want him ever finding out that she had deceived him. And he would if he came back. How long could her luck hold out? How long could she keep up the charade?

Taking the escalator down to street level, she let her mind drift in a momentary fantasy. Christopher and she celebrating their fiftieth anniversary in an exclusive restaurant, surrounded by children and grandchildren. Her hand would be on his, about to cut the five-foot-high cake. A tiny replica of them the way they'd been on their wedding day would stand on the top tier.

"Um, honey, there's something I have to tell you," she would whisper in his ear. *"I'm really my cousin T.J. and Megan is really my daughter."*

And then Christopher would drop the knife and walk out of the restaurant. Out of her life forever.

She wasn't even able to make him understand in her fantasy. She certainly couldn't hope to find the right words in real life.

Maybe she wouldn't have to.

The prospect didn't cheer her.

T.J. walked out of the terminal, looking for Emmett and the black stretch limo.

Odds were that once Christopher was back in San Jose, concerns about business would swallow him up and he'd forget he'd ever said anything. After all, men took these liaisons lightly.

But she didn't.

She blinked back tears as she saw the car and began walking to it.

Just as well if he didn't come back.

The hell it was.

Emmett sprang to attention when he saw her, tucking the newspaper he'd been reading under his arm. One look at her face and he felt his heartstrings being tugged.

"You certainly look down-and-out." Moving nimbly, Emmett opened the rear door for her. He made a guess. "Mr. MacAffee find out at the last minute?"

T.J. shook her head. The interior of the car looked too lonely for her to bear. "Mind if I ride up front with you?" She turned her moist eyes to his and hoped he wouldn't notice that she'd been trying not to cry. "I could use the company."

Emmett offered her his handkerchief. She took it and dried her eyes. Of all the people he had ever driven around, Mr. Shawn's daughter had been the only one who had ever related to him on an equal footing. He thought the world of her and hated seeing her so unhappy.

"My pleasure, miss." He opened the front door for her before she could reach for it.

Rounding the hood, Emmett took his seat quickly and started the limousine. Expertly, he maneuvered the large automobile as if it was no more than a VW Bug, weaving in and out of traffic. Taking Century Boulevard, he entered the freeway.

Emmett decided to hazard one last guess, hoping he was right. He didn't want to think of her crying over a man. "Contract fall through?"

"No, the contract's fine." Theresa, at least, would be very happy. "Which is more than I can say for me," she whispered under her breath.

Making no comment, Emmett reached over to the radio. He turned the knob until he found what he was looking for. An oldies station.

T.J. looked at him in surprise, then smiled. Emmett hated oldies music with a passion. All he ever listened to was classical. But he knew she liked it.

"Thanks."

He nodded. "Don't mention it."

She sat back, staring straight ahead, trying to sort things out in her mind. She couldn't, not yet. "They're right about what they say."

"And what's that, miss?" His voice was soothing, low-key.

"About what a tangled web we weave when first we practice to deceive." It was more than something in a dusty book of quotations. It was now her life.

"Wouldn't know about that, miss. My life's very untangled."

She laughed softly. "You don't know how lucky you are, Emmett."

His small brown eyes met hers as he stopped the car at the light. "Oh, I don't know. Sometimes I would have welcomed a bit of a tangle." He gave her an encouraging smile. "Things have a habit of working themselves out. Wait and see."

Not this time, she thought. But she only nodded in response. There was no sense in discussing it. What was done was done.

THERESA WAS THE FIRST one in her path when she got off the elevator an hour later. T.J. had come to the office straight from the airport. Maybe if she kept busy enough, she just wouldn't think.

It was a feeble plan at best, doomed to failure.

Theresa was dressed in the subdued fashion T.J. always favored, her bountiful hair pulled back just the way T.J. wore hers when she came to work. Though she hadn't run into Christopher by design, Theresa had thought it prudent, though annoying, to dress the part she had reluctantly assumed until the man returned up north. Just in case.

She looked eagerly behind T.J. as the latter walked out of the elevator. There was no one with her. Theresa turned bright, hopeful eyes on her cousin. "Well, did you get him off?"

T.J. nodded. Never breaking stride, she continued walking down the hall to her office.

"Thank God!" With a dramatic sigh, Theresa pulled the clip from her hair and tossed her head. Her dark hair rained about her shoulders. "I can be me again." She shoved the clip into T.J.'s hands. "I didn't think I could stand this masquerade much longer." Combing her fingers through her hair, she followed T.J. down the hall, absently wondering what the hurry was. "You know, you really got the better end of the deal." She turned toward her own office and the change of clothes she'd brought in in the hope that they'd seen the last of Christopher MacAffee at the office. Theresa twisted a button open on her blouse. "I don't know how you can stand these drab clothes."

"They're comfortable," T.J. answered absently. Without thinking about it, she drew her hair back and caught it in the clip.

"They're awful." Theresa stopped and looked at T.J. She didn't look like a woman who had successfully driven home a major deal. "Are you all right? Anything wrong with the deal?"

The deal. The word echoed in T.J.'s brain. That was all that mattered. People, whole families, depended on their landing large accounts. And MacAffee Toys was a big one. She had to keep that in mind.

"The deal is alive and well. He's sending the final contracts back down via a courier as soon as they're signed."

"Good job." Pleased, Theresa hugged T.J. T.J. wasn't hugging back. T.J. always hugged back. Puzzled, Theresa peered at her face. T.J. turned away and walked into her office. Concerned, Theresa followed. "There is something wrong." She knew it was too easy. There was a catch to the agreement. "What?"

When was this hollow feeling going to let go of her? Her back to Theresa, T.J. squeezed her eyes shut to hold back the tears. "What could be wrong? We have a multimillion-dollar company on our books and an inspired commercial on the air, which the head of the company thinks is charming. Everything's wonderful. Couldn't be better."

Sarcasm wasn't T.J.'s long suit. Theresa became sincerely worried. But when she touched her cousin's shoulder, T.J. shrugged her away.

"T.J.—"

The last thing she wanted was to talk about it. Or worse, see pity in Theresa's eyes. "If you don't mind, I think I'll get out of these clothes and get some work done, all right?"

She knew when she was being dismissed. For once, Theresa let it slide. T.J. wasn't one to discuss her problems. Unlike her.

Reluctantly, Theresa obliged her and backed out of the office. "Maybe we can go out to lunch later?"

"Right," T.J. muttered to herself as she heard the door close. "We'll do lunch."

She stared out the window at the perfect day outside. She wished it would rain.

HE SUPPOSED HE WAS behaving like some lovesick adolescent, but Christopher figured he owed it to himself. He'd entirely skipped that portion of his life the first time around. He selected the next taxi queued up to the curb in front of the terminal and tossed his bag into the back seat.

"11737 Wilshire," he said in answer to the driver's raised brow.

The man nodded as he got into the cab.

Christopher looked out the window at the crowded lot, anxious to be there already. To see the look of surprise in Theresa's eyes when he walked into her office.

Yes, he mused, just like an adolescent. Or so he surmised. There had never been a girl in his teens he'd been smitten with. He'd been too busy being groomed for his position in the firm, constantly being reminded that the company, and its fate, would all rest on his shoulders someday. He was not to disappoint the generation that had come before. That hadn't left a hell of a lot of room or time for anything else.

And he wasn't exactly smitten now. At least, not only that. He was smitten, infatuated and head over heels. The whole gamut, up to and including wildly in love.

A horn blared behind them and the cabdriver muttered something in a foreign tongue that obviously wasn't very flattering. Christopher hardly heard him. His mind was elsewhere.

This was it—the woman he wanted to marry. He knew himself well enough to know that though this appeared like a snap judgment on his part, it wasn't. It was very sound.

He liked everything about her. Playing his own devil's advocate, he had tried to find a flaw, something to pick at, and couldn't. For a whole week, he'd tried, thinking that being away from her would naturally cool any fire he had felt.

It only fanned it.

The entire time he had been away from her, he'd been preoccupied. Snippets of the moments they'd spent together would replay themselves through his mind and he would drift off in the middle of meetings. People began to notice and to talk. This was completely out of character for him. It was chalked up as something to do with his recent illness.

Well, if this was being ill, he hoped he'd never get well.

Christopher looked down at the envelope on the cracked vinyl seat beside him. On impulse, he'd decided to bring the contracts back down himself rather than send them by courier, or Express Mail. He had never done anything on impulse before. But he wanted an excuse to see her again; he *needed* to see her again.

Like a kid, he thought with a grin. A kid who knew what he wanted.

More horns blared. He felt his impatience mounting. Christopher slid forward, leaning toward the driver. "Can't this thing go any faster?"

The driver snorted, waving a dismissive hand at the cars around them. "It could, if the traffic was moving, which, if you look, it ain't." Dark shaggy brows drooped over penetrating, black marble eyes as he looked over his shoulder at his fare. "Take it easy, mister. I'm doing the best I can. Whoever you're seeing'll still be there by the time I get you to Wilshire."

True enough, but it didn't dissipate the sense of urgency he felt. "I've wasted thirty-three years. I don't want to waste any more."

The driver just shrugged in response, turning forward again. Tourists. They were all the same. Crazy and in a hurry to get there.

CHRISTOPHER RELISHED the fact that his behavior was completely out of character for him. Normally, he would have had his assistant call her assistant and arrange a meeting. But that was before he'd met her. Now he couldn't wait to see the look on her face. Couldn't wait to touch that face, to hold her against him.

God, but he had missed her.

Getting off on the seventh floor, he hurried down the corridor to Theresa's office.

Heidi's myopic eyes were round as Frisbees as she recognized him. Jumping to her feet, the word *Mayday* flashed through her mind.

"Sir, wait. You can't go in there. She's in conference." It was the first thing that popped into her head.

"I won't say a word until she's finished," he promised, passing Heidi's desk. Knocking once, he opened the door to Theresa's office and then walked in, whistling.

In the middle of a call, her chair turned toward the window, Theresa heard the door to her office open and close. Heidi usually buzzed her before entering. Bemused, Theresa turned her chair around to face the door.

There was an incredibly good-looking man standing in her office. Well, well, well, Valentine's Day had arrived early this year.

"I'll call you back," Theresa murmured into the receiver, her eyes never leaving the stranger. She hung up before the person on the other end had a chance to respond.

A broad, inviting smile of welcome spread out over her lips.

The smile on Christopher's faded slightly as he stepped forward. He had the oddest feeling....

"Theresa?"

"Yes?"

He obviously had an advantage over her, she thought. But that wouldn't be for long. She intended to have one over him before the evening ended.

Christopher shook his head. Something was out of kilter. There was something about her.... "No."

Theresa blinked. "Excuse me?"

"You're not." He moved closer, looking at her. Studying her. She looked like Theresa, and yet... "Theresa, I mean. You're not Theresa." Was he losing his mind?

"I most certainly am." A flirtatious light entered her eyes as she laughed.

It was all wrong. Her laugh was all wrong. Different. It wasn't husky, wasn't melodious. And there was no dimple at the corner of her mouth when she smiled, he realized suddenly. Had he imagined all of that? No, he couldn't have. He couldn't have imagined the color of her eyes, either. The ones he was looking into were clear water blue, not brilliant the way they had been.

Completely turned around and at a loss, Christopher ran a hand through his hair, staring at the woman in front of him. Maybe he was hallucinating?

"Theresa Cochran?" he repeated dumbly. He'd made love to the woman, absorbed every nuance of her body into his. Why did it feel as if he was looking into the face of a stranger?

Nodding, Theresa rounded her desk, a huntress scenting her prey. "Yes, I'm Theresa Cochran. I've never been Theresa Cochran more in my life."

T.J. opened the door that connected her office to Theresa's. She'd been doing some preliminary sketches on the next phase of advertising for MacAffee Toys and wanted to run it by Theresa. Lately, she didn't trust her judgment about anything. Her brain felt leaden.

"Theresa, I—" The inside of her mouth turned to dust. "Christopher." His name came out on a barely audible whisper.

When he turned to look at her, she saw the flicker of doubt, then recognition pass over his face.

No! The single word screamed in her brain. *Not like this.* She didn't want him finding out like this.

Flustered, miserable, T.J. backpedaled as fast as she could. "Mr. MacAffee, Theresa's told me so much about you. This is an honor, finally getting to meet you."

A brave smile pasted on her face, she stepped forward putting out her hand.

Christopher felt as if he'd just stumbled into a mirrored room in a carnival fun house. With a few changes here and there, Theresa and the woman greeting him looked enough alike to be twins.

In fact, if she just loosened her hair, the woman in the doorway... The look in her eyes...

As if in a trance, Christopher took the hand she extended. He held it a moment longer than was necessary. Held it as he looked at her thoughtfully.

He saw the dimple at the corner of her mouth.

And then he knew.

Chapter Ten

"THERESA?"

Though in his mind, he knew, Christopher still couldn't make his heart believe it. Didn't want to believe that the woman he'd fallen in love with had deliberately duped him for some unknown reason. That would have made him the worst possible kind of fool.

Theresa felt as if she'd fallen into a foreign-language film where the subtitles had gotten scrambled. "No, I already told you, I'm Theresa."

"She is," T.J. told Christopher quietly. "I'm T.J." She couldn't draw her eyes away from his. They looked so dark, so forbidding. "Theresa, I'd like you to meet Christopher Mac-Affee."

The reason for the confusion had suddenly dawned on Theresa a moment before T.J. had said his name. The sinking sensation in the pit of Theresa's stomach widened at the confirmation.

"Oh, God."

Christopher didn't know what to say. What could he say? It was hard to form a coherent sentence while volcanoes were erupting all around him and the ground was shaking.

What the hell was going on here? Why had she lied to him about who she was? It didn't make any sense. All he knew was that she'd lied and that it hurt. Hurt like hell because he'd trusted her without reservations.

Her nerves knitted together furiously, and T.J. tried to keep a steady rein on them as she searched for a way to resolve this mess she found herself in.

Even as she did, she knew there was no way.

"Could you give us a minute, Theresa?" T.J. couldn't bring herself to look away, couldn't bring herself to look at anything except the deep, unreadable darkness in Christopher's eyes.

She should have told him, she thought in desperation. Somehow, she should have found a way to tell him. Now he was furious with her. But there still had to be a way to make him understand.

The tension in the room was almost physical, making it difficult to breathe.

"I can explain all this," Theresa began tentatively.

When he didn't look at her, Theresa laid a perfectly manicured, hot pink-tipped hand on his arm.

Christopher shrugged it off slowly, coldly. "I don't think anything needs to be explained. It's pretty evident." For whatever reason, she had played him for a fool. And he had helped her.

No, none of it was evident, T.J. thought fiercely. Whatever horrible thing he was thinking, she had to make him see that it wasn't true. That no harm had been intended. She couldn't stand having him look at her like that, as if he didn't know her. As if she'd done something awful to him.

"Theresa?" T.J. entreated her cousin.

Theresa understood and retreated. "I'll just be next door if you need me." Unless she missed her guess, her cousin had more at stake here than she had.

It took Christopher a moment to get his emotions under control. Rage was a completely new feeling for him. As love had been before it. Funny how the same person roused both.

The room was so quiet, he could hear her breathing. "Interesting way you have of conducting business."

His voice was cold, impersonal. His eyes were like sharp knives, cutting out her heart. She wanted to speak, but couldn't.

"Do you and your cousin sleep with all your prospective clients?"

T.J.'s eyes widened as if she'd been physically slapped. She couldn't believe that he could say that to her. Whatever she'd expected to hear, it wasn't that. "That's not fair! I tried to tell you but you wouldn't listen."

"Fair?" Temper flashed in his eyes like a grease-laden pan bursting into flame. He saw her tremble as she stumbled a step backward. And then something seemed to snap to attention within her. She held her ground. He could have wrung her neck. "You're a hell of a one to talk about 'fair.' You used me, Theresa. Or T.J., or whoever the hell you really are." Bile rose in his mouth and left a bitter taste. As bitter a taste as her deception left. "I thought you were different, but you're like all the others." He supposed that made him naive. Thirty-three years old and he was behaving like some hayseed from the backwoods.

Her head jerked up. She had no idea what kind of people he'd dealt with, but she had a pretty good idea. And she didn't like what he was saying. "Don't go lumping me in with people like that."

"Why?" he shouted into her face before he caught himself. He wasn't going to embarrass himself any more than he already had. Lowering his voice until it was a steely growl, he asked, "What makes you different?"

"I—"

He didn't want to hear elaborate excuses. He already knew how creative she could be. There were facts to deal with. "Did you or did you not sleep with me?"

T.J. felt as if she was being attacked. He wouldn't let her defend herself. "I did, but—"

"And do we or don't we now have a contract between us?"

This wasn't coming out right. He was twisting things around. What he was inferring wasn't true. She had to make him understand that. "Yes, but—"

That was his case, pure and simple. Pure and simple—that's what he'd thought she was, beneath the bravado. Talk about being a jerk—he took the prize. "Then how are you different?"

How could he ask? Didn't he know? "I don't do that sort of thing. I don't use my body to cement business relations."

He wanted to believe her. He couldn't believe her. "Oh, no?" The laugh was short, cruel. The sound cut right through her. "That's a little hard to believe. Don't forget, I was there."

T.J. clenched her hands into fists at her sides. She wanted to beat on him. To pound on his chest until she cracked that shield he had over it and freed his heart.

She lifted her chin defiantly. "I don't care what you believe." *Yes, yes, I do, damn you. How can you say these things to me? How could you make love with me and then say this?* "I just know what's true."

He turned from her and she grabbed his arm, jerking him around. The look he gave her almost turned her tongue to stone. But he had to hear this from her. He had to know.

"I didn't sleep with you because of the contracts, or because of business. It was just something that happened between us." He had to know that. Didn't he?

"Magic?" he said disdainfully.

She stared at him, dumbfounded. He was ridiculing her. Well, for her it *had* been magic.

"Yes, magic, for lack of a different word, or maybe it is the word. Magic, a spell. I don't know what came over me." Backing away from him, she threw up her hands as she began to pace about the office like a tiger searching for a way to escape out of its cage. "Damn it, I don't even kiss on the first date."

Tears were stinging her eyes and she drew in a deep breath, hoping that would somehow keep them from spilling out. She wouldn't let Christopher see her cry. He'd probably accuse her of using tears to make him feel guilty.

Swallowing, she turned to look at him, remembering the way it had been between them. Remembering the shimmering moment when she had thought he loved her. "It just felt as if you needed me—"

He had needed her. Or thought he had. But he refused to give her that satisfaction now. "Oh, then it was pity that had you making love to me."

She ignored the sarcasm. "And I needed you." Her eyes challenged him. "Now you can believe me or not, but I've never slept with anyone else except for Megan's father."

Megan. Something else she'd lied about. How many more lies were there? Probably too many to count. "Then she isn't your niece." There was no emotion in his voice and it was all the more chilling for that.

T.J. blew out a long, shaky breath. "No, she's my daughter."

Maybe, if he'd thought about it, he would have surmised as much. But he hadn't thought. Hadn't been able to think. She'd seemed to infiltrate every portion of his brain. Like a virus.

One he was damn well going to be inoculated against. "What else wasn't true?"

"Nothing." He didn't believe her. She could see it in his eyes. Why should he?

Why shouldn't he? she demanded more fiercely.

She was getting herself all tangled up. "Everything else was true. Everything I told you about the company." T.J. drew closer to him. "And everything that happened between us."

He had to believe that, she thought. He just had to. She couldn't bear it if he thought she'd lied to him about that.

He struggled with the temptation to crush her to him. God help him, even after all this, he still wanted her. Which made him an even bigger fool.

Christopher turned from her, from her haunted eyes and from the scent of her hair that was driving him crazy with desire. "You'll forgive me if I cast a jaded eye on that."

Suddenly he had to get out of here. He started for the door.

Throwing herself into his path, T.J. made one more attempt. "Look, you were set to meet Theresa, insisted on it. 'Company policy,' we were told. Theresa really wanted your contract."

He felt his mouth twisting into a mocking sneer. "Apparently—"

Gaining momentum, T.J. wouldn't allow him to interrupt. "And then she was in a car accident—"

"Oh, please—" Did she think he was that naive? Car accident. Was that the best she could do? He would have given her more credit than that.

"She was," T.J. insisted. When he made a move to open the door, she placed her hand on his chest. Taking him by surprise, she managed to shove him back. "It was a minor accident, but the paramedics took her to the hospital and the doctor insisted on keeping her there for observation. She'd had a hard enough time scheduling this meeting with you and you were already on your way. She was afraid you'd be annoyed when she wasn't there and take your business to another company."

"Why didn't you just tell me she was in an accident?" That would have been the logical thing to do.

T.J. wished now that she had. "Theresa has a reputation for being flighty. She was afraid you'd just think she was putting you off."

Theresa, or T.J., he amended, had a point. He probably wouldn't have believed the excuse. He didn't think he did now.

She was losing him, she thought in desperation. "So she asked me to substitute for her."

He paused, reflecting. What was to keep her from lying further? Burned, he wasn't about to grab the red-hot skillet handle again so quickly. "Is that the story you two cooked up? Very creative."

Frustration clawed at her. What did it take for him to believe her?

"We didn't cook it up. It's true. You can check with the hospital. Harris Memorial. And if *you* hadn't gotten sick, you would have toured the offices, made your decision and left on the evening flight." Didn't he understand that? "But you did get sick and the rest just happened."

No, he wasn't going to be made a fool of twice. Served him right for believing in something as ethereal as love. "Conveniently."

What was the use? She wasn't getting through to him. Surrendering, T.J. backed away from the door. "You can say it happened any way you want to, but I just told you the truth."

"The truth." He echoed the word, mocking her. "New experience for you?"

How could she have given her heart to a man who didn't have one? T.J. dug her nails into the palms of her hand. She wasn't going to cry. She wasn't going to give Christopher the satisfaction of seeing her heart breaking in front of him.

She lifted a shoulder carelessly and let it fall. "You can believe me or not, the choice is yours. The facts are what I said they were. That, and one more thing."

Was she going to rub salt into the wounds she'd created and profess undying love? Did she really think he was that gullible? "And that is?"

She wanted to tell him she loved him. But what good would that do? He wouldn't believe her and that would leave her without the least bit of pride. Better that he never know.

Instead, she told him what had originally put her on this rocky road to nowhere. "That we are the best company for the job." T.J. thought of the figures she'd requested. The ones that had just arrived. "Marketing has been keeping tentative tabs on your sales. The bears are flying off the shelves."

They were. He knew that for a fact. His own people had called him with the news just before he'd boarded the plane. It was one of the things he'd wanted to tell her. Along with something else, something very important. Something that no longer mattered.

He was grateful he'd found everything out before he'd made a complete fool of himself.

It was cold comfort to him.

His eyes searched her face. He thought of the way he'd rushed here to see her. She'd probably have a good laugh over that, wouldn't she? "It was just business with you, wasn't it?"

If he really thought that, maybe she didn't want to be with him after all.

The hell you don't.

She shut the voice, and her feelings, out. Somehow she was going to get through this. And past it. She had to.

Lifting her chin, she answered, "There are people depending on the company for jobs. Families with bills to pay, kids to send to school."

She was giving him his answer, he thought. She was saying yes.

"Save it for a card commercial," he snapped. How could she? How could she have used him this way? Didn't she think her company could stand up on its own merits? Or did she think that he was so feeble-minded as to be led around by his desire? "I would have given the contracts to you, anyway. You didn't have to sleep with me."

The sanctimonious bastard. "No," she agreed impassively. "I didn't."

Couldn't he tell that she cared, that she'd fallen for him the moment she'd seen him walking in her direction? That she wasn't the type who would just give her body for the fun of it? Never mind that he was supposed to think she was Theresa, he should have *known*. Making love with her, he should have known.

But he didn't.

Her mouth hardened. "Consider it a bonus." She squared her shoulders and looked past his head. "Now if you'll excuse me, I have some small children to lead astray."

His eyes bore small holes into her. What the hell gave her the right to be sarcastic when he was the wounded party?

"Fine," he bit off. As an afterthought, he threw the manila envelope on Theresa's desk. "There are the contracts."

The envelope fell on the desk with a thud and then slid off onto the floor. She didn't even look in its direction.

"You're staying with the company?" She would have thought that would have been his final revenge, to pull his business.

"Sure." The laugh was without humor. "As you pointed out, the bears are flying off the shelves. I'd be a fool to turn my back on good business. And I've already been enough of a fool, haven't I?''

And with that, he walked out of the office. The slam of the door vibrated into her very soul.

She was still standing there, staring at the door, her hands clenched at her sides, when Theresa reentered. She picked up the manila envelope and put it on the desk. Quietly she crossed to T.J. and placed her arms around her cousin.

"Are you all right?" she asked softly.

No, she wasn't. She was never going to be all right again. T.J. wiped the tears away with the back of her hand.

"Sure, I'm fine. Just fine." Her voice nearly broke but she managed to get it under control again. "I made love with him when I was playing you."

She didn't know why she was even saying it. Theresa had probably heard everything. All of L.A. had probably heard.

A soft, sympathetic smile played on Theresa's lips. "Did I enjoy it?"

T.J. shut her eyes for a moment before answering. "Yes. Very much."

Theresa's heart ached for T.J. It wasn't often her sympathies were stirred, but a stone would have ached for T.J. right now. She brushed back a loose strand from T.J.'s face. It was flushed, she noted, as if T.J. was trying very hard not to cry.

The streaks along her cheeks gleamed.

"By the look on your face, I'd say I enjoyed the week I had with him more than the week I had here."

T.J. looked at her cousin sharply, her feelings exposed, raw. "This isn't funny, Theresa."

"No, I can see where it wouldn't be." Theresa gave her shoulder a little squeeze. "I can go after him for you and try to make it right."

She had no idea what she'd say to the man, but she'd come up with something. She'd never seen T.J. so upset, not even when she discovered that Peter had been cheating on her.

But T.J. shook her head, stopping her before she could leave. "Don't bother. Nothing is going to make this right."

"I can be very persuasive if I have to be."

T.J. knew what that meant. That was all she needed, to have Theresa "persuade" Christopher. "Not with him you won't."

Theresa raised her hands in surrender. "Hands off, I promise." She dropped them to her side, growing serious. "I just want to see you smile again."

"I will," T.J. promised. "In time." But not anytime soon.

Theresa had her doubts. She glanced toward the door. Maybe if she tried to talk some sense into Christopher, tell him that it was all her fault.

"I can—"

T.J. didn't want Theresa interfering. This was between her and Christopher. "No."

Theresa wasn't accustomed to being voted down. "But—"

This time, T.J. placed a restraining hand on Theresa's arm. She was firm on this. "No, Theresa. If he comes back, he comes back on his own, not because you bent his arm. Or any other part of him," she added pointedly. She released Theresa's arm. "I told him the truth. That should have been enough."

If he cared about her half as much as she had about him, T.J. thought, it would have been.

Theresa's expression was skeptical. "In all fairness to him, how is he supposed to know which 'truth' to believe? You did lie to him."

So now she was taking his side? "Because you asked me to."

Theresa shook her head. Men were very sensitive creatures when it came to their egos, no matter what they let on. "He doesn't care about that part. You lied to him once and maybe he's afraid of believing you now. Maybe he's afraid you're still lying."

It made sense, but she didn't want sense. She wanted Christopher. She wanted him to have faith in her no matter what. "He should know the difference."

"Why?"

T.J. avoided Theresa's eyes. "Because people in love do."

Theresa took her face in one hand and looked into T.J.'s eyes. Love. She'd had no idea. She'd thought only passion had been involved. This made it a great deal worse. "That bad?"

T.J. drew her head back, and then sighed. "Yes, that bad."

Theresa sank down, leaning against her desk. "Oh, T.J., if I'd known this was going to happen, I would have never asked you to take my place."

"Why?" Still smarting, T.J. looked at her. "Because he's handsome and you would have wanted him for yourself?" She was accustomed to that. Theresa had gone after someone she'd cared about more than once and whisked him away before she'd ever had a chance. It was in Theresa's nature to be competitive when it came to men.

Theresa took no offense. "No, because you're hurting and I don't want you to be."

T.J. looked at her cousin sharply. The smile came to her lips slowly as realization set in. "You mean that, don't you?"

"Yes." Theresa rose to her feet again. "I might be a world-class witch sometimes, but you're my cousin and I do love you." She laid an arm around T.J.'s shoulders. "I don't want anything to hurt you."

"Thanks."

Theresa bit her lip. She hated for it to just end this way. Particularly if T.J. loved the man. "Are you sure there isn't anything I can do?"

"No, there isn't anything anyone can do. Not now." *Not ever,* T.J. added silently.

"Do you want to go home? Pamper yourself? Soak in a hot tub? Make a dart board with his face on it?"

T.J. laughed, a tiny spark returning. All of those were Theresa's methods of dealing with things, not hers. Besides, she didn't have a photograph of Christopher that she could use.

Nothing but the image in her mind.

"No, I want to work." T.J. looked at the drawings she'd placed on Theresa's desk a hundred years ago, before the world had crumbled. "Here." She spread them out. "What do you think of these?"

Theresa looked at her skeptically. "T.J., now?"

"Now." She paused. "Please."

"All right." Theresa nodded and looked down at the drawings.

Chapter Eleven

It had been, T.J. thought as she dragged herself out of her office, one of the longest days she could remember ever putting in. It hadn't been because of the number of hours she had been here. It was a standard eight-to-five day as far as that went. No, the problem was with the date itself. Valentine's Day.

This one had been particularly bad for her.

Maybe it was just her imagination working overtime, but everywhere she turned, it seemed as if thoughts of Christopher would assault her. They would race through her mind unannounced, making her remember. Making her ache.

Today was supposed to have been special for them. Today Christopher was supposed to have returned from San Jose and taken her out for the evening. Perhaps even given her a card. Some silly little thing she would have cherished forever.

Except now, of course, he wouldn't. They wouldn't ever see each another again.

The hell with him. The hell with everything. T.J. mumbled a good-night to Heidi and kept walking.

At one point, the day had become so hard to endure that T.J. had decided to leave early. She never got the chance. Today, of all days, Theresa had waylaid her with a project. She'd been forced to remain until now, working out details and watching a parade of flowers and gifts arrive for Theresa.

Didn't matter, T.J. told herself, walking down the hall. She didn't need any of that. Tomorrow this fanfare would be over and she could just continue with her life. Alone. With Megan, she corrected silently.

But alone where it counted.

Damn him for ever coming into her life.

She had to stop dwelling on him. It was over. Over almost before it was begun.

No, she amended, punching the down button on the wall. That wasn't really true. It had been begun, all right. With a parade and confetti and a fifty-piece brass band marching down the center of town. And ended, she thought sadly, with the same amount of noise.

She'd hoped.

Wished.

T.J. pressed her lips together as the elevator arrived, banking down her emotions. Emotions that threatened to run riot through her. There was no point in raking herself over the coals about this anymore. Life went forward, not back.

Even on Valentine's Day.

The silvery doors of the elevator yawned opened. Stepping forward, she was forced to quickly step back again. There was a forest of plump red roses fairly choking out of a long white vase directly in her path. All she could see of the person carrying them were jean-clad legs and hands attached to the slim column of alabaster.

Another delivery. She sighed. *Some of us have it and some of us don't.*

"Second door from the end," T.J. mechanically instructed. More booty for Theresa. Flowers, candy and an array of boxes she could only assume were lingerie had been arriving for her cousin all day.

"Gee, thanks," the profusion of roses responded.

T.J and the deliveryman then did a sashay that looked like a mating dance, exchanging places until T.J. was the one on the elevator and the deliveryman was out in the hall.

Leaning over, T.J. pressed the first-floor button. As the doors closed, she saw the deliveryman craning his neck around the side of the arrangement he held as he tried to make his way down the hall without a mishap.

Didn't matter if he had one, T.J. shrugged to herself. One bouquet more or less, Theresa would never notice its absence. She'd given up wondering how Theresa managed to know so many unattached males.

T.J. banked down her sour mood. It wasn't fair to be annoyed with Theresa. Theresa couldn't help it if she attracted men like honey did bees. And bears.

The thought of bears resurrected an image of Christopher in her mind.

No, she upbraided herself. No more Christopher. Ever. Some were meant to have romance in their lives and some weren't.

Until now, it really hadn't bothered her that much, apart from the hype of Valentine's Day.

Hype, she reminded herself tersely as she made her way through the parking lot, that she was as guilty of promoting as the next person.

Maybe more so. After all, she'd been the one to push MacAffee Toys into the holiday.

She couldn't chastise herself about that. It was what she was paid for. To have ideas. T.J. got into her car and slammed the door. Hard.

Right now, the wrong ones were plaguing her no matter how she tried to block them.

Annoyed with herself, T.J. turned up the radio.

"And now, this one is for all you lovers out there. Elvis, singing '*Love Me Tender*,'" the disc jockey announced as she pulled out of the lot.

Muttering under her breath, T.J. shoved the first handy tape into her tape deck.

A deep male voice began singing that it was beginning to look a lot like Christmas. T.J. left it on.

THE DRIVE HOME was virtually accomplished on automatic pilot. Under oath, T.J. couldn't have said how she'd gotten there. She just had. Mercifully intact.

With a flick of her wrist, she aimed the garage door opener at the closed dove gray door. The hinges on either side creaked as it opened to admit her.

Maybe, she mused driving in, just this once she'd take a page out of Theresa's book. She'd pamper herself with a bubble bath right after she put Megan to bed.

A really hot bubble bath, T.J. decided. With any luck, she'd purge Christopher out of her system once and for all.

He didn't belong there anyway.

Getting out of the car, she saw a flicker of pink out of the corner of her eye. Curious, she walked around the back of her car and looked out.

There were rose petals strewn in her driveway. Pink rose petals. The breeze had ruffled some of them, but from the looks of it, they formed a trail.

A trail of rose petals?

Puzzled, she followed them and found that they led to her front door.

She would have said that Megan was responsible, except that there were no roses in her garden and the petals looked as if they had been deliberately arranged to form a path to her door.

T.J. couldn't begin to make heads or tails out of it. Maybe it was someone's bizarre idea of a joke. If that was the case, she was far too tired to be amused. She still didn't understand why Theresa had insisted she remain until five. Theresa was usually the one ushering her out the door if she showed the slightest inclination to leave early.

Who knew? Who knew anything, T.J. thought irritably. All she wanted was for today to be over.

Unlocking the front door, T.J. discovered that the lights were out. They shouldn't have been. But the only illumination in the house was a small, eerie light coming from beyond the living room.

T.J. caught her lower lip between her teeth. This was getting to be really strange.

Venturing in, T.J. looked around. Nothing. No one. Where was everybody?

"Cecilia? Megan? I'm home." She paused, waiting. "Where are you?"

There was no answer.

Nerves began to manifest themselves. Her purse slipped from her slick fingers. As she bent down to pick it up, she saw that the rose petals were inside the house, too. Leading away from the door.

Heart quickening, T.J. had no choice but to continue to follow the trail. It extended through the living room into the dining room, where it stopped abruptly at the table.

It didn't even look like her table. There was a fine white lace tablecloth spread over the cherrywood top and it was set for two. The light that had guided her through the house was coming from two tall, tapering candles set in silver stands.

A light scent of berries was in the air.

Rather than a covered dish containing dinner, in the center of the table, between the two candlesticks, was a small, white teddy bear. His clasped paws were beribboned to help him hold on to a velvet box.

Just like in the commercial.

It was a joke.

Angry now, T.J. fisted her hands at her waist. She raised her voice. "All right, Theresa, this isn't funny." Her voice echoed back to her. It was all she heard.

Theresa had been exceptionally kind to her today, as if she understood what she was going through. But this sort of thing was her speed. It had Theresa written all over it. And she was carrying the joke too far.

"Enough." T.J. looked around the empty room. Unease nudged a place for itself beside her anger. Why was Theresa doing this? It had to be Theresa. Who else would have gone to this trouble for a prank? "Come out, come out wherever you are. Game over. Go home."

Still no one.

"All right, I'll see this through," she called out. "I'm reaching for the bear." T.J. squeezed it, just the way the woman in the commercial had.

Instead of "I wuv you," the bear said, quite audibly, "Flip my switch."

Surprised, T.J. stared down at the small bear. "Is that anything like ring my chimes?" T.J. shook her head. "My God, I'm talking to a stuffed bear."

But she turned it around and found the tiny switch. Flipping it, she heard a click and then the sound of a man's voice.

Christopher's voice.

She dropped the bear. It continued talking.

"Forgive me. I've been an idiot."

T.J. scooped up the bear, then looked around, her heart slamming against her rib cage. "Christopher?"

Was he here? Had he come back to see her? Why—?

"Right here."

She swung around. He was standing in the doorway behind her. He hadn't been there a second ago. There was no time to think, only react. T.J. dropped the bear again and flung herself into his arms.

Oh, God, he thought he'd never be this happy again. For a moment, watching her, he'd been afraid that it was too late. But it wasn't. She was in his arms and it wasn't too late.

Lowering his mouth to hers, Christopher kissed her, kissed her like a man back from the dead. Because that's what he was. Back from the dead. The living dead. Without her, he'd only been marking time. He just didn't know it until she'd entered his life. And then left it again.

"Wait a minute." Wedging her hands between them, T.J. pushed him back. She searched his face for an explanation. "What's going on here?"

"I'm keeping our Valentine date." *And my sanity,* he added silently.

"What date?" she asked incredulously. Had he forgotten what

he'd said? "The last I saw of you, you were walking out of my life as fast as you could go. What happened?"

"I had time to think and came to my senses. I did nothing but think. Of you." He coaxed T.J. back into his arms. He never wanted her to be out of reach again. "No matter how hard I tried not to, there you were, inside of every report I read, within every dream I had, sitting in on every meeting I tried to conduct."

His mouth curved as his eyes tried to absorb her. He'd been so afraid that he had lost her.

"You might say I was haunted. My father always told me to face up to whatever I was running from." It was the one good piece of advice the older man had given him. "So here I am."

T.J.'s eyes narrowed. She didn't want to let herself get carried away. She was afraid to. "So this is a showdown?"

"No, it's a show up. I've showed up the way I was supposed to."

He paused, debating telling her. But there were going to be no more secrets between them. That meant on both sides. Still, if he told her, she would know he went on doubting her story until it was confirmed by outside sources. He knew that might not go down well.

Christopher took his chances. "I called the hospital."

"Hospital?"

He nodded, then recited the information he'd been given. "One Theresa Cochran had been admitted overnight the day I arrived in L.A."

Finally, he had to believe her. She couldn't have very well bribed hospital personnel to lie for her. "Why would I have lied about that?"

The answer was simple; at least it had been for him at the time. "Because you lied about who you were."

Were they going to go over old ground after all? "I already told you, there was a reason for that."

He didn't want to argue about that. Or about anything, ever again.

"Yes, you did, and I guess, seeing it from your point of view, you might have expected me to be inflexible." A smile spread over his face as he remembered making love with her. "Instead of the flexible man I turned out to be."

She could read his mind. It wasn't hard. "And agile. Don't forget agile."

It was going to be okay, he thought. He hadn't blown it. "I might need a refresher course when it comes to that."

She couldn't think of anything she'd rather do more. But they weren't alone. Or were they? "Where are Megan and Cecilia?"

Meticulously, Christopher had taken care of everything. "Theresa's. I asked if they could stay there for a while." He smiled into her eyes. "Perhaps the night."

"Theresa's?" T.J. echoed. "Does she know about this?"

"She knows."

He knew he wouldn't be able to pull off this apology alone. He'd needed an inside accomplice. Theresa had seemed the likely choice. Once contacted, Theresa had been more than eager to help. She'd been the one to suggest Megan and Cecilia remain at her house overnight.

"And she didn't say anything to me?" Theresa could never keep a secret.

"I asked her not to." The woman had promised, probably afraid that he would pull the contract if she didn't keep her word. It didn't matter. All that mattered was having the woman he loved here in his arms like this. "Did you receive my flowers?"

T.J. laughed. They could hardly be called flowers now. "All down the driveway, all over the house."

It took him a second to understand. "No, not the petals. I mean the flowers I sent to the office. I timed the delivery for just when you were leaving. Three dozen long-stemmed roses."

She thought of the huge bouquet that had gotten off the elevator and she groaned. Her first flowers for Valentine's Day and she had given them away. "I sent them to Theresa."

Maybe he wasn't home free after all. "You didn't want them?"

"No, I mean, I didn't know they were for me. I thought they were for Theresa. Flowers and things have been arriving for her all day." T.J. shrugged helplessly. "I'm sorry." More than Christopher could possibly guess, she thought. "I figured it was just another one of her admirers."

She looked so upset, he kissed away the furrow between her brows. "It wasn't. It was one of your admirers."

"Admirer," she corrected. "No plural." She raised her eyes to his. "And do you? Admire?" she added.

He grinned, his eyes touching her. Loving her. "I intend to. Closely," he whispered. *For the rest of my life.* Christopher held her against him, looking down into her face. A face he'd missed so much. "So, what are you doing Valentine's Day?"

She laughed. That was an odd question. "I'm spending it here with you now."

She'd misunderstood. Not that he could blame her. "No, I meant Valentine's Day 2010."

T.J. blinked. He wasn't making any sense. "What?"

Releasing her, he crossed to where she had dropped the bear and picked it up. He handed the stuffed animal to her. "You're not finished with the bear."

T.J. cupped her hand around the gift. "He has more to say?"

"He has more to give." Christopher indicated the box in the bear's paws. If it hadn't been wrapped up so tightly, it would have fallen when she'd dropped the bear. He saw her hands were trembling as she untied the red ribbon.

"How did you get him to sound like you?" She fumbled with the knot.

Christopher was tempted to help her with the ribbon. Instead, he shoved his hands into his pockets. "I had the designers rig a tiny microrecorder in his stomach. I thought 'I wuv you' just wouldn't do the trick this time."

It would have, she thought. T.J. finally managed to get the ribbon off. She placed the bear on the table. If fell on its back. Taking a deep breath, she opened the box. Her eyes stung. Oh, God, she couldn't cry now.

"It's a ring," she whispered in disbelief.

"I know." The next few seconds would tell him if he'd been a fool or not. "I picked it out."

She raised her eyes to his. She couldn't believe—refused to believe—"For me?"

He raised one shoulder and let it drop carelessly. "It's too large for the bear."

T.J. stared at it again. "But it's an engagement ring."

She wasn't taking it out of the box. Why wasn't she taking it out of the box? Was she going to turn him down after all?

"People usually give them when they get engaged." Christopher took a deep breath. It was time to go all the way. "That is, if you want to be engaged to a jerk."

"No, I don't." T.J. paused, looking up at him. She saw the look of bewildered disappointment in his eyes. He didn't understand, she realized. "I want to be engaged to you."

Relief flooded him. Taking the ring out of the box, he slipped it on her finger. Christopher gathered her into his arms again. It *was* going to be all right. "You know, I should have gone with my first instincts."

She couldn't help it. T.J. extended her hand and watched the candlelight dance on the diamond, making it catch fire. "Which were?"

He laughed when he saw what she was doing. She made him think of a little girl with a precious new trinket. He couldn't wait to shower her with more "trinkets."

"That you were the woman I'd been looking for. Smart, funny, warm. Not to mention a terrific kisser." He thought for a second, growing serious. "I suppose it was easier not to believe it. It's a scary thing."

"What is?"

His eyes touched hers. "Happiness."

T.J. laced her arms around his neck. "Want to be scared together?"

"I'd love it." He brushed her lips with a kiss, whetting his appetite. "And you."

"Nice to know," she murmured. Tempting him, she leaned her body into his. "Because I'd hate to think it was a one-way street."

He wanted to hear it. Needed to hear it. "Then you do love me?"

"Of course I love you." Her eyes were teasing him. "Do you think I go around accepting talking bears from just anyone?"

"No, I guess maybe you don't." He couldn't remember when he'd been this happy. "Never" came to mind. "Happy Valentine's Day."

Just as he lowered his mouth to hers, she asked, "Say it."

Puzzled, he drew his head back. "Say what?"

"My name." He hadn't really called her by her name, except for that one time. She wanted to hear the sound of it on his lips without anger. "Say my name."

"T.J." She didn't look like a T.J. T.J.'s were cool, efficient. They weren't warm, giving women. They didn't flow through their lovers' hands like heated mercury. "You know, I like the sound of 'darling' better." The smile faded from his face, to be replaced with a look of love. Everlasting love. "Happy Valentine's Day, darling," he whispered against her mouth.

It was hard to imagine a heart singing, but hers did. This had turned out to be one hell of a day after all. "Happy Valentine's Day."

And it was. If asked, the stuffed animal on the table could bear witness to that. The record button had accidentally been turned on when it fell.

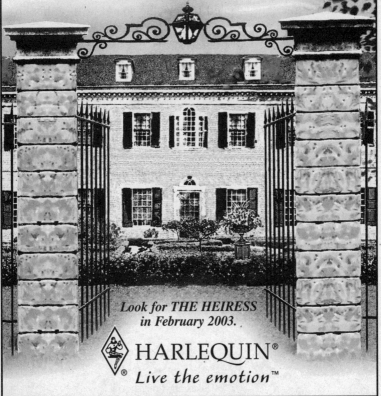

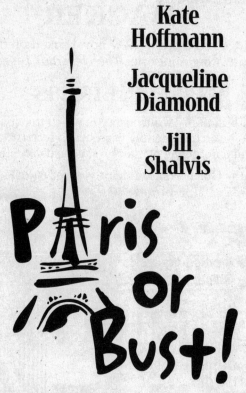

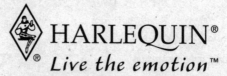